MW00618359

Lockett's Crucible

A Novel by

T.J. Johnston

James Lockett Novels

The Boys From Kalamazoo

Volume 3

Copyright © 2019 by T.J. Johnston

All Rights Reserved – No part of this book may be reproduced in any form without permission in writing from the author, except a reviewer who wishes to quote brief passages in connection with a review.

This book is a work of historical fiction. Any resemblance of fictional characters to actual persons, living or dead, is entirely coincidental.

Johnston, T.J.
   Lockett's Crucible : a novel / by T.J. Johnston

   ISBN 978-0-578-46578-4
   1. Michigan—Tennessee—Kentucky--History—Civil War, 1861-1865—Fiction. 2. Stones River, Battle of, 1862—Fiction. 3. Murfreesboro—Middle Tennessee—Fiction.   4. Perryville, Battle of, 1862—Fiction. I. Title. II. Series: Johnston, T.J. James Lockett, Boys From Kalamazoo novels.

Dedication

For my mother, who taught me the joy of reading.

<u>Foreword</u>

Lockett's Crucible is a work of historical fiction, but like all of the books in the series, I have taken great pains to be as accurate with the history and the context as possible.

Part of our fascination with the time period is that the history itself does not need a boost from the writer's imagination very often. It is vibrant and full of surprises on its own. All it really needs are some fictional characters to live it and weave it together.

While James Lockett and Blair's Independent Regiment are fictional, their travels, travails, battles, and observations are straight from history. At the end of the book, I have included a Historical Background section for the reader, so that they can see where my fictional characters merely substituted themselves into someone else's shoes in history.

Middle Tennessee and Kentucky

(with selected railroads)

==============================

Section I – Buell's Crawl East

Section II – The Race to Bluegrass

Section III – The Hangman's Noose

Section IV – Murfreesboro

Section V – The Slaughter Pen

==============================

Section I

Buell's Crawl East

Chapter 1

June 1862
Tennessee

The crackle of gunfire was distant and sporadic now, an echoing reminder of the sudden skirmish from an hour past. As usual, the Confederate raiders had melted away as quickly as they had appeared.

Lieutenant James Lockett watched two groups of blue-coated Minnesotans half-heartedly swishing their bayonets through the tall grass. One group came to a halt and gathered over what must have been a dead Rebel, though Lockett could not be sure. The thigh high grass obscured whatever had captured their attention.

"If the Minnesotans think they'll find something valuable on one of those dead Rebs, then they're dumber than they look," Sergeant Milton Bosworth grumbled.

"Don't know. The Reb cavalry fellows are mite better off than their infantry," Private Patrick McManus argued, as if reading Lockett's thoughts.

Lockett was not surprised that McManus could do that. They had known each more or less since birth, growing up on neighboring farms in far away Kalamazoo, Michigan. The calamities that they had seen and experienced in Missouri and Tennessee had only made them closer. Even though Lockett was now an officer, the result of one foolhardy act of courage, he and the red-headed private were inseparable.

"Rebel cavalry, bah!" Sergeant Bosworth grunted.

"Of course, they're better off only because they have been pickin' our army clean for the last hundred miles," Patrick McManus added.

Like the rest of General Don Carlos Buell's army, Lockett and his little company were frustrated and sickened by the events of the last month. The army had won a pivotal battle at Shiloh just a few months ago, paid for in a galling price of blood, but the army was now in retreat. At least, that was how it felt to Lockett and the others as they trudged eastward. Told that they were to protect the vital rail supply line and to counter Confederate rumblings in the eastern part of the state, all they really knew was that this had become an increasingly slow and hot march away from their victory.

Lockett watched one Minnesotan hold something of value over his head with a cry of triumph. It was nothing new to see either side pick the dead clean after a battle or skirmish, though it still gave the tall officer an unsettled feeling.

"The Reb cavalry are better supplied than we are, course it is our stuff they have." Bosworth agreed with McManus. "I've lost track of how many times Forrest and Hunt Morgan's men have cut our supplies and communication."

"At least this time, they made a mistake and strayed too close to the main body," McManus responded.

An officer on a horse, apparently one of the Minnesotans, rode up to his men. He tried waving his men back into order, but even from across the field, Lockett could see the men only grudgingly stopped their search.

"Time to bury the dead," Bosworth remarked.

Lockett nodded and was about to lead the trio off, back to their regiment, when something flickered from the corner of his eye. He turned his head, wondering what had glinted from the tall grass. There was nothing there.

Then suddenly, a Rebel officer leapt up from the grass, sword in hand, heading straight for the Minnesotan on a horse. The other Minnesotans gave a cry of alarm, and the officer on his horse reached at his side for either his sword or revolver, but he was too late.

In one motion, the sword cut across his torso and the Rebel's other hand yanked the Northerner from the saddle. Launching himself into the saddle, the Rebel charged into the group of Minnesotans. He swung the sword wildly, but it was really the horse that did the rest, scattering the men to the left and right.

He spurred the horse into a full gallop, cutting across the field obliquely away from a second group of Minnesotans. But this second group had seen their officer fall and had the time to react. Picking up their rifles, they hurried to aim at the fleeing rider.

However, the Rebel was not done yet. Freeing his feet from the stirrups, he slid across the saddle, placing his right foot in the left stirrup. He clung to the side of the racing horse as it galloped by. At the speed with which he was moving, it was a stunning sight.

Clutching the side of the racing horse, he ducked behind the mane, shielded from the shots that whistled over the now empty saddle.

"Patrick," Lockett said, unnecessarily, since McManus had already unslung his Dimick Deer rifle.

Seemingly in the clear, the rider started to put himself in the saddle.

"Take the horse," Lockett ordered in an even voice.

The former sharpshooter took careful aim.

At this point, Sergeant Bosworth was still readying his own rifle, nodding absently to Lockett's commands.

The shot from McManus's rifle echoed and was true. The Rebel was still in the process of getting his feet back in the stirrups when the horse was struck. It swerved violently and lost its footing. Then its hind legs seemingly somersaulted over the front, throwing the rider wildly into the sky.

"C'mon," Lockett said, his voice showing some urgency for the first time. In a dead run, he took off for the spot where the Rebel had landed, eighty yards away.

"I ain't never seen anything like that trick ridin'!" Bosworth exclaimed, as he pounded along beside him.

I have, Lockett thought to himself.

The Minnesotans reached the Rebel first. Dazed, he was yanked to his feet only to take a rifle butt to the face. The soldier then reversed the rifle and aimed at the fallen Rebel.

But it was two shots from Lockett's revolver that they heard next. Frozen, the Minnesotans looked at the tall officer who ran toward them with his revolver pointed straight in the air.

"The man is my prisoner!" he shouted fiercely.

"He's done in the captain!" shouted back one of the Minnesotans.

"Go tend to your captain then," Lockett said. He glared at them with steady gray eyes, and despite the wrath they felt, they wavered, particularly when McManus and Bosworth caught up with their long-legged Lieutenant.

"I said, go tend to your captain," Lockett repeated in the menacing voice. Reluctantly, the Minnesotans departed.

The Rebel rose to one knee.

Even smeared with dirt and bloodied by the rifle butt, Lockett recognized the features and knew that he had been right. He was the younger, spitting image of the last man whom Lockett had seen ride like that.

"On yer feet, Secesh," Bosworth growled, roughly grabbing the man under the arm, "You're lucky to be alive, and I ain't talking about that fancy ridin'."

"True, Billy Yank," the Rebel answered with that now familiar Tennessee lilt. "And at whose hand was I delivered?"

Lockett shook his head and did not answer, not directly. "This war is the damndest thing," he grumbled. He looked at McManus and gestured at the Rebel. "Patrick, Milton, meet Anna's brother, Ambrose Tucker."

Chapter 2

Word of the encounter spread quickly through the encampment. It was no secret within Blair's Independent Regiment, especially those in Lockett's small half-strength company, that Lieutenant Lockett had spent considerable time with Anna Tucker back in Savannah, Tennessee.

The dark-eyed preacher's daughter had earned their admiration and loyalty. They all knew of her daily efforts in the hospital tents on the banks of the Tennessee River, tending to the many wounded from both sides after Shiloh.

The sights and smells of these hospitals made cowards even of the bravest men. One in ten would die, but every soldier knew it would have been worse without the selfless actions of those like Anna Tucker.

Yes, the men admired her. And no, it was no secret that their sometimes solemn, gray-eyed lieutenant was sweet on her.

However, what was a secret, a secret that Lockett even kept from McManus, was that Anna Tucker and her preacher father were not what they seemed.

They were Rebel spies.

By the time that Lockett had realized the truth, he was so closely tied to the Tuckers, both by appearances and emotions, that he had felt compelled to rescue the preacher from a Union trap. It had been a frantic and compromising day, where the preacher had returned the favor by protecting Lockett from the bushwhacker, Bloody Bill Coulter. It had left Lockett more conflicted than ever.

But that was history now, or so Lockett had been trying to tell himself for the past month.

Reverend Tucker was dead. Anna had left western Tennessee for her Aunt's. And Lockett was on this interminable march with General Buell where every day he found himself more morose and dejected than the day before.

Things had seemed so simple when he and his friends had left little Kalamazoo. Things were far from simple now.

And now Ambrose Tucker was here…

Anna's brother, who had supposedly been coerced and conscripted into the Rebels' service before Lockett and his comrades had swamped Savannah with their wounded from Shiloh, was his prisoner.

To McManus and Bosworth, it was a bizarrely silent march back with Anna's brother. Both Lockett and Anna's brother were curiously preoccupied with their own thoughts.

Not to mention that neither McManus nor Bosworth could figure out how their Lieutenant had known right away who the Confederate was.

The man bore some resemblance to his sister, but not so much that they ever would have made the connection. And yet, James had somehow made the connection instantly?

Patrick McManus, in particular, found this more than a little unsettling. He knew everything that there was about his old friend, or so he thought, but there was something more going on here, something that he did not know about James. This realization was more discomfiting to him than the sight of Rebel cavalry or infantry.

Meanwhile, Lockett's mind was also awash in thought. All that he could hear was his heart beating loudly in his chest. The silence and lack of questions meant something to him too. It meant that Ambrose Tucker knew who he was. That could mean only one thing. Ambrose had seen Anna. So Anna had mentioned him in some way to her brother, but what had she told him?

Did Ambrose know exactly who he was? Did Ambrose know exactly what had transpired with his father? Did Ambrose know that he was the Union officer who had helped Reverend Tucker, a Rebel spy, escape a trap?

So Anna had seen her brother, but how much had she told him?

* * *

It had been a fitful night of sleep for Lockett. Before his duties and the day's march began, he knew that there was one thing he had to do.

The dark had yet to fully give way to the light, but the morning cook fires were already starting to be extinguished, hissing as their embers turned dark and smoke twisted into curls in their lambent glow.

Nearby, the detachment from Illinois readied the small group of prisoners. Ambrose Tucker was the lone officer that they guarded, and as such, he was treated a sight better than the others.

Lockett had come with a tin cup of coffee for Anna's brother but was surprised to find that Tucker already had one.

"Not as good as the coffee we stole off your supply line two weeks ago," Ambrose Tucker remarked as he swirled the liquid in the dented tin cup.

The man's ease and lack of concern at being a prisoner struck Lockett as a type of contempt and arrogance. Both of these were characteristics that he despised in men of all shades. Lockett's frown was hidden by the darkness, but the annoyance in his voice was not. "You seem pretty pleased with yourself considering that you're a prisoner."

Tucker shrugged.

"Doubt you'll feel that way by the time you get to Rock Island."

"I'll be exchanged before then," Tucker said confidently.

This time it was Lockett's turn to shrug. He knew that there were still plenty of prisoner exchanges going on. Both sides had the inventory.

"I fig'gured you would come to see me off," Tucker said with a tone that hinted neither at civility nor hostility.

In the glow of a distant campfire, Tucker gave Lockett a small smile. It was not like the smile of his sister, Lockett thought.

From their first encounter, Lockett had noticed that Ambrose Tucker had dark eyes like his sister, but that is where the similarities ended. While Anna's rounded features, easy smile, and lively eyes gave one the impression that she was interested in whatever one had to say, Ambrose Tucker had a leaner, wolf-like confidence on his face, and his dark eyes seemed to stare right past Lockett. The thin smile that he wore gave the appearance that he knew something that the other did not.

14

Lockett studied him for a moment and was surprised that Anna's brother brought someone else to his mind, Orrin Long, his nemesis. Lockett scowled at the remembrance of the treacherous Long.

"I think we both knew that I would come, Ambrose. I would have to at some point."

Anna's brother had brought back a quick flood of memories last night. It had been impossible to stop his mind from flitting back to his time in Savannah. All of his self-control to block Anna from his mind had been made impotent.

Lockett gulped a third of the coffee that he had originally brought for Tucker. It looked like he needed it more than the Rebel anyway. With the nightlong memories, he had scarcely fallen asleep before Sergeant Bosworth's gruff hand had shaken him to start the day.

"So you knew who I was in that field?" Tucker started, his eyes following the actions of the Illinoisans around him instead of looking at Lockett. "How did you know?"

"Horsemanship," Lockett replied simply. "I've only seen one other man try that sidesaddle stunt to avoid fire."

He would never forget the image of Anna's father, Reverend Tucker, lame in one leg, aging, yet somehow swinging himself into that position along the horse's flank then galloping through the bushwhackers to give Anna and him a diversion…

"Father?"

"Yes, when Anna and I were cornered by bushwhackers. I never saw anything like that before… thought that I would never see anything like it again either."

"I guess it didn't work for him either," Tucker said grimly.

"No," Lockett said slowly, "Not in the end, but he did save Anna and myself." There was an awkward pause. "I don't think he ever thought he could accomplish more than he did. He knew what he was doing." There was another pause as the two men stood awkwardly in the darkness. "Anna told you all this, I assume?"

"Yes," Ambrose Tucker answered, looking around to make sure that there were no others within earshot. "And what you did, Yankee, makes no sense to me."

It doesn't make much sense to me either, Lockett mused. He

was no traitor, but he had tried to prevent Anna and her father from being captured as spies. Had he done it to protect her, or had he done it to protect himself?

"How is she?" Lockett finally asked.

This time it was Tucker's turn for a sad look. "She's taken it poorly. Oh, she's not weepy-eyed, but she and father were close. Her spirit is quiet, and that is not like her."

"No, that would not be like her," Lockett agreed. It was said in friendly way, but it stirred something else in the Southerner.

Tucker's features narrowed into a glare that was visible in the growing hues of morning. "You speak with a familiarity that disturbs me." After a breath, he added, "But I suppose that should not surprise me." Still, there was a steely-eyed glare.

Seconds passed before Tucker finally added, "I look at you and wonder... what possesses a man to betray his country?"

"Isn't that what I should be asking you?"

The retort stung Tucker whose face flashed anger. There was a physical tenseness from his shoulders down to his clenched fists. "I have, and always will be, loyal to *my* cause, Yankee. I have never strayed. Can you say that? What makes a man betray his own colors and help the other side?"

Lockett had asked himself that question many a time and knew that he had no answer.

The war continued to crawl on with devastating destruction, and he was... he was... a fool! He berated himself silently. He was a fool, and always would be until he met an empty, untimely death at the point of some bayonet or unseen minié ball!

"So why did you do it? You don't believe in that ape, Lincoln, do you? So help me escape, Yankee. Come back with me."

Lockett blinked in surprise, and his jaw hung open. He had not expected that sort of response.

"Escape? Are you crazy? And you're wrong about my motivations. I would never betray the Union or my brothers in arms trying to put down your rebellion."

Tucker looked disappointed and somewhat surprised.

"Escape?" Lockett repeated, shaking his head.

"Yes, escape. You tried to help Anna and my father escape. Now, help me escape."

"You're crazy."

"I think it is you who's crazy, Yankee."

"You are sitting in the middle of Buell's army. You think that you can escape?"

"With some help."

"Not from me."

"I know *all* about you," Tucker threatened.

Both men knew what he was getting at.

"You think that would work?" Lockett laughed to cover up his concern. "You're a prisoner who will say anything. That is what anyone would think. Besides, you would incriminate your own sister and dead father to free yourself?"

"There is nothing incriminating about being a patriot."

Lockett snorted again. He knew that he was putting up a good act, but it was an act. The threat of his secret coming out was real. "No one would believe you. They all think that the spy was Bloody Bill Coulter, and Bloody Bill was killed. That probably even led to another officer's promotion."

Lockett didn't really know if Orrin Long had received yet another promotion for supposedly killing the Savannah spy, but nothing would surprise him along those lines. It would be the height of irony though if he had to rely on Orrin Long's own hubris to protect him from Ambrose Tucker's claims of treachery.

There was a long pause. In the distance, there were a couple of shots as sentries emptied their rifles as precautions, worried that the morning damp had ruined their powder. Finally, Ambrose Tucker shrugged, and he smiled good-naturedly, as if he had never made any threat.

"Very well. Very well. Looks like I will just wait to be exchanged."

Chapter 3

--the diary of James Lockett
Mail made it through today, but little in the way of supplies.
There was still no letter from Daniel. My brother has not
answered one of my letters in a long time now. My concern grows
by the day.

* * *

"This ain't no work for soldiers. Look at me."

Patrick McManus looked at the man who had muttered the words, knowing that every man here felt the same way. His fellow soldier's face was streaked with dirt and smudged down the middle with railroad tar, giving Levi Thickle a badger-like appearance.

While both men's jackets had been set aside from the beginning, the blazing Tennessee sun had turned the thin shirts into soaking rags with more dirt and tar on them than anything else. Each man's clothing looked like it had been wrapped around a railroad tie and dragged across the ground, which was how most of the exhausted soldiers felt. And it was true what Private Thickle had said, they had a very un-military appearance at the moment.

"Levi, if you want to look more like a soldier, you could go work in Lieutenant Fulkerham's crew," McManus responded wryly.

Thickle scowled and did not bother to look at the other company's work crew. He stripped off his soiled shirt, joining a growing group of Lieutenant Lockett's men who were barebacked. Their jackets lay in a pile next to their stacked weapons, nearby just in case the Rebels decided to go for more than the edges of General Buell's army today.

Lieutenant Fulkerham's men, on the other hand, still labored in their woolen blue jackets at their officer's insistence.

McManus's comment ultimately drew no verbal response from Thickle, who turned back to his labor. McManus, of course, truly agreed with him. This was no work for soldiers. They were no army now, just common laborers for General Buell, fixing the Memphis-Chattanooga rail line as Buell's army slowly crawled eastward to Chattanooga.

The pace was agonizingly slow and frustrating. Rebel cavalry would sweep ahead, tear up the rail line. Buell's men would repair it and move forward, knowing that a week or two later the Rebels would either sweep ahead or behind them again and re-interrupt the line. It seemed a pointless exercise to McManus, but he had been in the army long enough now to know that the army was full of pointless exercises.

Patrick McManus left his farm with James Lockett and two other friends, ultimately becoming part of Birge's Western Sharpshooters. It seemed like years ago now with so much that had happened in between.

He had nearly died of disease in Missouri and returned home to find that his young wife had passed away in his absence. He then re-enlisted in the 12th Michigan with James, fighting at bloody Shiloh from beginning to end, and now he was repairing railroads with Blair's Independent Regiment, which most days more resembled a crew of laborers than soldiers.

Taking a drink from his canteen, the young Irishman looked at the others.

The big German, Otto Klugge, was coming up the embankment, a railroad tie over each shoulder. He spoke little English, but he did the work of three men.

Behind Klugge, as usual, was young Adie Graham. Four years short of his twentieth birthday, Adie was never too far from Klugge, although it was more because Klugge needed him rather than the other way around. Adie was the only one who could translate the man's guttural German into English. At this moment, Adie's slender boyish frame was slowly dragging a single railroad tie behind him. The tie made a rut in the ground like a farmer plowing his field.

That was where I should be, McManus thought to himself, back in Kalamazoo working on the farm. Somehow, he doubted he would ever do that again. He was here in this war now, and it did not seem like it would ever end.

"Ready?" Thickle's voice said, interrupting him.

McManus turned back to his work. He picked up the heavy sledge hammer and battered the iron spike through the railroad tie that Thickle had arranged into place.

Thickle started on the next tie. "Ain't got no point," he said to no one in particular, "These officers ain't got a tinker's clue what they're doing. We repair the line, and Johnny Reb rips it back up. Why fix it in the first place? The officers know this ain't working. Why, just look at our lack of supplies. They cain't even re-supply us from the line that we just fixed, already cut off by Forrest or Hunt Morgan or whoever runs these Reb horses. They ride circles clean round us."

McManus made no answer because none was necessary. He knew that grumbling was how Levi entertained himself through the monotonous or back breaking moments.

"Excepting Lieutenant Lockett, of course," Thickle added. It was an obvious after-thought. Thickle, like all the others, knew that McManus and the Lieutenant were close. It was an unusual bond that crossed the officer-general ranks threshold. Though in Lockett's case, it was perhaps more understandable since he had started out as a common private, eventually promoted to officer for his actions in the Hornet's Nest at Shiloh.

McManus paid no attention to Thickle, although mention of James did make him reflect on his friend as he hammered another set of spikes home.

James was, after all, the reason that he was here in Tennessee hammering railroad spikes. Every man in the army had their own reasons for being here. There were a few abolitionists, adventurers, cutthroats, thieves, and everything in between. In his case, he was here for friendship. James was the closest thing that he had to family now, especially since his wife died.

McManus had re-enlisted after that bad experience in Missouri for one reason only and that was to protect James. He had done that well so far, but with James... Well, trouble always seemed to find him.

* * *

-- the diary of James Lockett
A mile of progress today. The men are exhausted. Colonel
Blair says that tomorrow we will be on flanking duty. It is a job
for the cavalry, but since we have none, it will be our job to watch
for any prowling Rebels. Still, the men will cheer it. It is far
better than the work on the railroad.

* * *

The relentless northern Alabama sun beat down on them. It was mid-afternoon and the heat was at its most torturous. At least the day's march was over even though it seemed that they had scarcely started or made much progress. The reason for this brevity was not truly known to Lockett: lack of supplies, need to repair the railroad as they went along, the heat, or just a general lack of urgency to reach their destination of Chattanooga? It could have been any of these.

At this moment, the reason for the Army of the Ohio's sluggishness was not paramount in his mind. Honestly, he was just glad to be under the white canvas of Colonel Blair's tent with the other officers of their small regiment. Sweat still dampened his face and dripped steadily down his neck and back, but it felt twenty degrees cooler in the shade at least.

The other officers looked much the same. Lieutenants Williams and Fulkerham stood near each other, as usual. Their jackets were fully buttoned up to their neck. They both fancied the broader tarpot hat, which each had tucked under an arm. Like them or not, Lockett had to admit that the two surely looked the part of an officer.

Lieutenant Renaud stood next to Lockett, amiably chatting with Lieutenant Pope. The French Detroiter was the lone officer who seemed capable of liking each of Colonel Blair's small officer corps. Heavily bearded, Lockett wondered how Renaud was able to keep such facial hair in this heat.

Pope gave his mule like laugh at whatever Renaud had

remarked. Pope was a genial enough fellow, but if there was anything that Fulkerham and Lockett could agree on, it was that Pope was generally a weak officer.

Colonel Laurent Blair re-entered the tent. His officers came to quick attention, and he waved them at ease, laying a piece of paper on his small writing desk.

"General Orders Number Twenty-Four from General Buell," he said simply. In their short time together, Lockett had seen that the Colonel was very direct and not much for small talk or airy speeches, even more so as this slow march went on. "It's nothing new from the General. You are to remind your men of the importance of protecting the constitutional rights of all citizens, including those in rebellion."

Some of the frowns and stiffening postures did not surprise the Colonel. He knew how his men felt about General Buell's long-standing conciliatory policy.

"We ought to be punishing them, not protecting them. Spare the rod, spoil the child," Fulkerham muttered just loud enough for the others to hear. The statement went unanswered, but there were heads nodding.

Lockett, on the other hand, viewed the policy with mixed feelings. His experiences in Missouri immediately flashed into his head. He had seen what could happen. There were far more sinners than saints in this army.

The sight of little Amelia's blood flowed into Lockett's head, quickly followed by the sneering face of Orrin Long. Back in those early days, he had been surprised to see a Union officer and some of the men robbing a Missouri homestead or attempting an assault on the inhabitants.

It had been less of a surprise the second time. He had tried to stop Orrin Long and his cronies, but in trying to wrestle the gun free, it had gone off, shattering little Amelia's head.

The blood had been everywhere. Some nights when Lockett woke up, sweat dripping off his face, he would swear that he could feel her blood on his face and hands.

Yes, he knew what some men were capable of.

* * *

The rifles were stacked and the usual smell of the cook fires drifted up into a dirty brown haze over the camp. The air was heavy and still, seemingly holding the smoke down like blanket over the sweltering camp. There was not even enough breeze to make a single blade of grass wave.

Lockett turned at the sound of a horse approaching. The sound was rare these days. Before departing on the march, General Buell had ordered that officers like Lockett were not permitted to ride horses. Many of the officers grumbled greatly at having to leave their horses behind, but it did not bother Lockett as much.

He preferred to walk, despite the fact that Anna Tucker had left him her father's horse. Thunderbolt was as impressive of an animal as his name. Lockett had never ridden anything remotely like him, but he was no horseman. It was probably just as well that he had left the horse behind before he killed himself on the charger. Thunderbolt was now in care of a shopkeeper in Savannah with instructions that it be given to his friend, Ainsley Stuart, when Ainsley had recovered enough from his wounds. Of course, he wasn't sure that Ainsley would ever be able to ride it considering that he was now missing a foot, courtesy of a Rebel shell at Shiloh.

War had made for some strange friendships, Lockett mused. While he himself was just a poor farmer trying his best to keep their little farm afloat after his father's death, Ainsley was close to royalty in Kalamazoo: wealthy, educated, and with an important father. Now, James carried Ainsley's family sword. It only seemed right that Ainsley have the majestic black horse in return.

So lost in these thoughts, Lockett did not notice that the horse and rider had reined in at his tent. It was one the Anderson troopers from Pennsylvania, General Buell's personal bodyguard. "You Lieutenant Lockett?" the rider asked.

"I am."

"General wants you forthwith."

"General Buell?" Lockett asked with some astonishment.

"If you're the Lieutenant Lockett who captured that Reb a week back, then yes."

Lockett arrived at General Buell's headquarters with bewilderment and a serious sense of dread. He had a hard time imagining what this could be about and every scenario that he could envision was not a good one. Had Ambrose escaped? Had Ambrose told someone of how Lockett had helped Rebel spies escape capture in Savannah? What else could it possibly be?

The Anderson trooper had instructed Lockett to wait next to the fence one hundred yards from the headquarters and said he would be summoned. That was nearly two hours ago. Although it was far from the hottest part of the day, he could feel himself melting in the sun. Across the way, there was the shade of some trees, but he did not dare wander over for relief. General Buell's lengthy reputation as a stickler suggested that would be a terrible idea.

Finally, a captain emerged from the tent and headed straight towards Lockett.

"Follow me, Lieutenant Lockett," he said simply, turning without another word, fully assured that Lockett would be on his heels.

"May I ask what this is about?" Lockett asked as he trailed the man.

The captain ignored the question. He ushered Lockett into the tent where he saw Ambrose Tucker calmly sitting on a camp stool. The captain ushered Lockett to the corner and then departed, leaving the two of them alone.

"What's going on?" Lockett demanded, but in a quiet voice.

"Your army is without honor... and good sense," Ambrose Tucker answered. He was in a particularly cheerful mood, clearly amused by what was going on.

"What are you talking about?" Lockett hissed. The two hours baking in the sun had sapped his patience, but Tucker just looked at him with a calm, gloating face.

There was a rustling at the tent flap, and Lockett turned with the frown still on his face before realizing that he was standing before General Buell. Lockett blushed and snapped to attention. "Sir," he said, saluting.

General Don Carlos Buell was a stocky, deep-chested man. Though not towering, he cut an impressive muscular figure and wore a full, but trim, gray-flecked beard. He looked at Lockett with a narrowed gaze.

"I understand that you two are friends," the General began. He paused, waiting for Lockett to answer.

24

"More like we have a mutual friend, sir," Lockett answered cautiously, "I only met Lieutenant Tucker when I captured him a few days back, sir."

General Buell tapped a finger on his thigh, seemingly disappointed with the answer.

"May I ask why I am here, sir?"

"You are here to talk sense to this... this man..."

Tucker interrupted with a bemused laugh, "These Yankees want me to take an oath of allegiance, James."

Buell glared at the interruption, and Lockett worried for Ambrose's safety. General Buell had a reputation of no tolerance for insubordination. In fact, the rumor in camp was that the General had nearly been court-martialed in his younger days for slicing the ear off of an insolent private during the Seminole Wars. Some said that he had killed the man outright merely for disobeying an otherwise benign order.

Instead, Buell turned suddenly and spoke to the captain behind him, whom Lockett had not even noticed before. "Captain Harrison, you will explain the situation to Lieutenant Lockett so that he can convince his *acquaintance* of his foolishness."

Buell marched abruptly from the tent, and Captain Harrison motioned for Lockett to follow him outside.

Once they passed the guard at tent flap and were out of ear shot of the tent, Captain Harrison turned to Lockett. "It's quite simple really. The general wants the man to take the oath of allegiance to the Union. Once the man does that, he is free to go."

"Free to go?" Lockett asked.

"Free to go. Pardoned."

"Just like that?"

"The other prisoners all took the oath earlier today. That man is the only one left."

"The other prisoners are gone?"

"Sent home with promises that they won't take up arms against the Union again. The general believes that this will help persuade the locals of our good intentions. That all this army is interested in is re-establishing the union under one government and constitution."

Lockett looked uncomprehendingly at the captain. He was all for convincing the Southerners of their good intentions, even though he knew that there were plenty in both armies who wouldn't understand the words 'good intentions', much less the actions, but it seemed particularly foolish to assume that a simple oath would fix everything and that those men would not take up arms again, especially once their property was threatened by an invading blue army.

"Ambrose is the only one left?"

"Yes, are you daft, man? I just said that," the captain answered with exasperation.

"And Ambrose refuses to take the oath?"

"Says that he cannot promise not to take up arms again."

"Shouldn't we be thankful for his honesty? And what do you want me to do about it anyway?"

"The man's a damn fool."

"Maybe, but at least he seems to be an honorable one," Lockett said stubbornly.

"You don't understand, Lieutenant. Your friend seems to think that he is going to be exchanged."

"He's not my friend."

"Regardless, the point is that he will not be exchanged. Things are too fluid in this theater. We don't know that the enemy has anybody to exchange, nor do we have a good way to contact them."

"Plenty of men have been scooped up by Hunt Morgan and Forrest over the past two months. I'm sure that there are plenty who could be exchanged."

"You don't understand, man. You are as stupid as all of these other damn country bumpkin volunteers. Just as the General always says, you volunteers have no concept of how to run an army."

Lockett ignored the insult. "You want me to convince him to lie to us? Or lie to himself? Or both?"

"The general wants no prisoners right now. This army is having a hard enough time feeding itself. It does not want to feed a prisoner too."

He's just one mouth, Lockett thought bitterly.

"So, convince him, Lieutenant."

"And if I can't convince him?"

"Convince him."

When Lockett returned to the tent, Ambrose Tucker was still seated in the same rough camp stool. He smiled grandly when Lockett entered, obviously entertained by the entire episode.

"So they sent you to change my mind now?"

Lockett pulled another stool so that he sat across from him. "They want you to take the oath of allegiance."

"I'm not going to do it," Tucker said lightly.

"Because?"

"Because I don't believe in this union! I have a country to fight for and that country is Tennessee's, not Abraham Lincoln's. I'll not pretend otherwise."

"You won't put down your arms?"

"Never, not until we've won this war."

"What if you don't win, Ambrose?"

"Then, I'll be dead and I won't have to worry about putting down arms anymore."

"A fight to the death for you then?"

"That is what this is, Yankee, and you won't win such a fight."

Lockett's face twisted into a mixture of a frown and a nod of agreement. "Most likely not when our generals let you go every time we catch one of you."

They lapsed into silence for a moment before Ambrose Tucker continued. "So that is it? That is how you were going to get me to take the oath?"

"I'm not going to try to convince you of anything," Lockett answered bluntly.

"Funny thing, though. You are starting to make me wonder if I should take the oath then, but I still think not. I was raised better than that. It would be wrong to knowingly lie like that. Besides, I will be exchanged anyway."

Lockett looked at him. Again, this war made for some strange realizations. There was still something about Ambrose Tucker that he did not like. The haughty attitude, the confidence, the desire to fight to the death for something that Lockett could not understand... All of it.

Yet, though he disliked the man, there was still something admirable about Ambrose Tucker. It was the importance that he placed in honesty and honor. It would be so easy to just take the oath and then conveniently forget about it an hour later when he was safely back with his people. Who would ever be the wiser?

"So what other tricks do you have?" Tucker mocked, "What next to get me to sell out my country and my honor?"

Lockett stood calmly and straightened his jacket before saying anything. "Nothing, Ambrose. We're done here. Don't take the oath. Keep praying that you get exchanged before they send you to Rock Island or someplace. Get that exchange." He looked squarely at the Tennessean. "And then let's hope that our paths *never* cross again. Let's pray that fervently." He turned without another word and left the tent.

Chapter 4

-- the diary of James Lockett
Two miles of progress today. The Rebels did a hasty job in this
section of the line. Most of the material could be reused. It was
quick tear up only. Still, our progress is so slow. How can this
war end if we never reach our destination? This rebellion can
only be put down by force, by victories, by blood and killing. I
have no wish to see more of the latter, but how can it end without
it? If we need to capture Chattanooga, then let's march to
Chattanooga.

* * *

Two days later, Lockett laid on his back reading his journal in
the glow of the evening. He had intended to write of today's
actions, as monotonous and routine as they had been. It had been
another crawling mile of track work, back to camp, and futile
hopes for putting some real miles of marching in. But before he
could write more entries into his beloved journal, he found himself
looking at past entries from his time in Savannah. Of course, he
had not written any of his final interactions with the Tuckers, lest
his journal be read by prying eyes and someone learn his secret.

He flipped through the pages and re-read April, starting with
the day that he had first met Anna Tucker. He didn't need to re-
read the account. It was burned in his memory. It had been in that
tent hospital when he had gone to find his friend, Ainsley Stuart.

Of course, the day that Ainsley had been wounded was another
day that he would never forget. There was the hour after hour of
horrific killing within the Hornet's Nest, then the sight of Ainsley
falling, of his mad dash with Patrick, carrying Ainsley all the way.
Finally, there was the thoughtless desperation of their eventual

charge into the Rebels, which was the action that had suddenly propelled him to being an officer.

Those were memories that he wished to leave behind. But that first day with Anna...

Her flawless face, that bursting smile, how she somehow kept everyone's spirits up... How she was oblivious to the horrors of the hospital tent around her, and how she made things better.

Lockett had never been the love struck type. There was too much work and responsibility for that. But that was what made Anna's presence so life-changing and unreal to him. Of course, those silly dreams that he had harbored deep inside were all dashed now.

He now knew her true motivations. The army had moved on from Savannah, and so had she. He would never see her again. Perhaps that was just as well, because he doubted that he could handle the conflicting emotions.

For weeks, he had been forcing himself to forget her. It had not been easy to attempt, but now after Ambrose, it was impossible, Lockett thought to himself.

"Sir, come quick, sir!"

It was one of his men, Oliver O'Leary, who was supposed to be on picket duty.

"What is it?" Lockett said, jumping up and grabbing his rifle instinctively.

"Trouble with Lieutenant Williams's men. Easier if you come see," O'Leary answered cryptically.

They arrived just as Lieutenant Williams arrived and looked at an unexpected scene. Adie Graham and Otto Klugge stood confrontationally across from two of Williams's men, one of whom had blood dripping out of one nostril.

Behind Adie and Otto, there were five blacks, four of whom looked like escaped slaves to Lockett's eyes based on their tattered clothing. The fifth one, conversely, had a washed, clean-shaven appearance and wore higher quality clothes that were in better shape than Lockett's own dusty and patched blue.

"What's going on, Adie?"

"They're just looking for some food, sir," Adie burst out.

"Your men are disregarding a direct order," Williams corrected, scowling at Lockett.

30

There had long been animus between the two men, but Lockett's tried to keep an even tone. "Still looking for someone to explain what is going on here."

"My men were relieving yours from picket duty, and just in time from the looks of it. As they arrived, they saw your men talking to these here slaves and letting them through the lines."

"They just need food, sir," interrupted Adie. The act drew another scowl from Williams and a gentle nod of reproof from Lockett.

"When my men interceded, that is when your ape slugged Peters." He pointed at Klugge.

The burly German gave no reaction to being called an ape, if he even recognized the word.

"You know the standing orders, Lockett," Williams said, pointing at the five refugees. "No contraband."

"They're not contraband; they're people, sir," Adie retorted.

"I'll not stand this insubordination one more time," Williams warned, while Lockett gave Adie his own look of warning. It was not like the boy to be so fired up and willingly unruly.

"Lieutenant Williams is right, Adie. You know the standing orders. You can't let them into camp."

"Sir," Adie pleaded, "They just want food."

"We don't have food to give," Williams replied angrily. "Our own rations have been cut thanks to those Rebel marauders."

"Suhr," one of the five spoke up. He was the one with the nicer clothing, and he did not seem to have much in common with the other four. Not only were the others in far different condition, but their faces plainly held a guarded look as they watched the argument. The speaker, on the other hand, did not seem to wear the same hunted and tired countenance. "We don't want a hand out. We can work for the food."

"Really? And what can she do?" Williams scoffed, pointing at the lone woman in the group.

"She's good at doing laundry, suhr," he answered, seemingly taking no offense at Williams's tone.

"What's your name?" Lockett asked.

"Amos, suhr."

"Are you escaped slaves?"

"No, suhr," Amos answered uncomfortably. There was a

pause.

"Of course they're slaves," Williams said irritably, and Lockett was prone to agree with Williams for once.

* * *

"Are you lucid?" Colonel Blair demanded. The commander of Blair's Independent Regiment glared at Lockett with his icy blue eyes. His skin flushed to nearly the color of his thick reddish, brown hair. In frustration, he pulled at his bushy side whiskers, which wrapped around his ears, across his cheeks and into a moustache.

Lockett was used to waking before the dawn. That was life in the army, not to mention his prior life on the farm. However, the summons this morning from Colonel Blair was unexpected, and he found himself foggy. Sluggishly, his brain tried to connect what Colonel Blair was so irate about.

While the colonel had a temper, and though their backgrounds were as different as could be, Lockett had often found himself surprised at how well they got on. He had expected the worst, but the former banker had given Lockett respect based on what had happened at Shiloh.

Respect or not, this morning, the red rimmed glare was square at him.

"No, lucid is not the word. Deaf. Deaf is the word, Lockett! Deaf in hearing and deaf in listening. Do you know the difference? No, of course not. You *know* the general's orders regarding the slaves!"

Lockett shook himself, his mind slowly clearing. This was about Adie and those escaped slaves? "Yes, sir," Lockett finally answered as the Colonel caught his breath. "The general's orders are that they are not allowed in camp. I told Private Graham that. Are they in camp?"

"In camp? Mercy, no. Then there would be real hell to pay with General Buell. Lockett, no contraband is allowed in camp, but that is only half of General Buell's orders. The other half is that they are to be reported to the local authorities."

"Report them? I was not aware of that, Colonel, but why would I want to report them? And who would I report them to exactly?" he asked, truly puzzled.

The icy glare that Blair had focused on Lockett now turned into a scowl, and he looked at the tent opening. "Why report them? You would be reporting them so that they could be returned to their owners. That's the obvious reason."

"Sir, returning them to their bondage wouldn't go over well with some of the men."

"And with a different group of the men in your same company, it would go over perfectly well," Blair replied. "You know that just as well as I."

Lockett could only agree with Colonel. The army had a mixture of feelings on the matter of slaves and slavery. For some, slavery was the whole reason that they were in the army; for others, they did not think much about it. And while yet others may not care for the institution of slavery, that did not mean they wanted the slaves trailing them around and held them in low regard.

While Lockett knew what his own feelings were, having sat through innumerable sermons on the matter from Reverend Bailey. His belief that slavery was evil and corrupt only made obedience to General Buell's orders more difficult.

Colonel Blair lowered his voice to a hush. "Don't think that I don't agree with you. I know what you are thinking. If slavery isn't no more at the end of this war, then what have we fought it for? Yes, I know, Lockett. But these are the direct orders from the general. We can't just ignore them. It's not about our feelings on the matter, Lockett. These are the General's orders, and he means no deviation. He has a very strict, if not peculiar, thought on how the country should be. He has been clear that we are not here to fight for the slaves. He believes that we are fighting this war to return the country to *the way it used to be* and nothing more."

"Begging your pardon, sir, but that is impossible. The country will never be able to go back. Battles like Shiloh have seen to that. Too much blood was spilled, will still be spilled, to ever go back, even if that was the right answer. General Buell was at Shiloh. He should know that!"

"Lockett," Blair said, shaking his head. "Damned if I don't like you, but sometimes you say the most ignorant things. You are a mere lieutenant and a tossed up one at that. This is a general that you are talking about. If he ever heard you talk like that, or even a colonel like me, he would hammer you back into the dirt before you knew what happened. You see what I am saying?"

"Honestly, no, sir."

"Lockett, Lockett. You see, General Buell is married to a Southern belle. She brought slaves into the marriage. No one will be changing his mind on the disposition of slaves, so find a way to abide by his orders... or at least look like it."

"Sir, it is one thing to turn them out of camp, but we cannot turn them over to authorities. Besides, I don't even know who that would be. At this point, in these parts, aren't we the local authorities?"

"I thought you were a farmer, Lockett? You sound like a lawyer."

"So you are ordering me to try to find some local authorities in the morning?"

Blair hesitated. "No, the march continues in a couple of hours. There is another section of track that needs repair... I have no time to let you wander off in search of some local constable. Tell them to disappear. If some other regimental commander was to become aware..."

"Yes, sir," Lockett said coyly.

"And try to keep any other slaves from interacting with our soldiers, for their own good."

"Yes, sir."

"And, Lockett... we never had this conversation. Do you understand?"

"Yes, sir."

"No, of course, you don't."

"Yes, sir."

"By Lucifer, Lockett, I can see it in your eyes. You want to stick your neck out for some slaves who just wandered out of the woods? No, don't answer that. I know the answer. I saw you do it for Private Klugge before."

"Otto Klugge has become one of my best soldiers, sir."

"Of course, but someday, Lockett, it won't work out for you so pretty, this habit of yours."

Chapter 5

Lockett sat wearily on the edge of the dried up creek bed. The men had fallen out for a brief rest. He took off a shoe and looked it over. The front half of the sole was flopping freely again. It wouldn't be much longer until the whole thing came apart.

Milton Bosworth joined him. "Sorry, sir, thought that I fixed that good the other night."

"Not your fault, Milton. The leather is just rotting away. It won't hold the stitching."

"I better try again anyway. Ain't gonna want to do this march without shoes."

"True," Lockett agreed, "It's a sad state of things when my best chance of better shoes is to take them off a dead Reb after a skirmish."

"Most likely, they'd be barefoot too," Bosworth chuckled.

"Of course, even if we were supplied, all that might mean is that I end up with a pair like yours." He pointed at the ill-fitting and bizarrely wide shoes on Bosworth's feet.

"Ain't that the truth. These pontoons... They don't even look like shoes."

"I think you might be able to fit both feet in one shoe, Milton."

"Ain't tried that, but you're probably right," Bosworth grimaced. "Hard to imagine how someone could make shoes like this. Even a blind man could tell these ain't the shape of person's foot, and I ain't the only one with pontoons. Five or six of the boys have the same, damned near a miracle that we can even walk in these without falling over ourselves."

Lockett exhaled loudly and leaned back in the dry grass. "What a crazy time this is, Milton. A crazy time. I wonder sometimes how we got here."

For once, Bosworth was quiet, not sure how to take his

lieutenant's musings. They had been together a couple of months now, and Bosworth knew that he could depend on this officer, unlike his old officers in the 53rd Ohio, but sometimes he did not understand the lieutenant.

"How did you end up here, Milton?"

"Sir?"

"I mean, I know that you came from the 53rd. I know that just like the rest of us in my company that we were all at Shiloh, left over from shredded units."

"We're from all over," Bosworth's head bobbed, "Ohio, Michigan, Illinois. Why John Messern is even from Kaintuck."

Lockett nodded, "I mean, why did you join the 53rd Ohio in the first place?"

"Oh, well, seemed like the thing to do, sir. The Union and all…"

"Not to free the slaves like Adie?"

"Ain't no supporter of slavery, but it ain't my problem either. No, I want the country to stay together. We got laws and constitutions. George Washington didn't beat the British and give us our freedom so that some renegades could all go separate ways."

"Renegades? That's strong."

"Basic folk don't want to go."

"You sure about that, Milton? They fight like hell."

"They had laws, even here in Tennessee. They voted to stay in the Union, and still, the renegades forced them to break off."

"And still most of them fight like hell."

"They fight like hell, sir, because we are here. If the renegades had just left well enough alone, then we wouldn't be here and the rest wouldn't want to fight us."

Lockett looked at his burly sergeant, a little surprised at the philosophical depth that he had just heard.

"They voted to stay in the Union, and yet, here we are," Bosworth repeated.

Lockett knew that was true, but he was surprised that Bosworth knew that as well. Perhaps, he had picked up that tidbit about Tennessee's vote during their time in Savannah.

"One country, sir, under one flag. It's simple."

Lockett wasn't sure that it was really that simple. He also

36

knew that his own motivations were more complex and maybe more convoluted.

"What about you, sir? Why did you join?"

Lockett bit his lip before answering.

"For the slaves, sir?"

"No, not for the slaves, although I think that they should be free to do what they want to, like you and I. No, I volunteered to stop my younger brother from volunteering."

"I don't understand, sir."

Sometimes Lockett wondered if he understood himself, but he answered, "My father died when I was a boy. As the head of the house, it was my job to keep us alive. My brother, Daniel, is a fool, a rudderless fool, always off in search of fun or adventure. I knew he wanted to volunteer, and he'd probably get himself killed."

"So you tried to take his place?"

"The farm has to be run still. The farm is what provides for my youngest brothers and my mother. He's the only one capable of doing it besides me."

"So by volunteering, you force him to stay on the farm, and you take his place as cannon fodder?"

"That's about it."

"Sir?" Bosworth said hesitatingly.

"Go on."

"Sir, I don't mean no disrespect, but that sounds like a crazy idea."

"You mean because I might get killed then instead of him?"

"No, sir, not that part. That part don't sound so crazy. I reckon that is why we fight so hard and the Rebs too. We all have brothers whether by blood or bond that we would fight to the death for. Every battlefield has something like that. No, it is the other part that sounds like it ain't gonna work."

"What other part?"

"The part about forcing him to stay on the farm. If he's the spirited boy you describe, he ain't gonna think sense and stay on the farm. He'll probably hate you for trying to make him stay on farm, and he'll spend every waking hour figuring a way out."

* * *

The blue jacketed horse troopers had trotted into camp with their normal imperious attitude. Lockett and all of the other soiled and dusty infantry men had watched them with poorly disguised contempt.

"Like to see *them* put this railroad back together since they're the ones who can't keep the Rebs at bay," Levi Thickle grumbled to the knot of comrades.

For once, Lockett was inclined to agree with the acerbic Thickle.

"Their horses look better fed than we are," Oliver O'Leary griped.

"They didn't run into any Rebs between here and Kentucky this time," Adie remarked.

"That jus' means that Forrest and Hunt Morgan decided to let them through," Thickle replied. "They're still out there."

Amidst the murmuring agreement, Lockett thought it strange that the Rebel cavalry leaders had such admirers within the Union ranks. But it was true that Nathan Bedford Forrest, John Hunt Morgan, and their respective raiders could seemingly do as they pleased behind the lines. Of course, they knew the land, and there were plenty of locals willing to help them.

Lockett watched one of the Union cavalry lieutenants talking to Renaud and Colonel Blair. He was a small, bow-legged man, perfect for riding a horse, Lockett amused himself with the thought. So focused was he on that man that Lockett did not notice Milton Bosworth coming over from a group of fellow sergeants that included a couple of the cavalrymen.

"Got some news, sir," Bosworth said.

"Mail?" Lockett said, not bothering to hide his hopes.

"Sorry, sir, not that," Bosworth answered, knowing how anxious his lieutenant was to hear from home. "No, other news, sir. The rest of regiment has left Michigan. They should join us in a few weeks."

Blair's Independent Regiment was a volunteer regiment outfitted by Colonel Blair himself. As a wealthy banker, it was his contribution to the war. But the regiment had been only a half strength group, short on men and officers. To this group of Detroiters, Lockett's own company of post-Shiloh detritus had been attached.   Initially, Lockett had been sour on the arrangement, but over time he had come to respect Colonel Blair, and he especially liked the fact that the regiment was short on officers. This meant that he could command his own company as a mere lieutenant. However, while the news of the reinforcements was good news to most, to Lockett, it was horrible news.

"Men and officers?"

"Yes, sir," Bosworth answered. "According to the trooper, it's a full complement."

Lockett frowned and tried to keep his mouth shut, but the look said it all.

The furrowed brow did not flummox Bosworth though, who added, "It'll be all right, sir. A lot can happen between now and then."

"Like what? Getting killed?" Lockett snapped. He instantly regretted the harsh words, but he turned nonetheless and walked away, wondering about the faceless captain who would be coming to take away his company and his men.

* * *

--the diary of James Lockett

Still no mail, so no news from Daniel. The cavalry did bring other news. Reinforcements and replacements will be joining our regiment soon from Detroit. To boot, Fulkerham's captaincy came through. So he does not need to worry about his company. The man has never seen a battle, but one year in West Point does wonders. Amazing how the professional soldiers treat the volunteers. Without us, there would be no Army, but they treat us as if we are in the way. And it is not just young lieutenants and captains. I saw General Buell himself today berating Colonel Blair and another volunteer regimental commander for slackness, when there was no slackness to be found. If the General thinks that this provides respect for his superiority, it is lost on us.

* * *

Adie slipped back into his bedroll. He could hear Prosper T. Rowe's usual prodigious snoring above the sound of the insects, but all else was quiet. Satisfied, he laid his head back and closed his eyes.

There was the crunch of footsteps in the dry grass nearing him, but Adie kept his eyes closed and feigned sleep. The steps came closer and stopped next to him. A rough hand grabbed his shoulder.

"I know you're awake, Adie," came Milton Bosworth's gruff whisper. "Where have you been slipping off to?"

Adie sat up. He was quiet as he contemplated trying to lie to the sergeant.

"You're going to get yourself shot, going out near the pickets in the dark of night."

Adie stayed silent, recognizing now that Bosworth was not alone. McManus stood behind.

"No, you won't get shot, will you, Adie?" McManus corrected after a pause, "That's because you know the pickets tonight, and you gave them a warning, didn't you?"

Adie's blink of surprise went unnoticed in the dark of night. "I'm not deserting."

Bosworth snorted in amusement. "Of course, you ain't deserting, but what are you doing?"

"They don't want trouble," Adie said slowly, "But they need food."

Neither McManus nor Bosworth was surprised by the answer, but they had wanted to hear it from Adie.

"You can't go helping every contraband who approaches the army," Bosworth said.

"And what food?" McManus added, "If you're giving them part of your rations, that won't work for long for either of you. You're already a wee wisp. You'll shrivel into nothing."

"If I want to give my food to someone, whose business is that?"

"It's not your food, Adie," Bosworth said, "It's the army's food, and they give it to you so that you can stay in condition to pull a trigger."

Adie frowned. "I'm just trying to follow orders. They're not allowed in camp...."

McManus cut him off. "Those weren't orders, Adie, to go out into the woods. The orders part was to keep them out of camp.

You shouldn't be providing any assistance. You'll get the Lieutenant in a heap of trouble. Imagine what Fulkerham or Williams would do if they heard that we were feeding the contraband?"

"I won't stop trying to help them, Patrick," Adie said stubbornly.

McManus wanted to smile at the determination of the scrawny youth, but there was one other thought that overrode all others. "Don't get caught, and you got to do it without the Lieutenant knowing or calling it anything like official."

"You know our Lieutenant," Bosworth added, "We don't need to give him any trouble. Trouble finds him well enough on its own."

* * *

Ambrose Tucker dug inside his faded butternut jacket for the louse.

"Pointless task," Lockett remarked to him.

"True. They care not whether it is officer or enlisted, nor Billy Yank or Johnny Reb." Tucker was in high spirits which was to be expected. This was the day that he had promised would come. He was being exchanged after all.

"They plague us all," Lockett agreed.

"I was wondering if you'd see me off this day," Tucker commented, changing the subject and giving up on the hunt for the louse.

"I was wondering that myself."

"Fair trade, though," Tucker apprised, "One of us for three of those Yank riders. Even deal."

For a second, Lockett thought it was another jest, but then he realized from the look on Ambrose Tucker's face that he was serious. Lockett found himself wondering if that was what the elder Tucker had been like in his younger days when he had ridden in Mexico.

"I see that your brief time in captivity has not changed your impression of yourself."

"And why should it? It was just my bad luck that you happened upon the scene. If it weren't for your man's marksmanship, I would have ridden clean away."

Lockett shook his head silently, unwilling to engage the man in the argument, even if he knew what to say to it.

"So in a matter of hours, Lockett, I return to the South. Any messages that you would like to return with me?"

Lockett was caught off-guard by the offer. "Messages?"

"I shall let Anna know that you are well," Tucker offered.

Lockett paused. What would he have Anna know? He wasn't sure himself what he could say to her even if she was standing in front of him.

"No message, then," Tucker laughed after the pause, "Then I suppose this is farewell until next time, though as you said before, you should pray that there is no next time. In this world, that is unlikely to have such a cheery outcome as this day."

Lockett frowned. The man was beginning to irritate him greatly, as was this whole situation.

"I have no message," Lockett said tersely, "And I do pray that we never meet again, Ambrose."

Chapter 6

Adie waited for the tell-tale night bird call to respond. After a second, he heard the usual response, and then he showed himself from his crouched sentry provision. He yawned. The extra sentry duty that he had volunteered for came at the cost of some precious sleep, but he did it without a second thought. It was the easiest way to accomplish what he wanted to do.

Levi Thickle and some of the others obliged without hesitation. They all knew why the youngster was volunteering for extra duty and could not understand it, but if it gave them a moment more of rest, they were happy to do so. Rest was precious, and the idea of volunteering additional times to stay awake all night and then march the next day without rest was madness to them. Sentry duty was so boring and exhausting that the men joked about needing to sit on their bayonets to stay awake, and the penalty for falling asleep on post included court martial and even death.

"It's not much," Adie said apologetically as Amos and Hal appeared from the shadows.

"It never is," Hal said with a frown. He was the older of the two ex-slaves. Thick-shouldered but somewhat stooped with a streak of gray hair on the left side of his head, he always said little, and when he did speak, it was usually in a grumble. Comically, he reminded Adie of Levi Thickle. Of course, he would never tell that to Levi, who would not take kindly to being compared to a slave. Though he was young, Adie had grown up understanding that not everyone thought slavery the great evil that he and his family did.

"We're grateful... Adie," Amos answered. The final word took physical effort to say. Adie had long since informed them that they should address him as Adie, and not Master Adie or any other derivation.

43

"We'd be better off stealing food," Hal answered, "Either from the army or the people."

"Foolish talk," Amos said, ignoring him. He wiped sweat from his smooth brow.

Even in the dark of night, the air was heated, and the humidity clung like a second skin. Smooth-faced, unlike the bearded Hal, Amos was a picture in contrasts to his fellow escapee: close-cropped hair, refined features, and nicer clothes than Hal's rags, although the clothing was quickly becoming more tattered and worn. Amos's outlook was also different in many ways.

Adie had learned in their previous conversations that Amos had not worked in the fields like the others. He had actually been a somewhat skilled laborer and given a surprising amount of authority and freedom as a sort of supervisor in his master's distillery. As a believer in abstinence from alcohol, unlike nearly all of his comrades, Adie found it ironic that someone with such skills trailed along behind the army, and that the only one who knew of those skills was the one person who could care less.

"The cavalry said that there is a supply train in route. It should reach us in a week. That should help with what we can muster together," Adie explained. He knew the other Abolitionists in the ranks, and between them, they shaved their own rations and scrounged what they could for Amos, Hal, and the others.

Adie hoped the cavalry was right, and that the Confederate raiders were nowhere to be found this time, because at this rate, there would be little to share in a week's time. They needed a supply train.

* * *

The familiar jangle of canteens and rifles, tramping feet, and time-passing talk in the ranks sounded again. It was another day of marching, another day of dry dirt roads, dusty throats, and sore feet.

"Walk with me, Adie," Lockett said, as they moved ahead of the column, surprising Adie with the extra attention. "So how are your unofficial friends doing?"

"Patrick and the sergeant told you, sir?" he asked worriedly.

But Lockett just smiled. "No. No one told me. I just knew

that you'd be taking care of things. Are they still with us?"

"Yes, they trail the column. The rear guard actually likes it that way. They figure it will give them extra warning if the Rebs sweep up from behind. They figure they'll take a few shots at escaped slaves before they take shots at us."

"Tell me about them, Adie. What are they like?"

"Well, what do you want to know, sir? I can tell you more about Amos. He does most of the talking."

"He was the smooth faced one? He's their leader?"

"No, I don't think I would say that he is their leader. I'm not even sure that the others even like him, but they let him do most of the talking with me."

"They don't like him?"

"The others worked the fields. Amos didn't. He worked in the distillery."

"Distillery? Don't let the others know that. They'd have him putting up a still in a heartbeat," Lockett said, only half-joking. "What about the others?"

"Don't know as much about them, sir. I usually only see Amos and Hal. Hal, well, he's not the pleasant sort. I'm actually surprised that he hasn't gone his own way yet. I know that they are anxious for the army to turn north. I tell them that we are heading east to Chattanooga, and we ain't going north, but they still follow right along. I guess they figure it's safer to follow us than set out on their own northwards."

"Probably," Lockett agreed, "If I were them, I'd probably do the same. They got a long ways to go to reach some actual safety. I can't imagine what I'd do if I were in their shoes."

Adie nodded in agreement.

"I can't imagine that I'd make it," Lockett added. "Strange country, don't know your way, no friends to help…"

"There are some friends, sir. There's the underground railroad."

Lockett shrugged, "But how do you find that, Adie?"

"I don't know," Adie admitted. He was about to add something else when Lieutenant Williams caught up with them. Williams allowed himself a glare at the young private before addressing Lockett.

"Lockett," he said, "The colonel has informed me that we'll be stopping about a quarter mile from here. All officers to report to him when we do."

Colonel Blair's meeting had been brief and matter-of-fact. They were setting up camp and sending out forage parties immediately.

The promised supply train had been intercepted by Morgan's raiders. There would be nothing in the way of supplies coming through this day.

* * *

Patrick McManus whistled tunelessly while he whittled. The small figurine that he was carving with a preposterously large bowie knife was still not taking any recognizable shape. Looking up, he set aside his labors.

"Is that what I think it is?" he said to his other messmates.

Milton Bosworth looked in the general direction. "You mean, Otto with the other Germans from the 9th Ohio? He's always with them if he ain't with the 32nd Indiana. Them Germans, they stay together. Course, they're the only ones who understand him other than Adie."

"No, not that." McManus pointed to the small cadre of men reappearing from behind the row of dusty tent canvases.

Bosworth looked at the four men. He recognized the tall, thin frame and taciturn, pinched face of Colonel Fry, General Buell's Chief of Staff. Something about the man's gaunt cheeks and bushy moustache reminded Bosworth of his schoolmaster, switch in hand.

There was another younger officer with him, who Bosworth assumed was part of General Buell's staff, as well as two civilians walking alongside, studying the camp as they went.

"You mean them?" Adie put in, pointing at the group.

"Yes. You think they're doing what I think they're doing?" McManus asked.

"That all depends," Levi Thickle commented, "What do you think they're doin'?"

"Those two look like locals. I think this is another group coming into camp to hunt for their runaways."

46

"More'n likely," Bosworth agreed. "Those two probably asked General Buell for permission to search the camp for 'em."

McManus grunted. He didn't like the idea of Southerners walking through their camp, and he wasn't the only one.

"Stupid," Levi Thickle grunted, "If we had 'em, we should put them to work on fixin' that dang railroad, rather than having us melt away in the sun."

The Southerners peeked inside a tent with a closed flap and then another and moved on past a row of tents with their flaps open.

"General Buell's standing orders," Bosworth shrugged, "Play nice with the locals. Don't break into their homes. Don't take their property."

Adie instantly opened his mouth, but Bosworth waved him quiet. "I know, I know, people ain't property, Adie. You know what I mean."

"Another fool Buell decision," Prosper T. Rowe rhymed, trying to add some levity.

"He wants to be all friendly and such to 'em, but they're still Rebels," Levi Thickle complained.

"Not all of them are Rebels," Bosworth pointed out.

"Too many of them are. 'Sides, how can you tell which is which?" Thickle grunted, always eager for an argument.

"They could take an oath of allegiance," Prosper suggested.

"I give them plenty of oaths while I shoot at them," Thickle declared, drawing laughs.

"Still, the sergeant has a point," Adie said.

McManus gave himself a small smile. Adie was the kid of the group, but he was increasingly willing to speak up for himself. It was strange to watch him grow over the past couple of months. Like many of the men, he considered Adie a sort of younger brother.

"They aren't all bad," Adie continued. "Just look at Miss Anna back in Savannah. She nursed our men back to health."

"Good friends with Lieutenant Lockett too," Thickle cackled, drawing protective frowns from McManus and Bosworth. "No offense," he added, seeing the looks. "It's true that Miss Anna was good to us, but what about her brother? He's a Reb. You just can't tell, and that's my point."

"Well, we can't fight them all," Adie said, "How are we supposed to be one country again if they're all against us?"

"You're starting to sound like General Buell now. What do you want, Adie? You want to be nice and go back to the way it was, slavery included?"

"Course not!"

"It is plum difficult to see which way to go," Prosper said, "Better that I be a private than a general for that decision! Don't know which way is right."

"It is hard to say," McManus agreed. He spoke less frequently than the others, but when he did, they listened. "Not sure that we can win a war by being friendly though. You saw Shiloh. We all did. After that... seems like the only way to win this is to kill the other fella before he kills you. And if that means grind 'em down so that they don't have food to march with and bullets to shoot with, then that is what we ought to do." He paused. "I don't like the answer. I have no ill will against most of these people."

"So what do we do, Patrick? Burn their towns down as we go?" Thickle said in a surprisingly reflective tone.

Adie too looked at McManus, who shrugged.

"Levi's got a point," Bosworth agreed, "That's what General Mitchel had been doing to northern Alabama before we got here, and now look at the place. We gots bushwhackers and more bushwhackers. We gots no food for us or the animals. We're even having to take the time to rebuild bridges that our own side burned down just a month or two ago."

"Like I said," Prosper concluded, "There ain't no good answer. Of that, we can all agree."

"Agreed," McManus nodded.

"And," Bosworth added, "I think that we can all agree that we don't like the idea of them coming into our camp to look for their fugitives. Besides, we don't even know they own any slaves. They might just be coming into camp to get a count of our numbers so that they can pass it on to Forrest or Hunt Morgan."

* * *

Patrick McManus joined Lockett at the lip of the gulch. At the bottom, half-coated with red dirt and dust, the charred timbers of the railroad bridge could still be seen.

The engineers were sizing up the situation.

"It's going to take a few days to repair this one," McManus remarked as Lieutenants Renaud and Pope joined them at the edge.

"Not much left of it," Lieutenant Pope gawked at the sight, "Forrest or Hunt Morgan this time?"

"Neither," Lockett answered grimly, "General Mitchel and his men burned this one down two months ago, or so that engineer over there told me."

"Our General Mitchel?" Pope asked.

"The one and the same."

"While Buell marched west to Shiloh back in the spring, General Mitchel marched south and has been raising holy hell down here."

"Burning bridges?"

"Among other things," Renaud answered, "Zey're ze reason zat so many here already have a hatred of our army."

"He's not a believer in our General Buell's philosophy of reconciliation?" McManus remarked.

"General Buell and General Mitchel are not on friendly terms, let's just say that."

"But why'd he burn the bridges?"

Renaud shrugged. "Could have been for a good, ro-buss reason. Maybe he was worried zat Bragg would send reinforcements to Corinth?"

"Either way, we have another bridge to build," Lockett frowned.

"Look on ze bright side," Renaud said.

"What's that?

"That creek is all dried up. It'll make it easier to build a bridge."

Lockett snorted in amusement. "Given our empty canteens, I'd rather that the stream had water and lots of it."

After two days, a rickety-looking replacement spanned the gulch. The engineers pronounced it fit, but of course, there were no trains of supplies coming to truly test it. A lack of available locomotives still plagued their long supply line back to Memphis.

If it weren't for the supplies coming overland via the northern roads from Nashville, they would have nothing at all.

But today, the biggest problem was the water or lack thereof. And it was the water situation that prompted Lockett to approach Colonel Blair this morning.

"As per the General's orders, we move out in an hour. Are the men ready, Lockett?"

"More or less, sir. Six more are infirmed today."

"Heat from yesterday or water?"

"Probably both, but it is the water situation that I wanted to see you about, sir."

"What about it? I know that we are low, but the quartermaster reported that each regiment still has two barrels of water. Won't last long I know, even with a shrunken regiment like ours, but there should be water in eight miles."

"For starters, sir, no offense to the quartermaster, but we don't have two barrels. More like one and a quarter, but the worse part is that one barrel, sir. I saw it myself today. It's fouled. There's more scum in there than water. The men drink that, and we will have a lot more than a couple who won't be able to keep up, even at the pace that this army moves."

Colonel Blair's blue eyes turned icy, and he glared at Lockett. "Well, Lockett, that may be, but I don't see what we can do about it. I can hardly make water appear in this barren place! We march to the nearest water, which is in eight miles."

"I think that I have a solution, sir," Lockett answered evenly, not put off by his superior's temper.

"Oh, do you? What, are you going to steal some from one of the other regiments?"

Lockett looked quizzically at his colonel.

"Yes, Lockett, I have been hearing the rumors of some food disappearing from others, and don't pretend like I am unaware of where at least some of that is going. I know there is a number of contraband trailing us, including those that your young private has befriended."

"Sorry, sir, I am not sure about any food, but I do have some reliable information on water. There's a spring not far from here, and it is more or less right along our path."

"A spring? And how do you know this exactly?"

"A reliable source, sir," Lockett replied cautiously, "But I think perhaps it is best if you don't know."

Colonel Blair paused. Slowly, the tense look on his face softened. "Very well."

"So when we break for camp tonight, sir, I'd like permission to take a squad and check this spring. If it is there, then we can fill our supplies, perhaps for the whole army..."

"But for now, we keep this amongst ourselves?"

"Exactly, sir. It's best that we claim we stumbled upon it by accident, if you know what I mean."

Colonel Blair pulled on his long side whiskers while he thought about it. Finally, he nodded. "Very well, Lieutenant. You have my permission for some foraging once we reach camp tonight."

* * *

Adie Graham yawned mightily even though it was near three in the afternoon. It had been that type of day so far. They had been up before dawn to pack up camp and then marched through the morning and into the afternoon.

They were tired, thirsty, and hungry. It was a bright, sunny northern Alabama day, and the heat had worn them down.

"Ain't gonna be much left of these fields after this drought," Prosper T. Rowe remarked. A long blade of brown-yellow grass poked out from his gap-toothed mouth.

Patrick McManus toed the bone dry dust. Nothing was going to grow here with this summer's lack of rain. Most of the creek beds were dry too, which contributed mightily to their current problem of empty canteens.

Lockett walked back to the knot of men. He had sent Adie out immediately upon finishing the march to find "his friends". Now, outside the camp lines, their small detail was joined by Adie and the escaped slaves, Amos and Hal.

"Milton, rifles, cartridge boxes, and spare canteens only?" he said.

"Yes, sir. Fifteen men like you asked." Milton Bosworth nodded in the direction of Adie, surprised that the contraband had been allowed this close to camp. There was obviously something afoot. "They coming too, sir?"

"That's right."

"Forage duty, sir?" Prosper asked.

"Yes, Prosper, and a good chance at finding a spring."

The final word had a magical effect.

After a hot, tiring march, one might have expected a grumble or two about being assigned to forage duty, but there was none. The thought of finding some water and maybe even a little food was enough motivation for their tired feet.

"Within the normal limits, sir?" Bosworth asked.

Lockett nodded. "Yes, there's still General Buell's standing orders about their personal property. It's theirs unless they are obvious Rebels, in which case, we 'purchase' it. But the spring is God's own, so we are welcome to that. Now, let's get started."

"What about them, sir?" Prosper pointed at Amos and Hal.

"They're our guides."

"Guides, sir?"

"Amos happened to mention to Adie the other night that he had been through this area before. He says there is a farm about a mile from here, a spring too. If we're lucky, it will still be flowing."

Again, the word "spring" brightened the mood.

"That's the reason for the spare canteens. We'll bring back a present for the rest of the company. If there is good water there, the quartermaster can bring all his barrels later."

"By God, would be nice to have some good water for the next stretch of this march," Prosper remarked to no one in particular.

They tramped along a narrow, two track wagon trail. There would have been little room for a wagon; it was barely enough for two men to walk shoulder to shoulder. The trees were close in, and their branches required some to be held as they made their way. It was still green, although some of the trees seemed to be suffering from the dry conditions also. Their leaves were yellowing and some were already beginning to drop even though it was just early summer.

"You were here before?" Adie asked Amos.

He spoke in a hushed voice, as he had been conditioned to do with Amos from their many nighttime clandestine meetings. Adie was more used to Amos's birdcall, alerting Adie that they were coming than he was to actually seeing the man's face in daylight.

"Once," Amos answered. "The springs are known for their healing powers. My master wanted to see if it he could distill the magic from the waters."

Adie looked at him. Amos was no longer clean shaven. There were patches of scruff on his otherwise smooth face. Adie wondered if Amos was joking with him.

"Magic? Really?" Adie answered. He peeked over his shoulder at Hal who followed them with a sullen look on his face. Further behind Hal came the soldiers. The small squad watched him with curiosity as they followed Adie and the two runaways on the trail.

"Did it work, Amos?"

"Of course not," Amos laughed, "It's just sweet water, that is all. But that did not stop my master from selling it for its magical healing powers."

The narrow trail split and without hesitation, Amos directed them to follow the left fork.

"For only being here only once, you sure seem to know the way," Adie remarked.

"When you are a slave, every new road is a possible road to freedom someday. You remember every turn." Amos said it with a seriousness that gave Adie pause. As if to prove the point, Amos added, "There will be a large stump of a fallen tree around the next bend." And there was.

"Did you... did you ever try to escape, Amos? Before now, I mean."

A pained look slowly came across Amos's face. He looked straight ahead as he answered in a softer voice. "No. I was too scared until now. Maybe my lot was too easy compared to the others. I thought of it often, even had a small opportunity when my master took me to Nashville. I looked so long at the cargo on the wharf near the river and dreamed of what it might be to be free. Could I hide in one of boxes? Could the steamer take me north? But then what? There were so many slavehunters in that city. Surely, they would find me.... And if I ran and was captured..."

He still looked straight ahead. The pain had increasingly etched itself into his face with each word, and with each word, Adie felt more ashamed that he had asked the question. Still,

Amos continued on.

"All of the hostile eyes in that town... It was a town known for arresting abolitionists, even ones who did nothing more than carry pamphlets on the subject... If I was captured, then would my master sell me further south? For the fields? I couldn't bear the thought. I am a coward, Adie," he finished, glumly looking down.

"You are being too hard," Adie said hastily. "That is not true. You are here now." But the words did nothing to change the fugitive's mood, and Amos lapsed into silence.

They reached the edge of the small field, across which lay a small house, barn, and two small outer building.

"Where is the spring?" Lockett asked.

"Beyond the house there, not even a quarter mile."

"Looks deserted," Bosworth observed.

There was no movement to be seen.

"Perhaps," Lockett said cautiously.

"Should we head for the spring?" Bosworth questioned.

"No, we will see what we have here first. You take half of the men and approach the house, Sergeant." He looked again at the sun-beaten homestead. There was no movement, but the farm had clearly not been in a state of abandonment for very long. "I'll take the other half and check the barn. Food and only food, Milton, remember?"

"Of course, sir."

"If that house is deserted, remind the men to keep their fingers to themselves. We only want food, and what we find, we write them script for."

"Yes, sir."

Lockett knew that Milton had selected some of the better, more trust-worthy men, ones less likely to steal, but Lockett would not take chances, not after what he had seen in Missouri. The temptation was still great for many of the soldiers, and it did not hurt to remind them that he was watching.

"Lieutenant, suhr," Amos said gently. Lockett looked over, and Amos nodded gently in the direction of Hal. There was an unspoken question between the two men, and Lockett nodded his assent. As soon as he did, Hal headed off to the clump of trees and the two small outer buildings.

Meanwhile Bosworth took his half of the squad and headed for the farmhouse.

McManus fell in step beside Lockett as they headed for the barn. "What was all that about?" the red head asked.

"Hal?"

"Yes, been wondering why he was with us to begin with. I can understand Amos since he knows the way, but the other one?"

"Hal has his own reason for being here. Amos asked if he could come along, and I said 'yes' after he told me why." He looked over in the direction of the outer buildings, but Hal had already disappeared in the trees. "He's looking for his brother."

"Brother?"

"His brother was apparently sold to this farm many years ago. He wanted to see if he was still here."

"If he was, it doesn't look like it now."

"Probably not," Lockett answered. It was difficult to tell from the state of the fields how much attention they had received. The drought had seen to that. "Seemed no harm in letting him check."

"But what if his brother was here, what then?"

"What do you mean?"

"He wouldn't have just left. He'd have helped his brother escape, and you would then be breaking General Buell's orders. I mean, if it was Daniel, you wouldn't just say hello and then leave, not without him. You'd do whatever it took to help him escape."

Lockett frowned. He had not really thought much about what would happen in that case. Yes, what then, he wondered silently.

"The Colonel made it clear to all of us that we aren't to encourage more of 'em to follow us," McManus pointed out.

"I don't know," Lockett said sharply, "But let's cross that bridge when we come to it. And today doesn't look like that day."

Adie pulled on barn doors. "Locked from the inside, sir."

"There is a window over here," Levi Thickle said from the side. "I'll climb through."

After a moment, there was the scraping sound from the back of the doors, and then they were swung open to reveal Levi Thickle and a startlingly empty barn.

"Been plum cleaned out," Thickle said as the others entered the structure.

The barn was old and its tinder dry walls had seen better days.

In some places the wood was rotting away, but what stood out was that the barn itself was completely empty. No kit, no tack, no animals, no tools. The only things in the barn were an enormous pile of horse dung in the back and a ladder leading to an equally empty loft.

"Farms deserted," Thickle commented to no one in particular.

"No surprise," Amos replied, "They would not be friends of your kind."

"Didn't leave a thing behind," Adie said with some wonderment.

"They had enough warning, as slow as this army is moving," Thickle grumbled.

"Check anyway," Lockett said. "Look around. Check the loft." He had been hoping that there would be some food to supplement their half-rations.

The men checked the stalls, loft, even the outside, but there was nothing.

Lockett gazed out the front of the barn. It looked like all they would return with was some water from the spring. The sun would be setting in a few more hours. They would need to hurry to that spring.

"You need a shovel," Amos said to Levi Thickle, who happened to be standing near the copious mound of horse dung.

"A shovel? What the hell for?"

Amos pointed at the pile.

"Why the hell would I clear up their horse shit?"

"You don't understand," Amos said patiently as Lockett walked over. "You see, there is no one who knows more about hiding something than a slave."

"What in tarnation is he talking about?" Thickle frowned, looking over at Lockett.

With a small smile, Lockett said, "Go find a shovel, Levi. There was a shed across the way. If there is nothing there, then check those small outer buildings."

"Sir?"

"We need to clear this away, Levi. I see what Amos is getting at. If you wanted to hide something in here, then cover it with something that no one wants to poke around in."

Thickle looked skeptical but nodded and disappeared in search of a shovel.

Patiently, the men waited for Thickle to return from his search while Lockett contemplated splitting his small party even further to go in search of the spring. Ultimately, he decided against it. All of the men would want that first cool drink directly from the spring. That would be their reward for the foot-wearying day.

The yell from beyond the barn startled him with a jolt.

"Yankee! I know y'all can hear me in there. We got your man."

Everyone leapt to their feet, and Lockett raced to look out the front of the barn.

"Yankee!" the yell repeated.

"Patrick, get up in the loft," Lockett ordered, "Tell me what you see."

From his vantage point by the front door, Lockett could only see a handful of dismounted riders. One had Levi Thickle by the collar with a shotgun pointed at him. They were in the open space, roughly fifty yards from the barn and doubly more so from the house.

"Now, come on out and surrender, Yankee. No one needs to die!"

The barn was quiet when McManus broke the silence. "I see about twenty total. There are some others in the tree line to the left, just beyond the ones in front."

When there was no response from the barn, the man holding Thickle tried again, "Now, be smart, Yankee. We know you're in the barn. Your man already told us. Now come on out!"

Lockett studied the man holding Levi Thickle. There were four others near him. From Lockett's angle, he could not see the others that McManus said were in the treeline.

"Shall we hole up here and fight it out?" one of his men asked.

"Everyone, make sure that you're loaded," Lockett said while he thought about their next move. Normally, he would have agreed with the man, but as he looked around the barn, there were three problems with that option. For starters, the thin, rotted wood would offer no protection from the heavy slugs. In fact, as thin as this wood looked, it was likely that a shot would blast through the front wall and clear out the back wall. Worse, there was no opening on the south side of the barn. Anyone with half a brain could approach from that side without any defense from the inside. And then there were the sheer numbers. Twenty wasn't so bad, a fairly even fight, but his men were split in two groups. The farmhouse across the way was just far enough away that it would be difficult for Bosworth's men to offer any meaningful support from there, especially with an approach from the south side.

"Y'all ain't got all day to decide, Yankee," came the yell, now sounding a little exasperated at the lack of responses. "Don't make me burn y'all out of my uncle's barn!"

"We gonna let them dig us out of here?" Prosper T. Rowe asked.

"It's not defensible," Lockett declared.

"Give me a gun," Amos said.

"Can't," Lockett answered, walking over to the ladder leading up to the loft. "You know the standing orders. I'm not even supposed to see you. Now you want me to give you a gun? I can't give you a weapon, Amos."

"But if we die?"

"We aren't going to die, Amos," he said with a confidence that surprised the black man and reassured his men. "Patrick, catch." When the red-head poked into view above him, Lockett tossed up his rifle.

"This will give you two shots at least. With the first, make sure you take out the speaker."

The former sharpshooter nodded. He knew that he could get two. That still left another eighteen or so.

Lockett turned back to the rest of the men. "Bayonets," he said simply.

With that, there was the clang of the two foot long swords sliding over the metal barrels.

"Give me a gun," Amos repeated.

"I don't have an extra," Lockett said calmly, looking out the opening again. He pulled his sword free from the scabbard and his Starr percussion revolver from its holster.

"You're going to take on twenty Rebel cavalry with six men?" Amos asked.

"They're not Rebel cavalry. More like some local militia," Lockett replied, still studying the men outside. Their weapons looked old. He could see two shotguns and one that looked like an old blunderbuss. He couldn't tell what the others were carrying, but by the way that they stood, they did not look like regulars to him. One looked nervous, and a couple were inattentive, or at least, that is what he told himself. "They'll skedaddle quick enough."

Amos looked doubtfully at him.

"Patrick, what are the ones in the tree line doing?"

"Not much of anything."

That too was strange to Lockett. By staying to the treeline, those men were putting unnecessary distance between themselves and the barn, plus there was a fence line in the way. Regular army would have taken up position at the fence line, he was sure of that.

"Alright, men, this isn't Forrest's cavalry out there. They're local farmers, and they're not expecting a fight. On Patrick's signal, we come out of here, screaming like demons. Straight at'em, don't stop until you are among them. Ready?"

They nodded.

"Alright then, Patrick."

"Yan..." the speaker started his yell again, but it was cut short by the crack of a Dimick Deer Rifle.

The man staggered backwards with a stunned look, and Lockett and his men burst from the barn, yelling like demons as instructed.

Lockett's long legs quickly carried him in advance of the others. Sword waving in his left, Starr revolver in his right, he covered the ground quickly. The reaction was slow from the militia, and it seemed that he had covered half of the distance before there were any shots. Then urged into a rush by the sight of the silvery bayonets carried by the small group of blue coats, the militia men fired their shotguns and weapons. Many of the rushed shots flung high, though one created a small dust cloud to the left of Lockett's whirling feet. Lockett was hoping that from the corner of his eye, he would see Bosworth and his men erupting from the house, but they too seemed to have been caught by surprise by his sudden charge.

A couple of militiamen were already inching backwards, and Lockett fired a shot from his revolver in their direction. A few others, however, steadied themselves and aimed at the tall, rapidly advancing Yankee, but a second shot from the barn loft cut down one of them. Still, the other raised his musket and fired. Lockett felt the ball whip under his outstretched sword arm and heard the sickening thud of ball meeting flesh behind him.

There was no time to turn around and see who the unfortunate victim was. And then he was among them, slashing the sword down across the forearm of the nearest man. Nearby, Levi Thickle wrestled on the ground with a man, desperately trying to work the man's weapon free.

There were other shots from the tree line, but where they were aimed and with what success, Lockett could not tell. Then, there were new yells coming from the direction of the house. Another militia man raised his spent shotgun and swung wildly at Lockett. Lockett ducked and fell awkwardly, losing his grip on the revolver, and three blue coats surged past him. One attempted to skewer the man with his bayonet, but missed and was knocked aside by a back swung shotgun.

It was Adie, Lockett realized as he hurried to his feet. Too late. A swung musket caught the youngster in the ribs, knocking Adie onto his back with a cry of pain. The militia man raised the butt of his gun over Adie's head.

Lockett reached for the revolver desperately but then something flashed past him. He finally grasped his gun, but by then the flashing bayonet drove right through the militia man just before he could crash the fatal blow onto Adie's head.

The suction of the bayonet was so great that as the man toppled over backwards, the bayonet rifle was ripped from the attacker's grasp, from Amos's grasp. The militiaman fell straight onto his back with the rifle sticking out of him at attention before falling to the side.

The other militiamen were now running back, heading at full speed towards their comrades in the trees. Sporadic fire from Bosworth's men and another shot from the loft hurried them on their way. A couple of ineffective shots from the tree line answered them.

"Reload!" Lockett ordered, "Independent fire."

Finding what cover they could, the men crouched and reloaded. Their rifles spat into the tree line at the scarcely visible enemy. Amos retrieved his procured weapon from the chest of the militiaman and kneeled next to Lockett. Lockett looked at him.

"I believe your man's name was O'Leary," Amos said

somberly.

Lockett nodded, his brain recalling that revolting and too familiar thud of ball and flesh. That was who had been on his heels during the charge, O'Leary.

"Get his ammunition and reload."

"I don't know how to reload."

The rifle fire from his men snapped at the distant tree line. His men were fighting in groups of two from kneeling positions, just as he had been training them to do, and they could feel their advantage now. The distance was a distinct benefit for his men and their rifles. The militia muskets returned fire from the tree line, but their older smoothbore weapons did not have the accuracy from this range.

"Milton, if they start to make for the fence line, then we charge as well," Lockett yelled across to Bosworth, but he wasn't sure if Bosworth heard him above the sporadic din. If Lockett had been in charge of the militia, that is what he would have done, cut the distance and take advantage of the limited cover, but the militia showed no interest in exposing themselves to the run across the pasture to the fence.

Lockett took O'Leary's rifle from Amos and started to reload. "So you followed our charge without a weapon and grabbed O'Leary's when he went down?"

Amos nodded. A couple more of Lockett's men fired, while others hurriedly rattled their ramrods in their barrels as they reloaded.

"So, I guess you are not the coward you feared," Lockett commented, unable to suppress a wild grin, thrusting the ramrod down the barrel. Seeing the surprised look on the Amos's face, "Yes, I heard you talking to Adie."

There were a few answering shots from the trees, but not many now. Perhaps the rest of them had shotguns too. The range was too great for them, Lockett thought as he eyed the fence line and decided that it was time to give them more to think about. "Carry a message to Sergeant Bosworth for me?" Lockett asked Amos.

"What is it?"

"Tell him to provide fire as my group advances to the fence line. Once we are there, have him sweep to their left flank. See those rocks and trees there? Have him take up position there.

They'll have no choice once we take that."

Amos nodded and took off at a full run for Sergeant Bosworth and his men. The order was passed on but to no matter. By the time that Bosworth's men reached the rock and trees, the enemy had fled.

Chapter 7

--the diary of James Lockett
Never have so many soldiers agreed on one thing without
dispute. The water from Amos's spring was the sweetest water
that any of us have ever tasted. He was right too about the dung
pile in the barn. Below it we found a trap door, though there was
little in the dug out room. It was scarcely worth hiding, which just
shows how little is left here after armies come to and fro.

* * *

Lockett reached General Buell's headquarters with Colonel
Blair's weekly report in hand. He was familiar with the exercise
now. Every week, General Buell required each regimental
commander to submit a report on ammunition levels. The
commissary and quartermasters had to submit one on foodstuffs
and supplies. Lockett imagined that was increasingly easy for
those two since there was little of either, especially food. Of
course, if the report wasn't just the way that General Buell liked it,
it would need to be redone. It was bizarre to Lockett that the
penmanship was of more importance than the fact that they were
down to half day rations and the animals even less.

"James," greeted Lieutenant Jones from the 15th Ohio. He
held his own regimental report in hand. "Another important duty
fulfilled?" he joked.

Before Lockett could answer, his stomach growled audibly.

Jones laughed. "A better timed answer, I cannot imagine.
Here," he said, pulling a small apple from his pocket. "Sounds
like you need it even more than I do. Just don't let the General or
his staff see it. Best to eat it later. Don't want him asking us
where it came from. I prefer to march in straight lines."

By this point, the Army of the Ohio was well aware of General Buell's orders regarding the protection of property and his uncanny ability to spot violators. Punishment was always swift. One man had been forced to drag a railroad tie behind him in a perfect rectangle for 12 hours. Another three men had been forced to march around a violated fruit tree for 24 hours.

"Thanks," Lockett said, quickly stuffing the apple in his pocket. "Your men have had some success."

"Natural born thieves some of them," Jones grinned, "But they don't forget their officers."

Lockett shook his head ruefully. "All this work to repair the Memphis-Chattanooga rail line and still no supplies to be had."

Jones nodded. "The line behind us is in good shape now, or so I'm told, but there are no locomotives available."

"And the river is too low for transport," Lockett frowned.

"Even if it wasn't, I doubt they could get enough steamer captains to bring their ships this far. Too many bushwhackers."

"Excuses," Lockett said sourly. "Can't feed the men on excuses."

"If we could, we would be the most well-fed army in history," Jones laughed.

* * *

July 1
--the diary of James Lockett
We have arrived in Huntsville. It is a handsome town, but rumors that we would have food and supplies waiting turned out to be nothing more than rumors. We will have to scrape by. Despite all of our efforts to repair the Memphis-Chattanooga line, it seems that we will never be supplied by that. Now, the focus is repairing and securing the two lines from Nashville. A number of regiments have already been pulled from the main body to garrison certain sections of those two north-south lines. They are shorter sections of line, so perhaps it will work. Chattanooga is not far now.

* * *

"This is no way to run an army," the gray-haired man grumbled to Lockett. The older man scowled, making his white and gray stubble furrow into unkempt rows above his sagging jowls. "I know exactly why your general has suggested that I follow you and your men on this hapless mission. With all the goings-on in Huntsville, I should still be there covering it! But of course, your general is even less free with *that* information than normal. As if, that is even possible..." He punctuated the last with a hacking cough that lasted a full minute.

Lockett glanced at Lieutenant Renaud, who looked back at him with a bemused smile. Neither man knew quite what to say to this newspaperman, Silas Hoskins. Certainly, they had not asked him to accompany their two twenty-man squads on this day's march to Huntsville's sawmills. Much like the reporter, they too thought this was a mundane task. They could at least agree on that.

"Mr. Hoskins," Lockett finally said, "I..."

But he was interrupted by another hacking cough, which was only halted after Silas Hoskins took a hearty pull from a silver flask.

"Followed this Army for three months," Hoskins interjected, "The only thing that moves slower than this army is how long this cough has lingered." His face had turned into a bright red, either from the vigorous coughing or the flask.

Diplomatically, Lockett nodded, "I'm sure all involved had hoped for a quicker resolution."

Hoskins spat grotesquely to the side. "That is what I think about this army's pace and their stone-walling of the press! Buell won't tell us a damned thing! I would have hoped for more from a standard line officer such as yourself."

"You were saying zat you should be in Huntsville," Renaud said, trying to change the subject.

"Of course, we should!"

"And why is that, Mr. Hoskins?" Lockett added, gratefully taking Renaud's lead. "What is so interesting there to your readers in Indiana?"

"That should be patently obvious, young man," he fumed, "The Indianapolis Daily Journal readers would, of course, be interested in the trial proceedings."

"Ah, General Turchin's trial," Renaud replied, nodding.

The trial of General Turchin was the current talk of camp. Brought before General Buell for his plundering of Athens in response to Rebel provocation and hostility, General Turchin's trial was on many minds.

"Don't tell me that this has gone unnoticed, young man. I spend considerable time in your camp. I know all that goes on there."

"It's true, Mr. Hoskins. It is the subject of the day."

"As well it should be," Hoskins started and then finished with another coughing spell. "A court-martial for fighting rebellion and insurrection? Exactly what is wrong with this army! Tearing this army apart from the inside! That is what that Southern-loving Buell is doing."

Renaud nodded, but Lockett remained stone-faced, actions like General Turchin's made him think of his time in Missouri. It made him think of little Amelia.

Lockett stared into the distance. He did not see the red earth cotton fields of northern Alabama. Instead, he saw the hungering eyes of Orrin Long. He could feel the wanton ill-regard of Long and his cronies. He could see the terror in little Amelia's eyes.

Renaud and Hoskins had still been talking when they noticed the peculiar look on his face.

"James?" Renaud asked.

"Yes," Lockett said snapping out of it, "Just thinking."

"About General Turchin or that traitorous General in charge?"

"About Missouri, Mr. Hoskins," Lockett answered, "Things are not always so clear cut in this war. I don't know about General Turchin, but I saw things in Missouri, things that deserved a hanging, not just a court-martial."

Hoskins stubbled and jowled face reflected his surprise. "Is that so? Didn't realize that your regiment had been in Missouri."

"It was before I joined this regiment. I was with Birge's Western Sharpshooters then."

"So you are saying you've seen nasty things too. Well, I can tell you that is nothing compared to what they would do to *us!* Nothing indeed! Why, if they had a chance to put a boot to your throat, young man…"

"Mr. Hoskins," he growled, "There are elements within every army who are eager to steal, assault, and kill without provocation.

I don't know what happened in Athens with Turchin, but I have seen enough to know that nothing should be assumed." He had not intended it, but his words were said with an edge to them that startled both Renaud and Hoskins.

It took Hoskins a breath to recover his stride, but he was not to be put off. "You sound every bit the Rebel lover as General Buell," he retorted. "The next thing I know is that you will say you even agree with him countermanding a Congressional order."

"I have no idea what you are referring to," Lockett answered evenly.

"I am talking about how General Buell is refusing to obey Congress's mandate in regards to the treatment of fugitive slaves."

"What mandate?" Lockett asked.

"Ah, hah. Exactly," Hoskins's face warped into a fleshy smile of victory. "In March, Congress passed a mandate to prohibit, and I do mean *pro-hibit*, the return of fugitive slaves to their owners, but I have seen with my own eyes that Buell has let Secesh into camp to look for their prized African possessions, and I have heard with my own ears that he insists that fugitives be turned away and returned to their owners. Utter disobedience of his own Congress! That's what it is."

"Since March?" Renaud asked.

"March," Hoskins repeated in triumph.

"That is news to us," Lockett said slowly, "And I, for one, don't agree with letting Secesh into camp. But that doesn't mean that putting the torch to Southern towns is necessary either."

"That's your opinion," Hoskins said, "I'm sure that there are others like you, but plenty who are not, including Turchin's own men. Why, the officers for the 19th and 24th Illinois will resign if he is court-martialed! They've told me themselves."

By the time that they arrived at the sawmills, the mood was as heavy and still as mid-summer Alabama air.

"Fool's errand," Hoskins grumbled again. His face was as red as could be, and he had perspired completely through his garments.

The sawmill sat absently next to the river tributary. Even in the dry summer that it was, there was enough flow to power the mill, but there was no activity. It was silent, and the lone person to be seen was asleep under the broad branches of the river's willow trees next to the mill.

"You zere!" Renaud called twice before the man opened his eyes.

The sergeants had the soldiers fall out for a much needed rest while the two officers walked over to the willow trees.

Lockett and Renaud rousted the man from his nap. After determining that he was indeed the owner of the mill, they explained what they wanted.

He was a short, balding, older man with a club foot. At first, he looked at their request with a quizzical stare of disbelief and then one of obstinacy. In a polite but firm tone, he drawled that he had no interest in doing business with Yankees. The strength of his reaction surprised both of the two officers. Both Lockett and Renaud had expected their offer to be welcomed. After all, they had permission to offer him a substantial sum.

"Y'all don't understand," he answered.

"You can say zat again. We offer you ne-uw work, and you zay no?" Renaud muttered.

"Mr. Plumlee," Lockett tried again, "You do understand that we are offering to pay for the work? We are paying in good U.S. currency, not worthless Confederate paper. We want planking from your sawmill. You are obviously not very busy now. We are offering a fair price for the work."

"Y'all are the ones who don't understand," Plumlee answered again.

"Won't you go out of business without work?" Renaud said puzzled, looking again at the empty mill.

"It's a generous offer," Lockett added, "Given the size of the order, you can make a lot of money."

Plumlee shook his head. "Can't spend money when yer dead."

"Mr. Plumlee, ze closest Rebel army is a hundred miles from here," Renaud said.

"That is an exaggeration, Frenchie, but it ain't the regular army that I'm worried about. It's the bushwhackers. They won't take kindly to me doing business with the Yankees, not after what you've done to some of our towns."

"General Buell has not harmed any of your towns," Lockett said patiently.

"Maybe General Buell is a gentleman, but he ain't the only general in your army. Sorry, but it ain't safe for me to do work fer y'all."

"What if we doubled the price?" Lockett said, looking at Renaud and knowing that they weren't authorized to do quite that much.

"No difference, sonny. Ain't going to make y'all planking for your bridges… Bridges that you'd use to conquer the rest of the South."

Lockett frowned and looked at Renaud. Both were unsure what to do next when there was the sound of a woman's voice screaming.

The two officers whirled around and did not see any women, only their men lounging in the shade. Of course, there was no time to count heads. Instantly, Lockett wondered if one of the men had wandered off and been overcome by some impulse. Or was it something else?

"It's coming from over zere," Renaud said, pointing to the thick growth and gnarled trees that leaned out over the small river. "Sergeant Pampleau!" Renaud motioned towards his dependable, heavily bearded French Detroiter sergeant.

The hulking sergeant, who looked more like a fur trapper than the farmer that he was, quickly summoned Renaud's men and they crashed into the brush.

"Levi," Lockett called out to Levi Thickle, wishing that Milton or Patrick was with him now instead of back at camp with rest of the company, "Defensive positions." He wanted to follow Renaud and his men into the commotion in the brush, but he fought the compulsion. It might be nothing, but old instinct had been learned hard.

He surveyed the terrain for the best possible defensive position. The crux would be a crumbling fence line and a copse of trees beyond the sawmill. Instructing his men, they quickly took up positions and listened to what had returned to silence. An ominous tranquility hung in the heavy, humid air.

Minutes passed, and Lockett's impatience grew steadily. He was contemplating sending a man off in search of Renaud when there was an abrupt series of shots fired in rapid succession. After a second's pause, there were more shots fired in reply, and he could hear someone calling out something in French.

Shortly after, he could hear hooves beating, coming closer.

But they were on the other side of the river. Five horsemen and one woman came into view. The men had rifles slung to their backs. They rode on, mocking the blue-coated soldiers on the opposite side of the water. Two of the men fired revolvers aimlessly in their general direction, and two others waved their hats wildly, greatly pleased with themselves.

"Bushwhackers, sonny," the sawmill owner said, idling up to Lockett as the riders turned and rode off into the distance.

"I'm quite familiar with bushwhackers," Lockett snapped, slamming his revolver back into his holster.

Minutes later, Renaud and his men trudged back into view. They were grim-faced and silent. At the head of the group, four of them carried the lifeless body of Sergeant Pampleau.

"Damn," Lockett said softly, knowing that Pampleau was a good, dependable man. Renaud relied on the sergeant the same as he relied on Patrick and Milton.

Lockett left Plumlee and joined Renaud. His friend was ashen faced, save for the smear of his sergeant's blood that he had absently put on his own forehead as he had crossed himself.

"It was a trap," he said softly. He paused, trying to compose himself before continuing. Finally, he added, "Zere was a clearing beyond ze brush. Zis was lying in the clearing."

He held up a blue bonnet. "When Pampleau and ze others went into ze clearing to look at ze bonnet, zat is when zey opened fire from ze other side of ze water." He gripped his Gaulic jaw. "No warning. No chance. Devious devils."

"Others?" Lockett asked.

"No. They were not good shots fortunately. Only Pierre was hit… but that is enough." Renaud walked away from him and back to his men.

Lockett stood there, feeling his friend's pain and impotence. That was the problem with leading. Every death felt like a personal failure. He didn't notice Silas Hoskins making his way over to his shoulder.

"Still think General Turchin is wrong?" Hoskins asked slyly.

Lockett whirled with such suddenness and violence that the stubble-faced reporter stumbled backwards and would have fallen had Lockett not already grabbed him by the collar.

"You want to see blood!" Lockett snarled. He pulled out his revolver. "How about we start with yours?"

The look of pure menace on Lockett's face shocked the reporter. He mumbled unintelligible words as he looked wide-eyed at the demon face in front of him, sure that he was about to die.

Instead, Lockett threw him to the ground and stalked away.

* * *

July 29
--the diary of James Lockett
The mood of camp has not been so high in quite some time. Supplies have arrived from Nashville! We are finally back on full rations. It is hard to believe that we survived on half-rations for so long. Now that we are back on full rations, it seems almost a gluttony, if hard tack biscuits and rancid bacon could ever be gluttony!

The supplies arrived two days after Amos and his comrades left us to head north. I know that Adie gave them all he could before they left. He probably wishes that they had stayed those two more days so he could have secreted something more substantial for them. At least I don't have to worry more about Adie starving himself anymore.

July 31
--the diary of James Lockett
Orders have arrived today, but they are not for Chattanooga.

Oh, what a difference two days makes. From the peak of optimism to this woe!

General Bragg and his Rebel Army arrived in Chattanooga. We have lost a race that we didn't even know we were running. Chattanooga is now theirs, and we are to march north to protect Nashville. I fear that Shiloh and our other gains that were paid for in such rivers of blood are slipping away.

Mail arrived also, but there is still no news from Daniel or anyone else.

Patrick tells me not to be alarmed. He reminded me that there are bushwhackers and raiders in Tennessee and Kentucky. The mail could have been waylaid anywhere. Still, I see the look in his eye. He does not believe it either.

There is something wrong. We can both feel it. Is there some disease sweeping through town? Is that why Daniel has not written? Has something happened on the farm? If Daniel himself cannot write me, then why has no one else either?

Section II

The Race to Bluegrass

Chapter 8

Ambrose Tucker watched the gnome-like, heavily bearded teamster slash down on the hapless mule again. Cursing up a storm with such volume that it seemed to echo, the teamster whipped the mule repeatedly, but the stubborn animal refused to budge, and the stationary wagon blocked the entire bridge.

"Get those wagons moving again," bellowed the quartermaster's assistant, "They're slowing down the entire column!"

"Trying, captain," the gnome said.

"Give me that," the captain said, snatching the whip. He too whipped the bony animal to no avail.

Much more of that and the animal's bones would start to show through, Ambrose thought to himself. He looked at the long line of wagons stacked up behind them. The current delay notwithstanding, they had made excellent progress, he thought to himself. They were rolling unimpeded through Tennessee and would soon be in Kentucky. In this race to Louisville against the Yankee General Buell, General Bragg was off to the quick start that he needed. The cavalry was reporting no movement by the Yankees yet, so General Buell seemed unaware that they had even left Chattanooga.

The gnome and quartermaster captain were now arguing over how best to move the animal and wagon so that the rest of the wagon train could proceed. They were currently debating the merits of shooting the animal and dragging it aside.

Oddly, as if it was listening, the mule started moving on his own, his cohorts following.

"Stupid animals," a dapper major next to Ambrose Tucker remarked.

"Stubborn as a stump, mules can be," Ambrose agreed.

"No, I mean stupid because it doesn't realize that we would never shoot it to unblock the train," the major grinned, "Beasts of burden are too valuable to this army for that." He laughed heartily, not in the least put off that the young lieutenant next to him did not think his joke was laughter worthy.

Finished with his jest, the major added, "The General is ready to see you now, Lieutenant Tucker."

"Lieutenant Tucker, I knew your father," General Bragg started.

Ambrose Tucker felt a twist of discomfort as the man's heavily browed stare bore into him. The older man's thick beard wrinkled with disgust. "Bad business about your father. Sorry to hear of his passing. He was a soldier we could have used, his injury and all."

Ambrose nodded. There was an urge to explain to the General that his father had been acting in the best interests of the Confederacy, serving as a spy for her. Clearly, the General did not know about that aspect, but the opportunity to speak up to the commander of all Confederate forces in Tennessee did not make itself available.

"Shame that he chose to be a man of God. Of course, there is no place in the Army for men who have chosen that path. General Polk is the living example of that," he said sarcastically. General Bragg studied Tucker's face for any flicker of emotion at his bald-faced slap at one of his own generals. Every man in the army knew Polk as the 'Bishop General.' He was after all a bishop in the Episcopal church and was well known for his Sunday sermons. "The man is utterly worthless at disciplining his men," Bragg added. But with hardly a breath, he snapped into a new subject.

"Your father and I were in Mexico together. Fine, fine horseman. As fine of a horseman as I ever saw. Obedient to his duty too." He paused, perhaps expecting Ambrose Tucker to remark that his father had spoken of Bragg before. But this was news to Ambrose Tucker. His father had spoken of many of the men that he had served with, men who were now generals in both the North and South, but he had never mentioned Braxton Bragg.

Bragg rubbed a hand across his thick beard, a beard so thick that it obscured nearly every iota of skin on his face, save his eye sockets and nose. In a serious tone, Bragg added, "I am in need of an aide to carry messages for me. When I saw your name on the exchanged list, I naturally thought of you. I assume that you are at least half the horseman that your father was, which will do nicely."

"An honor, sir."

Bragg gave a dyspeptic scowl at the interruption. "Of course, it is an honor," he said, as if confused by Tucker's comment. "Do you have a fast horse? And can't be skittish at all around the sound of the guns."

"I do, sir."

"Very well. The major must be nearly finished by now drafting the copies. You have the honor of carrying our marching orders to General Hardee for me. Soon we will be liberating Kentucky from that Yankee horde."

"An honor, sir," Tucker repeated.

"Major!" Bragg growled, "Are you done yet?"

"Nearly so, sir," the major answered, "Just copied the abolition demagogues section and only the last sentence now... Soldiers, the enemy is before you and your banners are free. It is for you to decide whether our brothers and sisters in Tennessee and Kentucky shall remain bondmen and bondwomen of the Abolition tyrant or be restored to the freedom inherited from their fathers."

September 1
--the diary of James Lockett
The month of dawdle has finally ended. First, we lose this race to Chattanooga, but instead of engaging the Rebels, General Buell spreads his army out across countless garrisons to protect Nashville. While our regiment protected another railroad crossing from marauders that never appeared, General Bragg and the Rebels seem to have duped us again. All this time, we thought that Nashville would be the next target, but the Rebels have grander plans. Today, we learned that General Bragg left nearly a week ago. They are marching north towards Kentucky, though our generals still fear that Bragg will swing west towards Nashville. We are to form up to defend the approaches to the city.

Some of boys think this is non-sense. They are sure that the

Rebels are headed north. If they're right and the generals are wrong, then we will be chasing the Rebels after giving them a good head start. At the rate things are going, we will be in Ohio sooner or later.

* * *

"Like mewling little kittens," Milton Bosworth grumbled to McManus. "Look at 'em." He pointed at the newly arrived replacements.

After so many months of supposed reinforcements arriving to turn Blair's Independent Regiment from battalion sized to a full regiment, it seemed hard to believe that the men were finally here. And now that they were here, now what, McManus thought to himself?

James would no longer lead a company? They would all answer to some new Captain? At least James would have seniority on the other lieutenant who would be assigned to their motley company of Shiloh veterans, but it would not be James in charge. He prayed that he could trust this new captain the way that he trusted James, but he knew that would be impossible.

He looked over at Milton Bosworth, who was studying the newcomers as any sergeant would. Though burly, Milton was usually the good-natured sort, yet at the moment, he looked anything but good-natured as he glared at the newcomers from afar.

The gaggle of soldiers stood around talking, laughing, and generally displaying high spirits. Their blue uniforms looked particularly bright, unfaded, and clean as compared to those that Bosworth and McManus had become accustomed to seeing over the past months.

"They need us to come find them rather'n finding the right camp on their own. A wasted lot this will be," Bosworth continued to grumble. He was not slowed in his criticism by the fact that McManus said nothing in return.

"Who's in charge here?" Bosworth bellowed to one knot of the freshly scrubbed.

A thin, red-haired lad turned his boyish face to the grizzled sergeant. The others did not even bother to halt their joking and laughing.

"Captain Bibb," the lad said, "But he's off trying to figure out where we go next."

"Which regiment are you?" McManus checked.

"Blair's Independent Regiment."

"Not yet you ain't," Bosworth grumbled. "You ain't even found our camp yet."

But before the lad could answer, a voice fairly yelled, "Patrick!"

Puzzled, McManus turned his head to the side, towards another knot of new men.

He frowned and cursed aloud.

Cursing was as common as bad food in the army, but McManus rarely did it. The sudden outburst shocked Bosworth. If he had not already been in such a foul mood himself, he would have found it funny. Instead, it caused unease.

"What is it, Pat?" he asked.

McManus gave no answer and stared at a bright-eyed, brown-haired youth. The baby-faced lad broke off from the others and headed straight for them. McManus stood rooted in his spot and watched with a hard look.

"What?" Bosworth continued. "You know him? Who is it?"

McManus muttered something and pulled on his jaw.

"What's wrong?" Bosworth repeated.

"Milton," McManus answered slowly as the youth approached them, "That's Daniel."

"*The* Daniel?"

"Yes," McManus said tight-lipped, a clenched fist behind his back. "This is going to be bad," he thought aloud. He turned to Bosworth. "Yes, that Daniel. Daniel, James's brother."

* * *

"What's wrong with you? Aren't you glad to see me?" Daniel groused. He stood beneath the shade of an enormous oak tree while his brother paced furiously in front him.

James Lockett opened his mouth, but again, no words could come out. So he clasped his hands behind his back and stalked back and forth in front of his younger brother.

"I am your brother," Daniel continued, "And yet, you treat me like, like, I dunno... Some stranger or worse! Aren't you glad to see me?"

"Glad to see you?" the elder Lockett sputtered, "Glad to see you? Hell no, I am not glad to see you! You damn fool, what are you doing here?" His jaw was clenched, and his face was flushed bright red with anger.

"You and Patrick, you both treat me like, like..."

"Like someone who is not supposed to be here, Daniel! That's what! What are you doing here? What about the farm? Mother? The twins? Who is taking care of things?"

"They can take care of things themselves. My place is here in the army, in this great struggle."

"Your place is on the farm," Lockett growled lowly through gritted teeth.

"You can't tell me where my place is, James."

"You idiot! Of course, I can, now more than ever. This is the army, and I am an officer. You are not. I can tell you to go clean out the latrine with your hands if I want!"

Despite the strength of the reaction, the younger brother was not cowed by the vehemence. "Well, maybe that part is true. But I am in the army now, James."

"How did this happen?" Lockett muttered, turning away from his brother and looking up at the gray sky. It was more of a rhetorical question, but Daniel answered anyway.

"I slipped away to Detroit. I knew that they were looking for more volunteers for your regiment. I'm old enough to make my own decisions, and I enlisted."

"You are old enough to get yourself killed," Lockett corrected. He closed his eyes and could not stop the images of the corpses on the Shiloh battlefield, of their frozen rictus states. How many had they tossed into the stacked mass graves the day after the battle? With his left hand, he gripped his brow. "Oh, Daniel, what have you done?"

* * *

September 4
--the diary of James Lockett

We have new orders now. With all haste, we are to join the rest of General Buell's army and chase Bragg north. It would seem the boys were right. It was Kentucky that the Rebels were after, not Nashville. But as spread out we are, it will take days for us to gather together south of Nashville near some town called Murfreesboro before marching north in chase. We can only pray that this time we catch him.

* * *

September 6

"Tucker!"

The yell caused Ambrose Tucker to swing about in the saddle.

"Tucker!" came the call again, and this time Ambrose Tucker saw the origin. Behind a moving column of men, one of General Polk's aides waved his hat to catch his attention.

He cantered his horse around the butternut clad men and clasped a hand with the man. "Franklin, good to see you. How are you?"

"In the finest spirits," Franklin Witten said enthusiastically, "These are exciting days, that they are."

"Funny what a few days of rest can accomplish," Tucker said, motioning at the column marching by. Three days prior, the Confederate Army had arrived in Sparta, Tennessee. They had been exhausted. The hard, narrow roads through the mountains had worn down man and beast alike.

Beset by heat and thirst, straggling had reached a proportion that drove General Bragg into fits of anger. Still, his actual anger was far less than the rumored anger. Rumors had swirled through the marching, tongue-swollen army that General Bragg was executing stragglers.

The rumors were exaggerated, Ambrose Tucker knew. When he wasn't carrying the general's messages, he was at the General's beckon and call. Fuming and anger aside, there had been no executions, even though he would have liked nothing better.

The truth was that Bragg did not need to execute any stragglers. Those who fell out of line fainted from the heat and died often enough that no punishments were necessary. They had marched hard to put some distance between themselves and stationary Yankee army. While that laggard Buell and his dull-witted generals waited for them to march on Nashville, the Confederates had cleared the mountains and marched to Sparta, albeit leaving behind a trail of blankets, knapsacks, anything deemed too heavy to carry in the heat.

Even the three day respite in Sparta did not seem to have given the Yankees any inkling of their true plans.

Looking at the high-spirited men marching by, continuing their journey north to Kentucky, Franklin Witten smiled. "The three days of rest and local furloughs for the Tennesseans were exactly what this army needed."

"I thought that the furloughs were a mistake," Tucker admitted, "I thought we'd never see half those men again, but I've been proven wrong."

Witten laughed good-naturedly. "As one of those locals enjoying a short time at home, I am happy to prove you wrong, Tucker."

The two Tennessee horsemen chuckled together. They had known each other for a number of months, both had served originally with Colonel Morgan before their present assignments as aides and messengers for generals.

"Well, I have to admit to you, Tucker, that I was wrong about something too. I was one of the many Tennesseans pushing the generals to attack Nashville. But now... Watching this and seeing how open the way is, it is the right decision to head to Kentucky and bring them back into the Confederacy. Hopefully, there will still be some liberating left for us to do."

Tucker looked blankly at him.

"Haven't you heard?" Witten said. "About Kirby Smith?"

"Heard what?" Ambrose Tucker knew that Kirby Smith's smaller Confederate Army was already in Kentucky. It was with him that they were supposed to link up.

"Kirby Smith thrashed the Yankees in Richmond, Kentucky! Chased the Yankees from Lexington. They didn't stop skedaddling until they hit the Ohio River!"

September 6
--the diary of James Lockett

As we march to Nashville on our way north, I fear the worst. Oh, Daniel. How do I keep him safe now? We finally move to confront Bragg, and surely there will be a point where the two armies meet, and then what? How can I possibly keep him safe now?

Milton Bosworth looked sideways at Patrick McManus. It had been nearly a week since the newcomers had joined the regiment in middle Tennessee, and it clearly impacted his now morose Lieutenant. If he didn't already know that his Lieutenant was an abstainer, then he would have been sure that the man was sour headed from another night of too much alcohol. Lieutenant Lockett scowled at everything and said little. He did not appear to have shaved in a week.

It seemed like only a matter of days ago that he had pulled himself out of similar state after leaving Savannah and Anna Tucker. That one had been understandable if Bosworth paused to think about it. This was too, although it was hard for Bosworth to say which drove the Lieutenant deeper into the depths. Was it the fact that he did not have a company now and instead reported to Captain Bibb? Or was it the appearance of his younger brother?

Back at that northern Mississippi creek bed, when the Lieutenant had explained his rationale for joining the army, Bosworth thought it was possible that he was setting himself up for such a scene, but now that it had come to fruition, the result was even worse than Bosworth would have predicted.

"I could try to talk to him," Bosworth had suggested to McManus, "Make him see mebbe that it's better this way. His brother could have enlisted in a different regiment. Better this way, right?"

Poker-faced, McManus shrugged.

"I mean, ifs I had a younger brother, I'd want him where I can see him, right?"

"I don't think words will help him now, Milton," McManus finally said. "Time, just time. He'll be all right."

"Hope that you are right about that," Bosworth said dejectedly. "The men need him, especially the new ones. They're green as spring grass, and Bibb? He reminds me too much of my old officers in the 53rd."

"Every officer except James reminds you of the yellow ones in the 53ʳᵈ, Milton."

Bosworth nodded grudgingly. "Most aren't worth a wooden nickel, Patrick."

"It will be all right. James just needs a new mission. We need to march on Bragg. That is what we need to do. Sitting around camp, stewing, that is not helping him. We were supposed to march north days ago, and I thought that the march to Chattanooga was a slow eternity! But this confusion is beyond absurd."

"Ain't that the truth. First, we crawl towards Chattanooga, only to find Bragg gets there just before us, and now what? We creep back north. Then what? We need to fight Bragg, not sit outside of Nashville. Now, he's moving north while our generals sort out what to do."

"The war won't end by sitting here," McManus agreed, reflecting on how much that sounded like something that James would say.

September 11
--the diary of James Lockett
Orders have come down finally. We move after Bragg. It took days to pull the army back together from the various garrison postings. Then we waited again. Wait, wait, wait. It should be General Buell's middle name. The Rebels were supposedly east of Nashville in Carthage, and the Generals thought that Nashville might still be the target, but Bragg has moved on, and now everyone realizes that Louisville must be the target. So we finally head north to catch them with General Thomas's division staying behind in Nashville just in case.

A more bedraggled army has never been seen short of the Rebel army. We hardly resemble what we were when we left western Tennessee. Disease has taken a quite a few. We are half the size that we once were, and we never fought a battle. Those who are here have the most threadbare and patched uniforms that anyone in blue has ever worn. We were supplied and ate well enough at our posting southwest of Nashville, but many of the others do not look so hearty.

And now we must chase Bragg. He has a good lead, but it is not just Bragg that we are chasing. Apparently, a separate Rebel army under Kirby Smith left Knoxville for Kentucky three weeks ago. We won at Shiloh because two of our armies merged before the Rebels could pick us off one by one. Now, the shoe is on the other foot. We need to engage Bragg before he joins with Kirby Smith.

* * *

Ambrose Tucker dismounted his horse and removed the sealed orders from his saddle bag, handing them over to General Hardee's adjutant.

"Bring us news of a Yankee surrender, Lieutenant Tucker?" the man joked.

"Soon enough, soon enough," Tucker answered cheerily, patting his steed.

"He looks like he needs some water. I'd direct you to some, but…"

"I know. Such as it is. Can't say that I've ever seen a summer as dry as this one."

"We are even having to post guards over the dregs of some of the water holes to stop the men from sickening themselves on it."

"Saw one such on the way here," Tucker said with a sad shake of the head. "It was a near mutiny. The men were convinced that the water was being protected only so that the generals could have some." The other man just shook his head in silent disgust.

"In any case," Tucker added, "I'm to await General Hardee's response."

"Can't offer you any water, Lieutenant, but there is a good shade tree over yonder. You can wait there."

Tucker nodded. "The General would like a quick response."

"Anxious today, is Bragg? Well, we are making good progress. General Bragg needn't worry. We will beat that laggard Buell to Louisville with no problem. We'll cut him off from all his supplies, and he'll surrender."

"We'll need to get to Munfordville first. Once we beat them there, they'll be cut off," Tucker replied.

"You a Kentuckian, Lieutenant?"

"Tennessee."

"Ah, you seem to know your way around these parts, thought

perhaps you were a local."

"Been through here once with Colonel Morgan on one of his raids."

"That explains it. So is it true what they say about Kentucky?"

"And what might that be?" Tucker asked, plucking a cluster of burrs off of his trouser leg.

"General Hardee has been told that the presence of our army will embolden those under the Yankee heel. They say that our army will swell with 25,000 anxious recruits."

"I've heard the same," Tucker answered. "That's why the wagon train is carrying thousands of extra muskets. Those anxious recruits will need to be armed."

Chapter 9

The newcomers had spent weeks trudging south from Michigan to join their comrades, only to spend a matter of days with them before turning around and heading back north. The frustration among the original core of Blair's Independent Regiment was palpable, yet for Daniel, the thought never even occurred to him.

His thoughts were consumed with wonder, and the only disappointment was that he had not done this sooner. The freedom, the new sights, and the bonds of new friendships were even more exhilarating than he had guessed they would be. Even James's reaction did not dim his feelings. He had expected such a reaction from him, and he partly wondered if perhaps he should have joined a completely separate regiment, but then of course, he would not have made the close friends that he had now in his messmates. John Bouma was like a twin brother, equally enthralled with life away from the farm, and Vaught... Well, Vaught was like the older brother that Daniel had always wanted. He had taught him so much already, and how the women flocked to the man while they were in Cincinnati! Daniel had never seen anything like it.

John Bouma tugged on Daniel's arm, interrupting his thoughts. "Do you see that?" he said excitedly.

"See what?" he asked, looking at his tow-headed 'twin'. Then Daniel looked to his right and saw the erect officer on horseback trotting past the column with three staff officers trailing behind him on their own muscled steeds.

These were no plough horses like those Daniel was used to seeing. These were immaculately groomed creatures that looked like they could streak across a field in the blink of an eye.

"It's General Buell!" Bouma said enthusiastically. "Shouldn't we give him a cheer?"

"He would like that," Levi Thickle muttered with disgust, but if young Bouma heard the comment, he gave no indication.

Daniel could only agree with his friend. The man was the picture of a leader. Lean and athletic looking in the saddle, his trim gray beard suggested nothing but wisdom. With a leader like that and with spirited men like the newcomers, there could only be one outcome, Daniel believed. The only sad thing was that once they caught up to the Rebels, they would surely rout them, and the war would be over. He should have joined earlier, he decided.

At the outskirts of town, Daniel and the others had been greeted by mostly womenfolk, heckling them from second story windows or their front doors. Some had merely hissed. Others called out to the "blue bellies" that it was good riddance, or that they were marching off to their graves, or how General Bragg's army would slaughter them.

The newcomers were startled by the animosity. The older core of Blair's Independent Regiment said nothing but returned the hateful glares with ones of their own.

At times, only the momentum of the marching column was all that prevented some of them from veering off the road and into the various vociferous households.

An hour later, Blair's regiment reached the center of Nashville. Here things were different.

Next to Daniel, his new friend, Robert J. Vaught, sighed as they marched on.

Vaught had hoped to spend some time in this town before their orders had been changed. Nashville had always been a good town for him and would be even better now by the looks of it. There were more saloons and bawdy houses than Vaught remembered. No doubt, this was the influence of an army's presence.

Even now as they marched by, he could see other blue coated soldiers standing and watching them march by.

"Provost guards," Prosper T. Rowe said from behind them, "Don't look cross-eyed at 'em, kid."

At first, Vaught thought that Rowe was talking to him, which would be strange to call him 'kid', but then he realized that he wasn't the only one taking in the sights. Young Daniel Lockett's eyes were flitting between the provosts and the scantily dressed women of the whorehouses, many of whom watched from the second floor balconies.

The marching soldiers and the provosts mutually studied each other. There seemed to be few townspeople. Vaught knew that most of the whores were not locals.

"Them provosts also take special pleasure in cracking heads on a good soldier boy, and this town's worse than most. Been hearing bad things about Colonel Truesdail, the man in charge," Prosper T. Rowe added.

"Andy Johnson's always asking for more troops. Maybe he should use the ones that he has for something more useful," John Messern complained.

Vaught did not know who Andy Johnson was, but the original part of the regiment had been in Tennessee long enough to hear stories of the paranoid military governor, Andrew Johnson, plus the scheming head of the provost guard, Colonel Truesdail.

"Eyes front, soldier" Milton Bosworth barked at Daniel.

"C'mon, sarge, he ain't never seen a woman like that before," cracked one of the men, drawing laughs.

"Ain't got those types where he's from!" another hooted.

Two streets further down, there was another house that Vaught reminded himself that he ought to visit when they returned. The sign said saloon, but the half-dressed women on the front step and balcony said something else. Vaught caught the eye of one, who waved, gesturing him to come in, laughing, knowing that was not possible this time as the troops marched on. But both of them knew that there might be another time.

"That one gots an eye for you, Vaught," someone remarked. They all called him Vaught. None of them even knew his first name, or much about him in general, and that was the way that he liked it.

"They always do," Vaught said with a crooked grin, "Didn't you notice that in Cincy?"

The other man chuckled in agreement, and Daniel Lockett looked at Vaught with some wonder. Everywhere they went, it was hard not to notice Vaught. Men and women alike always seemed to notice the large, athletic man who possessed a strange charisma. And naturally, that charm and confidence had a particular effect on the women.

"Aw, Nashville," Vaught laughed, "We hardly knew ya."

"Maybe we'll be back after we whip the Rebels," Daniel said.

"Probably, kid. Probably."

* * *

"That's the shame of it," Captain Baxter Bibb explained, pointing to the railroad tracks that ran parallel to them. "There would be little difficulty catching this Bragg if we could just use the railroad..."

Lockett gave a small nod, but no other reaction, to suggest that he was listening to his new company commander. His head throbbed, probably from a poor night's sleep. He had awakened in a cold sweat from another dream of little Amelia. When he had finally been able to fall back asleep, he had surprisingly dreamt of Anna Tucker. While such dreams were good, waking to reality made them particularly sour.

Compounded with those lost dreams, his mind was still stunned by how everything had crumbled in a matter of days. Not only had Daniel showed up and the army had let the Rebels slip north, but he had lost control of his precious company with the arrival of the new officers.

There had been times when he had cursed his promotion from the ranks, but now he realized how much guilty pride he took in it. He liked to control things, much more so than taking orders from someone else, especially someone like Baxter Bibb, Esquire.

"...If Hunt Morgan had not blown up the twin tunnels north of Gallatin on the Louisville-Nashville line last month, we could quickly make up the ground on Bragg."

When Lockett made no comment, Bibb frowned. "I say, you aren't much for conversation, are you, Lieutenant Lockett?"

Lockett tried hard to prevent his disgusted mood from seeping into his voice. "Sorry, sir. Agree with you, sir, about the rails that is."

"And we shall need to talk to the sergeants about keeping the company tighter up. Some of the men are starting to straggle..."

Lockett did not see any stragglers. If Bibb thought that they were straggling now, just wait until ten miles from now, or worse, three days of hard marching from now. The men were keeping up for now, although a few did try to march on the outside edges of the dirt road in a futile attempt to avoid some of the choking dust that those ahead of them were kicking up.

"... And at the next opportunity, I shall want the men to practice some of the infantry tactics."

"Yes, sir," Lockett answered without enthusiasm.

"You've read Hardee's book on infantry tactics, I assume."

"No, sir. General Hardee from the Rebel side?"

"Yes, that one. Shame he is a turncoat. His manual for the infantry is superb. I have been studying it since we left Detroit. I have a copy with me. You are welcome to study it for yourself." Bibb paused abruptly. "You know how to read?"

"Yes, sir."

"Excellent. I know that you were a farmer, Lockett. Not all farmers, well, you know…"

Lockett said nothing. He had learned very quickly that his new commander was a lawyer and a successful one at that, at least according to himself.

"Very good, very good. I can see why they raised you from ranks then. The men need learned men to lead them. Yes, very good indeed. That is how we will beat down this rebellion. Simple really, how far knowledge can go."

"I didn't know you were a mathematician, sir." Lockett knew that the bile in his throat was reaching a dangerously high level.

"A mathematician, Lockett? No, I'm a lawyer. I thought you knew that? A mathematician? Why on earth would you say that?"

"You were saying, sir, how knowledge will lead us to victory. It is simple math, sir. We win when we kill more of them than they kill of us. The more that we kill, the sooner it ends. We kill more by having more guns shoot at them than they can shoot back, and we shoot and reload faster so that there are more minié balls in the air than they can withstand."

Bibb looked strangely at Lockett, who looked straight ahead, grim-faced. Bibb was about to say something when suddenly his expression changed, and he laughed aloud. "Oh! You are joking! I see! Very good, yes, very good indeed! You had me for a moment, Lieutenant. A mathematician! Very good indeed! Never realized you were such a jester."

Lockett said nothing in return. There was nothing to say.

September 12

The trail of dust rose up behind General Buell's army for miles. Whatever Rebel cavalry was watching them would surely be reporting back to Bragg that the Yankees were finally on the move. The two armies marched parallel tracks through middle Tennessee towards Kentucky.

Somewhere east of their dust trail, a separate revealing cloud was being kicked up by the Rebel Army and their wagon trains. But how far north of their own position? That was the question as Buell's army churned along with surprising alacrity.

The few newcomers notwithstanding, they were an army of thinner men than they had once been. Their uniforms were faded and patched, but they marched with a foot-hardened pace that the newcomers struggled to keep up with, even though the journey was only in its early days. It was not at all like their slow marches across northern Mississippi and Alabama during the summer. They were pushing hard, and Lockett was surprised that this army could actually move so quickly when its mind was put to it.

Lockett stared eastwards across the bluest sky, but there was no parallel dust trail visible to him. He knew that General Bragg and his Rebel army was out there somewhere, and beyond that there was another Confederate army, already deep into northern Kentucky. He had not believed the newspaperman from Chicago who told him that Confederate General Kirby Smith was already near the Ohio River after winning a victory in Richmond, Kentucky a week ago.

He could imagine the chaos and concern in Ohio. This was no small, mounted raiding party. Bragg had an army of infantry, with a second army waiting to be linked up.

It was Lieutenant Renaud who brought his attention back to their own columns.

"What do you zink of the ne-uw men?" the French Detroiter asked.

He too had received some of the reinforcements, and he too had lost sole control of his company. His company was now commanded by Captain Billard, the only Frenchman among of the new officers. It made sense to all that Billard be the captain of a company of French Detroiters, but most of Renaud's company were farmers and hunters who had grown together under Renaud. Billard was the son of a foundry owner, and at this point, the men resented his presence.

"There is no time to train to them," Lockett replied. He paused. He knew that the speed of the march was crucial. "They need training. What little I have seen is that they are slow with their weapons and incapable of following simple commands."

"We all were at one point."

"But we have seen enough now to know how important that is."

"And what of your brother? Have you spoken again?"

"Very little," Lockett responded cautiously. He was uncomfortable that his intentional estrangement was so well known.

"Is he learning?"

"Learning?" Lockett snorted, "Not about the things that he should." He looked forward. He could see his brother marching about 50 yards ahead of him. Daniel was taller than Lockett remembered, though not as tall as he was.

"He is friends with zat man called Vaught. You should keep an eye on him," Renaud warned.

Lockett knew who Vaught was. The man was hard to miss among of the newcomers. All of the newcomers gravitated towards him. He was tall and handsome. Smooth-faced, he had a muscular square jaw that looked as if it had been chiseled by some sculptor. Broad shouldered, he walked with a confidently erect posture that belonged on a General from West Point, not some lowly private.

"What do you know about Vaught?" Lockett asked. "I know he is one of my brother's messmates, along with that boy with shock white blond hair."

"Bouma, I believe, is his name. Yes, he was zere too."

"Where?"

"Gambling with some of my men. Zey are convinced zat Vaught cheated zem, but zey have no proof."

"Did he?" Lockett asked

"Perhaps, but it does not need to be true to have trouble follow. I feel something unusual about Vaught."

Lockett nodded. There was something about the man that did not fit.

"Your brother should be careful hanging about men like him."

Lockett pursed his lips. There were plenty of men who gambled. There was little to do besides that in the army. It was nothing unusual, but a man with a reputation for cheating was another matter.

"I guess it is good that we are on such a hard march then. The men will have little energy for much else."

"Perhaps, but marches always come to an end at some point, mon ami."

Lockett agreed, but he also knew that there was little he could do about it now. He was sure that his brother would brush off any guidance at this point.

* * *

Franklin Witten flagged down his friend, Ambrose Tucker. "I see more of you now than when we served together with Colonel Morgan."

"True," Ambrose said, taking the proffered hand, "Although some days I miss the action."

"Not enough danger as a messenger?" Witten laughed.

Tucker shrugged.

"Course, you heard about General Chalmer's man? Adkins is his name, I believe. Had a run in with some Unionist bushwhackers, barely escaped by the skin of his teeth."

Tucker patted his handy LeMat sidearm. "I'm ready should the occasion arise." He pulled the heavy sidearm from its holster.

"You mean not everyone in Kentucky is happy about our arrival?" Witten said laughingly, "I guess they have not read General Bragg's 'Proclamation to the People of Kentucky.'" He lowered his voice an octave and recited the printed message that had been shared with the army and the people of the bluegrass state. "We come not as conquerors, but to restore you to the liberties of which you have been deprived by a cruel and relentless foe. If you prefer Federal rule, show it by your frowns and we should return where we came."

"Yes, I guess Adkins' bushwhacker was frowning broadly

enough."

"No matter," Witten said, "Chalmers captured Cave City and the Yankee telegraph."

"Really? Cut the Yankee telegraph line?"

"No," Witten said with a shake of the head and a sly smile, "He didn't cut it."

"What? Why not?"

"Decided it was better to just listen in on it. Now, we know the disposition of the garrison at Munfordville, and the status of reinforcements."

"Oh," Tucker said, impressed, "That was clever. With our vanguard arriving in Munfordville by the end of the day, we should be well placed to capture it."

Witten nodded eagerly. With that long bridge in our possession, we will really have that devil Buell in a hard spot."

* * *

Daniel Lockett stood unsteadily, his face wracked with discomfort.

Darkness still had its hold on the morning, but the sergeants were rousting the men and camp was being quickly broken down. Another day of marching would start in a matter of minutes.

The novelty of the marching had worn off. He wished now that they had just stayed north, someplace like Cincinnati would have been nice. He had liked the Queen City with its hustle and activity and that big Ohio River where the black stacks of the steamers moved back and forth like an army of smoke belching trees towering over the waterfront buildings.

They had spent four days in that town, awaiting orders that would direct them to Blair's Independent Regiment's latest location. Those four days had been the most interesting of his seventeen year-old life, and exactly the reason that he had joined the army.

Cincinnati was a true escape from sleepy Kalamazoo and the drudgery of the farm.

He and John Bouma had followed their other messmate, Vaught, around to its taverns and gambling halls. Daniel had never known that places like that could exist, nor be as interesting to observe. There were so many different people, some in fine dress and some in sweat stained dockmen's garb, and the girls...

Vaught had been to Cincinnati before, he seemed to have been about everywhere before, and he led the two boys from place to place. And the amount of money that Vaught could make in one night of gambling! Daniel had never seen such money in his life, and it came so easily to Vaught in just one night of card playing.

"Come on, Daniel," John Bouma interrupted his thoughts. "Sergeant Bosworth called for all men to fall in."

Daniel looked at his messmate and friend. He had met the young Dutchman when he had first arrived in Detroit to muster in. Discovering that Bouma was also from west Michigan, the two had struck up an immediate friendship. Equally young as Daniel, the blond haired, blue eyed John Bouma was an easy-going youth, and he too was anxious for the adventure that the army promised.

And while thus far the army had provided little entertainment for them, the third member of their mess more than made up for that. Vaught was far older than the two boys, but for some reason, he seemed to have taken the two youths under his wing.

Daniel didn't know where Vaught was from, if he even had a home. Vaught seemed to have lived everywhere and regaled them with stories from his time in Chicago, St. Louis, and even New Orleans. All of the newcomers, not just Daniel and John Bouma, were drawn to him, although they had quickly learned not to play cards with him.

"Daniel, come on," Bouma urged again.

Daniel frowned.

John was not usually so diligent, but as he arrived in formation just in the nick of time, Daniel was thankful for the warning. Still, his belly was sour, and his head pounded from the drink that Vaught somehow found last night. The last thing that he felt like doing was marching more miles this morning, and he didn't need Sergeant Bosworth bellowing at him either.

The burly sergeant seemed to have taken extra interest in bullying all of the newcomers, but particularly himself, Daniel thought. He suspected that it was James's fault. It was just the type of thing that he expected from his brother, only he would have predicted that James would do it himself and not through somebody else.

What did surprise Daniel was how little Patrick McManus had spoken to him. Patrick had always been like an additional older sibling to whom he could go. Patrick had always listened to him before, even when James would not, but the Patrick McManus that Daniel had observed around camp was not the Patrick McManus that he remembered from the farm.

This Patrick McManus was quiet and serious. The Patrick that Daniel had known in Kalamazoo was quick with a smile or a joke, someone who did not take things so seriously and who knew that when times were tough on the farm that only meant that they were bound to improve. Patrick had always said that this was his endless Irish optimism shining through, but Daniel was not seeing that in Patrick now.

"Shoulders straight," came a friendly whisper in Daniel's ear.

He looked to his left. Vaught had quietly joined him in the ranks. With some wonderment, Daniel thought that the man sounded as fresh as could be. Vaught had drank three times as much as he had last night, but the man smiled and gave no hint of the pounding head and roiled stomach that plagued Daniel.

"Your brother is having weapons inspection before we set out," Vaught said softly, "Though how anyone can see anything at this time of the morning, I have no idea."

The sergeants were working from opposite ends of the ranks, inspecting the rifles of each man. There was never an issue with the older members of the company but not so for many of the newcomers.

"Dirt!" Bosworth bellowed at one soldier. "Step forward!"

How he could tell in the dim light of early morning, Daniel was not sure.

"Dirt and rust!" he snapped at another. "Step forward!"

Bosworth reached Daniel's section of the ranks. He checked John's rifle. "Passable," he grunted, handing the rifle back to Bouma.

Next, he took Vaught's rifle and inspected the firing mechanism in the first pinkish glow. Vaught stood nearly a head taller than Bosworth, and he stood by confidently.

Bosworth examined the rifle painstakingly and then raised an eyebrow. Wordlessly, he handed it back to Vaught.

The sergeant stopped in front of Daniel next. He looked

squarely at the youth first, his burly, grizzled appearance contrasting sharply with the younger Lockett's cherubic face. "Dirt!" he glared after a half second's inspection of the gun. "Step forward!"

At the end of the inspection, seventeen men had stepped forward, all newcomers. Daniel watched his brother slowly pace in front of the men, while Captain Bibb watched from behind.

"You men will be on punishment duty after today's march for the next week for failing to keep your weapons in perfect working order." James Lockett stopped and looked at the men in the front middle. His head turned left and right to look at each of them, though Daniel felt as if the gaze had skipped right past him. "A weapon that will not fire is a weapon that will not kill the enemy. I promise you that the enemy's weapons will have no such problems. They will kill you or the man next to you if you do not kill them first!"

But Daniel did not hear anything that his brother said after 'punishment duty.' He was already so tired, and the thought of extra duty after another long day of marching burned him. He silently cursed his brother.

* * *

Ambrose Tucker watched the Confederate army take a brief break from its march. It was strange being a messenger and not a regular. He was on alert that General Bragg might need him to deliver an urgent message, for every message was urgent, but there were long periods where he had little to do. It was very different from his time with Colonel Morgan, where there was never a moment's rest.

He imagined that Colonel Morgan, a native Kentuckian, would be very pleased now, given that the Confederate army was back in Kentucky. Although Ambrose Tucker wondered what the Colonel would say about the reaction of the Kentuckians so far.

The expectation had been that the army would swell with volunteers, but so far, the reaction was muted in terms of volunteers. Womenfolk had cheered their arrival with the waving of handkerchiefs and cheering calls, but the men had not joined their ranks. He could not tell if caution and a belief that the

Yankees would be back were to blame, or if this was their true reaction. He wasn't sure what to make of Kentucky at this point.

Either way, it had not dampened General Bragg's spirits at all. They had reached Kentucky days ahead of Buell, and they could beat him to Louisville now. They could select the ground of their choosing. They could link up with Kirby Smith. They had a bounty of good possibilities to pick from.

And today, they would continue to plunge deeper into Kentucky. Hopefully, the lead infantry elements would reach Munfordville by nightfall.

September 14
--the diary of James Lockett
They tell us that we are in Kentucky now though it looks no different from here. Colonel Blair says that General Buell and the lead elements have reached Bowling Green. I cannot remember a faster three days of marching. Surely, we must be close to Bragg now. But that is all for tonight. I am too weary to write more.

* * *

Ambrose Tucker watched the men trudge back, away from the town of Munfordville and the fort guarding it.

"A shambles, that is what it was," Franklin Witten complained to him.

Ambrose held the bridle of his horse and watched the wounded struggle back. One used his musket as a crutch. Two others pulled a small handcart that was loaded down with four men. A trickle of blood dripped from the back of the tilted cart as it was dragged along.

"General Chalmers should have waited for more of his men to arrive. He was so sure that the Yankee garrison would surrender just at the sight of our flag. After this, now it will take the rest of Bragg's army to root that garrison out of there," Witten frowned.

"General Bragg won't be pleased by any delays," Tucker remarked aloud.

"Seen enough now to know that," Witten added, hauling himself up into the saddle. "Doubt that Bragg will bypass this garrison and allow it to linger in his rear, but the longer this takes, the closer that Buell gets to us."

"No matter if Buell does," Tucker said indignantly. "Those Yankees can't stop us."

"You sound like General Hardee," Witten laughed. "He'd just as soon fight them anywhere, but he says that Bragg won't fight until we've linked up with Kirby Smith."

"Maybe," Tucker shrugged. "But we know that Buell ain't at full strength either. He left Thomas's division behind in Nashville. We know that thanks to their telegraph."

"I best get back to General Hardee. He'll want to know that the advance has halted."

September 15
--the diary of James Lockett
We have joined General Buell's lead element in Bowling Green.

The sun was nearly down below the horizon as Lockett sat next to his men. It had been less than a full day's marching for them to meet up with the vanguard. The army now halted while the generals decided what to do next. Somewhere up ahead, Bragg's army waited.

"We march tomorrow, Lieutenant?" Private John Messern asked.

"Hard to say," he answered, looking around the camp fire. There were seven men around this fire, all from his original Shiloh core. To this point, they had not mixed with the newcomers, which Lockett knew was a problem, but he could not bring himself to address it. And since Captain Bibb had made no mention of it, he let it go. Though in the back of his mind, he knew that they would need the new men to work together.

"I say there will be a battle tomorrow," Private Charlie Adams declared.

"God help us, if so," Levi Thickle muttered, "These fresh fish ain't ready for that." He forked a thumb towards the nearby camp of newcomers.

"None of us were ever ready for that first battle, eh, Levi?" Lockett said pleasantly.

"I sure warn't," Prosper T. Rowe chuckled. "Our company had

hardly even drilled with our muskets before Shiloh. Half the company ran after the first shots. The other half war' so dazed that we sent a volley of ramrods at the Rebels with our second shot." He laughed loudly. "Them Rebels knew then that they had us. Imagine seeing a twenty ramrods flying through the air!"

"So you think that we will fight them at Munfordville, sir?" Messern questioned.

"Looks like it. They're blocking the path to Louisville. Of course, they need to finish off the garrison there. Hopefully, the garrison can keep delaying Bragg long enough for the rest of our army to reach 'em, but a garrison won't be able to hold out forever."

"There are some bluffs near the river," Messern commented, "It won't be an easy go. Good ground to make a stand." The lone Kentuckian in the company looked off into the distance, imagining the ground in his mind's eye.

"If that is the case, then Buell won't fight," Thickle complained, "He'll march us around. He ain't got stomach for a fight like that."

"Not so easy to find another way across this river, Levi, not for an army."

"Buell still won't fight."

Lockett said nothing, but he was inclined to agree with Levi. General Buell did have a reputation for espousing a belief that outmaneuvering the enemy was always better than defeating the enemy directly.

"We gonna to see any of your neighbors joining up with Bragg, John?" McManus asked Messern.

Messern shrugged. "The ones who would have become Rebs already joined up months ago." He paused. "I have a brother and cousin over there, somewhere in Hanson's Brigade."

"Kentucky is a slave state," Thickle said to no one in particular.

"True, but we are a Union state for a reason," Messern defended. "Bragg will find few friends there beyond the ones that he already has."

"That Hunt Morgan is a Kentuckian, ain't he?" Thickle continued in an argumentative tone.

Messern stirred next to Lockett. "You trying to say something, Levi? Why don't you just come out and say it?"

Lockett put a gentle hand on Messern's shoulder and eased him back. "Let's save the fight for Bragg tomorrow. Levi's not saying anything about you or Kentucky. This is Levi that we're talking about. He'd argue that a tree did not contain enough wood if he thought it would get under someone's skin."

* * *

"If the damn man doesn't surrender, then we will have no choice but to assault the Yankees," Ambrose Tucker heard General Chalmers complain. "With Buell approaching from the south, we can't have 4,000 men positioned directly in our rear, even it if is a garrison of 4,000 store clerks. Damnation and hell fire. The bastards!"

Ambrose Tucker could only grin as he saw General 'Bishop' Polk wince at Chalmers's language.

"Then we will just have to crush the man," General Cheatham said. "He'll regret his foolishness. He may have 4,000 men in his garrison, but we'll storm their defenses, and there will be no mercy once the men's blood is up."

"But in the time that takes, Buell will get even closer, and we have not made our link up with Kirby Smith yet," Polk observed, "It's all about time, precious time."

"Then we had best hope that Buckner's plan works."

"Damnable foolishness, if you ask me. The garrison's colonel already knows that he is facing our entire army."

"We can tell that Hoosier that he's surrounded, but showing him a hundred cannon is something else."

General Chalmers looked unimpressed. He stroked his brown goatee thoughtfully before replying. "So he is such a fool that if we parade him past all of the cannon that we have and tell him that it is a fraction of what we will bring to bear against him, then he will surrender? Why don't we just polish them up while we are at it? Blind him into submission too!"

"I think General Buckner's plan will work. The Yankee colonel is not a regular army man. Who knows what he was before the war? A lawyer? The sight of those cannon will persuade him of the futility of resistance."

"Perhaps," General Hardee said grudgingly. He too had a low

opinion of men not from West Point. Both armies had plenty of volunteer leaders, few were worth much in his view. "Perhaps, perhaps. In any case, we will know in two hours."

* * *

Hours later, Ambrose Tucker mounted his horse and headed back to General Bragg's headquarters. He would sleep well tonight, full of the same elation that the rest of the army felt. General Buckner's ruse had worked.

The garrison had surrendered that afternoon. 4,000 prisoners had been marched off. 5,000 small arms had been added to the wagons that would be distributed to the swell of volunteers that was sure to follow this victory in Kentucky.

General Bragg had the army deploy south of the river along the hills. This now barred the Yankee's route to Louisville. They had the ground of their choosing now, and Yankees would have little choice but to come to them.

They could defeat Buell here and then march on Louisville. Other Yankee troops would be waiting there, but if they could face them one at a time, how could they possibly be stopped? Ambrose Tucker smiled at the thought.

* * *

Daniel Lockett swirled the rock hard biscuit in the remnants of the bacon grease as he slowly worked another bite over in his mouth. He chewed gently, patiently letting the biscuit soften, ever cautious about breaking a tooth on it. He hoped today would be a better day, a day with some activity. They had marched like fiends to get here, aware that Bragg's army was a mere day's march away, only to halt and wait for the rest of their army to reach them.

Their impatience was further soured by the news of the day. The surrender of the Munfordville's garrison had already reached their ears, but it was the sight of the 4,000 dispirited parolees marching through their camp that had frustrated them all and made a few despair for what might await them.

Paroled by General Bragg and the Rebels rather than trying to deal with the care and feeding of 4,000 men. Shoeless, weaponless, and seemingly prideless, the parolees were full of horror stories about the Rebel horde and the hundreds of cannon that awaited Buell's army in Munfordville.

Sergeant Bosworth had hustled the parolees quickly through the camp, threatening them with his fists if they lingered or opened their mouths again in front of "real fightin' men."

"It would make more sense to give them a weapon and turn them back around." Vaught commented as the last of the Munfordville garrison departed for points south.

"But they gave their word that they would not take up arms again?" John Bouma said in confusion, "That's how they got their paroles, right?"

Vaught gave a cock-eyed grin. "And how would the Rebels know if they broke their word?"

Before Bouma could reply, another sergeant rousted the men for yet another round of Captain Bibb's drilling. Captain Bibb seemed to enjoy drilling them on their right wheels and other terms that made no sense to Daniel, Bouma, and many of the other fresh fish. They did not seem to always make sense to Captain Bibb either since he seemed to consult some leather bound book from time to time. It was an aggravating exercise. It seemed that half of the time some of the men would turn the wrong direction and collide with others. The verbal abuse from the sergeants was continuous and particularly vociferous at those moments.

When they weren't trying to figure out their right from their left, then James was having the company repair fences and build barricades outside of camp. It seemed to Daniel that it was purely to keep the men busy. No one seemed to expect the Confederates to attack them; they all knew that the Rebels were waiting for them up at the river.

* * *

September 20

"Damnation!" General Hardee said for the second time. Even his well-known reserve could not constrain his frustration. He pounded a fist on the battered camp table. The worn wood cracked audibly, but no one in the tent paid attention.

"Your Kentuckians will be more than disappointed," Hardee said as he handed the written orders to one of his brigade commanders, General Roger Hansen. "I wouldn't blame them for being outright mutinous at these orders."

Hansen read the orders with disbelief, "General Bragg wants us to abandon Munfordville? March to Bardstown? But why? That will leave the way to Louisville open for the Yankees?"

"God damn it all! It is no matter that General Thomas has linked up with Buell, or that Kirby Smith has yet to link up with us. This is the place to make our stand!"

Another staff office spoke up, "We did a night march to get to Munfordville, marched 30 miles through the night to get here because it was so important, and now Granny Bragg wants to abandon it!"

"The men will not understand it," Hansen said dubiously.

"Nor should they," Hardee grumbled. He suddenly seemed to notice that there was still an interloper in the room, Bragg's messenger. "And what are you still doing there? You are dismissed!" he said angrily.

Ambrose Tucker stood unflinchingly. "My orders were to await your confirmation that you could begin in three hours."

"Confirmation?" Hardee said angrily, "Bragg wants confirmation! By God, I could shoot his damn messenger, would that suffice as confirmation?" His face was beet red with anger, and the faces of his staff and brigade commanders were equally hard.

But Ambrose Tucker still did not move.

Through a clinched jaw, Hardee muttered under his breath. He wrote two words on a scrap of paper. Rising to his feet, he angrily slapped the paper into the messenger's hand, "We will obey the General's commands, no matter how foolish and short-sighted they are."

Chapter 10

September 27

The clouds of dust filled the air, stirred up by the thousands of men marching on the choked roads. It was dust so thick that it obscured a man's own feet, both those fortunate enough to have shoes and those whose leather had worn out miles ago. It was dust that coated their faded blue uniforms from top to bottom. It matted their hair and sweat stained faces such that most men had only thin rivulets of white skin that ran vertically from their brows where the sweat had washed a path across the grime.

The dust clung to their already dry throats and swollen tongues. Men would collapse along the roadside. Some would rise again with assistance and squeeze into the overloaded and undersupplied hospital and supply wagons. Others would not be so fortunate. The weary and worn out would at first be stragglers. Then, when there was no one left to march past their exhausted bodies, they died along the road from the scorching temperatures and thirst. Their bodies would swell in the heat, and they would lay unburied by the side of the road, a rotting, stench filled feast for buzzards.

There was no longer any talking along the road. Parched throats were such that even issuing the most basic order took an act of self-discipline and willpower. Bodies and throats strained to conserve what little moisture they could retain.

Silently, thousands of Buell's men marched northwards. Their empty canteens jangled hollowly as they tromped along.

Most were still amazed that the Rebels had abandoned their fortifications at Munfordville, opening the way to Louisville. Some viewed this as salvation from God; others viewed it merely as another example of the inexplicability of this war; and even a few viewed it with disappointment, convinced that they could whip the Rebels if only they could find them, in spite of their condition.

The initial part of their march from Nashville had been a voluble mix of bravado and some disbelief that the Rebels had skirted north of them. Then there was apprehension about what lay ahead of them in Munfordville. And now... Now, it was a muted determination.

They marched past withered wheat, corn, and cotton fields. Some were tended by white farmers; some were worked by curious slaves who watched the blue army trundle northwards. Regardless of who tended the farms, the land was in bad shape due to the summer long drought.

There was nothing for the army to forage, even if General Buell had allowed it. A few isolated animals and morsels of food would appear in camps in the middle of the night, as the men and officers disregarded any orders in regards to foraging. Their desperation was strong, but there was little here to steal. The traipsing of the armies saw to some of that, but it was mostly Mother Nature's doing.

Even worse was the scarcity of drinkable water. Creeks and ponds were bone dry. What few scummy puddles remained were consumed by the men despite their wretched and wiggling appearance. Some men tried to hide the foul appearance by turning it into coffee, which oddly, the quartermaster still had plenty of.

It was the most foul water that the men from Blair's Independent Regiment had ever seen. Most of the men were from Michigan, and they were used to the cool, clear waters of their lakes and rivers, but the water here was water that they would never have let their cattle drink. Yet now, it was glumly swallowed by the men for their own survival.

Daniel Lockett silently marched along. For the first time, he second-guessed his decision to enlist. His once bright uniform was now a faded and dirty disgrace, and he marched along barefoot. One night, he had made the mistake of removing his boots from his blistered and swollen feet, but when he woke in the morning, they were gone, stolen.

He had fruitlessly tried to figure out who took them, but it was to no avail. He wasn't the only one with such problems. Other 'fresh fish' had similar problems, and it seemed to Daniel that some of the other regiments had it in for Blair's Independent Regiment. Besides having some newcomers, the regiment seemed to have a dubious reputation with many. No one seemed to know or care that at least one of its companies, his brother's, contained veterans from Shiloh. The other regiments discounted it since that company was put together from shirkers, scofflaws, and others remnant pieces.

It had taken a week since they had passed through Munfordville before Blair's Independent Regiment started to arrive at the edge of Louisville. The vanguard of Buell's army arrived a couple of days before, but it would be another week before the rest of his bedraggled army would stumble into the river town.

Local citizens watched in amazement as the unrecognizable army came in, day by day, with each regiment seemingly more dirty and battered than the one before it.

They were a sight to see. Patrick McManus noticed the locals' thunderstruck faces, but he felt no shame. In fact, he felt pride, as did a number of the other men.

It had been a long march from Nashville to Louisville, but the veterans knew how quickly they had accomplished this march. They may have looked like a rabble, even more destitute than the Rebel army, but they had beaten the Rebels in the race to Louisville.

They had marched with lightning speed, particularly in comparison to their crawl towards Chattanooga earlier in the summer. Their appearance notwithstanding, there was a new sense of pride that they felt. The town's citizens may look at them skeptically, but curiously, the army's morale was rising to new heights.

And Louisville had been saved. Local citizens who just days ago had been preparing to flee across the river by any means possible, including pontoon bridge, now felt some relief as the tens of thousands of dirty men marched into their town.

September 28

General Bragg paced slowly in front of his aides and staff. Consciously, he tried to slow himself as he talked and thought through this aloud. His mind whirled with the decision, and there was an urge for his feet to match his busy mind, but in front of the men, he could not allow that.

He took a long drink of water from a tin cup and forced himself still. Sweat dripped off his heavy brow and down into his thick beard. That was the heat, not anxiety, he told himself. They were all sweating heavily in the swelter despite being in the shade of his tent.

"Are you sure that you want to give temporary control of the army to General Polk?" Bragg's aide-de-camp asked, echoing his superior's own thoughts.

Bragg wanted to do no such thing. He would rather have left it to General Hardee, anyone besides Bishop Polk, but Polk outranked Hardee and army rules dictated that Polk would be next in command.

"It will just be for a few days," Bragg soothed his aide-de-camp, and himself. "Frankfort is not far, and this must be done. Polk can maintain position here in Bardstown, and I can return quickly if need be."

"Will this really work?" another aide asked.

Bragg fought the scowl down. The youthful aide who had asked the question was a fool. Clearly, he had not been paying attention when Bragg had explained this to them earlier. But the aide was the eldest son of an important bureaucrat in President Davis's administration. General Bragg needed to keep good relations there, so uncharacteristically, he smiled benevolently at the youthful captain.

"If you do this, will these Kentuckians finally volunteer and take up arms?" the youthful aide added.

To date, the promises of thousands of men joining the Confederate army had been empty. While the reception was warm, enthusiastic even in many of the towns, it was the women who waved and cheered their arrival. The men's response was muted, and a good many even disappeared into the woods.

General Bragg still had thousands of muskets in his wagons going unused. At first, they had thought that the response was timid due to concern that the Confederate army was here today, gone tomorrow, but now...

"They can volunteer if they wish," Bragg said, straining to bite back a sharply worded retort to the bureaucrat's son. "But that is not why I must go to Frankfort. We must officially inaugurate Governor Hawes as the true governor of the state. Once we have established a government, then we can start conscription in Kentucky like we did in Tennessee. That seems to be the only way to make the men from these states fight."

Ambrose Tucker flinched at the rebuke. The bitter statement startled him, but if there were others on Bragg's staff who took offense, it did not show. Apparently, the others were used to the General's prejudice against those two states now.

"Surely the establishment of a true government will be all that is needed to bring thousands of Kentuckians to our camps," the youthful aide declared confidently.

Braxton Bragg had seen enough to know by now that there would be no droves of volunteers, but he kept his tone even. "Volunteer or conscription, they will join us one way or another."

Ambrose Tucker frowned. The words of General Bragg's opening declaration to Kentuckians back in Glasgow rang hollow now, *If you prefer Federal rule, show us and we should return where we came...* But the problem was not the Cause, Ambrose thought angrily, the problem was General Bragg himself. Their Cause was just! It was liberty over tyranny! Yet, he too was bewildered by the reaction in Kentucky.

September 30

Daniel Lockett watched the horseplay in camp, but his mind was elsewhere. Perhaps it was finally having a full stomach and not having constant thirst after so many long and difficult days, but he felt out of sorts. They had been marching nearly 30 miles a day, waking at three in the morning, surviving on quarter rations. They had been terrible days. Hot, hungry, thirsty, plagued by flies and other insects. Men would fall out of line, unable to keep up. They had been good, hearty men too, yet the pace was too much. Only some had trickled back into camp over the previous three days. Where were the others? Daniel had no idea. Had they died right there on the road?

But most of the regiment had made it to Louisville, and despite the strange and even aghast looks that they had received, they were still viewed as saviors of the city. And now, bolstered by fresh reinforcements from Indiana and Ohio, their numbers swelled.

They should have maintained that sense of pride and relief. Instead the various camps were full of rumors and dissension. There were rumors that Buell had been ordered to relinquish command to General Thomas, and that General Thomas had refused. The men had shrugged off that rumor. General Buell had no friends in the ranks, but the fact that he was still in charge was something that most of the men were able to brush off.

No, the bigger news was the one that caused the arguments. It was all about what President Lincoln had done.

Emancipation!

The news of President Lincoln's Emancipation Proclamation had swept through their ranks as they had arrived in Louisville. There were some in the ranks who openly cheered the news and even sang a Hallelujah! But there were others who openly cursed it to such a degree that Daniel had to wonder if those men would desert and join the other side. And then there were others who gave no reaction. Were those men just too tired to care?

But now, days had passed. Their bodies and minds had started to recover, and there was constant talk and debate about it now. Slaves freed? Or at least freed in any state that was in insurrection? Oddly, that meant that the slaves here in Kentucky were still slaves, while those in Tennessee could be free? It puzzled Daniel, but he had heard the Abolitionists. They did not blink at it. They were confident that it would spread, and that it was only the beginning.

His brother, James, was walking toward him, eating an apple. He pulled a second one from his pocket and tossed it to Daniel. Daniel caught the apple, and silently, they looked at each other. Over the final days they had started to talk, but it was not much, mostly just a 'good morning' or 'how are you'.

"How are the feet?" James asked.

Over the final stages of the march, the blisters on Daniel's feet had become unbearable. Each step made it worse, and many times he thought about falling by the wayside like so many others had, but he refused to give in.

His friend, Bouma, had wondered what possessed him to keep

going on those bloody feet. But it was no mystery to Daniel. There was one reason, and one reason alone that pushed him to keep going. He was not going to give his brother the satisfaction.

"My feet?" he asked with a cautious squint, knowing that he had not mentioned them to James in their brief conversations.

"They were blistered something fierce," James said, taking a huge bite from his apple.

"How did you know that?"

James shrugged, chewed, and swallowed. Eventually, he replied, "You were staggering like a man on peg legs those final miles. Besides, I do talk to the men."

Daniel frowned at the last comment. If only his brother knew what the newcomers were saying about him, then he would not be so relaxed. They had just been whispers at first, maybe because the others knew that they were brothers, but then they ceased being so secretive. Newcomers like Winfield, Brewer, and Telford were bold in their dislike of their lieutenant who called for weapons inspections and firearm drill. Those three had ended up on punishment duty more than once, and their disdain for the young lieutenant was becoming increasingly bold, although when they were around the original part of the company, they wisely kept their thoughts to themselves.

"Have to say," James added, "That I wasn't sure that you were going to make it. You surprised me. Never saw that amount of gumption from you when we needed to work the plow."

Daniel scowled and stood abruptly on his still painful feet. He opened his mouth, but James waved him to silence. "Relax, I didn't mean to insult…"

"Well, you did!"

"Just saying that I was impressed, Daniel. Not every man made it. That was as brutal of a march as any army has made in such a short period."

Daniel relaxed slightly. "Yes, well, it will be good to rest after that."

James chuckled at the comment.

"What's so funny?" Daniel demanded.

"That was why I was coming over here. Better rest up tonight, we pull three days of rations and head out tomorrow."

"What? Where?"

"To Bragg and his Rebels, of course. With all of the reinforcements from the defenses of Louisville joining us, not to mention all of the new troops from Ohio and Indiana that have been raised to deal with this, there will be three full corps heading for the Rebels."

"If they stand and fight," Daniel said dourly, thinking of his sore feet. "They'll pull back again, and we'll march east across Kentucky? I don't think my feet can take it."

"You're the one who wanted to join the army," James said without sympathy. Part of him wanted the Rebels to stand and fight. After all, this war could not end just by marching around, despite what General Buell said. As James had long believed, for the war to end, they had to fight, and they had to win. On the other hand, no battle meant that Daniel would be safe.

October 4

Ambrose Tucker had departed days ago with General Bragg and his staff to begin the preparations, and he looked with satisfaction at the large inauguration day crowd.

Surely, this was the sign that the Kentuckians needed, Ambrose thought to himself.

The installation of a new Confederate governor would show Kentucky that the Confederacy was here to stay. Finally, those unused muskets would find some use in the hands of Kentucky born and bred soldiers.

The crowd bubbled with interest and conversation as they waited for the festivities to begin. It was a well-dressed crowd. There were certainly some well-to-do and important people here, Ambrose thought. The colorful dresses of the girls caught his eye, particularly since many of them were trying to catch his eye or some of the other young officers who were present.

Kentucky had a number of attractive girls, he mused. A dark-haired one made eye contact with him as she fanned herself coquettishly. Her dark hair reminded him of his sister, and his mind wandered to how she was faring with his Aunt. But before he could think much on it, a drop of rain fell on his shoulder with an audible plunk.

He looked up at the sky, but the solitary drop seemed to be a tease, and there were no other drops. Overhead the Stars and Bars flapped victoriously from the majestic statehouse. It was a red, white, and blue splash against a threatening sky.

He wandered over to General Buckner and Bragg's chief of staff. The two Confederate Kentuckians were talking with a knot of locals, all fancily attired for the occasion.

"...But I have heard that the Unionists are on the march," one of the local men said.

General Buckner laughed and smiled confidently. "Nonsense. It is just a mere reconnaissance force. If they wander too close to us, they will get a bloody nose that they won't soon forget!"

"There is nothing to fear," the chief of staff added reassuringly. "Today will mark a new chapter in Kentucky, a new chapter for all those who desire freedom from tyranny."

A few hours later, just before noon, Governor-to-be Hawes arrived with Kirby Smith's cavalry escort. There was an accompanying artillery salvo that startled the jumpy crowd before they realized that the booming cannons were just to welcome the new governor, not approaching Yankees.

As the band started up, the governor-to-be dismounted and shook hands with General Bragg and then individually with each of his staff. He coughed harshly between half of the introductions.

"He's recovering from typhoid," the chief of staff whispered to Ambrose before the final introductions were made.

Then, as it had been teasing all day long, large, heavy drops of water started to fall from the sky.

At first, it was merely a drop, drop, but then the sky opened up with a heavy drenching. The staff and dignitaries hustled into the statehouse. The large crowd lurched forward. The lucky ones were able to squeeze into the rotunda, but a significant number still stood outside in the rain.

Local son, General Humphrey, spoke first. Eventually, he yielded the stage to General Bragg. With a voice that easily carried across the statehouse floor and even out into the rotunda, the general excoriated President Lincoln and his Emancipation Proclamation, concluding by promising Kentucky greater liberties under the Confederate States of America.

It was then that Governor Hawes took the stage. The aging

attorney stood in front of the crowd and took a dramatic pause. Just as he was about to speak, there was the clear sound of cannon echoing in the distance.

Ambrose Tucker was standing next to middle-aged woman whose expensive frock was dripping with water, making a puddle beneath the two of them. "That was thunder, right?" she asked.

"Of course, of course," Tucker lied, wondering why there would be cannon fire so close that it could be heard inside the statehouse.

Governor Hawes continued his speech as if he had not heard anything and spoke for thirty minutes, never missing a beat as the cannon fire sound periodically throughout it.

Tucker was slipping his way through the crowd when he saw a drenched, gray uniformed captain enter the assembly room and head directly for General Bragg. He was able to catch up to the captain as he left and followed him outside, where the rain had faded to a humid drizzle.

"Franklin!" Ambrose called out.

"Ambrose," Franklin Witten greeted, mounting his horse.

"What's the news?"

"The Yankees are twelve miles from town."

"Twelve miles? Cavalry? Just reconnaissance?"

"Seems like more than that. They're in heavy force, just crossed the Kentucky River on the Shelbyville Road. General Bragg seems to think that it must be General Buell himself."

Reflexively, Ambrose took a step back and watched him disappear down the road.

Ambrose Tucker stood in the small ante room. Outside the room, a select group of Kentucky Confederates dined together, having been reassured that the cannon noise earlier in the day was nothing serious. But back in the ante room, General Bragg wrote out the orders that Tucker was to deliver to General Polk.

"We will evacuate Frankfort immediately," he said. "If the full Yankee army is converging here, we will need to leave until we can link up with General Polk and the main portion of our army. You will deliver this with the utmost haste, Lieutenant."

"Yes, sir," Tucker answered unnecessarily.

General Bragg scowled at the interruption. "Harrodsburg.

That is where we will gather."

Captain Franklin Witten burst into the anteroom and saluted. "General, sir, I believe it is time for you to leave. We have removed the planks from the bridges, as you ordered, but the Yankees could be here very shortly."

Bragg thrust the message into Ambrose Tucker's hand.

With no further ado, Tucker walked briskly for his horse, shaking his head at the oblivious diners in the outer room.

It was raining heavily, adding to the dismal scene as he galloped away for the long ride back to Bardstown and Perryville in search of General Polk.

But as he rode back towards Perryville, he had no idea that General Bragg's assumption was wrong. The main body of Federals was not headed for Frankfort. It was headed straight for Perryville.

* * *

Daniel Lockett and the rest of Blair's Independent Regiment marched quietly along. March, march, march...

The mood was grim, and tempers were short. It was water again. That was the problem, yet again. Now it seemed to curse them every which way, he thought darkly. They had run out of water again, and the streams and creek beds were bone dry.

Were it not for the total lack of drinkable water, Daniel would have found this part of Kentucky quite nice. They were about thirty miles beyond Louisville now, and the land had become hillier. Scrubby pines and timber lined the dusty road, but most men did not notice.

The thirst just drove men to the edge, especially so soon on the heels of their last difficult march. Just yesterday, the adjutant for the 21st Wisconsin had nearly been shot by his own men. The men had been on all fours lapping up the slimy, inches deep water that remained in what normally would have been a decent sized pond. For some reason, the adjutant had ridden his horse straight into it, angering his men so severely that the colonel punished the adjutant, if only to save him from being shot by his own men.

The cruelty of the water had only been increased overnight when a cloudburst soaked the entire camp. They had left their tents behind in Louisville, so they woke up thirsty and drenched. The men took to sucking the moisture right off their soaked, but filthy, uniforms. They all swore it was better than nothing.

"I don't know how much more of this I can take," John Bouma admitted to Daniel at the end of the day.

They were setting up camp with the rest of Starkweather's Brigade, where they had been assigned three days ago with the 79th Pennsylvania, 21st Wisconsin, and 24th Illinois.

Daniel was about to answer when he became aware of the sound of a disturbance in camp. It sounded like a fist fight, which was not all that uncommon, but larger, with more men.

Prosper T. Rowe ran by and tugged the two newcomers by the elbow. "Come on, have a look at this," he said excitedly.

They followed him over to where the 21st Wisconsin had pitched their tents. In the midst of the camp, they saw two local men with no shortage of bile or bravery as they engaged an entire regiment in a heated argument. Each of the locals carried a long whip and yelled back at the Wisconsinites. Then some of the Wisconsinites started pelting the Kentuckians with corn cobs.

"What's going on?" Daniel asked in puzzlement.

"Contraband," James answered, sliding over next to his brother.

Daniel took a moment to look around. Most of the regiment now stood with them and watched the scene unfold.

"Easy," James Lockett said, grabbing Adie by the shoulder as the younger man started to head over to the fray. "Not your battle this time, Adie."

"But Otto is over there."

"Not surprised. Most of the 21st seems German, and you two are usually over there with them every chance you get."

"But…"

"Let them handle it, Adie."

They could hear the two locals screaming back at the Wisconsinites. They could make out that they were looking for their two escaped slaves and did not mince words with what they thought about the Wisconsinites who hid them.

"Dumb bastards," Levi Thickle muttered. "Can't they see they're a little outnumbered."

"If it escalates into shooting, General Rousseau and

Starkweather, ain't goin' be happy," Prosper said accurately.

"They're looking for their slaves?" John Bouma said, "But they're free now, like it or not?"

"Not in Kentucky," John Messern spoke up, "Kentucky stood with the Union so it ain't covered by Lincoln's proclamation."

"Not yet," Adie said stubbornly. "But it will be."

"Hang'em! Hang'em! Hang the Secesh!" came a cry from one corner of the 21st. A length of rope was tossed at the feet of the two Kentuckians.

"Uh, oh," McManus said softly. This was going to be very bad, very quickly, they all realized.

It was then that General Lovell Rousseau, their division commander and a Kentuckian, rode into camp. He rode his horse straight into the middle of the fray.

"You will stack your arms and march thirty paces backward!" he ordered.

The Wisconsinites hesitated. Then three men stacked their muskets. A handful more followed suit, and then the rest grudgingly did the same and backed up as ordered.

"You there, Colonel Blair!" Rousseau yelled.

Lockett turned to see that the entire regiment now stood nearby, watching the episode.

"Yes, sir," Colonel Blair answered, saluting.

"You will march your men between the 21st and their weapons!"

There was a scurry of activity as the officers and company sergeants hustled Blair's men to obey the order. The 21st jeered them as they did so.

"You will load your weapons, Blair!" General Rousseau ordered.

There was a murmuring of disapproval from both regiments. Lockett and his men now faced the 21st Wisconsin with loaded weapons. A queasy feeling made him shudder.

"Now, 21st Wisconsin, will you follow my orders?" Rousseau bellowed.

"Only if consistent with our duty and our conscience!" came one loud cry from the 21st.

"Who said that?" Rousseau demanded.

Without hesitation, five men stepped forward proudly from the ranks of 21st.

Rousseau glared at the quintet but seemed at a loss for words.

The tension hung in the air for a moment, neither side wavering. Even the two local Kentuckians were silent.

Finally, General Rousseau turned to Colonel Blair. Calmly, he said, "You will do your duty, Colonel."

Turning to the two locals, General Rousseau frowned and said tightly. "You will now search the camp and be gone post haste."

One of the Kentuckians seemed to steel himself for a rebuttal, but after staring at all of the blue coated soldiers, their cold glares, and the gleam of the hundreds of weapons, the man changed his mind and wordlessly went on with his search.

The 21st , and even many of Blair's Independent Regiment, gave a derisive cheer an hour later when the two Kentuckians left the camp... empty-handed.

It was no surprise to Lockett that Adie was nowhere to be found until well after that hour.

* * *

It was another day and another march. Not much had changed. There was still little water, and what water there was could hardly be consumed. Again, most disguised it by turning it into coffee, although some members of the 79th Pennsylvania had found a stash of Kentucky liquor. They had swilled so much of it in place of water that a fair number were unable to continue to march, forcing their young colonel to destroy the remaining stores of it so that the rest of his disappointed troops could keep up with Starkweather's brigade.

But despite the monotony, trials of thirst, and tensions like the previous night's with the slaveholders, the spirits were high. In fact, at some point during the day, one company had taken up the song John Brown's Body. Before long, that entire regiment was singing it lustily and then the brigade as well. How much it swelled behind them, Lockett did not know, but it seemed as if the entire I Corp was singing gustily.

There were three Corps marching on parallel roads east. Their first objective was to meet at Bardstown, where Bragg's army had located after abandoning Munfordville, but the new objective was a town called Perryville.

The first objective had already been completing without firing a shot. Bragg had pulled back from Bardstown days ago. Cavalry reports and a string of Rebel stragglers pointed them to this new direction.

"So what do you intend to do?" McManus said in a low voice to Lockett as they marched along.

"Do about what, Patrick?"

"Daniel. I know that you always planned on keeping him safe, even after he joined up, but exactly how are going to do that? The Rebels won't run forever. Sooner or later, there will be a real battle."

Lockett said nothing at first. It was a question that he had been asking himself for weeks. Some days, when he was particularly aggravated, he decided that he would do nothing and let the fool get killed. Other days, he speculated that he could send Daniel back behind the lines on any fool's errand that he could think of. But deep down, he knew that he was pretty limited on what he could do.

October 6
--the diary of James Lockett
Yesterday was the Sabbath, and we had a brief rest from an early morning march. No such rest today. Starkweather's brigade is in the van, and so we were up and marching before light this morning. There are hungry bellies around. The rations that we drew in Louisville are gone now. The only food to be had is jayhawked from Secesh farms along the way, but today we are in Unionist territory. They line the roads and cheer us along. Neither that, nor the fact that it was the Sabbath stopped the 21st Wisconsin. One of their men was caught stealing a fowl and was tied to a cannon wheel for the night. Some of his messmates tried to free him during the middle of the night. Adie says that there was a near shooting between them and the other German regiment, the 79th Pennsylvania. Whatever it was, they resolved it in their mother tongue and walked away.

We are near the end of the day's march. This is our last rest before we halt. The road is hilly and narrow here. It is difficult to make progress, and the men are tired. It seems that we stop after every two miles, even though the boys are anxious to continue since rumor has it that the Rebels are retreating. With the exception of the 21ˢᵗ Wisconsin, the rest of this brigade was with us guarding railroad lines last summer. The boys are anxious to show what they can do.

October 8

Lockett's men rose stiffly and blundered about in the lightless early morning. With their brigade in an advance position of the main body of I Corps, they had been forced to camp without fires. Wearily, they tried to take stores and ammunition from the supply train that had been brought up during the short night.

"The officers tell us not to be tired, that we can sleep when we are dead," Levi Thickle grumbled to his knot of messmates and other soldiers. "As early as we keep rising, we really will die, right on the road. Officers!" He snorted the final word and then noticed Lockett behind him. "Not present company of course, sir," he added hastily.

"Of course," Lockett said without a smile. He was tired too, and the drawing of stores was turning into a confused fiasco. Some units, like his, needed minié balls for their rifles, but other regiments, particularly those fresh ones in Terrill's brigade needed musket balls for their older and inferior weapons. The quartermasters were having difficulty sorting out one from the other.

"This entire process is taking too long!" General Jackson thundered, butting his men into the quartermaster line. "We must put miles behind us this morning or Johnny Reb will be allowed to slink back. I will not have that! I will not!" He wagged a finger at the timid quartermaster and continued to demand action. The General turned to Colonel Starkweather and ordered his men back. General Jackson's were to get theirs sorted out first.

"At least our men got theirs before Jackson arrived," Colonel Blair remarked to Lockett.

"True, sir, but the rest of our brigade? This seems like it will take hours to sort out."

As Lockett said that, there was another rumble at another delay. The current stores were emptied out and the remaining wagons, while promised, were somewhere behind them, stalled on the narrow roads back west of their position.

Another hour passed before Colonel Starkweather gave Colonel Blair orders for Blair's Independent Regiment to march east with Jackson and Terrill's men. There was no point in them waiting around here while the rest of the brigade was stalled. They would rendezvous later.

Thankful to leave the confused situation and heated tempers, Blair's Independent Regiment marched eastwards with the rest of the van from I Corps. As a pink sun first poked over the ridge in front of them, they marched toward the battle for Kentucky.

Chapter 11

By 10 am, they reached a ridge top intersection called Dixville crossroads. The sound of distant guns had spurred them into a double quick march for the past forty-five minutes. They arrived at the high ground with their uniforms weighted down by sweat. Their throats were dry and crying out for water, but there was none.

Lockett stood next to Colonel Blair, who raised himself high in the stirrups of his equally thirsty roan.

"What do you see, sir?" Lockett asked. He could only see the smoke to his front right, but from his higher vantage point, the Colonel seemed enthralled by something.

"Oh? Nothing unusual," Blair replied with some embarrassment. It was then that Lockett remembered that for all his time together with the Colonel, this was the first time that Colonel Blair had seen a battle. He had not been at Shiloh like Lockett and his company.

A few blue coated stragglers came slinking back through the ridge top, seemingly drawn to others in dark blue.

"You're going the wrong way!" Levi Thickle jeered them. "The battle is up yonder!"

"Need us to show you where it is?" another chimed in.

The stragglers said nothing and started slink off in another direction.

"Which unit are you?" Prosper T. asked one of them.

"Sheridan's division," the answer came as the man disappeared into the brush.

"Sheridan?" Prosper T. said, looking at Bosworth. "Who the devil is that?"

Bosworth shrugged and shook his head.

"Must not be part of I Corps?" McManus theorized.

"Third Corps," Captain Bibb answered.

General Jackson and General Terrill began to issue orders. General Terrill placed his artillery on the high ground. The cavalry and infantry from Lytle's Brigade were ordered forward to carefully probe the woods and gully at the bottom of their position. As the only part of their brigade to be on the scene yet, Colonel Blair and his men milled about in the background, uncertain what to do beyond observe the goings-on.

"What do we do, sir?" Captain Bibb asked Colonel Blair.

"Wait for Colonel Starkweather and the rest of our brigade to catch up. If we are needed, General Jackson will call upon us, I am sure."

It was only a matter of minutes before the cavalry came racing back to the ridge top, reporting that there were Rebels in the woods below. How many, no one knew, but Lytle's Brigade was ordered forward in line of battle and ordered to hold the front slope of the high ground.

Another battery of artillery rumbled up the road from behind Lockett. He recognized the bespectacled battery captain from a few days in the march.

"It's the Coldwater Battery," McManus said, reading Lockett's thoughts again.

Lockett nodded. "First Michigan."

They all gazed down into the woods at the bottom of the ridge, a few hundred yards away.

It seemed empty for the most part. Occasionally, Lockett would catch a glimpse of butternut moving amongst the trees below, but the butternut blended in with the dreary October grass to such an extent that he wasn't sure if it was just his eyes playing tricks on him.

Regardless, the Coldwater Battery lobbed a few shells into the woods, but there was no response.

General Rousseau, the division commander for their brigade, rode up behind the battery, and Lockett wondered if this meant that the rest of the brigade was finally here. But Rousseau said nothing and just watched the Coldwater men fire a few more shells into the woods.

"Sir?" McManus said to either Colonel Blair or Lockett, "Do you see that?"

It was then that they all noticed the dust in distance, well behind the woods.

"The Rebels are retreating again," General Rousseau declared as he looked at the dust cloud. "There will be no battle today."

He looked to his left and spotted his aide. With a resigned wave, he beckoned the man.

When the aide arrived, Lockett could hear him say, "There will be no battle today. To the right down yonder is a creek. There might be nothing left than a few puddles, but I want that water. Send Lytle's and Harris's brigades down there."

* * *

Oblivious to the gap that he had just created in the line, General Rousseau rested at the top of the ridge. A quiet had descended across the entire field. Even far off to their right, where they had first sighted General Sheridan's gun smoke, all was still.

It did seem that the Rebels were retreating, in which case Lockett wondered why they were not more anxious to pursue them. After all, they couldn't be far if the rear guard was this close.

"Did you see that, sir?"

It was Prosper, pointing at the woods that was between where Rousseau's brigades had disappeared and Terrill's brigades presently waited.

"See what?"

"Thought I saw a Reb down there, Lieutenant... in the woods."

Lockett stared but saw nothing. "I don't see anything, Prosper T."

"Sure I saw something, sir. Sure as hellfire."

"You do have hawkeyes," Lockett admitted, "But I don't see anything."

"Wait! There, sir. See them now?" He pointed and Lockett did now see three men emerge from the woods.

"I see them too," General Rousseau spoke from behind, startling both Lockett and Rowe. "But they are Federals, like us."

Prosper T. looked dubiously at the general but said nothing.

"The Rebels have retreated. There aren't any within a mile of us, unless you count some of the stragglers that they are bound to have."

"Yes, sir, General," Prosper T. answered, looking skeptically at Lockett.

It was then that three Confederate batteries on a distant hill opened up and sent solid shells bouncing off the dry, rock hard ground. One of the balls bounded over the general's head. Another bounced twice and lodged itself into the thick tree behind them.

"By George!" Rousseau exclaimed, picking himself up from the ground and dusting himself off.

Nearby, the Coldwater battery wheeled their cannons around and took aim at the distant Rebel batteries, returning the salvo.

For the next hour, Lockett and his men crouched in the tree line. The artillery batteries dueled from long range. Their focus was the opposing cannon, but occasionally, a Rebel artillery shell would shriek into the woods, or more commonly, bounce into the woods where the infantry waited. When one of those shots did end up among them, James Lockett could not help but look over to where his brother crouched excitedly with some of the other new men.

Eventually, the rate of fire from both sides began to dwindle as they ran out of long range ammunition. In fact, the Coldwater battery pulled its cannon and caissons back as it retreated in search of the ammunition train.

Lockett turned his head to the other side and saw General Rousseau conversing with Colonel Blair, angrily gesticulating with his hands. The general had retrieved Harris's brigade in the past hour, but he was no doubt wondering where the rest of his Starkweather brigade was. They were his most experienced troops after all, even if most of their experience had been of the railroad guarding variety.

Lockett faced back to the front. The Rebels were out somewhere beyond that small strip of woods, somewhere among the rolling ridges and hidden troughs and valleys. He scanned the distance but saw nothing.

The country here was hill after hill, and while they held the high ground, those troughs between the hills could hide a marching army. A smart army could take advantage of that by staying below the ridgelines, marching undetected right up to their door step.

Another hour went by and Lockett occupied himself by pacing behind and then in front of the men. The new ones sat restlessly, not sure what would happen next. His old core, however, relaxed with seemingly not a care in the world. Patrick whittled another carving with that ridiculously large bowie knife. Prosper T. laid on his back with a blade of dry grass sticking between his lips. Levi, Milton, and John Messern debated how tall President Lincoln really was. Adie and Otto spoke quietly in their German.

Lockett walked away from the company briefly.

They were in reserve of Terrill's position on the Open Knob, and Lockett studied the path they would need to take if they were called up to support Terrill. There was a half harvested, withered cornfield. Stone and split rail fences separated them from a slight dip and then a rise up to the Open Knob. Below that, there was the long slope down into the woods.

Commotion behind him captured his attention. He saw the other officers with Colonel Blair so he headed for the grouping.

"… vorst tangle you've ever seen on the roads back dar!" one of the captains exclaimed. Lockett recognized him as one of the captains from the German 79th Pennsylvania. "Supply vagons und ambulances blocking de road. Terrible. Ve only got here vhen the Colonel decided to leave the road and march the men through the fields and woods."

Another officer appeared on the scene, one of Rousseau's aides. Orders were given out and the brigade was placed in support of Terrill's advance position. The 21st Wisconsin was placed in front on the Benton Road, facing the cornfield and fences. The 79th and 24th were to their right, finally filling in the gap that existed with Harris's brigade. Blair's Independent Regiment waited behind them, ready to support either flank depending on need.

Chapter 12

When the crackle of musketry sounded, the nearness of it startled them.

It was the tell-tale smattering of skirmishers engaging. It went back and forth for ten minutes, and Lockett waited for the louder, longer report of volley fire, but it did not come. The sound dissipated back to an uneasy silence, and he knew that one side's skirmishers had given up the fight, at least for now. But which side?

He did not need to wait long. A few dozen of Terrill's skirmishers emerged from a hollow, making haste for their own lines. A minute later, a mass of men appeared behind them. It was regiment after regiment. They wore a mix of butternut and dark blue uniforms.

"Are those our men?" Daniel Lockett asked, surprising James Lockett as he did not know that his brother had wandered over to him. "They're in blue?"

"No, that is the enemy, Daniel. Looks like some of them are wearing stolen uniforms?"

"Wearing stolen uniforms?" Daniel asked puzzled.

"Better than marching naked," Levi Thickle cracked from nearby.

A number of men laughed unusually loudly at the simple jest. It was the nerves, Lockett knew, as they all watched the amazing sight of thousands of men marching in line of battle.

There was a terrible pageantry to it, Lockett thought silently, and he was impressed with their order and how they dressed their ranks. These were no new recruits; this was an experienced mass of soldiers moving toward Terrill.

It was thousands and thousands, and sudden sight of them amazed the Federals. The rolling hills and troughs had hidden them completely from view. It seemed hard to believe that so many men could get so near to them without having been sighted before.

But as the Confederates started their way across the flat bottom, moving up to the hills that were covered with Yankees, they encountered the various rail fences and stone fences of the farms. The fencing broke up their carefully dressed lines. Some units were able to continue forward; others were stalled, and others yet were funneled into gaps in the fencing. Their sergeants pushed and pulled the men back into a line of battle. Despite the efforts, their cohesion was falling apart. Some regiments advanced before the others.

And then the Union batteries opened up.

The boom of their guns rang the ears of the Yankees, but it was a sight of the exploding shells and case shot that riveted their attention. It was appalling to see but also impossible not to watch, Lockett mused.

Daniel Lockett and the other fresh fish watched the gun battery with fascination. One of the gun crew used a leather gloved thumb to plug the vent hole. Another man on the crew used a wet sheepskin rammer to sponge out the heated barrel. Yet another member of the crew returned at a run with the cartridge that he had retrieved from the limber chest, kept back a safe distance away from the cannon. He placed the charge in the bore and the rammer quickly reversed his staff and rammed the charge home. Then the man at the back of the cannon unplugged the vent hole, and with a small wire tool, he stuck it into the vent hole and pricked the cartridge bag. The gunner finished sighting the weapon. The rest of the crew had already moved away from the mouth, and a lanyard friction pin was inserted into the vent hole. With a tug, the cannon belched smoke and flame, bucking backwards like an enraged beast.

And then the crew was off again, repeating the steps so quickly and automatically that Daniel was amazed.

Again, he watched the gunners load another spherical case shot into the bore. It was rammed down. The gunners stood back while the gun captain made a last sighting and the lanyard was inserted.

Seconds later, the spherical case shot would fly over the

marching Rebels. The timed charge would explode, and if the gunner had timed the fuse correctly, that one shell would explode directly overhead, showering the Confederate ranks with seventy-eight lead balls.

Shell after shell was launched into the Rebels, particularly from the far left of Terrill's position, where his guns were able to fire obliquely into the Rebels. The Rebels approach had been stealthy, but they too seemed to have little idea of what was in front of them because they had marched directly into a terrible crossfire.

If they thought that they were plunging into the Yankee flank, then they had miscalculated horribly.

The hollow below was a one sided charnel house.

But the Rebels were not giving up. It was the same dogged refusal to lose that Lockett had seen at Shiloh in the Hornet's Nest. They were coming again, more now, refusing to acknowledge the terrible blows that the Yankee artillery was inflicting.

More men came, and Lockett watched with a sense of foreboding as additional butternut uniforms joined the march. Their brown jackets blended in so thoroughly with the dry October weeds and the gathering smoke clouds that they seemed to disappear, only to reappear seconds later, moving ever closer to Terrill's exposed line.

The Rebels reached the foot of the knob, where again they encountered another fence. This fence was covered in brush and what must have been thorn bushes, Lockett surmised, because the progress ground to halt. Attempts to crawl over the fence were dulled by the presence of the interwoven tangle.

"They're confused," McManus said to Lockett.

And it was true. The Rebel officers were wildly gesturing, trying to get the men to move right, around the fence and maybe away from the still thrashing artillery shells. But many of the shells were missing now. Whether it was from the difficulty of getting their guns to deploy at a target so low, or perhaps the selection of the wrong type of ammunition, it seemed to Lockett that many of the shells were flying into the strip of brushy woods behind that fence instead of into the Rebels clustered around the fence itself.

Worse for the Federals, the cannon were now within Confederate infantry range. There was the roaring, elongated crackle of volley fire now coming from the Rebels.

Terrill's Ohioans returned fire from the top of the mound.

Minutes went by as the two sides fired muskets and rifles. The opposing lines were now thick with gunsmoke. Each side was effectively hidden from the other by their own smoke, but the assault continued as men fired blindly into the shrouds. Then the haze drifted towards the Rebels in the breeze.

From his position back and to the right of the conflagration, Lockett and his men had a better view than the combatants themselves. They could clearly see the flashes and even the men behind the curtain of pale, gray saltpeter clouds. The sound of the hammering was tremendous, but Lockett could see that the damage was not equal to the noise.

"They're firing too high," Bosworth explained to some of the new men. "You have to aim for their belts, even more so when on a ridge."

The Rebel line did not move forward, but it started to stretch from end to end, elongating on both sides. It neared the edge of Terrill's left flank, but most of the Rebels were off to the Terrill's right, engaging Harris's brigade, and even a few of the 24th Illinois skirmishers who had crept into the tall corn field.

They hid amongst the stalks, popping out to fire at the stationary Rebel line before darting back into the corn to reload. Then, they would reappear and repeat the whole process. The 24th's plucking and nipping at the edge of the Rebel line continued for ten minutes before the Rebels had enough. With experienced deliberateness, the three companies of Rebels loaded and waited. On their officer's command, their volley fire ripped into the corn field, shredding stalk and men alike. The skirmishers from the 24th continued their nuisance but with only a fraction of its former effect.

"When are we going to get into it?" Lockett heard one of men complain from behind him. He turned and saw Daniel's friend, John Bouma.

He made no reply. It would be soon enough, he knew. This was no brief skirmish. This was a battle, and he could tell that the Rebels were serious this time. It was then that he noticed a second line of Confederates approaching from behind the first. They would join up soon and have twice the strength.

He looked over his shoulder for Daniel.

Milton Bosworth saw the look and edged closer to his lieutenant. "Don't worry, sir. I'll keep a close eye on him."

Lockett nodded grimly but said nothing.

The roaring fire continued between the two sides, and Lockett waited with the men. The second line of Confederates was swinging the tide. Their fire from the bottom of the hill was growing, and the replies from Terrill's blue line on the top of the hill were clearly slowing. The cannon still fired whizzing loads of canister shot into the fence line below, but they too were reduced. All around the guns, Lockett could see a steadily increasing number of blue jackets on the ground. It seemed to him that soon the Rebels would muster the courage to push out from behind their thorny fence and surge towards those guns.

Lockett was not the only one who anticipated an impending Confederate advance, for at that moment, he saw Terrill's green 123rd Illinois rise from their position next to the cannon.

"Mercy, where are they going? What are they doing?" Captain Bibb said to no one in particular.

"Terrill wants his guns saved," Lockett speculated out aloud.

"He wants them to charge down the hill?"

Lockett squeezed the rifle in his hand tightly. He knew that he was the only officer who carried a rifle. It gave him some reassurance, even at a sinking moment like this. He knew some of the 123rd boys. He had met them on the march. They were as new as could be and had barely drilled before marching out of Louisville.

In dismay, Lockett and the others watched them ramble down the hill. It was unorganized from the beginning. One company marched off well in advance of the others, and they were quickly met with a hail of concentrated lead.

The main body began in two separate lines, and at first, it seemed that they had stunned the Rebels because the firing at the bottom of the hill slowed to virtually nothing. Then there was a sharp volley that staggered the front row of Illinoisans. Their progress was nearly halted, and then the second rank came crashing down into their own comrades. It overtook the front rank and squeezed off one volley. It was answered with horrendous fire from the front, right, and left. The Rebel line that stretched on and on was a wall of flame and an instant bank of smoke.

In seconds, a quarter of the 123rd was gone. Their cries and screams melded into the roar of gunfire. Those who could do so turned and staggered back up the hill. Many more fell on the way back up, shot in the back as they tried to escape the horror.

At the top of the Open Knob, Lockett could see Generals Terrill and Jackson trying to rally them, but these were spent men now.

Confederate artillery batteries opened up on the exposed knob. Gouts of black smoke erupted near Terrill's few remaining cannon. One Rebel solid shot exploded a cannon wheel into thousands of flying slivers, and the cannon crashed to the ground. Additional Confederate guns had arrived at a most opportune time.

Lockett's eyes were still following General Jackson when he saw him fall amid the crashing shells. Another one slammed off the top of the knob and bounded into a horse in a cloud of blood. A third shell battered a limber, sending a cloud of wood everywhere, yet miraculously, the contents did not explode.

Some of Terrill's gunners tried to bring up the horses to retrieve their cannon, but the fire was too thick and soon the knob was equally littered in the dead carcasses of the animals.

From below, there was a tremendous Rebel yell. Finally, the row of fence line was toppled over.

"They are going straight for Terrill now," Bosworth said, "Poor bastards."

Lockett watched, waiting for Terrill to rally his men in the face of the approaching butternut, but Terrill seemed consumed with the operation of one of his cannon. Whether he was aiming it, or trying to move it back, Lockett could not tell, but he seemed oblivious to the rest of his brigade's needs. All he seemed to care about was that solitary cannon.

The Rebels came forward.

The 105th Ohio tried to slow them, and it seemed that they had held them off, just 50 feet away from the guns.

"Four," Bosworth said.

"Four what?" Lockett answered in a puzzled voice, without taking his eyes off of the carnage to their front left.

"Why don't they send us in? We can reinforce him," Captain

Bibb said.

Lockett ignored him, knowing that this was a lost cause now. Terrill and Jackson probably should never have made a stand on such an open and exposed hilltop.

"Four what?" Lockett repeated loudly as Bush's battery behind them opened up, trying to pluck Rebels from the down slope beyond them without hitting any of Terrill's men.

"Four flags," Bosworth yelled back above the din. "I see four regimental flags going against the 105th."

For the next couple of minutes, the Rebels fired from their knees with steadfast accuracy, trying to bludgeon the fire from the 105th before they launched a final surge up the hill.

The 105th died bravely but died they did. Terrill and the last remaining men spiked the guns, plugging their vent holes by hammering soft nails into them, and then they ran for the woods 50 yards behind them, below the Open Knob.

An audible cheer went up from the Rebels. They had smashed Terrill's brigade, but if they thought the battle was theirs, they would be sorely mistaken.

On the ridge beyond the Open Knob another Yankee brigade waited, Starkweather's.

Chapter 13

Blair's Independent Regiment waited in the woods near the turn in the Benton Road. Ahead of them and to their right, the 21st Wisconsin waited in the small fenced cornfield. They had no one on their left; they had no one on the right.

Further, Lockett could see the rest of the brigade, the 79th Pennsylvania and the 24th Illinois, who at least had the benefit of being behind a sturdy stone fence.

"Do you think that is on purpose?" McManus said to Lockett, gesturing to the 21st Wisconsin.

Lockett could not understand why General Rousseau had placed the 21st there either. Was it because he remembered these high-principled troublemakers? After all, the General had nearly ordered Blair's regiment to fire on them.

Still, such a callous disregard seemed impossibly short sighted given the entire Corps' predicament.

"I don't know, Patrick," he said gently.

An eerie quiet was settling over the field. There was the occasional skirmisher's shot and the even more occasional ranging cannon fire. But the incessant musketry of the past two hours had paused as the Rebels readied themselves for the next hill.

"And where the hell is the rest of the army?" Levi Thickle complained. "Why is First Corps the only one engaged? Ain't we got three whole corps marching in parallel? Seems like ours is fightin' Bragg's whole army by ourselves. What is Third Corps doing off yonder? Sitting on their hands? And where in God's name is the Second Corps?"

"Shut up, Levi!" Bosworth snapped.

"Couldn't have said it any better myself," Captain Bibb muttered, although it was unclear if he was referring to Thickle's grumbling or Bosworth's response.

There was the sound of fire from down on the right and in the distance. It was then that Lockett remembered Lytle's brigade being sent off there to secure the water hours ago.

He wondered if Lytle was still on his own. It sounded like they had not been recalled. He didn't like the sound of that, but perhaps they had at least found some water. He was sorely thirsty already, and he knew it would be unbearable by the time this battle was over. They all would need to use their teeth to tear open the paper cartridges for their rifles, and the black powder would make for a powerful thirst, even on a normal day.

The firing resumed on the right, closer though, down somewhere near the 79th Pennsylvania.

Lockett paced behind his men. He did not like having to wait in reserve. The waiting frayed his nerves, especially now as he sought out Daniel's curly brown hair in the line of men huddled back by the trees. For a moment, he could not find him, but then he saw the statuesque frame of Vaught and saw Daniel lingering nearby. He contemplated ordering Daniel away from all this, giving him some menial errand, but he knew that was not possible. It would tar both Daniel and himself. All he could do was pray.

And he was not alone. A number of the men mumbled prayers. Others knelt openly and recited Psalms together.

General Rosseau galloped by, and their eyes followed him as he dashed down the line, past them and then past the 21st.

At the 79th's position, other blue jacketed men fled. What was left of the 80th Illinois had crumbled at the sight of so many Confederates approaching. General Rosseau rode to those fleeing men, beating some with the flat of his blade as he tried to get them to reform. One of them trapped the slender blade under his armpit and twisted violently, snapping the blade in half before resuming his dash away from the field.

Undaunted, Rosseau stuck his hat on the broken blade. Waving his sword, he raced along in front of the lines. Many men cheered, but Lockett could imagine that some were cursing his bravado and wished that he would get out of the way so that they could fire their weapons at the approaching Rebels.

Beyond Starkweather's men, the first of the Rebel assault landed its blows on Harris's brigade again. They came right up the hill to within twenty yards when a devastating fire soaked the ground with their blood, and they sagged back. The Union forces gave a mighty cheer.

But the Rebels were back again and again. Each time, their line seemed thicker and longer with more men.

Forty-five minutes passed and slowly Harris's men gave ground.

Colonel Blair rode up behind Lockett.

"Lieutenant," he greeted.

"Colonel, sir," Lockett said, "Begging your pardon, sir, but you make a nice target up there. Might I suggest that you dismount?"

"Nonsense," Colonel Blair replied with more confidence than he felt. "I wouldn't be able to see a thing from down there. I can scarcely see from up here. Why that corn must be eight feet tall! It is just about the only thing that has grown in these parts, and that is where the 21st Wisconsin is at, though I still can't locate them exactly. I can't even see their regimental flag."

"That is because they don't have one, sir," Adie spoke up from nearby. "They only mustered in four days before the march."

"No flag?" Blair said astounded. "But what will they rally around?"

"Are they even there?" one man piped up. "I don't see a one of them damned Germans in there."

"They're lying flat," Lockett explained. "A couple went down during Terrill's battle to spent balls, but I think it has more to do with that fact that Stone's battery is directly behind them, firing over their heads at the Reb batteries."

"If a cannon was shooting right over your head, you'd be lying flat too," Adie snapped indignantly in defense of his fellow Germans.

"As tall and thick as that corn is there, they'll be lucky to see the Secesh until they are right among them," Levi Thickle remarked in his gravelly voice.

"They'll have skirmishers out, Levi," Lockett commented.

"And what is left of Terrill's command is in a small gully in front of that," Colonel Blair added knowingly. "There will be some warning."

Suddenly, there was a smattering of cracks from the front of the cornfield. It was met with a tremendously loud volley fire, like the tearing of some mighty celestial sheet. There was a small response of musketry and then some cries of alarm.

"The skirmishers are coming back," Colonel Blair said with some concern from the saddle.

"That can mean only one thing," someone muttered.

The skirmishers came tearing back to their line where they halted. They were followed by the last of Terrill's men and General Terrill himself. The general ran past the startled 21st, yelling to them to meet the enemy with a bayonet as he kept running.

The major in charge of the 21st ignored him and instead tried to steady his men, ordering them to aim low. One of the cannon from Stone's battery sent a solid shot screaming right over the Wisconsinites' heads. Though the gunners fired low, it flew over the unseen Rebels as well.

The other cannon in Stone's and Bush's batteries remained silent… for now, but Lockett could see the gunners loading rounds of lethal canister. The problem would be where to shoot it. The guns were well positioned to fire at an enemy on the right or left, but anything directly ahead meant somehow avoiding the new men from Wisconsin.

A ghoulish Rebel yell erupted from the field, as if the ghosts of fallen men were rising from the corn.

Out of nervous habit, Lockett checked his Starr Percussion revolver. Were the percussion caps still on their cones? It was only the third time that he had checked in the last hour.

It would not be long now.

Shots were fired from the unseen in the corn.

The stalks rustled like a sharp breeze had suddenly blown in, and a number of ears exploded in showers of kernels. They could see a few of the Wisconsinites fall as well. Some of the shots flew into the woods where Blair's regiment was waiting also. One minié ball thudded solidly into a tree that Levi Thickle crouched by. He fell backwards in startled reaction.

Still, one could not see the Rebels as they fired blindly through the corn. The 21st held their fire, and then the first Rebels appeared. Upon the first sighting of their foe, the Rebels shrieked another Rebel yell, but it was drowned out by a point blank fusillade from nearly the entire Wisconsin regiment.

"By God, they are close!" Blair exclaimed.

"The batteries will be in trouble," Captain Bibb added in an odd voice that lacked concern.

Balls continued to zip from the corn. The first Rebels to appear had been obliterated by that volley fire, but everyone knew that there were more coming.

The 21st Wisconsin hastened to reload, but they were painfully slow. By the time they finished, a full wave of Rebels appeared, and that wave sent a crashing fire into the men from Wisconsin who had no protection amongst the slender stalks of corn.

The remainder of the 21st returned fire, a good many of them sending their ramrods flying with their shots in their haste and panic.

More Rebels arrived, easily overlapping the flanks of the 21st Wisconsin as seven Tennessee and Georgia regiments washed over and around them.

Daniel Lockett watched in horror. He had been focusing on the burly, red-bearded sergeant who had been shoving some of the 21st back into line, most by the point of his gun when his head exploded into a crimson mist. Aghast, Daniel watched the ten men near the sergeant drop their weapons, turn, and run at full speed straight towards him.

All across the slender line, parts of the 21st Wisconsin fled. A few of the Germans fought on stubbornly, if not suicidally, against the odds. A number of others tried to surrender, dropping their weapons, but they were too late as they fell to lead or rifle butts from the approaching butternut wave.

The entire front was disintegrating and in what seemed only a matter of seconds.

Behind Daniel, Colonel Starkweather ordered a bayonet charge to blunt the attack and save his batteries, but no one seemed to hear.

In panic, Stone's battery unleashed a hail of canister. Gouts of flame and smoke erupted from their barrels. The tin cans filled with dozens of lead balls spread from the mouth of the guns, like giant shotguns, turning men into little more than gristle, both Union and Confederate alike.

"Fire! Fire!" Captain Bibb and the other company commanders yelled in their own panic. Any thoughts of a bayonet charge were forgotten for the moment as the men poured lead into the conflagration.

Bodies fell in droves. Many of the Wisconsin men who were still fighting pitched forward, shot in the back by their own side. Those who could, tried to escape in any direction possible. Some tried to crawl away, afraid of their own fire, but the Rebel bayonets and rifle butts found them from behind. Others tried to dash back to the safety of Stone's cannon, but they ran into fields of fire from their own side, and they fell, shot through the front, cursing their own side.

"Reload, reload!" Lockett ordered his men. He had tried to halt his men from firing into the melee, but it was no use. He could see a few of the remaining Wisconsin men dashing straight towards them.

"Let them through! Hold your fire until they are clear!"

The Wisconsin men bolted past without breaking stride.

Daniel stared in shock at the white-eyed men and terror stricken faces.

One of the men nearly knocked him over as he sped through their lines. Others followed him, and their faces would be forever burned into Daniel's memory. A dark-haired one sprinted toward him with blood streaming like a fountain, most of his jaw gone. The bloody mess flew behind him like a tail as he raced, but with each step, the man slowed until by the time he reached Daniel, the man's pace was just a staggering walk. The blood no longer flowed behind him and instead just drained down his front. He fell dead at Daniel's feet without so much as a groan.

Beyond him, two other men tried to help a friend retreat. They each had him under the shoulder and made slow progress as the man's leg dragged behind them at a grotesque angle. It was slow going with their burden, but they would not leave him behind, even as they fell behind the rest of their retreating comrades. Just as it seemed that their torturous progress would be complete, one of them was shot from behind. He fell, twisting in agony, taking the already wounded friend with him. The last remaining

Wisconsin man heeled back around and was trying to drag the two of them to safety but not making much progress.

Daniel knew that he wasn't the only one watching the tragedy unfold, but no one moved to help them. The Wisconsinite dragged and pulled. It was a completely futile effort, but he would not give up. Daniel wanted to run out and help, but he was frozen in place.

Then the last Wisconsinite's head snapped back, and he fell lifelessly on top of his two friends.

"Reload!" Daniel heard Milton Bosworth's angry voice in his ear, "Or that will be us too!"

Another round of canister from Stone's battery showered the area with lead balls, but the gunners were falling by the second now as the Rebel infantry sought them out. The zip of minié balls was heavy around the guns, like a swarm of angry hornets. Balls winged off the barrels repeatedly, forcing some of the remaining gunners to take cover behind the wheels or under the guns themselves.

More and more Rebels emerged from the corn. There were more now than the first wave that had overrun the 21st, and they were as close to Stone's cannons as Lockett and his men were. More minié balls zinged off the gun barrels, and the Confederates headed straight for the guns that had blasted bloody holes in the 9th Tennessee.

The Confederates paused momentarily behind a split rail fence that lined the Benton Road. The air was now thick with drifting gray smoke.

From the woods, James Lockett instinctively flinched as a familiar zip zip of minié balls whipped overhead, one sounding particularly close to his ear. Nearby, Otto Klugge and Adie crouched behind a tree and quickly reloaded. Chips of wood flew from the tree as multiple balls clipped it.

There was one more blast of canister that hurled a whole file of Rebels from the fence line, but that was the last one. The Rebel muskets and rifles concentrated on the battery. The brave gunners who had fired were cut down in the hail. What was left of the gun crews crouched in the woods with Lockett or hid beneath the guns or beneath their dead comrades.

One gun crew desperately tried to pull their cannon back by hand, their horses all dead around them. They had barely made any headway when the first of them fell, then another and another before the last two crew members abandoned the gun.

Even more Rebels appeared, and they surged over the fence now, heading straight for the cannon.

But from the flank, the 79th Pennsylvania added their weight to the fight now. Their enfilading fire gave the Tennesseans and Georgians second thoughts about securing Stone's cannon from the open ground. So the lumbering weapons sat in the no man's land like tempting, teasing prizes.

The musketry and rifle fire hammered loud and constant.

Lockett lined his sight up on a Rebel officer waving a pistol in the air, admonishing his men to keep up the fight. Lockett took a slow breath and squeezed the trigger. The rifle kicked back hard into shoulder, and he noted with satisfaction that the officer toppled over backwards.

With his eyes streaming from the smoke and his mouth as dry as dust, Lockett tore open another paper cartridge and began the process of reloading his weapon. It was something that he had done a thousand times now, and he could do it with his eyes shut. In this case, he let his eyes wander to his men as he did so, and what he saw made his anger snap like a dry twig. He finished reloading, not sure that he had seen what he thought when it occurred again.

Slinging his rifle, he walked over to white-faced John Bouma and knocked the gun from the boy's hands.

"You have put the percussion cap on, you damn fool!" Lockett exploded. "How many loads have you done like that?"

Looking right through Lockett, the lad stared open-mouthed.

Growling, Lockett grabbed the rifle from another of his men, this one dead and pitched forward in a pool of his own blood. He jammed the dead man's gun into the lad's hands. It was not uncommon for a soldier in his first battle to load his weapon over and over without firing or without a percussion cap, but that did nothing for Lockett's boiling anger. Bouma's weapon was now completely useless for anything other than blowing up in his face.

Bouma stared blankly at him, completely befuddled by what was happening.

"Shoot and load! Do it right!" Lockett thundered.

Another pair of shots from the Rebels crashed through the

limbs above, showering him in twigs, but the fire was slackening now. The Rebels were surprisingly melting back into the corn.

Nearby, another newcomer was vomiting, and Lockett suddenly realized that he did not know where Daniel was. Usually, he was not far from Bouma. With a terrible sense of despair, he looked more closely at the pool of blood near his feet. His eyes tracked up from the boots to the casualty's head. His throat tightened.

But then in relief, he noted that the man had blond hair, not Daniel's curly brown hair.

But where was Daniel?

Before he could think about it anymore, a cry went up from the left, and then there was a thunderous volley followed by a Rebel yell.

Chapter 14

"They've flanked us!"

"They're going for Bush's battery!"

"Lockett! Lockett!"

It was Renaud sprinting towards him. The little French Detroiter waved frantically at him. "Zey've made a way around our left. We must reinforce now!"

"Company!" Lockett bellowed, not caring where Captain Bibb was or if he was even alive. "Follow me!"

He crashed off to his left. He did not look behind him. He knew that Patrick, Milton, and at least half would be following. He wasn't sure about the fresh fish, but there was no time to worry about that.

They crashed through the last edges of the thinning forest, and what he saw stunned him.

"Bayonets! On the double!" he yelled, though it was doubtful that anyone could hear him over the cacophony of the melee in front of him.

Blue and butternut mixed randomly around the smoking barrels of Bush's battery.

Lockett had seen battles before. He had lived through the smoke and shell of Shiloh and the Hornet's Nest, but he had never seen a fight such as this. While they all carried bayonets, they were, in fact, rarely used to draw blood. They were more of an instrument of terror and deterrence than anything else, but in front of him, he saw a hand-to-hand fight such that he could never have imagined.

Shots fired, knives flashed, bayonets stabbed, and rifles were swung in all directions. There was no telling which direction held friend or foe. Skeins of gray gun smoke wafted over all of them. Yells and cries of desperation mixed with grotesque screams of pain and agony. All was utterly intertwined.

Lockett and his men crashed into the jarring chaos and were instantly drawn completely into its swirling tornado. Lockett fired his rifle at a Rebel who had just pinned one of Bush's gunners to the ground with his bayonet, spearing the man like a piece of meat.

His shot spun the Rebel clear around, but Lockett had already shifted his attention elsewhere. He tossed the rifle aside and pulled out the double action Starr Percussion revolver with one hand and the Stuart family sword with his other.

Something whipped past his ear, but he ignored it and pulled through the first and auxiliary triggers on the double action revolver, firing aimlessly into a butternut knot of men. Again, he fired without seemingly affecting anything. He ducked instinctively, as a cursing Rebel came at him from the side, lunging with his bayonet.

Lockett twisted aside, and the menacing blade, already coated with some other Yankee's blood, narrowly missed him.

He chopped down left-handed with the sword on the man's extended arm and felt it clash against bone. The Rebel howled and dropped the musket but turned on Lockett with his one good hand, driving him back while clawing for Lockett's neck. Lockett staggered backward a step and fired his revolver into the man's midsection.

The slug stopped the Rebel in his tracks, but Lockett lost his balance as he stepped on the body of another dead gunner.

Tumbling over, he was aware of a swirling fight above him. For a moment, the battle seemed to have forgotten him. As he lay on his back, soaking in a gunner's blood, he craned his head and took in a thousand things at once.

He could see Fulkerham's company running at full speed, yelling like deranged men to join the rest of the regiment. Left of that, men from his own company mixed with Renaud's and a few of Bush's artillerymen. Adie and Otto Klugge fought side by side. Adie jabbed furiously with his bayonet while Otto held off two others using his rifle butt like a club.

Levi Thickle jousted with a scrawny but undeterred Rebel. Each man wielded their rifle like a staff, trying to batter the other into submission. Though smaller, the Rebel was getting the better of Levi when he was felled by an unseen shot that hit him in the leg. As he collapsed to the ground, Levi violently bashed his rifle butt against the soldier's head before he moved on and disappeared into the crowd of circling soldiers.

In momentary horror, Lockett saw Patrick pinned by a Rebel against a cannon wheel. The man had his rifle across Patrick's neck, pressing furiously. But just as Lockett began to fear the worst, Patrick pulled free his wickedly long Bowie knife and thrust it into the man's side.

It seemed that he saw everyone, everyone except Daniel...

Behind Patrick, two of Bush's gunners were trying to load a cannon amidst the mayhem. One jammed a charge into the muzzle while the other immediately rammed it home. He had barely removed his rammer when the bayonet from a Confederate speared him in the side.

Lockett lost sight of the cannon as another swell of men intersected his view.

They were more of his men. Some fell, but others frantically fought on like crazed animals.

Lockett rose to his feet in time to see a finely dressed gray officer heading straight toward him with two other butternuts. Behind them, more Confederates were joining the fight. A strange black regimental flag trailed behind them.

Lockett pulled on the front trigger, cocking the weapon, and then the front trigger hit the auxiliary trigger behind it, firing the Starr.

Missed. Again, and he missed. The three Rebels were then upon him. He pulled on the trigger of the double action weapon one last time and cursed. His final shot winged the lead soldier who was only 10 feet away.

The shot was enough though. The man's wounded arm let go of the bayonet tipped musket. It dipped, and Lockett was able to bat it away with his sword. The man's momentum carried him forward. Back swinging, Lockett's sword caught the soldier in the neck.

But the Butternut's comrade was there too. He pulled his bayonet back, poised to plunge it into the Yankee officer, but a rifle banged just a foot from Lockett. Equally stunned as the gut shot Rebel, Lockett turned to see John Bouma directly behind him.

Bouma looked at him for a split second before he too fell. The tow headed boy dropped to his knees. In silent wonderment, he stared at the blood pooling from his stomach.

But Bouma was not alone. More blue soldiers seemed directly behind him.

The gray clad officer in front of the black flag hesitated.

There was no hesitation from Lockett. With a guttural yell, he was upon the man, hacking down with his sword. Their swords met with a ringing crash that sent painful vibrations all down Lockett's arm, but he hacked again and again. His opponent was on the defensive and could only deflect the violent blows, stumbling backward. Lockett pounced further, coming close to the man and lifting a knee into his groin. The officer gasped and then never saw the blow that hacked down on the side of his neck.

Everything was a blur of smoke and blood.

A cannon fired in the middle of the hand to hand fighting, blasting a ten foot wide swath of open space from what had been full of fighting men just a second earlier. Blood flecked flesh seemed everywhere in the sudden gap.

With a desperation that Lockett had never seen before, he, the rest of the regiment, and the remaining gunners fought with a fatalistic insanity. It was fifteen minutes that seemed like fifteen hours, but eventually the Confederates sagged back. A few remaining fights sputtered and then were extinguished.

The Confederates had been beaten off... for now.

The ground was soaked with blood that actually puddled beneath their boots on the parched earth. Everywhere one looked, there were the blue, gray, and butternut bodies.

Gasping for breath, Lockett could not believe that he was still alive. He sagged back a step, weak on his feet.

There was a strange quiet across the space, broken only by the cries of the wounded for help. For the first time in what seemed hours, there was no sound of gunfire nearby; however, Lockett wasn't sure if he could trust his senses right now, as numbed and overextended as they were.

"What now, sir?" Milton Bosworth said.

Lockett looked over uncomprehendingly at his sergeant. There was a bloody slash on one side of Bosworth's head that coated his neck with blood. One ear hung half severed, and an arm dangled limply, dripping blood over his hand

"God in Heavens. You all right, Milton?"

"A few scrapes, sir," he said gruffly, "Nothing to complain about..."

They both heard Colonel Blair's voice in the background, and Lockett found himself surprisingly relieved to hear the banker's voice. The colonel was giving instructions to gather the wounded and to remove the cannon.

"We heading back?" Bosworth asked.

Lockett nodded. Both men would normally have cried out at the injustice of ceding ground that had been paid for so dearly, but not this time. They could see how few men were still standing, and both were certain that yet another Confederate regiment would rise from the gully and the cornfield. They could not defend this low ridge now.

There was a small cheer that went up from the remaining Blair men. Lockett and Bosworth turned to see Patrick and Prosper T. approaching from the front edge of the small hill. He was about to ask what the cheer was for when Patrick thrust the curious black flag into the air.

"We took their regimental flag!" Bosworth hooted.

McManus jabbed the flag onto his bayonet and hoisted it high over his head, causing another round of cheers. It drooped lifelessly in the still air as he headed for Lockett.

They embraced wearily while Bosworth removed the skewered flag and spread his arms out wide to look at it. The flag was really not black after all, more dark blue with a red cross and one star.

"First Tennessee ain't gonna forget us," Prosper added.

"We're not going to forget them either," Lockett replied, looking at the slaughter. Then he looked at McManus. "Patrick, you seen Daniel?"

The red head shook his head. "No, not for a good while." He scanned those still standing and did not see the boyish frame anywhere.

Chapter 15

They had only started to look for Daniel among the blue coated bodies that covered the ground when Captain Bibb reappeared. He looked remarkably unmarked, unlike the rest of them. They were dirty, sweat soaked, and bloody. Many had minor wounds, some multiple ones. Lockett in particular smelled of blood, mostly from falling into the pooled gunner's blood after his stumble.

"Orders to get those cannon moving," Bibb said, "We are falling back."

"I need to find my brother," Lockett answered gravely. His stone gray stare locked onto the captain.

"Orders," Bibb said, perplexed that Lockett did not immediately follow them.

"Let the gunners move the cannon. They got horses. I need to find Daniel," Lockett said with increasingly feverish fears.

"All of the horses are dead, and so are most of Bush's men," Bibb frowned.

Lockett was about to angrily rebut him when a few musket cracks sounded from the gully. It reminded him of the precarious position that they were in.

Captain Bibb's stare hardened. Patrick, Milton, and Prosper looked at him expectantly.

"Let's get those cannon moving," Lockett answered abruptly. It was not going to be an easy task, he knew as he looked around. The cannon were difficult to move by hand and bodies would need to be cleared from whatever path they took to allow the wheels to roll.

Bibb turned with a satisfied look and walked away to deliver the same message to another group of men.

As they headed towards the nearest cannon, Lockett looked

from Bosworth to McManus. "Milton, Prosper, help get that cannon moving."

"Yes, sir," they answered and jogged towards the idle weapon.

"And?" McManus said.

"We're going to look for Daniel among the dead and wounded. You take the left. I'm going to the right. Make it quick. Bibb is right. We need to clear out before the Rebs regroup."

McManus made his way to the left side of the ridge. There were bodies of all sorts strewn across the dried, trampled grass. There were some in blue, some in butternut, officers and common men alike. Many were dead, but many were still alive also. The wounded cried out to him for help, for water.

He looked at them, if only to confirm that none were Daniel. He had to step around and even over them to make his way. It seemed that every other stride required such a path alteration to make his way.

Most of the blue coated men were from Renaud's company in this section of the carnage. Ahead there was a literal wall of butternut. They seemed to have fallen in place on top of each other. Bent and collapsed at all angles, they nonetheless piled up in a small semi-circle around two blue bodies.

With a catch in his throat, McManus saw why. The burly German stevedore, Otto Klugge, was one of the blue coated bodies. It looked as if he had held off a whole squad of Rebels by himself before falling on this field, so far from his native Germany. McManus stooped to roll over the other blue body, even though he knew who it had to be.

Adie Graham stared back lifelessly at him. There were four bloody bayonet wounds in his stomach that spilled out his intestines when McManus rolled him over.

"No," McManus hushed. He stared at the lad for a long time, Daniel forgotten. Adie had annoyed many of the men with his outspoken abolitionist views, but he had also won over many of the men with stubborn defense of his beliefs. In the end, many of the men had come to affectionately view him as their own younger brother. His death would hurt them deeply.

"God, no."

McManus knelt and prayed quickly over his two fallen friends.

Otto and Adie were gone.

James Lockett scoured the right side of the hilltop.

He was vaguely aware of the activity from the remaining men to muscle the guns from this ridge. It took four men just to get it moving with another two or three to clear bodies from the cannon's path.

The surviving gunners were busy cutting harnesses and ropes from their fallen animals. They would need those to slow the descent of the cannon from rolling wildly down the backside of the hill. They would need them doubly so to pull them up the next ridge behind their current position.

That hill was steeper and longer than their current position. It was not clear to any of them that they could actually manhandle the guns up there without the assistance of horses in the time needed.

Lockett stepped over and around the bodies crying out for help. Single-mindedly, he ignored their suffering and searched for Daniel's face and curly brown hair.

He had traversed nearly the entire ridge when his heart stopped. Face-down in front of him was the small frame topped with curly brown hair. Blood had pooled around the body from a nasty gash in his neck.

"No," he gasped, kneeling into the blood as he rolled the body over.

Lockett twitched in surprise. It was not Daniel. The lifeless face that stared back at him was not his brother.

* * *

Patrick McManus and the rest of the regiment collapsed in exhaustion behind the sturdy stone wall that topped the ridge.

They had spent the past forty minutes breaking their backs to hurriedly get the cannon up to this location. What was left of Bush's gunners and Renaud's men took care of the limbers and caissons, while rest of the regiment worked the heavy guns up the hill. Fulkerham's company acted as a rearguard while the rest of them pushed and pulled each cannon.

The progress had been quick in hindsight, considering how far they had travelled in such a short time, but it had seemed slow to their protesting backs. Occasionally, the wheels would need to be blocked so that some men could switch in to help. Inch by inch, foot by foot, they had made their progress.

The fortunate wounded, those who were still ambulatory, followed them. All others were left on the bloody ridge, left to the mercies of the Rebels and their surgeons. There was no time to grab them. The entire brigade was falling back to this new position.

The 79th and 24th joined in this orderly retreat, although they too were down to half strength. A patchwork reserve force, what was left of the 21st Wisconsin and Terrill's brigade, waited in the woods behind Starkweather's three remaining regiments.

And so they waited for the inevitable.

At least this time, they had a nice stone wall between them and the Reb's balls, McManus thought wearily.

Levi Thickle angrily banged his empty canteen against the stone. It rang hollowly. In a fit, he chucked the canteen over the wall. "What I wouldn't do for just one drink of water right now!" he snapped.

"Don't you need that canteen?" Baker, one of the newcomers, said.

"What for? There ain't no water in this God-forsaken place. 'Sides, if we ever find any, there's a whole field of canteens out there that ain't gonna be used no more."

"They say this is the bluegrass state," Prosper added wryly, "But they should really call it the brown grass state."

"What I don't get," Thickle added sourly, "Is where is the rest of the damn army? We got three full corps in this army, but it sure seems that ours is the only one engaged. Bragg is hitting us with his whole army. Where are our other two corps? Sheridan is sitting on his hands, and we don't even know where the other corps is."

"You think we're seeing the whole of Bragg's army. How do you know that?" Baker asked.

"I can count, that's how. I can count how many regimental flags keep coming forward. It's too many to count, that's how I know!"

"That's just because you can't count very high, Levi."

151

The men laughed gently at the humor.

"Well, I know what I know," he said tiredly. "We all know that Buell is an imbecile. This just proves it. Why, he probably doesn't even know that we're fighting a battle today!"

While the men grumbled, Lockett closed his eyes and became lost in his own thoughts. Neither he nor Patrick had found Daniel, and Daniel wasn't with them now. No one had seen him, or Vaught, or a number of others for that matter.

The company had lost about a third of its strength in the chaos, and they were fortunate. Renaud's and Williams's companies had lost half their men, though both lieutenants had survived, which was more than could be said for their captains.

Still, Lockett could only let his imagination run away with itself as he wondered where his brother was. Had he been killed by a stray shot in the woods before they had rushed to Bush's battery? Had he been captured on Bush's ridge? Was he laying untended in a ditch somewhere? Was he one of the hundreds of men calling out futilely for help or water?

When the shelling resumed, no one was surprised or startled this time. The day had made even the newcomers accustomed to it. Those who were not already leaning against the stone wall scurried over to it as the Confederate shells came in. The first were slightly off target. They hit short of the ridge, although one of the shots landed further up the slope and bounded over the stone wall, still capable of decapitating a man.

But what was left of Stone's and Bush's batteries were to the right of where Blair's regiment laid, so most of the shots were in that direction, and Blair's men watched the exhausted gunners perform their duty. Soon the Union pieces were firing in reply.

From a mere 800 yards away, the artillery duel commenced and continued. Content to stay below the wall and out of the way, Lockett and the rest waited. Solid shells bounced in and amongst the gunners, but they seemed oblivious to it and as they searched out replies.

Behind the cannon, Lockett could see Colonel Starkweather and his small staff astride their horses, watching. A few shells careened nearby, but they settled their mounts and continued from that position. Lockett supposed this was one of those times where the most important role of a commander was to be seen and look unconcerned. If so, Starkweather was doing a fine job of it.

Then from behind their brigade commander, he watched a figure emerge from the woods where the remnants waited as that final reserve element. It took Lockett a moment to realize that the figure was General Terrill who had disappeared into the woods and had not reappeared until this moment.

The General gestured madly at Colonel Starkweather, obviously unhappy about something in the unit's disposition. Is Terrill trying to pull rank? Lockett thought to himself. The argument continued for another minute, although amidst the echoing cannon fire, there was no way to hear what the two men were saying. Regardless, it was clearly an intense disagreement.

With a final gesture, Terrill turned on his heel and marched over to the cannon. A Confederate shell exploded overhead, killing a gunner, but Terrill marched on as if unaware. He pushed aside the gun captain and began to re-sight the cannon. Bewildered, the gun captain stood to the side and looked at the general who rolled up his sleeves and began to work the turn screw to change the gun's angle of elevation.

More shells exploded overhead as the Confederates switched from solid shells to fused shells that sprayed deadly shrapnel.

Satisfied, General Terrill stepped back, but before he could fire his carefully aimed weapon, something hit him, and he staggered. It was difficult to tell with all of the explosions overhead if he had been hit by a chunk of exploding shell, but to Lockett, the reaction looked more like a man who had been shot.

Lockett had heard before of officers who were so unpopular with their men that they had been killed in battle, covered up by the chaos. He wasn't sure, but it looked to him as though he had just witnessed such an event.

Before he could think much more on it, there was a cry.

"The Rebels are coming!"

He peeked over the stone wall and saw the wall of butternut approaching.

"Two ranks," Captain Bibb ordered the company, "Wait for my command!"

It was a good idea, and Lockett found himself surprised that the man had thought of it. Perhaps, that had been somewhere in

Hardee's infantry tactics manual?

The Confederates made their way up the hill. It was slow going. The hill was steep and the ground uneven. Men would stumble, and the ranks would get disjointed.

Stone's and Bush's batteries switched their fire from the opposing artillery to the approaching infantry. They ripped gaps in the butternut line, but each time, the Rebels closed ranks and continued on.

"Steady!" Bibb ordered in a loud voice, "Not yet. Let them get closer."

Lockett paced over to some of the newcomers, determined to watch their action this time. He did not want to see any more ramrods flying or unfired guns being loaded and reloaded.

A few Rebels fired their rifles from long distance, and Lockett was vaguely aware of the zip zip of balls nearby.

Two feet away, McManus kneeled behind the low stone wall and squinted down his sight, looking for a Rebel officer, looking for someone who would pay for killing Otto and Adie. He couldn't get the thought out of his mind as he searched for a worthy target. He bypassed two younger looking officers. They weren't worth it, he decided. Finally, he saw an older officer with an expensive looking gray uniform, complete with a golden wreath stitched down one arm and a bright red tassel belt.

"Front rank, aim… fire!"

McManus anticipated the command a split second before the others, and he fired first. His vision was clouded by the erupting smoke bank, but he knew that he had hit the target. He scooted back to allow the second rank forward while he reloaded.

Another gout of smoke obscured their vision. When the drifting smoke did part slightly, it revealed a stack of butternut bodies on the ground.

Though not advancing any longer, the Confederates returned fire. Heavy slugs banged off the stone wall. Others flew over the elevated line, but some hit unfortunate soldiers in blue.

The two sides slammed away at each other.

The volume was heavy and loud. Men fell on both sides, but the superior position for the Federals began to take a toll, and the Rebels eventually drifted back.

The Confederates milled about in the distance, near the bottom of the slope and along the up slope of the Open Knob across the way. Lockett watched their officers trying to rally the men and absorb new regiments into a line.

"They'll be back in about ten minutes," McManus murmured.

Before Lockett could respond in agreement, the Rebel batteries opened up again. This time, the Confederates had been able to move a battery of their guns to the Union left flank, and the cannon enfiladed Starkweather's position. One particularly well-aimed shot landed parallel and just inside the stone wall. The solid shell bounced through the crowding soldiers, taking down a whole file of men in a cloud of dirt and blood.

This flanking battery seemed focused solely on the left flank position that Blair's men now protected. Levi Thickle cursed aloud with each shot. The men squeezed futilely closer to the stone wall that provided minimal protection from the flanking fire. Shot after shot came in, but there was nothing to do but bear it.

The other Rebel batteries, the ones on the Open Knob, still directed their fire on the Union cannon, but Lockett and his men did not notice it this time as they tried to burrow into whatever holes and depressions they could find from the flanking fire.

Lockett and McManus clung to the stone wall, knowing it was all a matter of aim and luck. One shot plowed the ground nearby, just feet away, but fortunately, it was on the other side of the stone wall. The explosion rang their ears and sent a shower of dirt twenty feet into the air. The wall quivered and echoed with the sound of metal casing lashing the stone. The top rock on the stone wall toppled from its position and landed on McManus's foot.

He winced in pain, wondering if it was broken, but knowing that if the shot had landed just feet to the right that he and James would be dead already.

Over the next ten minutes, the volume of shots began to decrease. The stamina of the gunners on both sides was wavering, as was their ammunition.

"Thank God, there is only one battery over there," Captain Bibb remarked.

"If the Secesh get more cannon over there, this position will be done for," Levi speculated.

"It will be dark by then," McManus responded.

The young Sam Baker peeked over the wall. "They're re-forming, sir!"

Ignoring the cannon fire now, Lockett and Captain Bibb sprung to their feet. They paced behind the line. "Make sure you're loaded!"

"Check those percussion caps."

"Stay below the wall until we give the order!"

The Confederates made their way down the slope of the Open Knob, across the thin strip of flat land, and started up the slope towards them.

The Union batteries again shifted their aim. More shots went into the butternut line, but they absorbed them as if they were nothing, closing ranks whenever an iron shell opened up a hole. Lockett watched from behind his men. The Confederate batteries on the Open Knob now joined the flanking batteries in focusing on the Union infantry behind the stone wall.

Off to his right, a shell exploded perfectly in front of the stone wall. Shrapnel whipped through the air and cut down a swath of Union blue.

More Union shells landed among the marching Confederates, but it was fewer and fewer. After a long day of firing both men and cannon barrels were worn out. It would be up to the infantry again to blunt this next attack.

"Steady! Steady!" Starkweather yelled to his brigade. "We will make these shots count."

Lockett wondered if he was saying that because he knew how few rounds his men had left. There had been time to draw more ammunition, but somehow, many of the supply wagons had been sent off in the wrong direction, towards Sheridan's men far south of where the actual shooting was occurring.

The Confederates picked their way up the slope, past their previous high water mark, which was designated by a coating of bloodied butternut uniforms.

"Front rank will rise," Bibb said loudly.

"Make ready," came another officer's order further down the line. Ominously, hundreds of weapons appeared above the stone wall and leveled themselves at the Rebels.

It must have been a terrifying sight to the Confederates, for their steady march checked in certain sectors. Hesitantly, many raised their own weapons, deciding that this was close enough.

"Fire!"

There was no call to aim. In the two tightly packed ranks, aim was of little consequence. Both sides seemed to fire at the same time. The sound was deafening, and smoke immediately obscured both sides.

The soldier in front of Lockett snapped backwards, landing at his feet. The man clutched at his collarbone.

After that initial cacophony of fire, there was an eerie near-silence, broken only by the screams of the maimed and dying. Then there was the rattle of ramrods in the barrels. Lockett could hear men grunting with effort as they forced the ramrods down the powder fouled barrels. After so much firing, there was a considerable residue to push through.

The fastest were already firing again. Those would be the more experienced men, and with some pride, Lockett noticed that the fastest of the fast were in his company. Hours and hours of drilling paid off now.

Their next shots plunged into the murky depths of the gray smoke that hung between the lines.

Satisfied that the men were re-loading and firing well, Lockett unslung his rifle and added his own shot into the cloud.

The bludgeoning continued time and again before the Confederates drifted back out of range.

Finally, Lockett and his men slumped against the stone wall and wondered if that would be it, or if there was time in the day for one more Rebel charge before the daylight would mercifully cede to the night.

Chapter 16

Lockett leaned with his back against the wall next to Renaud. The two lieutenants had their eyes open, but they were as silent as if asleep.

Lockett tried to lick his parched lips, but he had no moisture.

Renaud gave a small snort at the sound. "Ze men need to clean the powder out of z'eir barrels. Some of zem can't get the ramrod all ze way down." They looked at each other thinking the same thing. Normally, hot water would be poured down the barrel to rinse out the black powder. In a pinch, the men would urinate down the barrel to the same effect. "I'd order zem to piss down the barrels, but I doubt any of zem have piss!" They laughed softly at the absurdity of it all.

"Do you zink that zey will try again?" Renaud continued. It was the same question on the mind of most of the men.

"I would if I were them," Lockett shrugged. "They have to know how little we have left in us."

"My boys have done more zan any general has the right to expect of zem," Renaud added angrily.

Lockett nodded, and they again lapsed into silence.

He closed his eyes and tried to slow his mind, but he could not. He was exhausted, yet he could not rest. Besides Renaud's question, the question of where was Daniel reappeared. It thankfully disappeared from his mind during the last part of the battle, but in the lulls, it returned like a vulture to prey on his thoughts.

"Shames," Renaud spoke to him in his French toned accent, "Shames, look."

Lockett turned his head and to his amazement, he saw Daniel approaching from the woods behind their position. For a moment, he thought he was dreaming. Daniel and Vaught were walking straight towards them. Around their necks were a dozen slung canteens.

The two were greeted hungrily by the others.

"One drink then pass," Captain Bibb ordered, anxious to avoid a riot at the appearance of the water. Even though there were twenty some canteens, they would not last long in the thirsty ranks.

The first man eagerly gulped a deep swallow from the canteens while the others patted Daniel and Vaught on the back. The first man then sputtered and coughed roughly. "That ain't water," he gasped in a barely audible voice.

"Whiskey," Vaught said with his charismatic smile, "Couldn't find no water, but I found whiskey."

"One swallow, then pass," Bibb reiterated at the mention of the liquor.

James Lockett stared in wonderment at his brother. There was not a scratch on him. In fact, he and Vaught did not even remotely resemble any of the other men. His men's faces were blackened by powder, powder burns, dirt, and sweat, but his brother and Vaught looked as clean and untroubled as any soldier could at this point.

James Lockett's initial relief in seeing Daniel was now rapidly evolving into a deep disgust. There was no doubt in his mind where his brother had been. He had skedaddled to the rear when the fighting started! He bore no marks of fighting for the blood of his comrades, so many of whom they would be burying!

The shame and ignominy burned James Lockett. His brother was a shirker!

He grabbed Daniel roughly by the shoulder and steered him away from the men. Stunned, Daniel staggered along.

"Where the hell have you been?" he demanded.

Daniel spluttered, but James could not make out what he said.

"I asked you, where were you? You've been in the rear," he accused. His eyes narrowed, and his gaze bore into him like Daniel had seen a thousand times before. "Hiding? Were you hiding, Daniel?"

"No, no, not like that," Daniel protested weakly, but without the normal righteous indignation that he often put forth against his older brother's charges.

"A coward," James snarled in a low voice so that no else could hear. "You've been hiding with Vaught while the rest of us have been dying together!"

"No, not like that," Daniel repeated.

"Bouma is dead, you know!" James glared. "He died watching my back... There was no one watching his back."

He watched the shot go home, and Daniel looked as if he had been physically struck by his older brother.

"I didn't know," he said meekly.

"And now you show up because you think the day is done? Is that it?"

"No, not like that," Daniel said softly, but he was looking away now, unable to bring his gaze to his brother's eye.

"Well, you're wrong about that. There is just enough daylight for Johnny Reb to make one more push."

As if on cue, Bush's battery started up again, and there was a cry. The men moved back to their positions on the stone wall. The Confederates were coming again.

Section III

The Hangman's Noose

Chapter 17

And the Rebels did come.

One more time, they littered the slope with more dead. One last time, a brave few even tried to rush to the wall without pausing to fire their weapons, but there were too few who made the dash. They fell short, as did the last Rebel charge.

It was shortly after 4:30 by the time that third charge failed. With exhausted resignation, the Rebels fell back to the Open Knob and prepared to regroup for the next day. They had pushed the Union flank deeply during the day, at a steep cost to both sides, but darkness was beginning to settle in.

During the night, General Bragg came to the realization that he had launched nearly all of his forces against only one corps of Buell's army, not all of them, as he had first supposed. Aghast, he realized that his battered army would still need to face at least two new, entirely fresh, corps in the morning. So in the night, the Rebels abandoned the field.

Across the way, Union General Buell finally became aware of the battle that had engulfed part of his army throughout the day. He had supposed that the occasional noise which reached his headquarters was mere skirmishing, and that the reports of heavily engaged brigades were merely the nervous reactions of exaggerating commanders.

Realizing that he had missed an entire major battle, Buell began plans to put the rest of his army into action the next day to receive another of Bragg's attack, but of course, that battle was over, as was his career.

Dispirited by their Kentucky expedition, Bragg and the Confederate Army slunk back to middle Tennessee.

Their wagons were still full of the muskets they had intended to give to their Kentucky brethren. These same wagons were also disastrously low on food. The butternut ranks cursed Bragg's name and were sure that they would starve on the long march back to Tennessee.

Buell's army followed them south, but soon after, the armies settled back into their previous positions, Bragg in Murfreesboro and the Union in Nashville. And Washington replaced Don Carlos Buell.

It was now General William Rosecrans's army.

- the diary of James Lockett
Nashville again. While it might be a fine city outside of this circumstance, I detest being here. We are encamped outside the city, but not far enough away for the lures of the town to be avoided. Drink, women, and card playing establishments abound. Keeping discipline among the men is taking all of my energies, and I still fear that I am failing nonetheless.

"I don't know what you are criticizing them for, Levi," young Sam Baker remarked as the squad of twenty men marched along as part of their escort duty. Though one of the newcomers, Baker was now fully accepted by the rest of the company after Perryville.

"That jus' proves that you don't know Levi very well then," Prosper T. Rowe guffawed. "Levi's always complainin' or unhappy 'bout somethin'."

"And what has Levi got a problem with this time?" Sergeant Bosworth asked, rejoining the conversation.

"We were talking about Nashville, Sarge," Baker said. "I said it seemed like a fine town with some impressive buildings."

"It's gots some handsome ones," Prosper agreed, head bobbing.

"Well, for all those 'handsome' ones, they got some narrow and dirty streets. Got more horseshit in the streets than dirt… and when it rains?" Levi snorted derisively. "And the people? Ungrateful, secesh-loving…"

"Don't think anyone would be very happy about turning their city into an army encampment," Baker responded evenly.

"Not to mention turning it into the world's largest

whorehouse," John Messern added righteously.

"Now don't go tryin' to use logic on old Levi," Prosper winked.

"Still your tongue, Prosper," Levi said sourly, "That ain't no logic no how."

"But what about the statehouse?" Baker tried. "That is a fine building up on the hill."

"Overdone and out of place," Levi responded, "Looks like they spent all of the money on one building when they should have spread it out."

"C'mon, Levi," Baker said. He was still unable to see that no matter what he said that Levi Thickle was bound to disagree. "They even have some buildings with seven floors. Seven! Have you ever seen such tall buildings?"

"Old, dirty, dilapidated," Thickle answered, spitting on the ground for emphasis.

The provost officer in charge of their detachment swung his horse around and trotted over to them. Coal black eyes glared at them above an equally black goatee that hung over his neck like a veil. The jagged scar over his right eye only added to his vengeful stare. "That is enough talking in the ranks! Get your men in order, sergeant!"

Bosworth saluted and answered, "Sir, yes, sir."

"Good God, like I am in charge of bunch of chattering school girls not soldiers!" the provost lieutenant continued. "Wish to God that Colonel Truesdail could have secured some better soldiers for this, a menial task though it is! Gutter born, worthless fools!" He swung his mount around and headed back to the front of their small column.

"Regular bastard that one is," Prosper muttered, but quietly so that the man could not hear.

"Ain't all of the provosts?" Levi grumbled in rare agreement.

"Makes you glad for the officers that we have," Bosworth added softly. The other heads nodded in agreement, all except one. That one was Daniel Lockett, who heard the comment but could not agree with the sergeant's assessment. To Daniel, there was not much difference between the provost lieutenant and his brother, especially after Perryville.

Obviously, things had been strained between them before the

battle, but now? Now, his brother considered him a coward. He would not listen to Daniel at all or to his explanations that he and Vaught had carried a wounded comrade back to the surgeons and that they had gotten a little lost upon returning to the regiment.

James would hear none of it, and Daniel was conscious of the fact that James seemed to have turned the whole company against him, even the other newcomers. They all looked at him differently now. Their voices took on a different tone when speaking to him. They were all against him now! No one was willing to give him the benefit of the doubt.

Somehow, they did not seem to treat Vaught the same way. They treated the gambler the same as ever, even though it was Vaught's idea that they take the wounded man back. To boot, it was Vaught's idea that they take the northerly route back, and that they take the time to wait in the woods with some of the others who had fled the destruction that they were witnessing. They had all been Vaught's ideas, but it was Daniel that they viewed as the coward.

As Daniel reflected on the injustice of it all, it was the woman's cry that finally snapped him from that trance and reminded him of why they were here with the provost officer.

Their small detachment had been temporarily placed under the command of the provost in order to escort six townsfolk out of Nashville. They had retrieved the six men from the jail, old men all of them. Bent and stooped in both physical posture and spirit, the old men had shuffled out of the jail. With dirty, haggard faces obscuring their normal paternal looks, it was only the fact that their worn and soiled clothes were of a sharper cut that gave a clue to how far they had fallen.

They had once been men of power and privilege, and above all, pride. He did not understand why they were escorting these stumbling old men, nor why they could not speed the trip by securing a wagon for the forlorn group. He wasn't even sure what the men had done.

It was only when Daniel overheard Levi Thickle's answer to Sam Baker's same question that he understood.

The oath... it was all about the loyalty oath, Thickle had explained. With zero sympathy, the veteran soldier had explained that this "secesh trash" all refused to sign the oath of allegiance to the Union. As such, these men had lost their possessions and property, and they were now on this march with the ever-glaring provost officer, marching south to the town limits.

Of the six, all but one were bareheaded. Somehow, the one had retained an expensive looking bowler hat. That fact had not gone unnoticed by the provost officer.

"A fine looking hat if there was one," he sneered, stooping to snatch it from the man's head. "Three weeks in the prison and still no oath, and yet somehow allowed to keep this fine piece of craftsmanship?" He spun the round hat on his finger. "I do believe that our military governor, Andrew Johnson, was quite clear in his orders. You get nothing but the shirt on your back, filthy traitor!" The provost officer temporarily placed the bowler hat on his own head before reverting back to his martial ware. "I do believe it will look quite dashing on me, but only for when I am not on duty." He laughed to himself.

"Stop!" It was the woman's cry again. This time, they were close enough to make out that it was directed at them.

The provost officer looked at her but addressed the soldiers. "Keep marching," he said sternly.

"You can't do this!" the woman said in a shrill voice. She had parked her small carriage pulled by a one-eyed nag across the road, blocking it. "This is an injustice!"

"The injustice, madam," the provost officer said derisively, "Is that you are trying to prevent me from doing my duty." He turned back to the men. "March around her," he ordered, "And if any of these scum slow in the slightest, a harsh kick in the ass... or worse."

"Your duty?" she said in a strident and undeterred voice. She climbed down from the carriage and walked uncowed over to the mounted officer. "You have duty to imprison the innocent?"

The soldiers and their wards slowed ever so slightly, but they remembered the officer's glare and continue to march around the blockage.

"Well?" she glared at the officer.

Wordlessly, the officer slowly brought himself out of the saddle. Even without the benefit of a horse, he towered over her.

"If all of the Reb soldiers had the spirit of that little lass, we'd never win any battles," one of the soldiers muttered softly in

166

admiration as they marched by.

"These men," the officer said deliberately and then paused for dramatic effect, "Are *fully* guilty of their crimes... They are traitors. As such, they are fortunate to have been given such a lenient punishment as deportation."

"Traitors?" the young woman said angrily. "Has my father taken up arms against anyone? No, he has not. Has he done anything wrong? Do you have any evidence? None! None at all!" She followed angrily after the slow marching troops, leaving her carriage behind in the roadway.

"He was given multiple opportunities to prove his loyalty, and he refused. Now, you will..."

"You lie!" she snapped before he could finish. "You and your colonel took the keys to his bank and emptied it out. Thieves!"

"There was no theft," he answered. But for the first time, there was a lack of imperiousness in his voice. Her bold claims in front of non-provost troops had wrong-footed him.

"Liar!"

Her high-pitched accusation brought the anger back to his tone.

"Traitors forfeit their claims when they refuse to take the oath, and you would be wise, woman, to remember that we have plenty of your sort locked up as well! We know that Nashville is a den of thieves, Rebel spies, and traitors. Why just last week, the infirmary was robbed of all of its medicines, and who did we catch trying to exit the city? Townswomen with the bottles sewn into their petticoats! Shall we examine your petticoats to see what you are hiding there?"

She could see by the look in his dark eyes that the man would like nothing more, but she was unbowed. "You are all thieves, murderers, and kidnappers!" She looked accusingly at the detachment of soldiers. "My father is old and in ill health. He has done nothing wrong, and you turn him out of his own house and family! You force him to march miles to some unknown place where he has no family!"

"You are a tiresome woman," the provost officer said, shouldering her aside as he moved back to his saddle.

Off-balance, she stepped back on the uneven ground, and her heel caught the hem of the long dress. With an ungainly thud, she landed in the mud.

As she sat furiously in the muck, she saw one of the soldiers come out of the column and take one step towards her, but before the young, fresh-faced soldier could take a second stride, one of the prisoners shouted out, "Don't, Cora! Leave it be!"

She picked herself up from the ground, eyes blazing.

The provost officer smiled haughtily from atop his horse. "Sergeant, if she says so much as one more word, arrest her! I've had a belly full of her sort this week!"

"Don't, Cora," her father said again.

With a visible struggle for her self-control, she looked from the Yankee officer to her white-haired father in the middle of the group of prisoners. He was a frail looking man, and each of the soldiers could understand her concern given his sickly appearance. But he summoned a deeper voice than he had used before. "I will be fine, daughter, as long as I know that you are safe."

She clenched her fists and sadly watched the column continue away from her. Without bothering to wipe the clinging mud from her dress, she stared after them. She would not move from that spot until the column was out of sight.

Prosper T. Rowe turned his head as they disappeared for one last look. A traitor was a traitor, but there was still a ring of truth in her words that jabbed at him like a bayonet. He was not the only one. The once-jabbering soldiers said nothing as they marched on, remembering the hatred in her eyes. The soldiers could think of nothing else.

But there was one other thought in Prosper's brain as they went on. He had seen something that the others had not. He had seen Daniel take a step towards the girl during the confrontation that had ended up with her on the ground. He had seen the look on Daniel's face as he started forward to help her. For the first time, Prosper had seen Daniel do something that reminded him of the Lieutenant. Maybe they were brothers after all, he thought.

* * *

Ambrose Tucker watched the blue coated cavalrymen scurry back across the creek bed. No doubt they would head straight towards the infantry fortifications a half mile away. Ambrose and the rest of the mounted raiders were not so foolish as to follow.

Their ambush had been a complete success, and they had the two prisoners to prove it.

Ambrose chuckled to no one in particular. He was just glad to be back as a fighting man. He had served as Bragg's messenger during the slaughter in Perryville. Though he had to duck the stray shot, he had never fired his weapon and that seemed plain wrong to him. As it was, he could not in good conscience continue to serve a wavering general such as General Bragg any longer. So it was that he asked for a transfer back to Colonel Morgan and his raiders. He had done so without the hint of his frustration towards the general. Ambrose was wise enough not to burn any of those bridges, particularly since General Bragg still retained command.

When Bragg had gone to Richmond after the retreat back to Tennessee, Ambrose Tucker and most of the Confederate army figured, and prayed, that they would be getting a new commander, but General Bragg's friendship with President Davis was evidently stronger than good reason was.

The dithering that he had observed from the general in the lead up and during the battle of Perryville had left Ambrose convinced that they had thrown away a chance to crush the Yankees and re-claim Kentucky. Were it not for the dithering, they would not have thrown such piecemeal attacks at the Yankee's left all day.

But that was now in the past, and he was back with the men, fighting and watching the Yankees hole up in Nashville.

Chapter 18

Patrick McManus poked the fire with a stick and watched a few embers float up into the darkening sky. He and Lockett sat on logs and watched the orange flames. Behind them, they could hear the din of camp life. Prosper T. and John Messern were playing their fiddles. Others were laughing at some crude remark that Levi Thickle made at Sam Baker's expense.

"So what will you do?" McManus asked Lockett. It was a rare opportunity for the two of them to talk alone.

"What can I do, Patrick? He's a coward. No doubt about that. I can't unmake it."

"It was his first battle. Maybe he didn't…"

"Dammit, Patrick! Don't defend him. There is no defending it." He said the final words slowly, deliberating on each syllable as he said it.

He rarely got angry at McManus. Even so, his friend took the response in stride.

"Well, I don't know," he said gently.

"If there is anything good about this, at least we are not a normal company."

"What do you mean?" Patrick asked.

"Any other company would be filled with men from the same area. At least in this crazy, mixed up regiment, we're the only ones from Kalamazoo. Maybe people back home won't ever know about Daniel." He was about to add 'and any stain to the Lockett name', but he caught himself before he uttered the words, knowing how hypocritical they would sound. After all, there were some back home who thought that James Lockett had murdered a young girl in Missouri.

It was dark, but by the flickering light of the fire, Lockett could see the frown on McManus's face. He shook his head, knowing that they were thinking the same thing.

"You're right. I should not care. After all, half of the folks back home think that I am a beast, a murderer."

"Those of us who matter know better, James. We know about Orrin Long and his kind. We know it wasn't your doing that the girl died. We know."

There was a long pause before Lockett mumbled a soft, "Yes."

"James, we've known each other our whole lives. I know you. I know that when you put your mind to it that you aren't going to be stopped anymore than a river can flow upstream. And I know that you aren't going to commit murder. Hell, all of the boys here know it too, and they weren't with us in Missouri, and they haven't known you their whole lives like I have, but they would know too."

"We got some good men in this company," Lockett said softly, humbled by the words.

"Daniel's just young, and it doesn't help that he fraternizes with Vaught. Just give Daniel another chance. He's not you, James, but he's not a coward deep down either."

Lockett nodded. He wanted to believe McManus, but he wasn't sure. He debated whether he should seek out his brother.

But Daniel was not in camp at that moment. He was two miles away, following Vaught into an establishment that the older man had identified earlier.

It was a smoky, dimly lit place with a bar whose wood was as scarred and gouged as a plowed field. Despite its worn appearance, it was a crowded place. Every table was filled with a card player, nary a seat was available.

Stairs led up to rooms on the second floor, and heavily rouged and provocatively dressed women leaned precariously and suggestively across the railing above the men.

The place smelled strongly of sweat, cigar smoke, and liquor, but all that Daniel Lockett was aware of was the voluptuous, undergarment-dressed blonde staring at him with a knowing smile. Blushing, but unable to take his eyes off her, he fixated on her with a slack jawed look.

"Easy, Romeo," Vaught said with a firm grip on Daniel's shoulder. "You don't want to lose what little money you have so soon. We have a long night."

Blinking, Daniel tried to avert his gaze, but not until after the blonde winked at him. Flummoxed, he made himself face the other way. "There aren't any seats open at the tables," he said, trying to change the subject.

"No worry," Vaught said, "I like to spend a few rounds watching the tables first. Then I'll decide which table to make my way to. Let's have a drink and watch together. I'm buying."

The latter was important since Daniel had scarcely enough money to buy one drink. What he was supposed to watch for, he had no idea. But like a lamb led by his shepherd, he followed Vaught over to a tiny space at the bar.

As he squeezed in between two soldiers, it was then that Daniel noticed that he was different than most of the men in the gambling house. Besides the fact that most were older, he realized that most of the clientele were officers, not mere privates like himself. However, the lieutenants, captains, majors, and even a colonel would not notice the two privates because Vaught had instructed Daniel to hide their uniform jackets in the back alley before they had entered. Daniel now wore a simple brown jacket while Vaught wore an expensive looking green vest and trim brown jacket.

He looked much different in those clothes, Daniel thought to himself. Vaught had explained at the time that it was his lucky jacket, which Daniel believed, but now he guessed that it had as much to do with not advertising that they were humble privates.

They watched the various officers gamble, some winning, some losing. The amount of money being laid on the table stunned Daniel. He had never seen money like that. Even the games that he had seen Vaught win in Cincinnati paled in comparison. If it struck Vaught the same way, he gave no indication. In fact, he said little as he keenly studied each of the men around the tables.

Finally, one of the captains hung his head as he lost his last hand. Glumly, he left the table and headed for the bar, passing Vaught who was already on his way to fill the vacant seat.

The lugubrious captain sat next to Daniel and slapped a coin on the scarred bar top. The bartender came over and poured him a shot of whiskey.

The unlucky officer looked over at Daniel with a haggard appearance and large bulbous, red nose that seemed to turn ever darker as the whiskey burned its way through him. "I knew that I should not have tried to bluff that major," he explained to Daniel as if they were old friends. "It wasn't in the cards, so to speak." He laughed at his own jest while Daniel looked on blankly.

"Looks like I would have been better spent to sit at this bar and waste my money on this rot gut they call whiskey. I see that you are empty now too. Next drink on you, my friend?"

Daniel looked silently at him, unsure what to say, but the captain completed the conversation for him after two seconds.

"No? Very well, this one is on me then, but you will need to get the next one, my friend. After all that I lost tonight, I cannot afford to buy the drinks all night. We will need to share." He gave a cackling laugh that reminded Daniel of Prosper's horse neigh. "And of course, it will be a long night in here since the curfew has been placed for the night, and I have no desire to run afoul of the provosts."

Still, Daniel said nothing. In Vaught's pocket was a forged pass that Vaught had somehow procured for them. The pass said that Colonel Blair had given them special permission to be out past the 9 pm curfew, which the military government had established for all of Nashville. Of course, Vaught had plainly said that he had no intention of ever needing the pass; it was 'just in case'.

The captain with the large nose took off his boot.

Daniel stared quizzically at him, causing the captain's neighing laugh again. "I always keep a few extra coins in my boot, you see. That way when I have lost all of my money at the table, I still have a few bits for some drinks to drown my sorrow."

"I guess that is a good plan," Daniel replied.

"Captain Edward Blonton, at your service." He offered his hand to Daniel.

"Daniel Lockett."

"Pleasure, my friend."

Another two coins were slapped on the bar top, and soon the bartender had two more whiskeys in front of them. The captain picked up his shot glass and held it in toast. "Salut!"

Daniel looked blankly at him and started to bring his hand up in salute.

Blonton laughed heartily. "It's a toast, my friend, a toast."

"Oh," Daniel blushed. He downed the fiery liquid and gasped as it burned all the way down.

Blonton laughed good-naturedly. They passed the time talking, or more accurately, with Blonton talking and Daniel listening, or at least trying to listen. Despite his best efforts, he could hardly remember a thing that the captain said. At one point after another drink, the room spun crazily, and Daniel nearly fell over.

The gambling went on across the various tables, and the women came and went from the railing above it all. Later on, Daniel again noticed the voluptuous blonde. Blonton too noticed her, as well as the fact that his new friend could not take his eyes off her.

"She's the real thing, my friend. No doubt about that."

Daniel's head bobbed dumbly, although he did not understand exactly.

"There's so many in this town now, it's difficult for any of them to stand out, but she's one that does. Course, she is too rich for my blood." The captain laughed and shook his boot. There were no more coins rattling around in it.

Daniel turned back around and faced the bar. "No money here eit-er," he slurred, shaking his foot.

They were both wide-eyed in surprise when the blonde joined them at bar, leaning across Daniel's elbow.

"I see that we have caught each other's eye," she said.

Daniel looked at her. His head swam worse than ever, but he wasn't sure if it was the alcohol this time. Her perfectly round, rouged cheeks were dimpled on one side as she smiled at him. Her full, red lips curled back to reveal oddly white teeth, and she looked at him expectantly with the bluest eyes that Daniel had ever seen in his life.

She touched his arm gently, and it jolted him like a sting, but she paid no attention to his flinch. "You and your friend have been downstairs all night. Wouldn't you like to see what the upstairs looks like?"

Daniel's tongue tripped over his lips and he mumbled something unintelligible. "Just waitin' for my friend to finish his card game," Daniel managed on the second try.

She nodded in Vaught's direction. "Yes, I saw you two come in together, but there is plenty of time. I know his type. He'll be at the tables until dawn."

"I, I..." he stammered. His heart was pounding like a battery of cannon in his chest, and he licked his lips. His mouth felt as dry and parched as it ever had on the terrible march up to Louisville.

"He means to say, 'of course, my dear'. Indeed he does," Blonton added helpfully.

"I, I have no money left," Daniel said meekly.

"Well, perhaps I'll just show you around," she said demurely, giving him a slow wink.

When Daniel hesitated, Blonton pulled on Daniel's other elbow and whispered into his ear. "Don't look a gift horse in the mouth, my friend. Go now."

She lifted Daniel's hand from the bar top and gently led him away. He thought that her hand felt impossibly soft as he followed her up the stairs. At the top of the steps, he shot a quick glance at Vaught's table, but the gambler was engrossed in his game and did not notice Daniel disappearing down the hallway.

"And what regiment are you with?" she asked as she opened a squeaking door and led him into her room.

"Regiment?" Daniel said slowly, plucking at his brown coat. "What makes you think that I'm a soldier?"

She laughed softly. "Everyone here is a soldier. Besides, I can tell by your pants."

He looked down at his military issue blue pants.

"So what regiment?" she asked again. She slipped his brown coat off his shoulders and laid it across the lone chair in the sparse room.

"Blair's Independent Regiment, though there ain't nothin' independent about us. Orders for this, orders for that..." He felt so relaxed at the moment that the words came tumbling out of his mouth without even entering into his brain first.

"Blair?" she said with a purring voice, "I've never heard of it. Are you just mustered in?" She led him over to the bed and sat him down on it.

"No, it's not new. We were here before. Then Perryville." He blushed at the last word, remembering his fear and how he had eagerly followed Vaught away from the battlefield.

She noticed his blushing but mistook that for something else as she sat straddle across his lap.

"Perryville," she whispered in his ear. "Did you see much fighting?"

"We saw a lot," Daniel said hastily. "We lost half of the regiment there."

"Half," she said softly, "Are there many regiments at half strength?"

"A few regiments but not most."

"Half strength? Will you be getting reinforcements soon?"

"No," Daniel mumbled, feeling warm and relaxed, too relaxed, "*We* were the reinforcements." He was more conscious than ever that she was sitting across his lap. Her bosom was intoxicatingly close to his face.

She stroked his cheek. "I have not seen you here before. Will you be back, be a regular, or is your army moving out?"

"Moving out? No, we are moving into winter quarters," he said softly, his eyes locked on her wares.

"You look thin. Are you receiving enough supplies?" she asked as she ran her fingers through his curly brown hair.

"I guess so," Daniel answered in confusion, "I guess not? I'm not really sure."

As he spoke, there was the sound of commotion coming from downstairs. The normal droning din of the establishment was replaced by one individually audible voice and then commands. Someone was barking out an order?

The blonde leapt off the bed and rushed to the door. She opened it a crack and peeked down the hall.

"What is it?" Daniel said blankly. He stirred from the bed but staggered across the room, feeling the effects of quick movement and whiskey.

The blonde shut the door and retrieved his brown coat. Daniel was still gathering himself, lurching back to the bed and clutching the post like drowning man at sea. He did not see her slip a piece of paper into his coat pocket.

"You need to leave, quickly," she said.

"Leave? I just got here…"

"There's trouble. You need to go."

"R-rouble," Daniel slurred, "I can handle any t-ouble…" He forced himself erect and puffed out his chest.

"Yes, yes, I'm sure," she answered with some anxiety, "But I need you to go."

"Are you in t-ouble?" he asked stubbornly. "I can help."

"You can help by going." She gathered him under the arm and guided him to the window. "Out this window is the balcony. Go to the left. There is a trellis to climb down. Can you climb now?" she asked doubtfully.

"Climb!" He shook his head. "Can I climb? Why, I'm as nimble as a squirrel!" He tripped on the rug and staggered from her grasp and down onto his knees. Oblivious, he added, "Of course, I can climb down."

"Then you must go." She moved to lift the window sill.

"But when I will see you again?" he said in a mournful voice.

The sound of the commotion was upstairs now, and they could hear doors being burst into and the shrieks from the women.

"You must hurry. It's the provosts."

"The provosts!" Daniel said, feeling the fear suddenly latch onto him.

She raised the window, and Daniel clumsily stuck one leg over the ledge before hesitating. "Go," she said, impulsively giving him a kiss on the cheek, "There will always be another time." She pushed him out and shut the window.

Daniel sat on his backside on the balcony for a moment and tried to slow his spinning head. After a moment, he got up and staggered to the other end of the balcony. He was nearly to the other end when a figure stepped from the shadowed recess of another window. Gun drawn, the figure said in a threatening baritone, "Turn around real slow if you know what's good for you."

Daniel stopped. He looked over his shoulder uncomprehendingly at the shadow… and then its weapon. He had heard the voice before, but he could not place where.

The shadow had ushered Daniel back into the room, and they were not alone. The blonde was there, glaring at a short, stump like sergeant who had her by the arm. There was also an older woman dressed in a gaudy red dress whose eyes lit up when the shadow followed Daniel through the window.

"I pay you to avoid things like this!" the older woman hissed with a scathing glare.

"Your payments do not cover protection for traitors and Rebel spies," the shadow replied with an unconcerned, haughty voice.

Daniel turned and saw the face in the light for the first time. He knew now why the voice sounded so familiar. The long, coal black goatee, the jagged scar over the eye, and the hateful dark eyes... it was the same provost lieutenant whom he, Milton, and the others had accompanied a few days prior.

"There are no Rebel spies in my establishment," the older woman declared. She crossed her arms and tilted her chin defiantly.

"We are standing in the company of one right now."

"Utter nonsense," she retorted.

"Another word from you, Madame Bougeau, and I'll arrest you too. I don't fancy that you'll find our prisons as comfortable."

The threat had the desired effect, and Madame Bougeau made no other sound.

"Now as for you," the lieutenant said, turning towards the blonde. "You are going to tell me who else is in your little spy ring and how you get your information across to the Rebels."

"I'll do no such thing," she replied confidently.

"Oh, you will," he said with an expectant glare, "When I'm done with you, you'll wish that you had not been so brave at the beginning... After all, how do you think that we got your name in the first place?"

The threat penetrated Daniel's stupor, and he jerked his arm away from the provost officer.

"Whadda we do with the tadpole, sir?" the stocky sergeant said, pointing at Daniel.

"What do we do," the lieutenant mused. "What do you say, boy? You a Rebel sympathizer?"

"I ain't no Johnny Reb," Daniel snapped back. "I volunteered to fight 'em!"

"Out of uniform, are you? You a deserter?"

"N-no," Daniel stammered.

"You got a pass to be out past curfew?"

Daniel mumbled softly, knowing that his forged pass was

downstairs with Vaught, if Vaught was even still here. He did not realize that the comment about the pass was a joke until the sergeant started laughing.

"A pass to visit a whorehouse?" the sergeant laughed, "That's a good one, sir."

"Tear the room apart, sergeant. See what else you can find here. And don't forget to search her too."

"With pleasure, sir," the sergeant said. Greedily, he eyed the scantily dressed blonde.

There was no doubt where the search would start. The swarthy little sergeant squeezed her arm harshly while his other hand eagerly ran across her body.

"Get your hands off me!" the girl cried, but that only made him laugh.

Aghast, Daniel stared, frozen in place.

The blonde tried to twist away, but the sergeant's thick handed grasp yanked her back, tearing her undergarments.

"Stop," Daniel said to no one in particular.

"Hold still ifs you knows whads good for you," the sergeant growled at her.

She screamed again as the sergeant grabbed her tightly. Suddenly, she twisted and clawed at his face, catching them all by surprise. The sergeant howled and stepped back, red blood already bubbling from twin streaks below his eye and down his cheek.

But he had not let go of her completely, and in anger, he yanked on her wrist, bringing her momentum towards him as his other fist arced wildly, catching the top of her head.

Daniel's feet finally lurched forward towards the sergeant, but the man saw the clumsy movements coming. He released the girl and whirled around toward Daniel. With the skill of a man who had seen his share of bar room fights, he dipped a shoulder and launched a rage induced hook into Daniel's midsection.

The air exploded from Daniel's lungs, and he dropped to his knees.

But the momentary distraction had freed the girl from the sergeant's grasp, and she staggered over to the small chest of drawers. She reached into the top drawer and pulled out a small Derringer. She turned and began to swing around to aim the small, two shot weapon at the sergeant, but before she could pull the trigger, there was the louder report of an Army revolver.

Her snowy white skin pulsed with a spreading bloom of scarlet. She stood still for a second. Then, the bloom grew rapidly from her chest. She toppled over backward, dead as she hit the floor.

Wordlessly, Daniel tried to rise from his knees, but before he could, a revolver butt crashed down on the back of his head and everything went black around him. His last split second image was that of the dark red blood pooling out from the blonde, steadily spilling towards him. Her lifeless eyes stared hauntingly at him.

Chapter 19

"If he tries to kill him, should we let him?" Milton Bosworth murmured softly to Patrick McManus.

McManus gave no answer, but he was thinking along similar lines. The normally handsome Vaught already looked worse for wear with the swollen eye and blood crusted nostrils. If Prosper T. had not stopped them, Milton and he probably would have killed the man themselves.

When they had first discovered that Vaught and Daniel were missing at morning roll call, they had assumed some sort of desertion, which probably would have killed James on its own. But then, they had caught Vaught slinking back into camp, albeit by himself.

After learning from him that Daniel had been arrested by the provosts, neither he nor Milton could contain their tempers.

"So you were where, Private?" Lockett questioned Vaught.

The battered gambler stood at perfect attention, which was impressive given how sore his ribs were at the moment. When he had seen the provosts carry Daniel's motionless body out of the gambling bordello, he had thought that they had killed him. The sound of the gunshot was clear to all, even those at the tables downstairs. But Vaught did not see any blood on Daniel, and he learned from some of the provosts later that Daniel was just unconscious, although under arrest.

"We were at Madame Bougeau's, sir."

Lockett looked at him with shielded gray eyes, but there was a tightness in the jaw that the gambler recognized as a tell to the lieutenant's true state.

"And you say that the Provosts have him?"

"Yes, sir. They took him to the city jail."

"Did he say anything to you?"

181

"Uh, no, sir. He wasn't conscious."

"Not conscious?" Lockett said with the distress plain in his voice before catching himself. "I suppose he would not be the first suspected deserter to take a beating from the provost."

"Uh, yes, sir."

When Vaught paused, it was Bosworth who interjected, "And tell him the rest!" He glared at the gambler.

Vaught hesitated but then continued. "The other provosts told me that he was not under arrest for desertion. They took him to city jail because he is a suspected traitor and is guilty of helping Rebel spies that operate out of the whorehouse."

The color drained from Lockett's face, and he swallowed hard. The others mistook the look for something else, but to Lockett, a certain self-guilt started to set in.

"Helping Rebel spies?" he said softly, more to himself than to Vaught.

"Yes, sir. Not true, of course, sir. I don't know what happened, sir, but I'm sure that there is no way that they can prove it..."

Lockett did not hear any of the words. Instead, in his head, all he could think about was his growing guilt.

Was this some sort of cosmic justice? *He* was the one who had helped a Rebel spy, not Daniel! Was this the penalty then? Were the heavens seeking a balancing of the scales by having his younger brother pay the penalty?

"Helping a Rebel spy..." he muttered.

"...don't know what happened upstairs, but somehow, they think Daniel is mixed up with them."

"Helping a Rebel spy," Lockett repeated softly. Visions of Anna Tucker's fetching face filled his thoughts. He remembered riding through the forest to warn her father of the impending Union trap. He remembered the bushwhacker Bloody Bill Coulter nearly killing him and Anna. He remembered his relief as they clutched each other, hearts pounding at the end of the ordeal. He could feel her warmth and the pounding of her heart against his...

Oh, God! Somehow, this *was* all his fault, not Daniel's! If only Daniel had stayed back in Kalamazoo like he was supposed to!

Lockett looked into the distance with a blank look on his face.

The cosmic scales of justice were seeking to right themselves!

"What are we going to do, James?" McManus said, not bothering with the honorific.

There was no answer.

McManus laid a brotherly hand on Lockett's shoulder. "What are we going to do?"

The touch snapped Lockett from his swirling thoughts. "Do? Why, I'm going to go get him back. He shouldn't pay for my mistakes."

McManus and Bosworth looked at each other, unsure what mistakes their lieutenant could possibly have made or be referring to.

Lockett turned to the gambler. "I'll deal with you later, Private Vaught." He paused and looked at the man's battered face, wondering if there was anything that he could do that would have more effect than the communal justice which had already been done. He put the thought from his mind for now. He needed to concentrate on Daniel. He needed a plan of some sort. "I need to go see the Provosts now."

Daniel awoke in a puddle of water and mud. He was wet. His head throbbed. The stench of decaying mud and excrement filled the tiny cellar room where he found himself. A crease of light from a window high above illuminated the decaying brick work and dirt floor. By instinct, his eyes drifted to his feet and the glow of two eyes. With a start, he saw a rat that stared at him, as if waiting for him to die.

He kicked a foot and sent the rat retreating to a darkened recess.

His head pounded. Futilely, he tried to think. Where was he? What happened?

But then his body jerked as he remembered the last moments. The blonde, the pool of blood, the lifeless blue-eyed stare that seemed to focus straight on him...

Last night came back to him. He wretched, rolled to a side, and added to the foul smells of the room.

He was in a jail cell, he realized!

Good God! What had happened?

With long, quick strides, Lockett reached the small hill in Nashville that was capped by the impressive white steps and Greek pillars of the capital building. Below him, at the base of the steps, he could see the two cannon with two guards and their shiny, bayonet tipped rifles across their shoulders, stoically at attention. Further down the hill, there was a cluster of white tents and the rest of the city.

The cannon sat peacefully enough at the bottom of the capital steps, but the message was clear as they pointed out across the divided city. The Union Army was in control here, and there was to be no forgetting that. The Parrot rifled artillery was not aimed at anything in particular, not at the stately homes near the capitol, nor the church steeples just beyond, nor even the warehouses beyond that. But the message was clear, all were within the reach of the Union Army.

Below the capitol hill, the third stately house in, the one with the white picket fence was how it had been described to Lockett, was the Provost headquarters. It was a large and particularly well-adorned structure, brick with shining whitewash on the window sashes and shutters.

Lockett swung open the trim little gate and headed to the front door, which was guarded by another blue coated soldier carrying a bayonet tipped rifle.

The guard noted the Lieutenant's uniform and saluted Lockett.

"This Colonel Truesdail's headquarters?"

"Now that we tossed out the Secesh family that refused to take the oath of allegiance, yes."

"I have business with Colonel Truesdail," Lockett said.

The guard looked doubtfully at the tall, youthful looking officer. He was not the type who normally 'did business' with the Colonel, the guard thought to himself. But the man was an officer...

"His office is up the stairs."

Entering the house, Lockett noted the polished wood railings and expensive looking wallpaper as he took the steps two at a time. At the top of the staircase, there were a number of closed doors and a solitary open one. He selected the open door and saw a man behind a desk stacked high with paper. Behind the man was another closed door and from beyond, Lockett could hear the sound of angry voices.

The man behind the overloaded desk looked up when Lockett's frame blocked the sunlight that had been streaming through the rose glass window behind the stairs. He was a small man with pinched, suspicious, ferret-like features. He was clearly surprised to see someone admitted to the house.

"Who are you?" he snapped at Lockett.

Before Lockett could answer, the voices behind the closed door reached a new crescendo. "This is blackmail, damn you!" one of the voices clearly said.

It was answered with a softer voice, whose words could not be made out through the closed door.

"Well," the ferret-faced man demanded of Lockett, "State your business."

"One of our men was arrested for breaking curfew last night. I'm here to retrieve him so that our Colonel can properly punish him."

"Another scofflaw, eh? Plenty of those to go around these days."

Lockett nodded in agreement and that seemed to put the ferret more at ease.

"Last night you say? That is quick work that you are already here to retrieve him, but you see it is the Colonel's policy that each of those serve a punishment duty here first. Then they will be turned over to their regiments for additional punishments."

"He will be punished, I can assure you," Lockett answered.

"No doubt, Lieutenant, but the Colonel's rules are his rules."

Lockett paused, contemplating his next move and why he was even here in the first place. He had not really developed any plan on his way here. It was more of an impulse that he needed to get Daniel released. Colonel Blair did not even know about it yet.

Before the conversation could continue, the door to the inner office opened and a sharply dressed, but red-faced, civilian exited. He glared at the ferret and stormed out. Lockett stepped aside so that the man could leave and did not even receive a glance in return.

The ferret ignored the civilian and kept his attention on Lockett. "Of course, for a certain donation to the widows and orphans fund, the Colonel has been known to release a scofflaw."

Lockett doubted any monies ever went to the widows or the orphans. The only question in his mind was whether it was the Colonel or the ferret faced man pocketing the bribe.

"Orphans fund," Lockett said slowly, "Sounds like a worthy cause..."

"Very worthy," the ferret smiled crookedly.

"I'm sure that can be arranged."

"Capital," the ferret said, taking a ledger from the top stack of papers. "Now, what did you say this scofflaw's name was? And you did say last night?" He flipped the pages to the most recent entries. He squinted to assist his weakened eyesight, and his face hovered just above the page.

"Private Daniel Lockett."

The name made the ferret's face jerk up from the page. "Lockett, you say?"

"That's right."

"Well, then there has been some mistake. That's the name that the man in city jail gave this morning... And he was not arrested for breaking curfew. He was arrested as a traitor. He's a spy."

"Impossible," Lockett answered. "There has been some mistake alright. It is not possible that he is a spy."

"No, I remember the name quite clearly. He's the spy alright. No 'donations' can get *him* released."

"I'm telling you that it is not possible for him to be a spy. Where is he? I insist that you let me see him. This can be cleared up very easily."

"Insist do you?" came a dark voice from the open door to the inner office. A colonel with a heavy brow and thick moustache stared at Lockett with spiteful eyes. "In my day, lieutenants never insisted on anything, much less demanded to see a traitor."

"Colonel Truesdail," Lockett presumed with an even tone, "I believe that there has been some misunderstanding. One of our privates broke curfew last night. He's guilty of being a fool, no doubt, but I can assure you that he is not a traitor."

"You can, can you?" Truesdail said haughtily. "Well, I can assure *you* that he is a traitor, and that he will be hung like one."

The words struck Lockett like a slap in the face, and he noticeably flinched.

"Yes, hung like all traitors," Truesdail said, drawing out the last word and taking pleasure in the lieutenant's reaction.

"Hung? I'm sure that when the facts are made clear in his trial, then it will all be obvious that it was some sort of misunderstanding." But even as he was saying it, Lockett did not believe his own words. Against his wishes, he thought about Missouri and the death of little Amelia. Somehow, he doubted a trial there would have resulted in clarity to what had transpired or any justice. A trial there would have resulted in his hanging, and nothing for Orrin Long or his men.

"It will be a quick trial," Truesdail gave a snort. "Two of my best men are eyewitnesses."

"Eyewitnesses? To what?"

"The traitor attempted to help the Rebel spy escape by assaulting one of my men."

"What?" Lockett said, truly surprised.

"If it weren't for my Lieutenant's quick reaction, who knows what would have happened. That Rebel spy might have escaped, or maybe she might have a killed one of my men."

"She?"

"Yes, she," he sneered, "Women can be spies too... We knew that this whorehouse was a den of Secesh sympathy and even spying for Jeff Davis. What we didn't know was how successful they were. The paper that we took from the traitor after we arrested him was very detailed, a surfeit of information on our strengths and dispositions that General Bragg would no doubt like to have."

Lockett looked blankly at the colonel. None of this made any sense to him. Finally, he said, "Paper? You took information from him? From the private? What about the whore, sir? Did she say he was a spy?"

Truesdail snorted. "As if I would believe a word, a single solitary word, from a whore and spy, but no... She's dead, killed before she could kill my men. She'll not be able to alibi any friends or cohorts again." He snorted again with pleasure.

Lockett looked away. None of this made any sense to him... It sounded bad, far worse than he expected. He needed to talk to Daniel.

"Can I talk to him?"

"The traitor? Whatever for?"

"I'd like to hear his side of the story," Lockett said before thinking.

Truesdail's features darkened even more. "There is no other side," he menaced. "I've already told you the bare and ugly truth! You watch yourself, Lieutenant. I'll not stand in my own office have my veracity impugned!" He glared at Lockett.

"Not my intent, sir. I apologize," Lockett said stiffly. "I just want to understand what is clearly some sort of misunderstanding."

"There is no misunderstanding, Lieutenant. Your man was caught red-handed with the damning evidence. The Judas will hang like all Judases."

Truesdail turned to his ferret faced assistant. "Fetch Sergeant Greene. Time to officially inform this regiment's commanding officer of the filth that has been hiding amongst them."

Daniel stood wearily and half-heartedly explored the dim, ten by ten foot room. His head was exploding with the worst headache of his life. It was impossible for him to tell if it was due to the blow that he took or just from the drink. He had been hung over after a night in Cincinnati with Vaught, but this was something completely different.

His stomach roiled again, and he thought that he would vomit yet again, but there was nothing left, just misery.

He wanted to believe that this was a dream, but one couldn't smell in a dream, right? And this room smelled worse than any place he had ever been. He judged that this could not be dream, but he prayed that he was wrong.

What exactly had happened last night? Why was he here?

He had tried to help the beautiful blonde, and then…

He was in jail, but why?

She was dead. Those horrible images were burned into his memory, but little else about the night was. She was dead, and he was in jail. Why?

In his fog, he did not remember the accusations of Rebel spies, and even if he had, it would not have occurred to him that such was the reason that he was here now.

"You keep Colonel Truesdail waiting, and it will be both of our hides," the sergeant growled. "I need to deliver this and return immediately." Despite the fact that he was addressing an officer, the sergeant clearly felt no fear for insubordination. The provosts were a power unto their own.

Lockett frowned at the short, swarthy sergeant with the fresh twin gouges below his eye. Even before being addressed with the lack of respect due an officer, Lockett already felt a natural hostility towards the man. There was something about those in the provost. They projected an air of superiority that grated on all other soldiers.

They stopped as a stagecoach sped recklessly by, leaving a cloud of choking dust all the way down the dirt road. The haste of the stage struck Lockett as an interesting contrast to the otherwise leisurely pace that the army displayed in town. Anything unusual about it was lost on the sergeant though, who continued to grouse about lack of sleep and why it was necessary for him to deliver the message.

"Ought to bring my irons with me," he continued to grumble. "Where there is one vermin, there are always more. Likely, a number of this regiment ought to be arrested."

Lockett glared icily at the man but to no effect.

"Scum, that's what's they is. Ought to lock 'em all up so that we win this war. Win this war, and I can go home, back to my life."

"Do tell," Lockett snapped, "You had a prosperous life before this? Never knew that mucking horse stalls was such a rewarding profession."

"I was a man of the law," the sergeant glowered at the tall lieutenant.

Lockett was in an increasingly foul mood though. "I would have thought that your ability to take bribes would have been better here, as a provost with a war on."

The stocky sergeant balled his fists and jutted his jaw forward. "You got something to say, boyo!"

"I think I've already said it."

"If you wasn't an officer, I'd beat you to an inch of your life."

"Based on those gouges on your cheek, my guess is that you have had more practice beating women."

The sergeant's face turned purple, and his left eye twitched in seething anger. "And that whore Rebel got what was coming to her!"

Lockett took a step back and tilted his head as he looked over the sergeant. "You're saying that you were attacked by this Rebel spy last night? You were there?"

Before he could answer, a call came from across the way. "Halloo there!"

Lockett turned to see two men. One was a short, stocky man with flaming red hair poking out from all angles beneath a dusty derby hat. He was dressed in a civilian suit and carried a small bag in one hand and a slender cane in the other, although he did not appear to have need for the latter. He was accompanied by a tall, statuesque man who towered over his companion. The taller man had brilliant blue eyes and a husky, oddly tanned face with refined features. He too wore a tidy derby hat, but it sat atop a completely shaved head.

"Lieutenant," the red-haired man said, addressing Lockett. "Perhaps you can help us. Just arrived via stage from Chicago and am looking for the way to General Rosecrans's headquarters."

"We ain't headed that way," the sergeant snapped. He spat a stream of tobacco juice perilously close to the newcomer's leather shoes.

The newcomer looked curiously at Lockett, clearly surprised that the sergeant had answered instead of the officer.

"Now, ifs you would get outta my way, I have official provost business to take care of," the sergeant added.

"A provost, is it?" the red-haired man said appreciatively. "Well, we certainly don't want to detain you. What about you, Lieutenant? Are you a provost also? Can you point us in the general direction of General Rosecrans headquarters before you depart?"

"I'm not with the provost," Lockett explained, "And headquarters is mostly down the same road that we are heading. You can follow us, and when we get to that point, I'll send you in the right direction."

"Obliged," the red-haired man said, tipping his derby hat.

"Suit yerself," the sergeant grunted. "Let's go," he added, addressing Lockett.

The four continued down the street with the red-haired

newcomer joining Lockett at his shoulder.

"So what might you have done, Lieutenant," the talkative newcomer started, "Such that the provost is keeping close eye on you."

"Apparently something," Lockett answered slowly.

"You don't seem to be under arrest. Where I come from, we put irons on those fellows."

"I'm not under arrest. Colonel Truesdail, in command of the provost, wants the sergeant to deliver a message to my Colonel."

"You can't deliver it for him?"

"Apparently not," Lockett said with a shrug.

"And what is his story?" the sergeant interrupted with an annoyed tone, pointing at the bald companion. "He mute or something? He ain't said one word." The sergeant laughed, as if he had just made some joke.

"I parse my words with care," the bald man answered with a surprisingly educated elocution and a deep bass voice.

Taken aback for two seconds, there was silence before the sergeant grumbled, "Ain't that a trick. I didn't know I was with the King of England."

As they continued down the street, a muffled cry reached their ears, although Lockett could not make it out exactly. When they reached the edge of an alley entrance way, there was the sound of scuffle, and another cry, this one of pain.

Looking into the alley, Lockett saw two men beating a man on the ground. A third assailant stood idly by, holding a bottle by the neck in one hand while he picked a couple of coins and greenbacks off the ground.

"Hey!" Lockett yelled at the men. One of the two men kicking the man on the ground, paused, looked at Lockett for a second, and then resumed his kicking. The victim struggled to get to all fours, but another kick sent him flat on the ground. He was clearly in a bad way. His arms splayed against the ground, and he stopped trying to protect himself.

Despite the clear submission, the beating continued.

"Aren't you going to do something?" Lockett demanded of the sergeant, pointing at the rifle that the man carried. "You're a provost."

"Ain't my problem," he said, spitting another stream of tobacco juice. "'Sides, he's probably just another escaped slave trying to steal their money."

But Lockett did not hear him.

"Damn it all," Lockett muttered as he took off down the alley.

"Hey, stop!" the sergeant sputtered, surprised at Lockett's reaction.

Lockett ignored the cry and sprinted towards the fray.

"I said, stop!" the sergeant added in a bewildered tone. He took a step and then stopped with a shrug. "He ends up dead before I get my message to his colonel, then someone ain't gonna be happy, but it ain't gonna be me."

Unaware as to what was happening behind him, Lockett ran towards the two men kicking the man on the ground. Only at the last second did one of them realize that someone was hurtling towards them.

In a flying leap, Lockett crashed into the two men. One managed to dodge most of the blow, but the other was taken totally by surprise, and the collision drove him three feet backwards. He crashed to the ground with Lockett landing heavily on top of him. Lockett could hear the wind rush out of the man and then the painful rasping of the man's empty lungs.

The second man rose unsteadily to his feet, but it was the bottle-wielding third man who reached Lockett first. He swung his bottle in a wide arc at Lockett's head, but Lockett was already rolling to his feet and saw it coming. He ducked beneath bottle.

Balanced on all fours now, Lockett sprung backward like a cat as the man tried to backhand him this time with the bottle. It whizzed inches short of Lockett's face. Taking advantage of the man being off-balance now, Lockett stepped forward and fired a hard right-cross at the man's jaw. It connected solidly and sent the man staggering back.

Lockett was already turning to locate the last man when he saw a metallic glint from the corner of his eye. But before he could do anything, there was the sharp pop of a revolver and a cry of pain. As Lockett finished turning around, he saw the last man grabbing at his forearm with blood seeping between the man's fingers. A long knife lay forlornly at his feet.

"Be gone, or I shall aim at your head next," ordered a deep voice from the front of the alley. In his hands, the tall bald man held two revolvers, one trickling smoke.

Without another word, the bottle wielder gathered himself and his two cohorts, and they shuffled quickly out the front of the alley as the sergeant and the newcomers stood back.

Lockett looked at the black man on the ground. He was already trying to struggle to all fours. Lockett put a hand out and helped him to his feet. From the man's grip, Lockett could tell that the man would recover regardless of the signs of battery on his face. "Thanks, suh," he mumbled, rubbing his jaw.

Before Lockett could answer, the sergeant came up indignantly. "What the hell was that! Damn fool!"

Lockett ignored him and looked at the two newcomers behind the sergeant. The red-haired man was staring at Lockett with a strange bemused, knowing look. His larger friend just stared impassively.

"Thanks," Lockett said, "You're a good shot," he said to the taller one. "James Lockett." He offered a hand to the towering bald man.

"Octavius Matson," the bass voice rumbled. He reached out, and Lockett found his hand disappearing into a massive palm and iron grip.

The battered victim gathered up the coins from the ground and silently slipped out the back of the alley without a word.

"Who are you two?" Lockett asked, shaking the red-haired man's hand now.

"Pinkertons," answered the red-haired man.

"What?" Lockett said quizzically. "What's a Pinkerton?"

The red-haired man chuckled, "Maybe you'll find out." He looked at his companion, who gave no reaction. "Bobby MacDonald, at your service, Lieutenant Lockett."

* * *

Another gust of frigid wind warped itself through the tiny window at the top of the cell. Night had fallen, and the temperatures had quickly followed suit. Daniel huddled in a ball in the one corner of the cell that was dry. He sat like a small child with his knees tucked up under chin, and his arms wrapped around his shins.

He shivered and tried not to cry aloud, even though he knew the cold tears were sliding down his face. He knew now why he was here, and it seemed that he would be here forever, or at least until they hung him. The guard, who had earlier brought him a scrap of weevil infested bread and water that smelled of piss, had taunted him with the news that as a spy and traitor, he was sure to be hung by the end the week.

When Daniel had protested that he was no such thing, the guard had only laughed and informed him that there were two eyewitnesses, provosts no less! He was sure to hang!

So in the dark, the tears fell silently down Daniel's face. He had left the farm to follow his dreams. And now? Now, he was going to die! It was so unfair! It had gone so terribly wrong!

Chapter 20

It was first thing in the morning, and Lockett paused in front of the three story wood framed hotel. The Pinkerton men obviously did not spend much money on their lodging. Weather-dulled, faded, and mud-splattered, the hotel was going through a new life. The faded paint that had read "General Store" was still faintly visible beneath the only thing new about the place, which was the freshly painted "Hotel".

If Lockett was honest with himself, he wasn't quite sure what he could accomplish here.

One day ago, he had never heard of the Pinkertons. Even now, he had only a faint idea of what a detective did, but in his desperation, he was not sure where else to turn. Daniel was now a short trip away from the gallows, and he knew that his younger brother, while foolish and impetuous, was no Rebel spy.

Lockett also knew that no amount of words or pleading were changing the outcome, but perhaps some proof could? Daniel was an innocent by-stander. He had to be! Now, he just needed the Pinktertons to prove it.

The front desk, which also served as a bar in the converted store, already had a handful of customers even though it was early in the morning. Behind the bar, there was a wizened old man and a rather large, even intimidating woman. "What'll it be, soldier?" the old man said.

"I'm looking for Bobby MacDonald and Octavius Matson."

"Upstairs, second door on the right."

As Lockett looked in that direction, it just so happened that Matson was leaving the room.

"Lieutenant? Surprised to see you here," the curious looking bald man greeted him without a smile at the bottom of the steps.

"I'm here to see you and MacDonald."

"Bobby is already off and about. The early bird gets the worm, need to join him myself." He popped his trim little derby hat onto his domed head. "Welcome to walk with me, Lieutenant, but I can't keep the colonel waiting."

"Of course."

Which colonel of the many colonels in Nashville, Lockett did not know or care, but he quickly fell in step. While they walked, Lockett related his brother's predicament, repeating more than once of the certain innocence. Matson said nothing throughout, nodding occasionally to show that he was listening, but never interrupting him.

They passed outside of the city and into what Lockett knew to be General Sheridan's encampment. The white tents sprinkled the fields around a small crossroads. At the cross roads about 100 yards away, there were two small buildings.

Finally, Matson stopped his brisk walk and came to a dead stop. Turning, he looked serious-eyed at Lockett. "And you are telling me all this because?"

"Because the Pinkertons are detectives," Lockett answered with a sinking feeling, "And I thought that you might be able to prove Daniel's innocence."

Grimly, Octavius Matson looked at Lockett. "It is true that the Pinkertons are detectives, and maybe we could prove your brother was not involved, but we don't work for the sake of the truth. It is a business. I don't know what you could offer for compensation, and even if you could afford us, we are already fully engaged by the U.S. Army."

Feeling himself tense, Lockett answered, "I don't have much that is true, but nothing is more important to me. They'll be hanging him next week, and I won't let that happen. I can't."

There was an edge in his voice as he said it, and Matson took off his little derby. He looked down and studied the hat for a long pause before answering. Finally, he replaced the hat back on his head. "Very well. I believe that you would do about anything for this brother of yours." But before Lockett's hopes could rise fully, he added, "But I am in no position to truly help."

Sadly, Lockett was about to bid him good-bye when the Pinkterton added, "But I think perhaps there is something that you can do. That is, if you truly feel the way that you just said."

"I do…" Lockett added, but he was quickly interrupted by Matson's waving hand and sharp tone.

"Don't be so quick to say so," he warned, "You haven't heard what would be asked of you yet. There is a man in that little house who may be able to help, but I warn you, it will not be such a good deal. Most men… most wise men would say 'no' with all alacrity to what will be asked."

Lockett looked at the building, "Who is he?"

"That is the headquarters for Colonel Wilks. Know him?"

Lockett shook his head.

"Reports to General Rosecrans himself. Wilks is his head of intelligence."

Lockett nodded slowly.

"He's the boss, of sorts, at least for right now… And he has a problem that I wasn't sure that anyone could help him with, that is up until a few minutes ago. But I do warn you, my young lieutenant, go in with your eyes open and be sure that you know this, you see, what he wants won't be a normal task."

"What does he want?"

"I am sworn to secrecy so I cannot tell you, but it will be a hard bargain."

"To get Daniel spared from the gallows, I would do most anything."

"Do you know much about bargaining, Lieutenant?"

Lockett shrugged. "I'm a farmer, not a banker."

"Then know this about bargaining, he who wants something so badly will usually strike a poor bargain."

Lockett looked seriously at the detective. "You know how badly I want it, but the Colonel will not. I ask you to keep it to yourself."

The Pinkerton nodded assent and added a cautious hint. "Lieutenant, you won't be the only one who wants something badly."

"Then let's go see Colonel Wilks," Lockett said with determination.

"Before we do that, there's more that I think I should know about you, so let's stand here and talk for a bit."

* * *

197

As Lockett and Octavius Matson paused outside the converted headquarters, there was plenty of walking inside the humble frame structure. Tall and thin with a dapper black moustache and goatee, Colonel Emmitt Wilks paced furiously in his office.

"And what do they suppose me to do?"

Though there were two other men in the office, the question went unanswered again.

It was surely the fifth different time in the fifth different way that Colonel Wilks had asked the question, Bobby MacDonald thought to himself as he sat on the rough camp stool. At least this time, the question was more direct, although there still was no obvious answer to it.

Wilks turned to face his new aide who sat with the same attentive, but helpless, look that he had displayed all morning. MacDonald was not sure what to make of this captain. The younger man had a rich reputation, a reputation of someone perfectly deserving of the job, the right hand man of army intelligence chief. But so far, all that MacDonald had seen from the captain was an ability to fawn and watch... Watch, watch, watch, like a predator patiently waiting for something.

Of course, the captain had only been on the job for a week, and given that Colonel Wilks' problem had existed far longer, it was unfair to expect much more from anyone at this point. MacDonald decided that he was being too quick to judge. After all, the young captain was well known for rooting out and killing the Rebel spy who had plagued the army in west Tennessee earlier this year.

"It is really a job for the cavalry," Wilks expounded to his captive audience.

"It is. It truly is," the captain answered. "It is really the cavalry's primary mission."

"But our cavalry is worthless, out-foxed, out-ridden at every turn, and never a daring thought enters their head, not like our enemies unfortunately! Forrest and Hunt Morgan ride circles around us!"

"Literally," the captain added.

"They raid incessantly, behind our lines, even looping around the army."

"Why, even the supply situation is a mess, sir."

"Mess? Yes, yes, of course. At least that one is not my problem. No, my problem is worse. The General expects miracles! Miracles, damn him! At least, General Buell understood that some things were impossible."

MacDonald struggled to remain silent. The constant belly-aching was wearing thin.

"Washington does not help," Wilks continued. "The constant pressure that they put on General Rosecrans for action... Action, action, forward, forward. How easy to say that from Washington!"

Again, MacDonald squirmed uncomfortably on the stool. Of course, Washington wanted action. Of course, they wanted this massive army to move forward. Instead, since bloody Shiloh, there had been little action and rarely going forward. General Halleck dithered in western Tennessee. General Buell had been fired and replaced, and despite his spirited words, General Rosecrans had not moved forward yet either. It would soon be 1863, and at this rate, the war would go on for twenty years.

"Cannot blame General Rosecrans," Wilks said loyally, "No, I cannot. How can a general commit his troops without knowing the enemy's disposition, its strength?"

"A job for the cavalry," the captain agreed.

"But the cavalry is not up to the task. And yet, there is still a way...."

Wilks paused, and the captain finished the thought for him. "A spy right in the midst of the enemy headquarters but with no way to get the information out..."

"No good way," MacDonald corrected, finally adding a spoken word.

"No good way," Colonel Wilks mused, sitting down finally.

"There is the guide, McGowan," the captain answered.

Wilks frowned at the mention of the name and popped back to his feet for more pacing. "Unreliable and untrustworthy... In it only for the money... Good for certain errands, but not this."

"You could send one of your men through the lines to get the information," MacDonald added, knowing that the comment would only draw the colonel's wrath.

"Certain death!" the colonel spat. "I'll not order *another* one of my men to that. Besides, they don't know the country well enough to get there." He glared at MacDonald. "Well, Pinkerton man, what have you to truly add? We pay you well enough. How about if you go?" When that shamed MacDonald into silence, the colonel added, "No, I thought not. Don't know why Washington insists that we pay you. Not brought me one kernel of useful help so far."

It was at that point that Octavius Matson knocked at the outer office door.

"Enter," Wilks barked.

Matson entered the inner office and shut the door.

Wilks gave the tall, bald man a thinly disguised look of disdain.

"The hairless Pinkerton," Wilks grumbled, pacing again. "And what have you to say today?" He sat again. Without even looking at the tall man, he focused instead on the papers on his desk.

"The problem that you mentioned to us last night," Matson began, "I believe I have a possible solution."

That got Wilks' attention. His head snapped up, and he rose to his feet with his hands on his hips.

"A solution you say?" The colonel tried to sound coy but failed. The pressure that General Rosecrans had put on him to provide the numbers and disposition of Bragg's army was too great for that.

"I have a Lieutenant outside. He may be the man for the job."

"To go behind the lines? A local Unionist?" Wilks interrupted.

"No, not a local, Colonel. He would need that guide that you mentioned. But he strikes me as trustworthy and determined."

The colonel rose to his feet and paced behind his desk, shaking his head. "If he needs that McGowan, then trustworthy is only part of the job requirements. He would need..." he paused, choosing his words carefully in front the Pinkertons. "...courage, and large measures of it." The colonel sat again. Truly, the man needed to be as foolhardy as brave, but he did not dare say that aloud.

"This man has it. I understand that he was promoted from the ranks for that very reason."

Bobby MacDonald noticed that his colleague's statement had gotten the young captain's attention for some reason. The captain's eyes widened, and there was a sudden twitch in his face, as if someone had physically poked him.

"From the ranks, you say?" Colonel Wilks thought aloud, rising to his feet again. He tapped a finger against a cheek as he paced. "From the ranks..." he repeated to himself. He needed to demonstrate to the General that at least he *tried* to get the information, and though he would not waste one of his men on such an outrageous task, he was now thoroughly intrigued. "Bring him, Mr. Matson. Let me see for myself if he is... suitable... for the task."

The colonel continued his pacing, but Bobby MacDonald was now studying the captain.

The young officer said nothing, but there was a noticeable change on his face. No longer was there the supercilious fawning of a sycophant; now there was a hint of a grimace and of wheels turning inside his head. Something about what Octavius said is making this man think hard about something, MacDonald deduced. But what? And why?

The wait in the outer room had seemed interminable to Lockett. Though Matson had provided him with some hope, there was still doubt. Could this colonel really help Daniel? And what would he want from him in return?

From the moment that the Pinkerton had entered that inner office, the impotence and inevitably of it all began to creep back into Lockett's mind. Some things were just impossible to stop. He had seen that in the army too many times now: all of endless bloodshed at Shiloh, charge after charge of slaughter, yet knowing all along that they would not be able to hold that line on the sunken road, the dismissal of generals who won battles, the endless marching, the treachery of their own troops in Missouri...

Since he had joined the army, he had learned the hard way that things in life, not just in the army, but in life, moved with a certain inevitability that could not be avoided. It was like a terrible flood. Some events moved, washing aside all in their path. It was a foregone outcome, and no single person could prevent or even slow it.

In Missouri, he had seen Orrin Long's treachery coming, and in trying to stop it... well, nothing good had come of it. The girl had been killed; Lockett had been dismissed from the sharpshooters, and he was now forever branded, at least by some.

It all seemed so pointless. The longer he sat there, the more he wondered why he was even here. There was no way to stop the inevitable. And he had been foolish to seek out the Pinkertons in some futile hope at a miracle.

He had lost. Lost again. Like in Missouri. Like in Savannah. Savannah...

Anna was gone now too. That inevitability stung most of all, but to add insult to injury, his actions ultimately allowed Orrin Long to be given the distinction and laurels for having killed "the Rebel spy".

Pointless! Even knowing the truth of how it all transpired was no solace to Lockett.

The only good thing about that whole fiasco was that he had met Anna, but now she was gone to God knows where.

And then there was Daniel... Daniel was to be hung. There was no stopping it. The provosts had witnesses. Themselves!

And his brother had been his whole reason for joining the army in the first place, Lockett lamented. Now that too was foiled, squashed, defeated. What a fool he was!

"Lieutenant?"

Octavius Matson had exited the inner office without him even noticing.

"Lieutenant?" he repeated, "You all right?"

"Yes," Lockett answered. He physically shook himself and tried to hide the bitterness from his voice.

"Well, the Colonel will see you now. Good luck," he added in a barely audible whisper.

Lockett followed him into the inner office but stopped dead in his tracks just one step inside the door.

He was oblivious to the colonel seated behind the desk and to Bobby MacDonald on a stool in the corner. What he did see was the captain standing across the room from him, smooth cheeked, dapper moustache, combed and perfumed hair, and most of all, the knowing, reptilian smile.

Chapter 21

Orrin Long!

The rage seethed inside Lockett immediately and swelled by the second.

Captain Orrin Long looked back at him. His small, evil smile worked the corners of his mouth.

Lockett fought with all of his strength to turn his gaze away from his enemy and towards the colonel. "Colonel, sir," he said, although his mind was still locked in hateful remembrances of Orrin Long.

The cold sweat and miserable impotence that he had felt seconds ago had been instantly replaced. He could feel his heart pounding with anger. Fortunately, the inscrutable gray-eyed shield fell across his face to hide his thoughts.

Lockett brought himself to full attention. He focused squarely on Colonel Wilks, unaware that he had piqued a new level of curiosity in Bobby MacDonald, who from his corner stool had seen the flickering flash in Lockett's eyes.

"Lieutenant, Mr. Matson tells me that you might be the man for the job. A special job."

Colonel Wilks eyed Lockett carefully.

The intelligence chief saw a tall, wiry man with a gentle face who looked as if he was aging prematurely. To the colonel, Lockett looked, well, like any of ten thousand other men in the army. "So are you the man for the job?" He sounded skeptical and hopeful at the same time.

"Possibly. I'm not sure what this job is, but we may be able to make a deal."

"Deal?" Wilks said with surprise. "You said nothing of a deal, Matson?"

"A small matter, Colonel," Matson answered pleasantly,

"Nothing too difficult for a man of your well-deserved stature."

"You are not a volunteer for this job?" Wilks asked Lockett pointedly.

"I have been in the army for some time now, Colonel," Lockett answered evenly, "I would need to know what I am volunteering for *before* I volunteer."

The statement brought a frown to Wilks' face, and he rose to his feet. Across the room, Bobby MacDonald watched with interest.

"You serve your country? You serve the Union? Then you volunteer!" Wilks glared at Lockett, but the placid gray eyes of the lieutenant merely stared steadily back at him.

"I serve , sir... And I follow orders. Is this an order?"

Wilks turned away with a clenched jaw, knowing very well that he could not order a soldier outside of his own to do such a task.

"I need to know the job before accepting, sir... accepting a *deal*."

"Impossible! The matter is secret. If I was to tell you, and you said no? Impossible!"

The meeting seemed to be heading towards an abrupt and unsatisfactory end, when Orrin Long surprisingly interrupted.

"Colonel, a word with you in private, if I may?"

Wilks frowned and then nodded. Obediently, Lockett and the two Pinkerton men stepped into the outer office. It was near five minutes later when Orrin Long beckoned them back into the inner office.

The Pinkertons focused on Colonel Wilks behind his desk, but Lockett kept his eyes on Orrin Long. There was a pleased look on his face and that only increased Lockett's suspicions. Orrin Long was no peacemaker. He knew all too well that if Orrin was involved, it was for his own purposes and nothing else!

While they had waited outside, Lockett had tried to coax something out of the Pinkertons. What was this all about?

But whatever their roles or thoughts were, neither Pinkerton would compromise the apparent need for secrecy. Lockett thought that was a good thing on one hand, but he still felt disadvantaged to be the only one in the room who did not know what was going on.

Within the inner office, Orrin Long had taken his time convincing the colonel that they should hear Lockett out.

It was not for any reward nor good feelings towards Lockett nor for the benefit of the army. Quite the opposite...

The concept had sprung into Orrin Long's mind in a devious instant.

Having failed before to dispose of James Lockett, Orrin Long knew this was a golden opportunity. If this guide, McGowan, was as unreliable as everyone seemed to think, then the odds of success for anyone were almost non-existent.

Capture or death seemed inevitable for any fool on this errand.

As for convincing Colonel Wilks, the man was in a difficult spot, Orrin Long knew. Colonel Wilks needed to demonstrate some action to General Rosecrans, but Wilks did not view any of his own men as expendable. However, as Orrin Long had reminded his superior, this was a prime opportunity. Who could possibly be more expendable? The man had been a private mere months ago. As if reading the colonel's mind, Long concluded his argument that the army had thousands like Lockett. Why not see what this deal was that Lockett wanted? Lockett could be the solution to all of Colonel Wilks's headaches. At least this way, the colonel could demonstrate to General Rosecrans that he was trying to get the information.

Orrin Long tried not to laugh in delight as he ushered Lockett and the two Pinkertons back into the room.

"Very well, Lieutenant Lockett," Colonel Wilks started, "Captain Long has vouched for you as a man capable of doing this job. So tell me what you want from this 'deal'. If I think that it is something reasonable, then I will share the mission with you."

Lockett nodded. "My brother, Daniel, has been wrongfully arrested by Colonel Truesdail and charged with aiding the Rebels. My brother's only crime is being a green recruit who just arrived and entered a whorehouse at the wrong time. Nothing more. Colonel Truesdail has plans to hang him next week. I want him freed; he's just a dumb soldier."

Wilks frowned at the mention of Truesdail and tapped his fingers on the desk. The head of the provost guard? The wise soldiers were the ones who steered clear of Colonel Truesdail.

Wilks was unsure how to answer the request when Lockett

continued.

"And there is one other thing. Whatever this is that you need done, it must be difficult. I want a promotion to Captain made immediate upon completing it."

Instantly, Lockett noticed two things. Colonel Wilks nodded to the second request without a second thought, and from the corner of his eye, Lockett saw a stiffening in Orrin Long's body language. There was a brief silence, and Lockett focused on Colonel Wilks' face.

He could see the conflict on it. The man wanted Lockett badly but seemed hesitant to agree, particularly on the first part of the bargain. Sensing an advantage, Lockett pushed.

"Those are my terms, Colonel. If you cannot meet them, then don't bother telling me anything." It was said with a steely, almost demanding, demeanor that caught everyone off guard. There was a slight nod of appreciation from Matson.

Colonel Wilks reddened and tapped his fingers on the desk again.

In the silence that followed, Lockett thought that he had pushed too hard. Finally, Wilks stopped his finger tapping and said, "I will talk to Truesdail." He said it grudgingly and rose to his feet to resume his pacing.

"To be clear, sir, talking will not be enough. You must *guarantee* his freedom to me."

Wilks was not sure that he could guarantee that, but he was desperate and nodded his head.

"And the other part, sir?"

"The captaincy? Yes, of course, if you succeed, the General will be only too happy to grant you that." He did not add the silent thought that immediately came to mind - there were always plenty of captaincies that needed filling after a major battle.

"Well, then" Octavius Matson said, "All that remains is to tell him the mission."

"Undeniably," Wilks grunted, "Undeniably. Well, Lieutenant, what I tell you cannot leave this room, particularly for your own safety. But we require some information, information that awaits us in Murfreesboro. There is information there on General Bragg's plans."

"A spy?" Lockett said aloud, keeping the word 'again' to

himself.

"Undeniably, a spy. While I have my own famous spy catcher here in Captain Long, I have no good way of retrieving information from our own spy behind enemy lines."

Lockett fought the urge to laugh at mention of Orrin Long, spy hunter. If only they knew the truth, he laughed inwardly. Although if they knew the truth about Lockett's own actions, then they would not think him a good candidate for this job, seeing as how it was his secret actions that saved a Rebel spy back in Savannah.

"You want me to go to Murfreesboro?"

"Yes. Of course, we will provide you with a guide."

"If you have a guide, why do you need me? Why not just let him get it for you?"

Wilks shifted uncomfortably from one foot to the other. "McGowan?"

In the following pause, it was Bobby MacDonald who spoke up. "McGowan is a snake, Lockett. Wouldn't trust him further than I can throw him. He'll do this for the money, but nothing else. And if someone else pays him more..."

Wilks glared at the Pinkerton, but MacDonald only shrugged. "It's fair to let a man know what he is getting into. Our young lieutenant will be treated as a spy, not a soldier, if he's caught. Course, a quick hangin' might be the better of two options, considering what I have heard about the conditions in Confederate prison camps."

"It's a tall order," Lockett remarked. "You want me to go to Bragg's headquarters and back... with a guide of questionable loyalties? That's tall."

"Mighty tall," MacDonald murmured softly.

"Do we have a deal or not?" Wilks snapped. "It's no easy task to talk to Truesdail either. No doubt, I will need the General himself to sign off on it."

"You put it in writing, and we have a deal."

"In writing!" Wilks exploded. "My word is good as gold. How dare you!"

"I'm sure that the Lieutenant was not insinuating anything," MacDonald said smoothly, "But it is a war. Tomorrow is not guaranteed for anyone. By the time he returns, you may be a general assigned elsewhere."

"I want it in writing, sir," Lockett said without emotion. "I go, and Daniel goes free. I make it back, and I'm a captain. Fair?"

Wilks's face wrinkled into a scowl. He was over a barrel, and the tall lieutenant knew it.

"Very well, Lieutenant. Have it your way, though you have nothing to fear from me."

"Of course not, sir," Lockett answered, his eyes straying to Orrin Long.

"I will write your bargain for you. Then you will wait, while I have General Rosecrans himself sign orders for you to hand to your commander, detaching your services to me for the near future."

An hour later, Lockett departed with papers in hand. Bobby MacDonald and Octavius Matson joined him in quick lockstep as he made his way back to camp.

"I'm not sure that you know what you've done, Lieutenant, but I guess you got what you wanted," MacDonald said.

"It was the only way left to me."

"Never met this brother of yours, but I will now. We'll make sure that Colonel Wilks holds up his end of the bargain, though Truesdail's got some mighty fine pull around these parts."

"Appreciate whatever you can do," Lockett said simply, without breaking stride.

"Fool thing this, though. You got more guts than I do, or a death wish. Or both." He added the last bit with a chuckle but kept a trained eye on Lockett, testing if the words had any effect. "Humphh," he decided. "Thought I sensed a bit of the latter."

"Do you want something, MacDonald? Are you trying to talk me out of this, because it is a bit too late for that now?"

"No, no," MacDonald hastened, "Just trying to understand."

"Understand? Why?"

"Just my nature, you see. Curiosity. My mother always said it would be the death of me, always curious about things. Course, Mr. Pinkerton finds this a fine skill in one of his detectives. But I am curious. Curious about all this and what happened in there. That second part of your bargain was not planned, now was it?"

"No," Lockett admitted.

"Thought not. Changed when you came into the room, now didn't it? Something to do with that Captain Long. That's my guess."

Lockett shrugged. He was not sure what to tell the man. He was right, of course. He had not thought of asking for promotion until he had seen that smug face across the room. And he couldn't bear the thought of taking orders from the man again. Would have been better to be a major, he knew, but he did not think that Wilks would have gone that far. In fact, he was surprised that he agreed to the captaincy so easily.

"Whatever your reasons, Lieutenant. Get it done. We need that information. This army is rotting from the inside the longer that it remains inactive here in Nashville. Disease, whores, whiskey, insubordination. It's all there and growing by day."

"You don't need to tell me," Lockett grumbled, "I've seen this army strangled by its own inactivity since Shiloh. At this rate, the war will never end. We should have pushed on after Shiloh. Instead, Halleck crawled towards Corinth, and then we followed Buell back here. The war should have been over by now... before Daniel could have joined. Now? Now, I don't know. Don't know if we can ever win with these generals."

"Don't lose hope, Lieutenant. They ain't all scallywags. There's a few of these generals you can trust."

"Like General Grant? They got rid of him."

"Don't know Grant, but I've met a few others. You meet Sheridan, and you'll change your tune. A live one that one is."

Lockett shrugged. "Maybe so, but he sat on his haunches at Perryville while we took a helluva beating. He's got plenty left to prove to me and the boys, but right now, that does not matter a lick to me."

"True, you have more immediate concerns," Octavius Matson agreed. He put his hand on Lockett's shoulder. "I know Colonel Wilks has you returning here tomorrow morning, but meet with me at the crack of dawn at the hotel. There are some things that I can help with."

Oddly, there was genuine concern on his otherwise stoic face.

Chapter 22

Lieutenant Renaud was with Colonel Blair when Lockett returned to camp.

"Sir," Lockett said respectfully, "I have some orders from the General."

Blair accepted the paper from Lockett and read them. "Lieutenant Renaud," he said with a clenched jaw, "Will you excuse us?"

"Yes, sir," Renaud saluted and left the tent.

After the French Detroiter departed, Blair turned an angry blue-eyed gaze at Lockett. "What is the meaning of this?" he demanded in an ominous voice. He waved the paper in Lockett's face. "You are to be attached to Colonel Wilks' staff until further notice?"

"I am afraid that I am not at liberty to discuss it, sir. Colonel Wilks' orders."

"How do you know Colonel Wilks?"

"I don't, sir, not until today."

"This is about these recent goings-on, isn't it?"

Lockett hesitated, weighing what, if anything, that he could share with his commander. "In a way, sir, yes, it is."

"I know who Wilks is, Lockett. But what he wants with you, I don't want to imagine. It says here that you are attached indefinitely. I can't have that. I have a load of new soldiers and new officers. I need your experience. Do you think these men are ready for another battle? Ready for another Shiloh? Another Perryville? And what of your men? You think Captain Bibb can manage them in the next Shiloh?"

"Bibb has good men in the company. He just needs to rely on them," Lockett replied but only half-truthfully. The weight of Colonel Blair's words went straight to the pit of his stomach.

Patrick, Milton, Prosper, and the rest of them, what would happen to them in battle? He was abandoning them, and for what? Was this really possible? What had he gotten himself into?

"I can spare you for a week, but no more." Colonel Blair folded the written orders purposefully. "I shall talk to Wilks immediately about when you will return to us."

"It won't be a week, sir."

"This is about your brother, isn't it, Lockett?"

"I made a deal with Colonel Wilks, sir."

Blair glared at him. He visibly bit back his immediate response. Then he looked hard at him before answering. "A deal with the devil is more like it."

* * *

- the diary of James Lockett

Patrick took the news as I suspected. Secrecy or not, I told him all. He insisted on coming, but I told him it was impossible. The depth of hurt on his face surprised me, but there was no other way. It could only be this way. He refused to say it aloud, but I know what he was thinking. He thinks that he will not see me again. In the end, he embraced me like the brother he has always been. I will leave the diary and the Stuart family sword with him in the morning. There is so much more to say in my journal, particularly if this is the last entry, but I dare not use the night for it. Rest will be hard to come by in the journey. Tonight, I must sleep.

* * *

Lockett left before morning light without saying farewell to McManus or any of his men. It was easier that way, he told himself.

But the truth was that he could not bear to see the look on McManus's face again, nor did he think that he could refuse him twice in a row, and this was something that he needed to do by himself. He couldn't ask Patrick to throw away his life too.

As Lockett trudged to the Pinkerton's hotel, he found himself regretting that moment of cowardice though. He should have said final farewells to the men who had struggled and followed him so well, but it was too late now.

The sun was still not up when he reached their lodgings. "Didn't change your mind, I see," MacDonald greeted him at the door to his room. "Not that you could at this point." His red hair was plastered to one side of his head as if he had just woken up, but he was bright eyed and eager to usher Lockett into the room.

"No," Lockett admitted, "There is no going back... and no other way."

"Sure hope that brother of yours deserves this second chance. You might have to pay a mighty high price for it. Course, that is why we asked you to come here. I'd rather you didn't have to pay it." He sat himself down at a rickety table in the corner of the room.

Octavius Matson joined him. Reflectively, he sized up Lockett. The large man's quiet gaze was penetrating and unsettling. He was judging Lockett for something, although Lockett wasn't sure what for. He had already taken the mission. What was left?

Matson pulled a chair over and sat backwards over it so that he leaned forward over the flimsy wooden backing, which seemed unlikely to hold together against the weight of his muscular girth. Even in the dim light of the small lamp and candle, Lockett could see that there was something different about Octavius Matson. He wasn't sure if it was the trim brown suit that looked out of place, or maybe it was the freshly shaved bald pate, but there was something odd? Maybe it was just the way that man looked at him, as if he expected something from Lockett.

Whatever it was, Lockett could not quite place it, and MacDonald seemed oblivious to the silent thoughts in the two men's brains. He watched Lockett with a cock-eyed grin and none of his compatriot's stoicism.

"So what am I doing here?" Lockett finally asked the older man.

"Like I was saying, you've put yourself in quite a bind, my young lieutenant. Let's start with your most nettlesome problem."

"Which is what?"

"The colonel is going to tell you about your guide. Can't trust him."

"Which one, the colonel or the guide?" Lockett joked. When

both men looked stone faced at him, he lapsed into silence.

"Let me just say that your guide, this McGowan, is a skunk. Wilks might paint him evenly to you later today, but my advice is to not trust the man, not for one inch."

"Why not? And do I have any choice? I don't know the way to Murfreesboro, much less how to thread the needle between the two armies."

"For starters, McGowan was, or is, a slave hunter. That's how he knows his way through the country. He's no local, but he's been chasing runaways from Alabama to Ohio since you were born."

"His reputation is well-known in these parts and beyond," Octavius Matson interjected gravely. A flicker of a scowl passed across his face. It was one of the few times that Lockett had seen the man permit any emotion on his face, and it only added weight to his words.

"A slavehunter?" he repeated.

The word chilled him. He was no anti-slavery zealot. He had joined the army as a way to prevent Daniel from enlisting, not for the adventure, not for the cause of Union, and not for the cause of abolition, although the latter two were good reasons to take up arms in his mind. It was all about keeping Daniel out of trouble.

But now, a slave hunter? As a partner?

He had seen them before, even in Kalamazoo. With the protection of the Fugitive Slave Act, these coarse men had roamed the country for years, shielded by the law, hunting their human prey. Both fugitive and free black men were at risk of them. There was little to stop the slave hunter other than the subterfuge of a few local citizens.

In Kalamazoo, there were some of these citizens, mostly near Schoolcraft. It was an area that was well known to be part of the Underground Railroad. The slave hunters knew it too and would often come around, but they never came away satisfied.

"I can see by the look on your face that this gives you pause. Good." MacDonald added the last word with pronounced huff.

"Are you an Abolitionist, MacDonald?"

"I do travel with a black man as my partner," he answered with a bemused look.

Lockett blinked in surprise. "Black man? What do you

mean?"

MacDonald chuckled while Matson remained impassive.

"Well, go on, Octavius. He'll keep your secret."

The bright blue eyes looked right through Lockett momentarily. Then with some resignation, Octavius Matson spoke. "It is as Bobby says."

Lockett frowned dubiously at Octavius Matson. There was a husky tone to his skin, he supposed, but...

"My mother was a slave - raped by her master, as was her mother before her. Mine eventually escaped to Chicago, where I was eventually born. Though my skin is unusually light and my eyes blue as the Lake Michigan waters, I found very quickly that I was treated no better. That is, until I shaved the curly hair from my head and went where people did not know me or my mother. Instantly, I was treated with more respect and more opportunity, if only because people mistook me for a white."

"So then you became a Pinkerton?"

"Mr. Pinkerton cares not about the color of my skin. He knows full well who I am, but I have been able to serve the cause better when the world thinks I am a white man... usually."

Lockett looked on dumbly.

"Do you think that Colonel Wilks would have even allowed me into his office if he knew who I was truly?"

"Probably not," Lockett answered. Though there were plenty in the army who supported the cause of abolition that did not mean that even those men always viewed all men equally. Free was one thing to them, equal was another.

"So you work for the Pinkertons, but I still don't understand what that has to do with the Army, not to mention why I am here now? If you just wanted to warn me about this slave hunter, you could have done that before I left later today. Why did I need to come here before the crack of dawn?"

MacDonald paused at the blank look on Lockett's face. "I forgot that you don't seem to know much about the Pinkertons, or our boss Allan Pinkerton."

"No."

"Well, let me just share with you then that Mr. Pinkerton is no friend of the slaver. He managed a depot in Chicago."

"Depot? Like in the Underground Railroad?"

MacDonald nodded.

"I don't understand. Why are you telling me this? I have my hands full as it is. I can't do anything to help the Underground Railroad now."

Chuckling, MacDonald looked over to his partner, who frowned.

"You misunderstand, Lieutenant. We're not asking you to help the railroad. We're suggesting that the railroad may help you."

"Help me?"

"Mercy, Lieutenant. You are starting to make me wonder if we should continue." MacDonald looked over skeptically at his partner.

Octavius Matson nodded slowly.

"War and its strange bedfellows," MacDonald said softly. He pulled on his red whiskers.

"You're not making any sense to me, MacDonald."

"Allow me," Matson said, pulling his chair closer to Lockett. "This is all about McGowan and how we don't trust the man. For your sake, hopefully, McGowan's love of money is great enough that he gets you to Murfreesboro and back... but we doubt it. He gets half of his money now and half when you return. Maybe that is enough of an incentive, but he may just abandon you."

"We think that he'll cut and run when it's convenient for him," MacDonald added, "But this army needs that information to move forward, and we'd like to see you get back alive also."

"So we are about to share another option with you." Matson paused, and his eyes bore into Lockett in the flickering lamp light. "But what we tell you, you must take to the grave with you." He paused to let that sink in. "Those who work the Underground Railroad do so at great peril. Their only defense lies in secrecy and anonymity. Do you understand what I am saying?"

Lockett nodded solemnly. "I do, but why on earth would you be willing to share this with me?"

"We need the information," MacDonald said, "I fear General Rosecrans, like Buell before him, won't advance this army without it."

But it was Matson's answer that resonated. He placed a large, heavy hand on Lockett's shoulder. "My mother escaped by this route, as have countless brothers and sisters in bondage. No one wants that route protected more than me… But it was my suggestion that we share this with you. Why? Because I saw you in that alley. You did not see color. You saw right and wrong."

Lockett blushed and held up a hand. "Mr. Matson…"

"Octavius," he interrupted.

"Octavius," Lockett continued in an embarrassed tone, "In that alley… well, I did not see color because I did not know he was black."

But the answer did not change Octavius Matson's mind. He stood up and retrieved a small leather tube. He handed it to MacDonald who bent over the desk and unrolled a small scroll that was a map of the area, extending from Nashville down to Chattanooga. Rivers, roads, railroad lines, towns, small creeks, fords, paths, tiny crossroads, and woods were covered on the map.

"For me?" Lockett asked.

"For you?" MacDonald laughed, "God, no. But study it now. Commit it to memory. Know where the rail lines are, the rivers, the creeks, everything."

"Commit it to memory right now?" Lockett said, leaning over the map and noticing that there were no other symbols on the map. If this was the Underground Railroad, where were the stops? "Should I be looking for something in particular? Which locations have these depots?"

"Ah, you are a quick one, Lieutenant. That is why I think that you might be able to accomplish more than just killing yourself for Colonel Wilks."

"There are no markings for those," Matson took up for MacDonald, "It would be too risky to put those on a map." He tapped his temple with a forefinger. "The location of the Railroad is up here."

"In your head? What good does that do for me?"

"Well, I'll point to places on the map and tell you what is there. I'm going to tell you where you can go for help."

"You want me to memorize it? All of this? Now? In an hour before we leave for Colonel Wilks?"

"Can't afford to do it any other way," MacDonald explained.

"So listen closely, you don't have much time, and I have much to tell you," Matson added.

"But whatever you do, remember," MacDonald interjected,

"You take this to the grave with you. Don't let McGowan, or anyone else for that matter, know about these places. These are the stops for Mr. Pinkerton's friends, but they'll help if need be."

"My back up escape plan is the Underground Railroad?"

"Yes," MacDonald chuckled.

"I might be the first white man to use it."

"Not the first, Lieutenant."

"Really?" Lockett said with some surprise.

"Some whites have used it to get to Indiana, a few to Ohio too."

"Whites? Why?"

"Quakers, Lieutenant. There are Quakers in the South too, my young friend. When Jefferson Davis instituted a draft, a few of them found it necessary to escape the South rather than serve in the Jeff Davis's army. Some continue to make it out via the same path as the chained man and woman."

"The Underground Railroad," Lockett scratched his head. "Hopefully, it won't come to that."

"Hope ain't a plan, my lad. Now commit it to memory, and we'll tell you what to look for and how to prove yourself to them."

With his finger, Matson traced a line eastward and then northward from Murfreesboro. "So, for example, if you end up on this route, you look for the farm at the south end of the creek, near the bend here. There will be a small gated garden next to the house. If there is a ribbon tied around the gate post, then the stop is open. If not, then it is too dangerous and you will have to move on."

"So what do I do, just knock on the door and tell them that I am a Yankee in need of shelter?"

"Never fear, my lad. Before you leave here, I'll have taught you. Differs for different stops."

"What time is it?" Lockett asked, knowing that he needed to report to Colonel Wilks.

"You have a little over an hour. So there is no time to waste," MacDonald concluded.

Lockett shrugged in resignation and stared intently at the map. The Underground Railroad...

Chapter 23

"There is a stop that we need to make on the way to Colonel Wilks," Octavius Matson had remarked when they had left.

Standing here now, Lockett would never have guessed the nature or significance in Matson's bland comment. Across from him stood two generals, one of whom was the Army's overall commander.

William Rosecrans did not look like a general to Lockett at first glance. He had a friendly face dominated by a long flat nose with a neatly trimmed jaw line beard and moustache. His brown hair was short and well-parted on the side. Yet, he did have a dominating gaze and intelligent eyes as he studied Lockett briefly.

"So this is the man?" he said.

"Lieutenant James Lockett, sir," Lockett replied, giving his best salute.

The other general next to Rosecrans strutted over to Lockett. He was a short man, not even up to Lockett's shoulder, but everything from the man's quick stride to his flashing eyes spoke of unbridled energy.

"I need that information, Lieutenant," General Rosecrans added, "I hope you are up to the task." He turned and looked at General Sheridan.

"I am told that General Grant raised you from the ranks during Shiloh," Sheridan said with a surprisingly deep and resonant voice given his small stature. "Is that true?"

"Yes, sir."

"Then, that is all I need to know," Sheridan opined, "If Sam saw that much in you, then I am sure that you can accomplish this."

Rosecrans nodded thoughtfully. "Very well. Godspeed then, Lieutenant. There is no time to lose." He tilted his head and stroked his bearded jaw. "I must have that information."

* * *

Shortly thereafter, Lockett and the two Pinkerton men found Colonel Wilks, Orrin Long, and another man waiting in the colonel's office. The last was a large, unshaven individual who somehow combined a bear-like stature with a narrow, snake-eyed face. Even though it was early in the morning, he smelled noticeably of drink, horses, and body odor.

"Lieutenant Lockett," Wilks said, "This is your guide, McGowan." He offered no first name, nor any other information. McGowan, for his part, did not rise to greet Lockett and did not even bother to look at him. With uncanny accuracy, he nailed the spittoon in the corner with a voluminous stream of tobacco juice.

"I tolt you," McGowan began, "I don't think any boy lieutenant is up to this task."

"Your job is not to think," Orrin Long snapped before Colonel Wilks could respond, "Leave the thinking to those capable of doing so."

"It is of no consequence to you, McGowan," Colonel Wilks added, "You'll be paid the same whether it is a lieutenant accompanying you or General Rosecrans himself. I hardly see what difference it makes to you. Get him to Murfreesboro and back."

McGowan gnawed on the wad in his grizzled cheek. "Easier said than done, Colonel." The last word was said with more than a little spite and such insubordination that it would have had a regular soldier immediately punished. "This will be a hundred mile journey before we're done, easy. Them two lines are spread out for miles. Going around y'all and then the Rebs, that it'll be days. Ifs either side catches wind of us, we'll likely be kilt."

"You'll not be getting more money," Orrin Long interrupted, "Save your tale of woe."

"Y'all have no idea," he gave a gruesome brown and yellow smile. "Even whens we git around the lines, there be Reb patrols to avoid, plus the town folk themselves. If he ain't up to it, I ain't bringing him back." He thumbed derisively in Lockett's direction.

"You'll find me up to it," Lockett said, speaking for the first time.

"That so? Don't look it to me."

"I made it through Shiloh and the Hornet's Nest. Not many can say that," Lockett replied, staring hard at McGowan.

McGowan snorted. "Ain't no line of battle out there. Ain't no friends either. Jus' enemies and a whole slew of 'em."

The words ominously resonated with Lockett. There would be no Patrick, no Milton, no help of any sort out there. He would be truly on his own, unlike any time before. From the corner of his eye, he saw a sly smile crease Orrin Long's face.

"We're wasting time," Octavius Matson interrupted, bringing Lockett's attention back.

"And who the hell are you?" McGowan demanded, glaring at the Pinkerton with a look of undisguised hate.

"Mr. Matson is correct," Colonel Wilks said, trying to get control back, "This mission is of the utmost importance for the General. I want that information, Lieutenant Lockett."

"Yes, sir."

"I also want that spy protected. So, accordingly, we will use my normal protocols. Neither you nor McGowan will have all of the information required in the event that one of you is captured. We will use the usual pre-arranged signal, McGowan. Once you give that signal in Murfreesboro, then the spy will know you're there. The information will be left in a different pre-arranged spot on the following day. McGowan, you already know where to leave the signal, so if you will excuse us, I will tell Lockett where to retrieve the information."

McGowan grabbed his battered and soiled wide-brimmed hat.

"You too," Wilks added to the two Pinkertons.

"Of course, Colonel, sir," MacDonald said, and the two Pinkertons followed the guide out of the office, shutting the door behind them.

With the door shut, Wilks turned his attention to Lockett. "We have a bargain still," the colonel stated warily.

"I'll be fine, sir. I've seen McGowan's type before." Pointedly, he turned and stared hard at Orrin Long.

Wilks seemed to not to notice as he pulled out a small map.

"Take a look at this while we talk. The spy will leave the information for you here. South of town, there is the Garrett farm,

Unionists who fled Murfreesboro when Forrest took it from us in October. There is nobody there now. It's abandoned. Just beyond the farmhouse, there is a small family cemetery with a large oak stump in the middle. The information will be in that stump. But nothing will be placed there until McGowan makes his signal known to the spy. Understand?"

Lockett nodded. "Is the spy one of the Garretts, sir?"

"No, they fled, but the spy knows the farm, and this is our pre-arranged location."

"So we have retrieved information from here before, sir?"

"No," Wilks replied, shifting in his chair. "We made the arrangements, but the last time I sent someone to retrieve it, he was never heard from again."

"I see, sir."

"I hope you do. The General needs this information. He won't attack without a better understanding of Bragg's strength and plans."

"I'll get it, sir," Lockett said slowly, "We won't win this war by sitting here in Nashville."

Wilks grunted in agreement.

"So McGowan leaves the spy some sort of signal, and the next day I retrieve the information from the stump. I guess that I don't let McGowan follow me to that stump."

"It's safer for our spy that way," Wilks explained, "If you're captured, then you can't give away the identity of our spy or give the Rebels enough information to set up a trap."

"But what if both McGowan and I are captured?"

"Simple answer for that, Lieutenant," Colonel Wilks replied coldly, "Make sure you are not both captured... alive that is."

Lockett's gaze drifted back to Orrin Long. No doubt McGowan had received the same message. Now Lockett understood why Orrin Long suggested him for this mission.

* * *

Lockett and McGowan set out to swing wide around the lines before turning south. Mounted atop a skeletal brown nag, Lockett slowly followed McGowan. It was going to be a long trip for more reasons than distance alone. Given the condition of this horse, he was skeptical that the animal could even make it to Murfreesboro.

It was probably fortunate for the animal that they carried so little with them. Other than the bed roll and food, primarily salted beef and hardtack, they carried nothing with them except for weapons: each had a rifle, revolver, and a knife, while McGowan also kept a shotgun in a saddle holster.

Lockett felt strangely uncomfortable to be out of his Union blue jacket, and it had nothing to do with the brown jacket that was too short for his long arms. It just felt peculiar to be in such non-descript clothing. There was nothing that truly identified him as part of one side or the other, beyond his clearly Yankee accented voice that is.

To pass the time, he tried to remember when was the last time that he had been without a familiar blue coat. It had been months and months ago, back in Kalamazoo when he and Patrick had reenlisted.

He scratched an itch at his elbow and wondered if the brown coat had a louse or two. He did not want to think about where the borrowed civilian clothes had come from. They were thin, worn, and patched, but at least the heavy outer jacket would provide some relief in the event that the weather changed from its current mild state.

They clomped along in silence for most of the day.

"Two more miles then we stop for the night," McGowan announced as the sun began to set. "Ah know a place for the night. Tomorrow, we leave the roads and head south."

Lockett nodded, knowing that he was completely dependent on the man, like it or not.

McGowan's place turned out to be a battered tavern at a crossroads. Without hesitation, McGowan headed inside and ordered a drink.

Lockett frowned as he looked at the decrepit, weather worn structure. It looked like a good wind would knock it flat, and he had a sudden vision of his first encounter with the bushwhacker, Bloody Bill Coulter, back near Savannah. It had been in a place like this.

Unconsciously, his hand slid to the worn wooden butt of the Starr. Somewhat reassured, he followed McGowan inside.

There were three other men at the bar, as hard-bitten and soiled as McGowan. A large bellied, bearded giant manned a grimy counter.

"Leave the bottle," McGowan commanded him and slapped a greenback on the bar.

"Spending your money already," Lockett said.

"Ah git half now, half when you come back... course, they din't spect-ify dead or alive."

Lockett ignored him. "They expect this done quickly, McGowan. We leave at first light. Make sure you're in condition to do so."

"Who made you general, boy?"

"I'll be putting you on that excuse of horse one way or other."

McGowan downed a whiskey and poured another. "We go when ah'm ready, boy. Don't fah-get it." He glared at Lockett before downing another drink.

Lockett headed to the back corner of the room and maneuvered a chair. He leaned back against the wall and tipped his slouch hat over his eyes, but he kept his eyes open and was careful to keep a hand on the gun in his pocket. It was clear that even dozing might be dangerous tonight.

At first light, Lockett and McGowan were back on their horses. Despite finishing the bottle, McGowan was somehow still conscious though he wobbled as he mounted the horse.

They rode in continuing silence. After a while, they left the road for little more than a deer path. An hour later, they emerged to find a little used wagon trail which they followed to another deer path.

"You seem to know your way through this part of the country. You from Tennessee?" Lockett asked.

"Miss-a sip. And yes, ah knows the way. Been through these parts many a time."

"Hunting fugitive slaves?"

"Ya heard, huh?"

"I heard."

"So, yes, ah know my way, boy."

"Name's Lockett. My friends call me James. You can call me Lockett."

McGowan snorted at his attempt at humor.

"Boy suits you better." He took out a stubby, rusty knife and cut a plug of tobacco. "You have a problem with my profession, boy? You one of these slave-lovin' Northerners?"

"Would it matter to you one way or the other?"

"Ya don't need to answer, boy. Ah can tell by the way y'all so friendly with that Pinkerton. He may try to hide it, and he's got those blue eyes, but ah knows better. He gots some slave blood in him, don't he, boy?"

"I wouldn't know," Lockett said stiffly. They lapsed into silence again as their horses slowly picked their way through the tangled undergrowth of the forest.

"If you don't like the abolitionists so much, then why are you helping the North?" Lockett asked an hour later.

McGowan jammed more tobacco into his cheek and gave no answer.

"Shouldn't you be on the other side, especially now?" Lockett added.

"Now what?"

"Now that President Lincoln announced emancipation for any slave whose state is still in rebellion at the end of the year."

McGowan cursed lengthily about President Lincoln and his lineage. He only paused to catch his breath and spit a stream of tobacco perilously close to Lockett. "That's what I think of y'all's Pres-ee-dent!"

"Like I said, you seem to be on the wrong side," Lockett probed.

"Ah'm on my side!" McGowan said angrily, "But keep talkin' and that might change!"

Lockett took an amused breath, strangely pleased that he had been able to get under the man's skin.

* * *

Milton Bosworth was the first to see Daniel Lockett enter camp that afternoon, led by a tall, utterly bald man.

"Daniel?" he said in disbelief. "What are you doing here? Did you escape?"

Daniel shook his head somberly.

He looked to be in rough shape, the sergeant thought.

The others noticed his return and gathered around the lad with backslaps that threatened to knock the shaky youth over. His eyes were sunken into their sockets, and he looked as if he had not eaten in days.

Even so, it was the smell that stood out the most. He smelled as if he had been sleeping in a sewer.

"He did not escape, Sergeant," the bald man said.

"I see... And who are you?" Bosworth asked, looking up at the taller man.

"A friend of your Lieutenant," he answered mysteriously. "He asked me to make sure that his brother was delivered back to your camp, and that I give your Colonel this." He waved a folded piece of paper in his hand.

"What's that?"

"His pardon from General Rosecrans."

Bosworth's eyes widened. He had known how dire Daniel's position had been. Even when Patrick had told him that the Lieutenant was doing something to help his brother, he was doubtful that it would ever work.

"A pardon?"

"Indeed."

"From the General?"

"Indeed."

"General *Rosecrans*?"

"None other."

"I'll be damned," Bosworth whistled softly. "The General of the whole dadgum Army?" He looked wide-eyed at the visitor.

"Quite."

"How in tarnation did he do that?" He was completely mystified and in a bit of shock. "But let me take you to Colonel Blair."

He left Daniel in the care of his enthusiastic messmates, who welcomed him back, oblivious to the cost that their admired lieutenant had paid.

Bosworth could not wait for Patrick McManus to return from his detail with the quartermaster to tell him the good news! Daniel was back. The Lieutenant had done it!

He threw an arm around the startled Pinkerton. "You are clearly a friend of the Lieutenant, which means that you are a friend of mine, sir! What's your name? Milton Bosworth, at your service." He gregariously offered his free hand for the visitor to shake.

"Octavius Matson."

"By God, what a day!" Bosworth exclaimed. His spirits were flying higher than they had in months. "The Lieutenant did it," he repeated. "When Patrick told me that he was off doing something to help Daniel, I didn't believe that it could be so."

But the high spirits of the sergeant did not stir similar ones in Octavius Matson. Rather, the Pinkerton man felt a knot of guilt at seeing the excitement and pride that the man felt for his young officer.

"Patrick will be overjoyed to hear of this, like a third Lockett brother he is. Grew up on the farm next to them, you know."

Matson said nothing in return.

"How'd he do it? Did he convince the general that Daniel was innocent after all?"

"No," Matson said slowly, "It was more of a bargain."

"A bargain?" Bosworth answered in a mystified voice. "What in tarnation did the lieutenant have to give the General in return?"

Octavius Matson looked grimly at the flushed and enthused face of the sergeant. "Most likely, his life…"

* * *

Night came, and the temperature dropped. Lockett was weary to the bone and sore. He was not used to riding a horse for such a length of time. At points during the day he had contemplated getting off the sluggish nag and walking along with it. He resolved to do that tomorrow.

But as cold and tired as he was, he watched with some trepidation as McGowan built a small fire.

"You sure that is a good idea?" he asked.

McGowan snorted. "Look round, boy. There ain't nothin' here. When was the last time ya saw even a wagon rut today? Ya might as well be at the end of the earth now."

"Still seems like a risk to light a fire."

"Ah ain't freezin' to death."

"It's not that cold," Lockett answered, even though the thin blanket provided little warmth.

"Ah forget. Yankees like the cold," McGowan sneered derisively.

"Now Missouri, that was cold," Lockett said, remembering the bitter frozen weeks on the plains when so many of the sharpshooters fell ill. Disease had killed more than bullets.

"Bin to Mizzou, eh?"

"Before Shiloh."

They lapsed into silence and gnawed on their salted beef and hard tack. McGowan eventually laid down and propped his head on a saddlebag.

"Boy?" he asked, closing his eyes.

"What?"

"Ya ain't tolt me why yar' here. Ya already know that Ah'm here for the money."

"It's not for money."

"Then what? Wantin' to die young?"

Lockett frowned. Even if he wanted to explain it, he knew that McGowan would not understand.

"My reasons are mine and mine alone."

McGowan gave his usual snort. "Ain't nothin' to me, boy." The fire crackled and hissed, leaving Lockett to his own thoughts. One hand on the gun in his pocket, he closed his eyes and tried to get some sleep.

The next day of riding greatly resembled the last one. There were more deer paths, more twisting and winding, seemingly in every direction but eventually pointing themselves south.

They stopped at a creek and refilled their canteens with cold, sweet tasting water.

The horses were drinking from the water when McGowan's head snapped upwards at some sound, and he balanced on the balls of feet, alert to something that Lockett missed. The slave hunter looked in the direction of the creek.

The bank on the other side was higher and followed the creek into a bend further downstream. McGowan grabbed his rifle and shotgun and left the horses without a word. He began to creep toward the bend, a weapon in each hand.

Alarmed but unsure what was happening, Lockett grabbed his own rifle from the saddle holster and followed after McGowan. He caught up to him at the bend in the creek. Across from the bend, the forest thinned, and McGowan stared intently at the opening. Without scarcely taking his eyes off the scene, McGowan loaded the shotgun with bird shot.

Perplexed, Lockett looked at him as he reached his shoulder. "Birdshot?"

But McGowan did not answer him.

"What do you see?" Lockett whispered.

McGowan waved him to silence without taking his eyes off the spot.

Lockett looked into the opening with him. He stared for minutes straight when his eyes finally caught the movement from one tree to the next. It was a person.

McGowan reached at first for the rifle, but then stayed with the birdshot loaded shotgun.

Frowning, Lockett looked at him. The shot seemed too far for a shotgun, especially one loaded with birdshot. It would be better to use a rifle from this distance.

He assumed that McGowan was just being cautious in case there were others closer by, but all Lockett saw was that solitary figure, who now moved diagonally away from them. With the underbrush, he was only able to catch a glimpse of the person, though soon the person would cross into the open break in the trees.

McGowan raised the shotgun, balancing it on the log that he crouched behind.

Whoever it was had stopped behind the tree in the distance.

Lockett scanned the rest of the area but did not see anything else. Puzzled, he focused again on the tree. At first, he had feared that it was a Rebel scout, but there was only one person. It didn't make much sense to him. Where were the others? And why would a scout be hiding, cautiously moving from tree to tree? Regardless, they needed to avoid detection, and the person was heading away from them fortunately.

"Time to go," Lockett whispered in McGowan's ear, repelled by the intense smell of the man.

McGowan ignored him, patiently waiting for his target to move into the clear.

"Who is it?" Lockett finally whispered. "Calvary scout?"

"Runaway," McGowan answered. Just then, the figure began to move cautiously again.

McGowan steadied the weapon and looked down the sight.

"What are you doing?" Lockett hissed at him.

"Gonna shoot him. There's reward for the like, dead or alive. Alive though is twice as much. The birdshot should just slow him down. Then we can grab him."

"You can't shoot, someone will hear!"

"Ain't no one here but us three," McGowan said. His finger closed around the trigger.

Without a second thought, Lockett used both hands to snatch the shotgun away. Caught by surprise, the weapon slipped from McGowan's grasp without going off. He glared at Lockett with pure hate.

"Give me that back, boy, and I won't use it on you."

Lockett pointed it at him. "Leave him. You'll make more money from completing this mission than hunting any slaves." It was the only logic that he could use on McGowan.

"Ah can have both," McGowan growled.

"You have the mission and only the mission!" Lockett glared at him with his gray eyes.

"Ya gonna regret pointin' that gun at me," McGowan vowed, but he started to walk away, back to the horses. Lockett grabbed McGowan's discarded rifle as well and followed him.

When they reached the horses, Lockett tossed the rifle back to McGowan. He could see the temptation in the other man's eyes. The rifle barrel tilted upwards slightly.

The slave hunter scowled at the Yankee officer. His bloodshot eyes searched the tall Northerner for a moment of hesitation.

Lockett could almost physically see the thought pass through the man's brain, but then, the rifle dipped.

"Now, let's go to Murfreesboro, McGowan."

McGowan grunted something inaudible, slammed the rifle into the saddle holster, and swung himself up into the saddle.

"Ya owe me money, boy. Good money."

Chapter 24

Milton Bosworth manhandled Daniel Lockett by the back of his collar and shoved him towards Patrick McManus. The three of them were alone. The echoes of the camp could faintly be heard beyond the trees.

The two older men scowled at the lad with a ferocity that surprised Daniel. It made him defensive but not cowed.

"What's the meaning of this?" he snapped at Bosworth.

Neither of the veterans said anything at first. In fact, Bosworth looked at McManus, as if waiting for the Irishman to say something.

"Well, Patrick, what's going on here?" Daniel demanded.

"Impudent young pup," the sergeant muttered lowly, still waiting on McManus.

"Well?" Daniel asked again.

Patrick McManus took a step forward, but instead of saying anything, he launched a right hook.

Daniel could not have been more surprised. He did not even move an inch as the blow landed and knocked him off his feet. His eyes were open, but he said nothing from the dirt. It was unclear which stunned him into silence more, the strength of the blow or just the fact that he had been hit at all.

Finally, McManus spoke. "You've hardly been out of the provost's custody, and already, we find you back with Vaught?" He paused, grinding his teeth. His thick, red-haired grizzled jaw was set in a fierce scowl. "I've known you forever, Daniel. I've known you were a carefree spirit. I've known you and defended you against what your brother saw as laziness. I was wrong. You are a fool!"

"And an ungrateful one at that," Bosworth mumbled.

"What are you talking about?" Daniel said, rising to his

elbows.

"Vaught. That is what we are talking about. We tried warning you from the beginning about steering clear of the man."

"To do what, stay in camp? What good is that? I want to see the country. I want to see what is beyond Kalamazoo."

"Damned fool," Bosworth shook his head. "I can see now why the Lieutenant wanted to keep him on the farm."

"So this is about my brother," Daniel sneered, rising to his feet. "You aren't my brother, and you ain't my keeper either."

"The first accurate thing you've said," Bosworth replied, more to himself than anyone else.

McManus ignored both comments. "Vaught got you arrested, nearly got you put on the gallows."

There was a glimmer of recognition on Daniel's face. "Yes…"

"Yes, damn you. They were going to hang you."

"They can't hang a man for going to a whorehouse. They'd have to hang the whole army." But the belligerence was gone from his voice as he remembered the jail cell, and the tremor that he had felt all the way through his bones. When they had released him without explanation, it had been a tremendous relief, like waking from a nightmare, too good to be true.

"They weren't going to hang you for the whore," McManus added. "They were hanging you for aiding the enemy. A spy!"

"I ain't no spy," Daniel replied, but a certain meekness poked through in his voice as he thought about the cell again.

"I know you are not a spy," McManus said tiredly, "You're missing the point. You were in the wrong place at the wrong time. You were there because you've been hanging around Vaught, and he's trouble."

"He's just a gambler. Lots of soldiers gamble."

"Yeah? Well, this one nearly got you hung," Bosworth snapped.

"And as soon as James gets you released, you go right back to what got you in trouble in the first place!" McManus added.

"So that's what this is about? James sent you to do his dirty work? Where is he? I'll tell him a thing of two about trying to run my life."

McManus took another step forward, but Bosworth quickly snatched him by the arm. "Easy, Pat. He ain't worth it."

Daniel rose from the dirt and dusted himself off. The three of them stood there for seconds.

"You're right, Milton. He ain't worth the sacrifice, which makes what James is doing all the worse."

"Oh, and what is brother James doing?" Daniel mocked.

"I should beat you to a pulp, but it won't make me feel any better." McManus turned on his heel and stomped away.

"A bigger fool I ain't ever seen, and I've seen plenty," Bosworth said to Daniel. "Your brother is a good judge of character, but in your case, he's blind. You definitely ain't worth what he did."

"Fine, whatever you say, sergeant. Tell me where James is and I'll pay him back."

Bosworth scowled again. "Doubt you could ever do that, even if you were to see him again."

"What? Where is he? What are you talking about?"

"Gone. Basically took your spot on the gallows. The tall Pinkerton told me. To save your life, he's giving his away. He's gone, behind enemy lines to find Rosecrans's information. You weren't worth the sacrifice, Daniel. It's a waste of a good officer... and a good friend." The burly sergeant turned and walked away, his eyes tearing up.

* * *

Despite his dislike for the man, Lockett had to admit that McGowan knew his way through this part of the country. He seemed to know even the smallest trail and have a plan as well. For two straight nights he had directed them to different rocky, cave-like outcroppings, which was particularly welcome on the second night given the cold rain that was falling.

That night, Lockett had no second thoughts about the small fire that McGowan built, but the heat from the small fire did little more than turn his soaked clothes into a clinging damp.

"How many times have you been through this part of the country?" he asked, trying to forget the miserable conditions.

"More'n ah cain count."

"Why through here?" Lockett asked, flicking a weevil off of his piece of hardtack.

"Lots of slaves in here, more than western Tennessee where y'all came from."

"It did seem like there were more black faces in Nashville."

"Not as many as Miss-a-sip, but enough. There's the railroad too."

"Railroad?" Lockett asked.

"Underground Railroad, boy."

"Oh," Lockett nodded, thinking quietly of the Pinkertons' map.

"This area is on the way to Cinci-nata. They all try to cross the river. Probably caught over a hundred up near there," he bragged. "Caught some here too, but not so many."

"How many more days until we get to Murfreesboro?"

McGowan cocked one eye at him and said guardedly, "Enough."

"Enough?"

"Don't ya worry, boy. Ah'll git you there." McGowan rolled over and closed his eyes.

The rain of the previous night was gone by morning. Brilliant sun and a blue sky were visible through the branches overhead as they continued their journey.

Most of their path had been through briars, woods, and thickets to this point, but today, they came upon a wide, but shallow timber-cleared valley.

They halted at the tree line, and McGowan searched the flat expanse. A crow flew overhead, but nothing else moved. The fields lay fallow, untended, and at the far end, Lockett could see a cluster of small buildings.

"Ah don't see nuthin'," McGowan said, but he still didn't move from the treeline.

"What are you expecting to see?"

"Nuthin'," McGowan said simply, "But ya never know. Both sides have bin through here and back again. Used to be prime farm land."

"And what happened?"

"When we git to the other end, you'll see. Not much left of the manor now, jus' blackened timbers." He prodded his horse forward, and Lockett followed. "Yankees burned it to the ground. Said it was an accident, but only y'all believe that. And the slaves? Wahl, theys gone now too."

As they made their way through the valley and across the once fertile fields, Lockett scanned either side but saw no one thankfully. At this point, his own side was nearly as dangerous to him as the Rebels.

On the far side, he eventually saw the charred remains of the house. There was little left of it now. Nearby, there were a number of smaller out-buildings, slave quarters, and a barn that leaned perilously to one side.

To Lockett's surprise, McGowan turned down the path that led to the smaller buildings.

"Where are you headed?" Lockett asked. When McGowan gave no answer, Lockett added, "I should hardly think there is anything left to take from the place if both sides have already been through here as you say."

McGowan spat a stream of tobacco juice but said nothing. When he reached the first slave quarter, he slid off his horse. Shrugging, Lockett got off his excuse of a horse as well and started to follow him.

"Whar do you think yer goin'?" McGowan said harshly.

"Where are you going?" Lockett replied in kind.

"In there."

"The slave quarters?"

McGowan snarled at him. "Got to use a privy. Now, leave me. Go check that barn or somethin'. Maybe ya find something useful."

"You're going to use the slave quarters for a privy?"

"They ain't usin' it," McGowan snapped. He spat another long stream of tobacco juice, but for once it wasn't perilously close to Lockett.

Lockett rolled his eyes and let the slave hunter be. A couple of minutes later, McGowan returned. "Let's go," he growled, remounting his horse without waiting for Lockett. With a silent shrug, Lockett followed after his guide.

As usual, there was little conversation between the two of them over the next day and a half. The strange little valley was just a memory as they made their way back into the thickets and woods.

Their food was starting to run low, but McGowan still had no interest in sharing his plan with Lockett, nor provide any clues as to how close they really were.

By midday, they had reached a deep creek, deeper and wider than the others they had seen. McGowan veered away from their southerly course. Initially, Lockett thought it was because he was searching for a better place to cross it, but after bypassing a number of good options, it became clear to him that they were no longer heading south.

"Why are we going this direction? Why don't we cross and continue south?" Lockett asked, looking up at the late afternoon sun.

"Ya doubtin' my sense of direction? Ya think ah'm lost?" He laughed harshly, exposing his brown, sticky, tobacco-stained teeth. "Ah said, ya think ah'm lost?"

That was not at all Lockett's thought. He had seen enough to know by now that McGowan always knew exactly where he was heading.

"No, McGowan," he said calmly, aware that McGowan seemed eager for an argument "I want to know why we aren't going south anymore."

"Some things to avoid, boy. This ain't no as the crow flies trip."

"I know that, but we haven't headed south at all in the past few hours. How close are we? How soon will we get there? The general's need is urgent."

McGowan snorted and let loose a stream of tobacco juice.

Lockett reined in his horse. "I insist that you tell me."

"Ya *insist!*" McGowan said, laughing so hard at the word that he nearly fell from the saddle. He righted himself but continued laughing. Nudging his horse forward, he rode along slowly only stopping when he was forty yards ahead of Lockett. "Wahl, what are ya goin' to do? Stay there? Ya don't even know where ya are now?" When Lockett didn't move, he added, "Now, don't be a damn fool."

"I want an answer."

"Wit'out me, ya'r good as dead. Ya ain't got a choice but to follow me." When Lockett still didn't move, McGowan scowled, "Now, we are almost thar, at least for tonight."

"And how many more days ride to Murfreesboro?" Lockett

responded, finally prodding his horse forward.

"Don't rightly know. Depends on where Bragg has his cavalry. We'll have to be careful the closer we git."

"How long?" Lockett demanded stubbornly.

"Two, mebbe three days."

They followed the creek for another hour when it took a sudden turn southward and became substantially more shallow. Shortly before nightfall, they came to a small house in the clearing. McGowan headed straight for it.

"How do you know that no one is there?" Lockett hissed.

"Ain't no one there," McGowan answered with full confidence.

As they got closer, Lockett had to agree that the cabin looked deserted. The lone window was gone, as was the door. The stone chimney stood straight and tall, but the rest of the structure was falling into neglected disrepair.

They tied their horses to a tree and headed inside. Unlike the other buildings he had seen in the valley, this one had not been picked clean. There was not much inside the cabin, but there was a table, two chairs in the front kitchen with a few iron pots, and a cooking stand within the fireplace.

Next to the fireplace, a short hallway led to a back room which appeared to be a bedroom. In the short hall, there was a small built-in shelf that held a water basin and could have held other cooking utensils.

"You've been here before, I take it," Lockett said.

"More'n once," McGowan grunted. He looked at Lockett with a knowing glint in his darting eyes. "A Presbyterian minister and his wife lived here... Always thought that they were hidin' slaves but never found any."

"So where are they now? How did you know it was vacant?"

"Things happen to people who help slaves escape in these parts."

"What do you mean?"

"Ah mean shortly after your Pres-ee-dent Lincoln was elected," McGowan said with a voice full of spite, "Two slaves took off. Me and a posse followed 'em to these parts. That old preacher got the devil's tongue when Sam knocked down his wife on the way into this here shack."

He stopped, apparently at the end of the story, forcing Lockett to prod further. "So how did you know it was vacant?"

"Cuz then they was kilt."

"Killed? You killed them in their own home?"

"Not me. The posse. But they had it comin'. The old woman was kilt right where yer standin'."

Lockett looked down. Even in the dim light, he could see some discoloration in the wood flooring below.

"Never did find those damn slaves though," McGowan concluded.

* * *

"What do we do with him, sir?" Sam Baker looked expectantly at Sergeant Bosworth and then Patrick McManus.

Beneath an armpit, he supported the semi-conscious Captain Bibb.

Milton Bosworth shared a glance with Patrick McManus.

"Found him face down just inside the sentry line," Baker added.

Suddenly, the captain's head snapped upward, "Ser'g," he slurred with a big smile across his muddied face, "Mer' Christmas!"

"He's drunk," Baker said.

"Yes, I see that," Bosworth snapped sourly. "I've seen drunk men before, Baker."

"Sorry, sir."

"And stop calling me, sir. I ain't a 'sir'. I'm a sergeant."

"Yes, sir... I mean, yes, sergeant," Baker hastened, but he wore an amused grin.

"I say, ser'g. I said, Mer' Christmas!" Bibb repeated with a drop of spittle falling from his chin.

"It's not Christmas, Captain, sir," Bosworth responded. Beneath his breath, he added, "At least he ain't a mean drunk."

"Well, what do I do with him?"

"Put him in his tent," Bosworth answered tiredly.

As Baker shuffled away, supporting the hopelessly intoxicated officer, Bosworth turned to McManus.

"Honestly, Pat, what *are* we supposed to do with him? He's a grand enough fellow and all, but we can't have an officer who's falling down drunk every other night."

"The rate he's going, I'd say it was more like every night, Milton."

"Warn't so bad at first," Bosworth nodded.

"Perryville," McManus commented, looking down and toeing the cold dirt.

"Never saw him drunk until then," Bosworth concurred. "Ain't the first to see the elephant and turn hard to the barley corn."

"No, not the first."

"'Cept he's an officer, Pat, and the only one we got now. What's going to happen in the next battle? He'll get us killed, mark my words. Saw some of that at Shiloh. Hell, that is why our right hand companies collapsed that day. Those officers were worthless when sober, downright idiotic when drunk."

"He's not that bad," McManus answered in a dubious tone that doubted his own words.

"Pat?" Bosworth prodded.

"Yeah, well," McManus said after a second, "I know. We have a real problem."

"Should we tell the Colonel?"

McManus snorted. "The Colonel already knows, Milton. The Colonel is nobody's fool. He knows, but what is he to do? We're short-handed as it is after Perryville. Then, James leaves. What is the Colonel going to do? There's not exactly a lot of options."

"I don't like it, Pat. I've seen this before, like I said. No, this is real trouble. What are we going to do?"

"I don't know, Milton."

"We need the Lieutenant back. Mebbe when he comes back Colonel Blair can find a way to get rid of Bibb?"

Patrick McManus nodded grimly. More than ever, he worried for his lifelong friend. It had only been a matter of days, but he was keenly aware that they needed him, and McManus was equally sure that James needed them too.

* * *

After the past few nights, Lockett found this night to be an extreme luxury. They could sleep under a roof with a healthy fire in the fireplace. They had little food left to cook, but it was still rejuvenating to have some civilization again.

Lockett slept fairly well, even though it was a shallow slumber with one hand on the revolver at all times. Still, it was the best that he had slept since they had left. The comfort seemed to have the opposite effect on McGowan who stirred multiple times during the night. Lockett noticed him at one point get up and pace in the room. He half-wondered if the man was just more comfortable on the trail and unable to relax under a roof after all of these years. But the thoughts were fleeting as Lockett drifted off to sleep again.

In the morning, Lockett rose and prepared to head out. McGowan, on the other hand, made no effort to gather up his bedroll and instead stoked the fire. It surprised Lockett. To this point, McGowan had been an early riser and ready to go before he was most mornings.

"Let's go, McGowan. What are you doing?"

"The horses need to rest, boy."

Lockett looked at him strangely. "Rest? Mine is as broken down of a nag as they come, but it doesn't need rest. Besides, you already know that we have no time to waste."

"Very well," McGowan shrugged, "Grab that bedroll for me while I take care of this fire."

Lockett frowned. He had half a mind to tell McGowan to get his own bedroll, but he turned around and bent over to gather up the worn blanket. There was an audible and ominous click of a weapon being cocked behind him.

"Turn around real slow, boy," McGowan said.

Lockett turned and found McGowan had a revolver pointed straight at him.

"Ah din't forget that ya got the drop on me last time."

Lockett's eyes flitted from the gun to the pleased look on the slave hunter's face.

"Now, real slow like with just two fingers, take that revolver out of your pocket. Real slow. Ya think I din't notice that ya always had a hand on it?"

Slowly, Lockett obeyed and dropped the Starr. It landed on the wood floor with a thud.

"Kick it over."

"What's the meaning of this, McGowan?" Lockett asked instead, leaving the gun just at his feet.

"There'll be some friends meeting us here soon."

"Friends? I don't think you have any friends, McGowan."

The slave hunter smiled broadly showing all of his brown and yellow caked teeth. "True, boy. But they pay well. Given what you cost me with that slave, Ah'm goin' to enjoy handing ya over too."

"I thought you'd been acting strange the past couple of days."

"Thought Ah was usin' the privy!" he chortled, "Leavin' a signal for 'em. Lettin' 'em know we was here. Ya thought ya was so smart, so brave comin' out here," he mocked "Be a real hero, that's what ya thought."

"You don't know the first thing about why I did this," Lockett said slowly. His jaw tightened bit by bit.

"A damn *fool*, boy, comin' out here!" He laughed almost gleefully. "They should be here soon."

"So, what are you doing? Handing me over to the Rebs for money? Is that it?"

"Fig-gured me out," McGowan said sarcastically.

"This was the plan all along? Lure me out here, and hand me over for a fistful of dollars?"

"Not you, boy. Was supposed to be a major. They would pay more for a major. Now, a boy lieutenant? Ah won't git half of what Ah should."

"Seems like a complicated way of getting a lone prisoner. The spy is not real then, I assume."

McGowan shook his head. "The spy is real enough. That's the second part of the deal. They want the spy too. So why don't ya jus' be a good boy and tell me where that spy'll leave the information so that my Confederate friends can capture him."

"I won't be telling you anything, McGowan."

An evil look spread across McGowan's face. "Would have been easier for ya. My friends will git it out of ya one way or the other. Won't be pleasant. Now kick that gun over here, boy."

Lockett gave the gun a soft kick, sending it only half way between them. McGowan took a step forward and crouched to retrieve the weapon. His eyes only left Lockett for a second, but that was the second that Lockett was hoping for.

As soon as the slave hunter's eyes flicked downwards, Lockett took a quick step forward and fired a kick at the revolver in

McGowan's hand. The kick neither caused the gun to go off, nor caused it to fly from McGowan's hand as he had hoped, but it did send the slave hunter's aim up and to the right. McGowan stumbled back a half-step and started to move the revolver back on target, but Lockett was upon him, one hand wrestling for the gun. His momentum slammed into the slave hunter, driving both of them backwards.

They landed on the table, which could not sustain their weight, and McGowan crashed to the floor with Lockett landing on top. The impact on the floor did what the kick could not, and the gun slipped from McGowan's hand and went cart-wheeling across the room.

From atop McGowan, Lockett reached one hand for the man's throat. He looked into the man's hateful eyes and felt his fetid breath curling around him like some kind of specter. It was a vile decaying smell, equal to the stench of bloated corpses.

McGowan fired a punch with his free hand that caught Lockett in the side of the head, toppling him from his position. Dazed, Lockett staggered to his feet. With a growl, McGowan wasted no time in throwing himself at Lockett, driving him into the little hall between the two rooms.

Lockett was strong despite his lean appearance, years behind a plow had made that the case, but he could feel the other man's bear-like weight and strength overpowering him. McGowan slammed him into one wall and then another. Lockett tried to throw a knee into the man's side but to no avail. He tried to throw a punch but could not from their locked position.

McGowan smashed him into the wall next to the shelf, causing Lockett's hand to fly to the side, bashing against the underside of one of the shelves, which then gave way. The wind rushed out of Lockett's lungs, but on instinct, he was able to slip from the bear hug.

McGowan paused for just an instant to look at the shelving that Lockett's hand had crashed into. The shelf had folded back on a hinge connected to its underside, revealing a small vertical crawl space behind the shelf.

"I always knew they wuz here somewhere," McGowan muttered angrily as he looked at the exposed hiding space, just large enough for a fugitive slave.

The brief lull allowed Lockett to fill his lungs with breath, but it was of little value as the larger man threw himself back at Lockett, driving him into the front kitchen. Interlocked once again, they traded punches to the sides of their heads, but Lockett could tell that his did no damage.

"Ah'm goin' take pleasure killin' you, boy," McGowan exclaimed as he pounded Lockett's ribs with short, hooking punches. McGowan kept a fistful of Lockett's jacket as he slammed more right hands, driving Lockett backwards towards the fire place.

Pausing with the body blows, McGowan's large fist cut through the air, aimed at Lockett's head. Seeing it at the last second, Lockett was able to dodge it.

He knew that he was the quicker of the two men, but in such close quarters, that was of little value.

Still, as the slave hunter's blow found nothing but air, it put the larger man off balance. Seeing a potential opening, Lockett tried to use the man's own momentum to swing him into the kitchen fire.

But the slave hunter was too strong and ready for it. He held tightly to Lockett and pivoted with well-timed leverage.

With a terror induced cry, Lockett felt himself being flung face first into the well-stoked fire. The orange flames licked at his face as he twisted above it, finally landing on his neck and shoulder inside the fireplace opening at the edge of the blaze.

Chapter 25

His ears rang with his own howling screams. The smell of burning flesh filled his nostrils as if blasted in by a furnace bellows. He struggled to leap free from the flames, but McGowan's two thick arms held him in the charred coals on the edge of the fire. Flickers of nearby flames danced fractions away from his face.

The pain was like nothing that he could ever have imagined. Every inch of his body exploded in an excruciating overload, his toes, his fingers, not just his neck and shoulder. Even his teeth vibrated in pain such that it seemed they must surely fly out of his mouth.

The stench of burning flesh seemed to fill the room like a hideous cloud.

Lockett's feet kicked wildly and his arms flailed. McGowan's laughter reached his ears like some sort of distant echo. The flames were starting to smolder McGowan's sleeves, but he did not relent.

Screaming at the top of his lungs, Lockett squirmed but was held fast in the fireplace, despite his one last surge of strength. He was caught too awkwardly and had no leverage to free himself. Eyes closed, his arm flailed to the side one last time, grasping reflexively the iron poker that had fallen next to him. Seizing it, he stabbed backward with all of his strength.

It made contact with something, and the rigid lock holding him in the fire was broken. Instantly, his primal instincts launched himself out of the fire, and bare handed he swatted at the flames that were fueled by the little remaining fabric around his shoulder and collar. He swatted involuntarily, not realizing that nearly all of the collar had already burned away.

Gasping, he crawled away from the fire, finally looking for

McGowan.   The slave hunter lay on his side, an iron poker protruding grotesquely from one eye.

With a whimper, Lockett tried to move, but he could not even crawl. He tried to raise a hand but did not have the strength. His head swam in pain, and the room swirled in his eyes.   He collapsed backward.

Lockett awoke sometime later with the same smell of burning flesh all around. He tried to swallow but found himself as parched as could be. But by far worst of all was the pain that overcame all of his senses and thoughts. He wanted to howl in agony, but his body did not have the energy for that.

He laid on the floor in a near catatonic state for an interminable amount of time. Eventually, he became aware of sound. At first, he could not register what the sound was.   Then, with a dumbfounding realization, he recognized it, the sound of horses.

McGowan's Confederates were here.

Panic gave him strength that he had lacked seconds before, and he crawled away from the door intuitively. His crawling stopped at the hallway, when he realized that the guns were on the other side of the room. He paused, but with a sad realization, he knew that he would not have the strength to use them anyway.

"McGowan!" came a shout from outside.

From his shadowed recess on the far side of the room, he saw the horsemen ride by the opening. There were at least six, and he knew that he didn't have the strength to fight even one. Even if he could crawl to the guns, it was too many men.

A small cry caught in throat. He felt hopelessly alone.

His head sagged against the wall when from the corner of his eye he saw the opening where the built-in shelf was.   He remembered now his hand crashing into it during the fight.

A crawlspace!

With his last vestige of strength, he pulled himself to his feet and staggered over to the opening. He stuck his head through the opening and pulled himself into the space. He knew now why McGowan and his posse had not been able to find those slaves that night. The crawlspace behind the shelf was an ingenious, if not cramped, hiding space.

"McGowan, you in there?" came the call from outside.

"The horses are still here," remarked another voice.

Lockett pulled the flap shut and slid back the bolt that he had knocked free earlier, which re-locked the hidden hinge. In the pitch darkness of the hidden crawlspace, he sagged to the ground and listened to the Confederates enter the cabin.

"God almighty!" one exclaimed, "McGowan's dead. Look at him!"

"Where's the Yankee?"

Lockett could hear the murmurings and prayed that his hiding spot would not be found, but he was only vaguely aware of their rummaging and rumbling. The pain was too intense for anything else, and he found his head swimming again.

"Look around. He can't be far. There are still embers in the fire, and the horses are still here."

He had no idea how long they searched, because Lockett had once again passed out.

Section IV

Murfreesboro

Chapter 26

Lockett slumped against the leafless oak tree and closed his eyes. His life had never been one of leisure and ease, but he had never felt so exhausted. No long hours on the farm, no long marches, not even the cacophony and terror of Shiloh's battlefield compared to his current state.

His brow and jaw were still screwed in agony. The searing pain was not lessening across his shoulder, neck, and jaw. His limbs were lifeless, and he had no strength to move. He closed his eyes, yet the pain prevented any sleep. His early determination was now dissipating, and his own mind worked against him.

When he had awoken in the crawlspace, it had been morning. He had cautiously left the hiding place. The Confederates seemed long gone now, as were the horses, the weapons, and what little supplies he and McGowan had remaining.

His lips trembled in both pain and despair. He was countless miles behind enemy lines, and he wasn't sure what to do.

His belly rumbled angrily at its emptiness. His only drink had been hours ago at a small stagnant puddle, whose water looked so foul and full of scum that he hesitated to use the final drops of coolness against the still scalding sensation that ran from his neck to his fingertips. He could see that the burn did not extend past his shoulder, but what his eyes told him did not make the pain streaking the entirety of his limb any less.

He tried to focus his mind on the picture of the map, but it was getting increasingly hard to think. Was he even heading south still? Was the map accurate? Where was he exactly? He didn't really know. Even if he saw a landmark that would give him an important clue, he was in no state to recognize it.

He could continue south, but then where? There would be

patrols. What if he even made it to Murfreesboro, which seemed impossible now? There would be enemy encampments as well.

And he did not know who the spy was? How could he possibly find him? McGowan had taken the signal with him to his grave. Lockett had no way of alerting the spy to his presence.

Surely, it made more sense to turn around now. But in his exhaustion, he could not even imagine the journey back.

He leaned his head back against the tree and looked off into the distance. He was on a small knoll that looked across a shallow valley. It was an emptiness of dormant trees, growing darker by the minute, though that could be his own exhaustion and not the day itself.

Closing his eyes, he bemoaned his inability to sleep and the scalding pain that racked his body.

The smoke was thick and black, too thick to see through. He tried to move but was paralyzed. The black skein parted momentarily, and he could see friendly faces in blue coats through the curtain of smoke. He reached out for them but was rooted agonizingly in place.

Then with a start, Lockett realized that he had fallen asleep after all. Somehow during the long, torturous hours, he had managed to drift off into a tense sleep. Was it even the same day? The sun had long been up based on its position in the sky.

He wiped the sleep from his eyes and whimpered. The movement of his arm stirred excruciating tremors across his neck again. It snapped him more fully awake.

He moaned and turned his head slightly to the right, as if testing his neck, and that is when he saw it. In the distance, a faint trickle of black smoke coming up from the valley. It seemed to be moving, though ever so slowly.

Dazed, Lockett watched it for a full minute, drifting skyward and melting into the blue sky. The slow movement paused and settled into place in the middle of the valley. And then it finally struck him.

"A train," he said aloud to the empty woods.

"A train," he repeated, getting to his feet with renewed energy. Seized by a sudden idea, he made a stumbling journey down from the knoll and headed for the tree shrouded valley.

Lockett smelled it before he saw it. It was a scent that soldiers knew all too well, blood and infections.

At a large patch of evergreens, the tracks cut through the timber, and as Lockett carefully weaved through the last batch, he could now hear the familiar moans of the wounded and the sharp commands of an iron lung sergeant.

It was a small train of three cars, two flat cars and a well-worn passenger car. Across all of them lay Confederate wounded.

As Lockett peered through the trees, he could see that those who could move were now heading back up to the flat cars after having either relieved themselves or gotten a drink from a large stream that Lockett now saw ran parallel to the other side of the tracks. But most of the others were in no condition to move and just lay there on the railcars in powerless agony.

"She's nearly finished taking on water," said a voice from behind, startling him.

He turned to find himself face to face with a young private. His arm was in a sling, and his cherubic face was smudged with dirt, but it was the fleeting look of horror on the boy's face that Lockett noticed most. The boy could not take his eyes off Lockett's neck.

Finally, with some conscious effort, the gaping boy tore his gaze free and pointed to the left. "See?"

Lockett turned to see a small water tower whose boom hose was being turned away from the engine.

"C'mon, don't want to get left behind."

Lockett nodded dumbly and followed the lad onto a flat car.

"It's cold as hell on these flat cars," the lad added as they climbed up, "Course, it's better than getting assigned to the passenger car. Those poor fellows are in such bad shape, doubt they will make it to Murfreesboro."

Lockett maintained a blank look on his face, though his mind resonated with the final destination.

Murfreesboro!

Wordlessly, he sat cross-legged in one of the few empty spots, lowered his chin to his chest, and closed his eyes. To those around him he looked as if he were dozing, but now his mind was working furiously.

* * *

The train moved with an agonizingly slow pace. Whether it was the condition of the track or the condition of the passengers, Lockett had never seen a train move so slowly. At times, it hardly seemed to be moving faster than walking speed. But each slow clack from one rail to the next brought him closer to his goal, and each slow jolt elicited at least one moan from the many passengers.

Lockett kept his chin down and feigned sleep, cracking an eye open every once in a while. He knew that he could not afford for the lad to try to strike up a conversation with him. His accent would give him away in a matter of seconds.

The long quiet trip gave him plenty of time to formulate a plan in his head, but despite his best efforts, he could come up with little besides getting to Murfreesboro and getting off the train. After that, he had no idea what he would do. He needed to find the spy and then get back to his own lines, but how would he do that?

Oddly, his grim situation made him want to laugh and actually relieved some of the pain. He was such a long ways from Kalamazoo. How could he have ever imagined such a situation? It had been such a simple choice then: volunteer, go fight the Rebels, and keep Daniel on the farm. There was danger, to be sure, but it was the simple danger from lead flying or the random uncaring shot.

A scant year later, he had been booted from the sharpshooters, accused of a murder that he did not commit, not exactly anyway, though little Amelia's face still surfaced in his dreams with regularity. He had fought in the largest battle that the country had seen, survived, and even been promoted.

Then things had really become unimaginable. He had fallen in love with an angel of the battlefield, but she was a Southern angel who had betrayed him with her allegiance to the South and to her father. She had been a Rebel spy, and he had helped her.

And now? Now, he was lost behind enemy lines, in wretched pain, needing to find a Union spy, and somehow return to his lines so that his brother's freedom could be unequivocally secured.

The train whistle startled him, as well as the other dazed, half frozen wounded. He could feel the slow, but steady momentum of the train dropping away.

With his heart beating rapidly, the train came to a stop. A handful of townspeople and an equal number of gray clad Confederates waited on the platform.

Murfreesboro was bigger than he had thought. This was no one-shack stop. Murfreesboro had a long, full slate roof train station, and the town was well-kept and prosperous looking.

From the platform, two civilians headed immediately into the passenger car, doctors from what Lockett could gather.

He tried to move, but he found his legs incredibly stiff, to the point that they seemed not to operate. After a moment, he was able to get enough feeling in them to crawl to the side of the flat car. With a handful of people already ministering to some of his fellow flatcar travelers, Lockett tried delicately to climb over one last prone body, but in his discombobulated state, he stumbled, and his knee crashed down on the Confederate soldier's chest.

But there was no noise. The body just stared up at him with lifeless eyes. Lockett lurched over him and then dropped off the far side of the car, landing clumsily with a thud on all fours.

No one seemed to notice his exit.

With the busy station platform on the other side of the train, he had thought that he might slip off the far side and disappear in the woods while he gathered his strength and came up with an actual plan, but Murfreesboro was more of a town than he had figured. There were no woods conveniently next to the station, just houses, storefronts, an impressive macadamized pike, and narrow dirt avenues angling away.

A troop of Confederate soldiers marched down the pike. He did not know if they were headed for the train, but a moment of panic seized him as they seemed to be headed straight toward him.

Forcing himself to breathe, he chided himself for the brief moment of panic. He was just another anonymous soldier here, he told himself, but he knew that he could not remain anonymous for long.

His head was starting to swim again, and he paused to close his eyes. He could not afford to pass out now, he scolded himself. With a few more deep breaths and one last pull on his reserves, he fought back the dizziness.

He was about to head for the back of the train, skirting the activity, and disappear past the square frame houses when a peculiar feeling seized him, like someone was watching him. It was an intense feeling of self-awareness. Against his better judgment, he turned slowly and looked up at the face that was staring at him from atop the flatcar.

It was the shock of his young life.

Chapter 27

Lockett stared up into the face of Anna Tucker.

She gave an audible cry, and both were frozen in astonishment.

As he looked at her dark eyes and smooth features, he thought that he must be dreaming, delirious perhaps from the burn. He had been sure that he would never see that face again, that he would die somewhere, in some field in this war, thinking of her with that last breath. His mind's eye would one last time reflect on the smooth, perfectly symmetrical features. It would be like she was right there in those final moments, not some distant memory that he had tried so unsuccessfully to blot from his brain.

Except that she seemed to be right here in front of his disbelieving eyes. Despite the agony that wracked his body, there was a hopeful catch in his throat.

His gaze locked onto hers, fixated on the flowing dark hair, the aquiline nose, thoughtful brow, and most of all, the energetic brown eyes so full of vitality. These were the eyes that had first captured his attention in Ainsley's hospital tent. They made it impossible not stare in lost amazement at their beauty.

No, it was not possible that he was staring up at those same eyes now! He must have passed out! This must be a delirious dream!

And if so, he did not wish to awaken. Yes, he thought, perhaps he was dying now, and these were his last seconds. They said your life would flash before your eyes, but his last moments were to be consumed with visions of Anna. He had tried so hard to put her from his thoughts. How foolish, he realized now. She was to be his last thought!

He was rooted in place and could not move towards her, just like in some of those other dreams and nightmares he would have about soldiers in blue or butternut coats or little Amelia. And just like in those visions, she could not move closer to him either.

But it couldn't be a dream, another part of his brain insisted. He was in too much physical pain for this to be a dream. This was real!

Anna too looked at him, utterly stunned.

Neither could say a word, and they gaped silently at each other.

Lockett felt his heart pounding, thumping hard in his chest. Finally, he concluded that this was real. He was not dying. This was no delirium. This was real.

Perhaps he should have felt fear, he thought to himself later, fear of discovery, but he felt no fear, just shock and paralysis.

He opened his mouth to say her name, but no sound came forth.

Then slowly Anna made her way to a seated position, legs dangling over the side of the flatcar.

Numbly, he tried to get to his feet to help her to the ground, but he only made it to a precarious balance on his knees. Anna pushed herself off the flatcar and landed nimbly. She crouched next to him.

"James," she breathed, gently touching the unburned side of his face. She studied him, and he was suddenly conscious of what he must look like. He remembered the appalled reaction of the young soldier back at the water tower.

"James," she repeated, dropping her hand. Gently, she embraced him, cautious of the burned side of his body. She buried her face in the unscathed side of his chest.

"Anna," he whispered in her ear, as he returned the embrace.

Pain and calamities dissipated momentarily. He held her, feeling a joy like he had never felt before. It was a wordless, inexplicable moment of bliss, surrounded at an arm's length by a circle of pain and torment.

They held each other for a full minute. Finally, she lifted her head with tears in her eyes. "What are you doing here? What happened to you?"

He cleared his throat softly and found his voice to be little more than a cracked whisper. "It is such a long story, Anna."

"Are you a prisoner? Where is your uniform?" she asked in a hush. Her soft hands sought out and found his.

With his mouth near her ear, he whispered, "Not a prisoner.

I'm still a Union soldier… just not at the moment."

Anna stepped back and looked hard at him. Such an answer would have confused most people, but not Anna Tucker. Both knew that Anna would understand such a cryptic answer. After all, a fellow spy would know the meaning of the words.

The quiet was broken by another young voice from the flatcar. "Anna, I thought we were here to help the wounded," came the teasing voice.

Lockett looked up to see a blue-eyed teenage girl staring down at them with a mischievous smile. As Lockett turned his head, it revealed the burns on the other side of his face. The girl's smile dropped but only for an instant. Regaining her composure quickly, the young girl added, "And who might you be, brave sir? Anna, are you to declare a monopoly on the handsome rogues?"

The girl had an excitable and engaging charm.

"You already have a fiancée, Mattie," Anna laughed, stepping closer to him.

The girl, Mattie, raised an eyebrow at the movement and the easy familiarity of it. "I had no idea that our dear Anna had such an interest already. No wonder she has spurned so many offers here. You've been keeping secrets, Anna, haven't you?"

It was said in a whimsical way, but both Lockett and Anna Tucker squeezed each other's hand instinctively.

"Well, sir, keep the secret no longer. Who are you and where did you come from?"

Lockett clenched his jaw, and his mind worked furiously.

But it was Anna who answered. "His wound has damaged his voice… temporary, I am sure."

"Of course," Mattie answered, looking at the gruesome wound on his neck and jaw. "It will heal soon. Poor dear!"

"Let's attend to the wounded, Mattie. Then I can share our story with you."

"Of course, of course," she answered.

With complete trust in Anna, Lockett wondered what story that might be. At least, she would have a bit of time to concoct one, and he marveled at her quick thinking. The injury had damaged his voice? Indeed, such a brilliant idea would not have come to him with such lightning quickness. Anna always had been a whip smart girl.

Anna eventually led Lockett away. With the bustle of the train station behind them, they walked into a prosperous town like Lockett had not seen in quite some time. There were handsome brick houses, tall oak and elm trees that would no doubt provide relieving shade in the summer. In the center of the town, on a small rise so that its tall cupola would be visible from any point, there was a new and majestic courthouse. As they slowly walked past, the tall white pillars spoke to the prosperity of the area.

The streets surrounding the town square had trim looking store fronts, and beyond there were well maintained houses capped with clean, white fenced yards.

Cheerful faces and well-dressed individuals chatted casually on the plank sidewalk. Many waved or tipped their cap to Anna as she walked by.

He also saw a surprising number of black faces, slaves, Lockett assumed.

Anna steered them down an avenue away from the main square.

"Thanks," Lockett finally said, "Thanks for what you did back there."

Anna ignored the gratitude. "From now on, no more speaking from you. You mutter one word in that Yankee voice, and there will be no helping you."

Nodding appreciatively, Lockett whispered, "That was quick thinking, back there, I mean."

"I'm serious," Anna said. "No talking. None." She looked at him with surprising hardness. After a moment, he nodded, and she continued. "You will stay with us at Aunt Molly's. I'll have to convince her to let you stay. She won't like it, but it will have to be."

Lockett looked quizzically at her.

"Aunt Molly has both strict notions of propriety and also that I should be married off to someone of importance. She's seen what Mattie did and wonders why I refuse to do the same." She ignored Lockett's questioning look and continued on. "We will need a story, of course, so we will use the same one that I used to quell Mattie's curiosity. You are someone that I knew from Savannah. Father always said that the best lies are the ones that are closest to the truth." She smiled at the hidden meaning that existed between the two of them.

He would know, Lockett thought to himself. From the slightly upturned corners of her mouth, he could tell that a similar thought of irony had come to her as well.

They crossed over the broad Nashville Pike. Just slightly down, past the next tree lined avenue, they walked past a stately two story mansion. Two Confederate soldiers stood beneath the broad overhang of the large second story balcony. The home's slender pillars gave it a prominent appearance, and it reminded Lockett of the lordly home of Big John Moffit, back in Kalamazoo.

Anna followed his eyes. "You'll be interested to know that this is General Bragg's headquarters," she stated.

Lockett suddenly stopped. Careful that he only whisper despite the deserted street, "You don't have to do this, Anna. You don't know what you are getting yourself into."

"Neither did you when you first came calling on me in Savannah."

"You don't understand. I'm here as a spy."

"Naturally you are here as a spy. Why else would you be here and out of uniform? Murfreesboro is General Bragg's headquarters after all."

"Don't you understand what could happen to you?"

She laughed lightly, "Don't you understand what could happen to *you*? And yet, here you are."

A flash of pain shot through the side of his neck and face. The bolt did not go unnoticed. With a look of concern, she added. "Come. You need rest, and I need to look at that wound more. You can *whisper* the rest to me later."

Fortunately, Aunt Molly's house was a mere 120 yards further away. It was a small, white-washed house clustered with three others, but Lockett hardly noticed. His exhaustion was rapidly catching up to him.

"I was going to tell you to put on a good act of suffering to make my arguments with Aunt Molly easier," Anna said with concern, "But you can't fake that kind of color. Can you make it up the step into the house?"

He could scarcely remember making it into the parlor before

collapsing into a hickory backed rocking chair. His head was swimming again. Dizziness and sheer exhaustion were overtaking him. He struggled not to lose consciousness.

"Auntie?" Anna summoned.

Through slit eyes, Lockett saw a drab, older woman with a flour dabbed apron enter the room.

"Making some bread, dear, and what is that smell that…" Aunt Molly stopped in mid-sentence and mid-stride. "Heavens alive, who is this, and what is he doing here?" Her voice was tinged with indignation.

"Please, Auntie, this is my friend, and he needs help."

"Good Lord, look at his neck! Is he alive?"

"Yes, but he needs to recover."

Cautiously, Aunt Molly approached him and studied the raw, red, oozing burns on his neck, jaw, and lower cheek.

"I should say he needs to recover, but what is he doing here?"

"He's a friend…"

"A friend from where?" Aunt Molly interrupted, "And how did he get here?"

"The train with the wounded arrived today. Remember? I said that I was going down to attend…"

"Yes, I remember that. That was to attend to the wounded down there, not bring them back to my house."

"But…"

"And who is he exactly? A captain? Major?"

"Ah, well, no," Anna answered awkwardly.

"Well, take him back with the others."

"But Auntie, it's cold out. Others in town are opening their houses as well."

"I thought that the wounded were to be put in the church for now?"

"Some are, but we can't. He's a friend… a friend from Savannah."

"Friend, you say," Aunt Molly answered, studying her niece carefully. "Can't be having '*friends*' stay in the house. What would people say?"

"They'll say nothing, Auntie. It's a war. The wounded need places to stay. Besides it would be under your watchful eye. People would know that."

"Of course, people will talk, dear. You know so little about how this town works," she said, as if chiding a small child.

"It's a matter of Christian charity, Auntie."

That argument seemed to give the older woman something to think about.

"But where would we put him?"

"There is the small attic room across from your room, Auntie."

"But that is for Ambrose, dear. Where would I put your brother?"

The mention of Anna's brother provoked a moment of clarity through Lockett's fatigue. Ambrose? Here? A moment of alarm seized him.

"But Ambrose won't arrive until Christmas, Auntie. By then, James will be recovered enough to be back on his way."

"James, you say."

There was a pleading look in her niece's eyes, which was not normal. As poorly as she understood some of her niece's attentions, she rarely did ask for anything. Aunt Molly paused before adding, "Perhaps, he could stay briefly..."

"That is all he needs, Auntie."

"Well, what have you to say for yourself, James?" Aunt Molly said. "Making my niece beg like she did?"

"Oh, the wound has damaged his throat, Auntie. He can't speak right now."

"Can't speak?" Aunt Molly said, truly aghast. "Why good Heavens, he's a mute?" Her reaction was not one of sympathy, Lockett noticed, more like indignation, as if this was somehow a personal affront to her.

"It's just temporary, I am sure," Anna soothed. "He just needs to recover."

Aunt Molly shook her head. "Very well. You best attend to those wounds."

In his stupor, Lockett tried to portray a look of gratitude, but it seemed lost on the older woman as she waddled out of the room.

* * *

It was nearly 20 hours later when Lockett awoke and found himself staring up at the rafters in a strange, small room. The

259

space was occupied by his bed and a lone chair. There was no room between the bed, chair, and walls.

He vaguely recalled climbing the steps, supported by Anna, but it seemed like a dream. For a moment, he wondered where he really was. Had it been a dream? Had he really seen Anna?

If it was a dream, then the memory of it would entertain him for days, he thought. It had been a good dream. Instinctively, he touched the wretched throbbing of his neck. It was wrapped in a bandage with some sort of salve. He rubbed his fingertips together and wondered what the substance was.

He moved stiffly beneath a pile of blankets, curious what time it was. Though there were no windows in his little room, he could tell it was daylight from the light streaming in from the open door and the hallway.

With a grunt, he threw off the blankets and started to scoot to the end of the bed. Realizing that he had no pants on, he stopped with a start. Scanning the room, he saw no clothes.

He shivered as his bare feet hit the floor, but there were no clothes to be found. He checked under the bed without success and sat back down on the end of the bed to think for a second.

His head started to swim again from the effort, and he sprawled back so that he was lying on the bed with his feet still on the floor. He laid like that for a long period, trying to gather some strength.

Finally, he wrapped the blanket around himself and cautiously shuffled down the hall. He could hear nothing as he stepped down the bare plank stairs. As he rounded the bottom step, he came to an abrupt stop, finding himself staring eye to eye with Anna's Aunt Molly.

She gave a small cry of alarm that further froze him at the bottom of the stairs, but after her momentary reaction, Aunt Molly gathered her composure. "Good Heavens," she said, "You gave me a start."

Lockett nodded, mindful that he should not open his mouth.

"I'm not used to house guests," she murmured, "It was so quiet that I had forgotten that you were here... James, right?"

He nodded again."

"Can't speak, poor soul? Never understand my niece," she muttered, walking across the room, "Course I never understood her father either, and he was my brother, and I had known him all my years." She walked out of the room, leaving Lockett still standing at the bottom of the stairs. After a moment, she poked her head back into the room. "Well, aren't you coming? You must be famished."

Without waiting for an answer, she disappeared again and Lockett followed after her in his wrapped blanket.

"You look as if you have missed a few meals. I sometimes wonder what they feed you boys on the lines. I'm sure the Yankees do so much better. Some of the prisoners that Colonel Morgan paraded through town were down right plump. And those Yankees who occupied Murfreesboro earlier this year, why they never missed a meal!"

She offered Lockett a plate of cold chicken and bread.

"Anna should be back shortly. She is picking up more cornmeal for me. Getting harder and harder to come by, but such is the war." She looked at the blanket wrapped around him. "And of course, we will have to do something for clothes. I wanted to burn those rags you were wearing, but Anna insisted on washing them thoroughly." She paused awkwardly, recognizing that her word choice may not have been the most appropriate given her guest's condition.

"Disposed of," she corrected, "But the shirt and jacket are beyond saving. I have no other men's clothing in this house. No, indeed. Not certain what my niece will do about that, but she'll do something. She is the resourceful type."

Aunt Molly puttered around the kitchen, perfectly content to carry the conversation for both of them. Lockett hungrily ate the food she put before him, surprised at how hungry he found himself. Each bite seemed to make him more ravenous than before.

"Dear me, I nearly forgot," Aunt Molly said suddenly. She briskly walked over and pulled the curtains shut. "Can't have the town talking about how there is a half-naked man eating in my kitchen. Rumors and gossip, rumors and gossip. They would be talking about me like they do for Preacher Hornsby's wife or her sister. Can you imagine?" she said, facing Lockett, who paid her no attention and remained focused on the food and water. "They would think me a harlot. Indeed. Indeed. Yes, must find you some clothes." She saw the nearly empty plate. "You'll eat me out of house and home," she said, but she took his plate away and returned with more food.

"Auntie, I'm home," came the sound of Anna's voice from the front door.

"Back here, dear."

Lockett could hear the floorboards creak as she neared, but it was not Anna's laugh that he heard next.

"Oh, Anna," Mattie Ready laughed. "This is how you treat your guests? Poor man's got no clothes."

It was said jokingly, but Aunt Molly saw no humor in it. Her face turned a deep shade of red, and all she could muster was, "Anna, you didn't say that there was anyone with you!"

"I was only teasing, Miss Molly," Mattie said quickly. "I insisted on coming with Anna. Mother wanted me to deliver y'all an early Christmas present, this pie."

"She wouldn't take 'no' for an answer," Anna added, looking both bemused and sympathetic with her aunt's reaction.

"Mattie never was one for that," Aunt Molly grumbled.

Mattie Ready left shortly after that, promising to return with some of her brother's clothing for James.

Lockett anxiously waited for an opening to relate the rest of his tale and dilemma with Anna, but Aunt Molly gave little opportunity for the two of them to be alone. It was not until night, while Anna checked his wounds in the attic that he was able to whisper how he had ended up here.

It had been a long tale to cover, but Anna did not say a word until he had completely finished the narrative.

"I suppose that I am not surprised that you ended up on a fool's errand for your brother. Someday, I should like to meet him, although from what I recall of Patrick's description of him, he sounds nothing like you."

He shrugged, knowing that she was right, but the unconscious movement sent a jolt of pain down his side.

"But now what do you do, James? After you have recuperated, you need to return to your army."

"I need that information from the spy first."

"But you don't even know who it is, James? How will you even begin to figure out who it is?"

"If I don't return with the information, then all of this was for nothing."

"You could not help it that the guide they provided betrayed you. You can't stay, James. Murfreesboro is an armed camp. Eventually, someone will figure you out."

He nodded. "The longer that I am here, the more dangerous this gets, but it needs to get done nonetheless. I need to do this quickly. I do know a few things. This spy has been here for a while, so the spy is a townsperson. And I know the location where the information is to be left."

"But you said that you don't know the signal to prompt the spy to leave the information. That died with this McGowan."

"Sounded like a good plan at the time," Lockett whispered ruefully, "That way if one of us was captured, it would not allow them to capture this spy. But it does leave me in a fine kettle of fish now."

"Ambrose returns here on Christmas Eve, James. That's not an eternity. It's not enough time. It's impossible. Do you know how many people live in Murfreesboro? And that's not counting all of the slaves here too."

He looked at her in surprise. "I think that is first time that I have ever heard you say that anything was *impossible*, Anna."

She looked away angrily.

* * *

December 9

Anna examined his wounds up in the attic.

"How do they look today?" he whispered. He had lost track of how many days he had been resting, cloistered in Aunt Molly's house. His body still shook with pain at most points during the day, but days of rest, care, and Aunt Molly's cooking had restored some degree of strength back in his limbs.

"A little better," she said, still studying, "I was thinking that if they did not look better by now that I would need to bring a doctor here, and that might bring some uncomfortable questions."

"Anna?" Aunt Molly called from below.

"Coming, Auntie."

Lockett spied clothing hanging over the back of the chair, as she rose from it. "I'll be down in a moment," he whispered again.

When he came down the stairs to the parlor, Anna was putting on a winter shawl. "I'll be back soon," she announced, "Just a quick errand for Auntie."

"Can't have an early Christmas present go without response. I waited too long as it was," Aunt Molly added, "That would be poor manners, poor manners indeed." She handed Anna a covered basket of food.

Lockett motioned with his hand, drawing puzzled looks from both women. He tried again, pointing at himself and then at Anna.

"I think he wants to go with you," Aunt Molly guessed, earning a nod from Lockett. "You do look surprisingly better today. That would be my chicken soup, of course."

"Come with me?" Anna exclaimed, shaking her head. "No, no, James. I'll be back soon. I think you need more rest."

Lockett motioned again and shook his head.

"I don't think he is agreeing, dear. It wouldn't be a bad idea to have some male accompany you. There is an army of men in town, and some of them take to drink even early in the day!"

"The Ready House is not far at all," Anna said with exasperation.

"Still, this town is not like it used to be, dear. Soldiers, soldiers everywhere. Of course, it is safer than when the Yankees were here, but a soldier is still a soldier. And at this time of year, they won't need much reason to celebrate with drink. It's the death of men, my dear, you see. Take him, take him. Mattie left a jacket. I'll get it for you."

Anna glared at Lockett as Aunt Molly left the room. "You are a lunatic," she hissed. "You can't go walking around town, following me on errands."

Aunt Molly returned with the jacket and hustled them out the front door.

"I can't stay locked inside the house, Anna," he whispered. "How am I going to figure out who the spy is if I'm locked in your Aunt's attic?"

"You're crazy. James, we need to figure out a plan to get you back to Nashville. Forget about the spy."

"My mission was to bring the General back his information, and that is what I am going to do, Anna. If I don't, then they'll hang my brother and then probably me for failing."

Anna was about to argue that they would not hang James, but she clamped her mouth shut instead. Truthfully, she was not sure if she cared or not if they hung his brother. Anybody who would put James in this position was not someone to be mourned, although she did have to admit that seeing him again had thrown off the melancholy that she had secretly been feeling, even if it was under these bizarre circumstances.

She had seen many inexplicable things since this war had started. Regardless, she could not see how it was possible for him to decipher who this spy might be. Murfreesboro was considerably larger than Savannah, and she was a stranger to most of the town folk. She could not imagine where to start. On top of that, walking around this lion's den, the headquarters of the Confederate army, well, that surely seemed like an act of suicidal lunacy.

But she did not know how to persuade James. So he accompanied her to the Ready house. They walked silently down Main Street, past the town square and the new courthouse.

When Anna paused at the front gate, Lockett looked in surprise at the large two story frame house. It was even larger than the building that Anna had pointed out as Bragg's headquarters.

"This is it?" he whispered.

"This is it. Garden lot, twin magnolias, all of it. Mr. Ready is an important man, former Congressman, lawyer, and vocal Secessionist." She looked at him, questioning herself, but there was no hesitation on James's face. He looked her square in the eye and nodded resolutely.

"Let's go," he whispered, "But I'll let you do the talking." He winked at her, trying to take the edge off of the moment.

She gave a quiet, resigned chuckle at his audacity. He was normally the quiet, practical sort, a typical farmer, but she had seen firsthand in Savannah that he also had a hidden streak of boldness and bravery, as the bushwhacker Bloody Bill Coulter had found out the hard way.

Anna used the brass knocker, and the front door was opened by a clean shaven, neatly attired slave. He ushered them in from the cold. "Ah'll summon Miss Mattie," he announced while a separate slave entered the large front hall and took their coats.

On either side of the impressive entrance, Lockett saw large parlors. Most people would gape at the two large and immaculately trimmed parlors, but not Lockett. Rather, his attention was on the two slaves. He had never been in a house with slaves before, and he could not help staring at them. They were not like the contraband that followed the army.

These two, one older man and one younger girl, melded into the background with a practiced ease. They were there momentarily, retreating to the corners of the room. Both were quiet and observant with eyes averted. Normally, people would forget that they were even in the room. However, that was not the case with Lockett. He had a strange fascination with them. It was really another realm, one that was far removed from his toil in the dark earthen fields of Kalamazoo.

As Mattie arrived, the slaves disappeared, though Lockett was sure that they were still within immediate earshot.

Mattie entered the room and greeted them, even more excited than usual. Her bright blue eyes flashed triumphantly, and her cheeks were flushed. "Come in, Anna," she said enthusiastically, beckoning them to sit. "This is a surprise. So good to see you moving around already, James. Anna's care is working miracles!"

Lockett nodded appreciatively, though he winced as the movement sent a stab of pain down his side.

"I can't wait to hear your story once your voice returns. Anna is a wonderful friend, but she can be neglectful when it comes to sharing certain things, like mentioning you. I always knew there must be a secret beau, what with the way that she turned the others away."

Lockett gave a sideways look at Anna.

"And how did you meet, Anna? Come now, now you must share at least that story with me. I can see now by your devotion to him and how you turned away the other suitors, that this must be quite the story."

In spite of the danger of the question, Lockett felt strangely like laughing.

Anna, usually so poised and self-possessed, stammered and hesitated, even though she had practiced in her head for days how she would answer such a question.

"Dear me," Mattie giggled, "I have never seen my dear Anna

so flummoxed... That is a sign of true love if there ever was one." She laid a sisterly hand on Lockett's forearm.

Self-consciously, Lockett reached up with his other hand and touched the bandaged burns on his neck.

"Never you mind that, James. You'll be fit as a fiddle in no time. Why, you'll be helping my fiancée chase these Yankees all the way back to Canada!" The spritely girl bounced from Lockett's side and took the basket from Anna.

"From Auntie," Anna said, "Merry Christmas, early, to you and your family."

"Oh, she shouldn't have, but that is so nice of her. She makes the most excellent pies. Perhaps, we can make it part of our celebration dinner."

"Celebration?" Anna asked.

"Didn't you hear the news this morning? My future husband had another great victory two days ago. They should be returning in a couple of days. The messenger said that they would be bringing two thousand prisoners and a large amount of stores from their raid in Hartsville."

From the grandiose way she spoke, one would think that her fiancée fought them single-handedly, and Lockett found himself wondering about her beau. He was obviously with the cavalry if he was on a raid.

"They should be back in Murfreesboro soon. I shall introduce you to him, James. He is the most chivalrous cavalier. Do you ride? Perhaps you could ride with him after you are fully recovered."

Lockett looked at Anna with a curious look.

"He doesn't know who your fiancée is," Anna said simply.

"Oh," Mattie replied with some surprise. "That is easily rectified. He is the dashing John Hunt Morgan."

The look of instant surprise was so obvious on James's face that it made Mattie giggle. "I see that you have heard of him," she said, quelling her giggles by lifting a hand to her mouth. "But, of course, everyone has."

Lockett glanced, eyes still wide with surprise, at Anna. It was hard to imagine that such a young girl would be engaged to such an important person.

"You might as well tell him the entire story," Anna said to

Mattie.

"But, of course, it was before you arrived here in Murfreesboro, Anna, so I should tell him the story." With excited eyes, she turned back to James. It was clear that she enjoyed relating it and had done so before. "It started last summer when the Yankees were here. The louts and barbarians thought it was a game to slander the names of many a good Southern man. One of the men even had the gall to insult Colonel John Hunt Morgan, and in the presence of ladies no less! Well, I could stay quiet no longer!"

Lockett could easily imagine Mattie Ready having difficulty restraining herself.

"So I quickly told him how inferior he was to the good Colonel Morgan, who rode circles around the enemy, taking what he wished and defeating those who tried to oppose him! The newspapers keep us quite well informed of his many victories, you see."

She paused to take a breath, and Lockett had to catch himself from interjecting a question or two.

"Well, then, the Yankee demanded to know who *I* was," she continued "I told him that 'It's Mattie Ready now, but by the grace of God one day I hope to call myself the wife of John Morgan!'"

"She had only known Colonel Morgan a short time at that point. He had come calling once at the invitation of Mattie's father, the Congressman," Anna inserted, having heard this story multiple times from multiple places since arriving in Murfreesboro.

"Well, obviously, we chased the Yankees from Murfreesboro since the summer. There are no Yankees here now!" Mattie said emphatically.

Lockett fought to keep a small smile from creasing his face, but he stole a peek at Anna, who feared she was turning red from the suppressed amusement caused by the comment.

"Yes, there are no Yankees here now," Anna agreed, unable to resist.

"No, of course not, my beau, my John, made sure of that."

"Eventually, word of her encounter had made its way to Colonel Morgan," Anna explained, "So he came here to pay a call to show his respect for her confidence in him. And from there..."

"Of course, we are now engaged to be married," Mattie smiled brightly.

After a brief stay at the Ready's, Anna and Lockett returned to Aunt Molly's, where she worked her needlework from the rocking chair in the parlor. "Dear me," she said upon their return, "Perhaps it was too soon for you to be up and about. You are starting to look pale again."

She ushered Lockett to a seat, and he gratefully complied. Her observation was correct. Even though their time away had been short, he felt unusually tired.

Aunt Molly gave a maternal frown. "Too much, too soon. Too much, too soon."

"He can be difficult to slow down," Anna said, "Always a bit too stubborn for his own good." But she gave Lockett a small smile that warmed him despite his predicament.

"Sounds like someone else I used to know, my brother, your father."

The quirk of Aunt Molly's words was not lost on Lockett who closed his eyes. Two men, two spies but for opposite sides...

"He could never stay still," Aunt Molly continued, "Even when he fell from that horse, it didn't keep him down long. Up and moving before he should have been, that was him all right."

Lockett nodded politely. He had become more like Preacher Tucker than he ever could have guessed.

Chapter 28

December 10

Lockett sat in the parlor, soaking in the morning sun through the lone window. Anna was situated across from him. Aunt Molly, as usual, sat in her rocking chair.

He wished that Aunt Molly would leave the house, but she was clear that she could not leave the two of them without a chaperone. The only opportunities where Lockett could whisper his thoughts to Anna came in the moments when she attended to his wounds up in the attic. They were fleeting moments, and he still had too many questions for Anna, too many thoughts to share on where to go from here.

He felt tired, and his body still wished to rest, but he knew the clock was ticking. Anna had said that Ambrose would return on Christmas Eve, and General Rosecrans needed this information as soon as possible.

Lockett had seen the concern on Anna's face this morning when the subject had been broached. It did not look like Anna. The Anna that he had known in Savannah was so full of life and absent of worry that it seemed like she lived in a different world. And it was that sunny outlook of hers that drew the affection of so many of the desperate and wounded soldiers in that field hospital, not to mention entrapping Lockett himself.

Looking back and considering her double life, it was all the more remarkable that she had displayed no trace of worry and concern. But now... Now, he could see the brew of worry collecting behind those dark, enchanting eyes. He needed to hurry, he knew. The longer he stayed, the greater the likelihood that he would be discovered. The longer he stayed, the riskier it became for Anna.

If only he knew the signal that would alert the spy to his

presence, he sighed.

His brooding was interrupted by a knock at the door.

"Preacher Hornsby, this is surprise," Aunt Molly said, opening the door. "Please come in."

"Thank you, ma'am," he replied, removing his broad rimmed hat.

"I heard that you had a visitor, and I wanted to meet him."

Preacher Hornsby was a tall, thin middle-aged man. He had a thin, wispy hair with a stooping posture but a boyish, clean-shaven face.

"This must be the man here."

Lockett tried to rise to his feet.

"No, no, stay seated, lad. I had heard that you were wounded in the Cause. Ah, yes, that is nasty looking poking out from that bandage. How did it happen?"

"He can't speak right now," Anna interjected. "The wound, you see..."

"Pity," the preacher said. "You came with the other wounded on the train, I understand. How fortunate for you, soldier, that you knew people in Murfreesboro. Most of the wounded were from near here or Eastern Tennessee. It is odd to see someone from a Western Tennessee unit here."

He looked at Lockett, and Lockett felt a twinge of discomfort at being studied. Finally, the preacher continued, "Yet, if there is one thing about this fight for our freedom, it has brought people from far and wide. I was just with General Ector's brigade, and they are all Texans."

"Texas," Anna agreed, "That is a long way."

"Texans," Aunt Molly said with a face, "Would those be the scoundrels making such a racket the other day? Drunk as could be! And in the middle of the day!" Aunt Molly exclaimed in despair. "Why it made me wonder what kind of army this is? How does General Bragg get such success with such men!"

"Auntie," Anna chided gently. "They are not all drunkards."

"Seems like every Texan I've seen likes his liquor. Why, even your own father came back from that war down there with a taste for it."

"Auntie, you sound like you don't want them here, but just the other day, you were praising those who came so far to defend your home."

Properly chastened, Aunt Molly said nothing.

"Such is the cry for freedom," the preacher said, "They will come from all corners of the country to defend liberty."

"Indeed, indeed," Aunt Molly agreed.

"No more just cause than 1776 itself was," Preacher Hornsby added, and Lockett could feel a sermon coming on.

The preacher stayed for another hour, sharing news with Aunt Molly, much of it the same news on Hartsville that Mattie had related to them earlier.

Lockett feigned dozing in his chair after a while.

Finally, the preacher pulled an old time piece out of his waist pocket. "Time to go," he announced, "The generals do not like their daily prayer meetings to start late. I guess there is a war to run." The slim preacher gave a surprising belly laugh at his own joke, and he pulled on his coat.

Flurries were starting to swirl outside in spite of the blue sky overhead. After the preacher left, Anna stood. "Rather beautiful out there, Auntie. James, how about a short walk?"

"Is that such a good idea?" Aunt Molly asked.

"Some fresh air will do him some good, Auntie."

James nodded in agreement.

Anna retrieved his coat.

The blast of cold air stunned him momentarily when they stepped outside, but he was glad that Anna had suggested it. He needed to talk, and this was the only way.

She slipped an arm through his, and they headed up the deserted end of the street, away from the town center. "We won't be able to walk too far in this direction, some Alabamians have set up their camp not too far from here, but we can turn around before getting too close."

"Thanks," he said, "I've been getting desperate to talk to you."

She squeezed his arm but said nothing.

"I think I can cross the preacher off my list of potential spies."

"That is an understatement. Preacher Hornsby has quite the reputation as a Secessionist, a long-time Secessionist."

"At least I can cross two off my list. I don't believe Mattie is a candidate either."

"James, this is foolhardy. It's impossible. There are 1500

people in Murfreesboro and just as many slaves, not to mention all of the soldiers. What will you do, cross them off your list one by one? You don't even know for sure that there is still a spy here. He might have left."

"Do you have any idea who it might be, Anna?"

"Why? Because it takes one to know one?" she said sharply. They lapsed into silence for a moment. "Sorry," Anna murmured softly. "I just don't think that you understand the position you are in. Every minute that you are here…" She lapsed into silence and let the unspoken thought hang above them.

He reached for her hand. "I understand," he said, "And I admit that I am… am conflicted. I should leave, but I don't want to leave you… again."

"James, you can't *stay*." The words were both imploring and plainly practical.

"I know. Ambrose will be here in a matter of weeks."

"That is, if no one else has figured out who you really are before then…"

"Ambrose is the only one that I am worried about," he lied to himself. "Your idea about a throat injury was brilliant. That will deflect attention."

He paused before broaching the next subject, one that he had been thinking about since his first day here. "Anna, how much did Ambrose tell you about our encounter last summer?"

"Enough."

"Did he tell you that I saved his life?"

She hesitated. "He neglected to mention that, but Ambrose is very proud. I doubt that he would want to admit something like that."

They stepped to the edge of the road as a troop of horsemen filled the roadway and trotted past them. Slowly, the riders sauntered into the distance.

Anna though was still contemplating James's last words. With a peculiar look, she teased him with a twinkle of merriment in her dark eyes. "So," she started and then paused as the twinkle dazzled him, "When will you save Aunt Molly?"

Lockett looked at her in confusion.

Anna smiled. "I mean, you've saved all of the other Tuckers at one point or another. Me, Father, Ambrose…"

It was her old smile, the one that had been burned into Lockett's memory and dreams. It was the smile from Savannah that had enthralled him from the beginning; it was the smile that had leaked into his thoughts at moments around the cook fires; it was the smile that creased his mind in sudden flashes as he waited for the Confederates at Perryville.

He could not help but feel the warmth course through his body at seeing it again. A wide grin came across his face, and he stared at her. It was as if both were under a spell and could not move or look away.

It made him want to stay, war or not. How could he leave her again? He just couldn't! How could he live without seeing that smile each day? Still, he answered, "I will leave before Ambrose gets here, Anna. I promise you that. One way or another, I will leave before then."

Anna took a long breath and then gave an acquiescing nod. "Then we should start figuring out *how* you will get back."

"I already have a plan for that, Anna. I just need help figuring out who I was to meet. There is a spy here somewhere, and I need their information."

He left unsaid what was on both of their minds. She was a Rebel after all, a former Rebel spy at that, and here he was talking about finding information to benefit the Union army.

The sheer irony of what he was saying was not lost on either of them. She clasped his hands and buried her head in his chest.

"I hate this war," she managed to utter through the mutual emotion.

They stood frozen, wishing that moment together would not end. Yet, they both knew that it would be fleeting, more fleeting than the flurries on a blue sky day.

Chapter 29

December 11

Daniel Lockett snapped wide awake with a start. His heavy, panting breath left a fog in the cold night air, but it could not be seen in the pitch black. His eyes flashed around the tent while his mind grappled with where he was. Finally, he sighed in relief, realizing that it had been a dream, just a nightmare.

As his breathing regulated, he knew that there would be no more sleep this night, again... He wished that he could find a way to push the nightmares from his head. He had tried to ignore them at first. Then, he had tried a different tack and tried to remember all that he could, but neither tactic expunged them from his memory. Each night, the gruesome sights came back, always the same...

There was the pool of blood, so red, thick and viscous, almost like molasses, as it spread in a broadening pool. Slowly and inevitably, it approached him.

In the dream, Daniel watched the blood come closer and closer, he wanted to move, to back up as it neared, but he could not. His legs were frozen in place, and ever so slowly, it reached him. It was then that Daniel realized in his dream that he was not standing, rather he was lying down and the blood would lap up against his face. He could feel the heat, not just warm, but hot, like it was burning his skin.

He would try to roll away, but all that could move were the eyes in his head, and as he struggled to move, they would eventually glance out across the crimson flood until he saw the source. It was the girl. He did not know her name. He just knew that he had been with her ever so briefly, and now she lay on the ground. A wretched gunshot wound gaped at him and the lifeless eyes stared at him. They were not accusing eyes; they were not imploring eyes; they were nothing, just staring into nothingness.

The blood was rising by then, covering his nose and mouth so that it was getting hard to breathe, and it was then, always then, that he awoke with a start.

* * *

Aunt Molly continued to sweep the floor of the parlor area where James dozed.

She had spent the morning working laundry at the cold tub in the back and then moved on to straightening the entire house. She worked without stop and seemingly without notice of James. She talked to herself all the while.

He supposed that she spoke to entertain herself, and it had taken him a while to realize that she was not addressing him as she harped on the quality of soap now with a war on, the lack of a decent straw broom, how easy it was for mud and dirt to be tramped into the house, the noise that the soldiers made in town, how certain women paid too much attention to the soldiers, and how certain women paid too little attention to the soldiers.

After a while, he found that her constant prattle was like a steady drone that relaxed him, and he snoozed contentedly, only waking up when the wide hipped woman bumped his chair as she attempted to dust an end table.

She looked at him but made no apology. Perhaps, she thinks me a lazy lout, he mused. He was unaccustomed to such inactivity, which did make him fidgety at times, but on the other hand, his body was demanding sleep like it never had before.

A gust of wind blew against the window and rattled the pane, drawing their attention.

"Going to be cold soon, mark my words," Aunt Molly said. "I'll need to split more wood."

Taking the hint, Lockett waved to get her attention. Pointing to himself, he then made a chopping motion with his hands.

"Why, indeed, that would be helpful," she said.

He rose from the chair and stretched his back. It would be good for his muscles to do some work, he decided as another blast of wind rattled the glass. He looked out the window and saw two women walking past the house. One jostled the other as the gust knocked her off stride.

"Preacher Hornsby's wife, Ruth, and her older sister, Mary," Aunt Molly said, following his gaze, "Poor dear lost her husband last year." She noticed his questioning look and accurately guessed the question on his mind. "Consumption, not the war. My, no. They are too old to be fighting. Then she moved in with her sister and the preacher."

Lockett nodded. He wasn't sure which sister was which, but it was the second day in a row that he had seen the heavy set one out for a walk.

"The wood pile is in the back," Aunt Molly said with a polite cough.

With a small grin, Lockett rubbed his hands together and wondered how much strength he would have to swing the axe.

* * *

The news had taken Murfreesboro by storm.

As Lockett accompanied Anna to the general store in the afternoon, he was struck by how many townspeople were outside, putting up bunting, wreaths, and garlands. He wasn't sure that he had ever seen any place so excited for Christmas.

As they entered the simple two story frame building of Tompkins General Store, Anna was greeted by the animated Mrs. Tompkins. The pudgy-faced woman with gray hair in a tight bun grasped Anna by the hand. "Isn't this the most exciting news that you have ever heard?"

Anna looked blankly at her.

"The news, dear, the news!"

"I guess I have not heard this news," Anna replied.

"The President is coming, child, coming here to Murfreesboro! Can you believe that?"

"Here?"

"I know, isn't that the most wonderful news? Our little town has never seen the likes!"

"Manners, Millie." From behind the counter came a thin elderly man with a cane. "Can't you see that Miss Anna has brought her guest?" He reached a free hand out to Lockett. "We heard about you, young man." They shook hands, and the shopkeeper added, "Mattie was here yesterday, told us all about you. Don't worry about replying, we know about your throat."

Self-consciously, Lockett reached up and touched the bandage that covered his neck and jaw. Only the tips of the burn on the lower half of his cheek were visible.

"So you are the one who caused Anna to send away all of the others?" Mrs. Tompkins queried, eyeing him. She did not look impressed.

"President Davis is coming here? To Murfreesboro?" Anna asked, trying to change the subject.

"An incredible honor, eh? Our town has seen nothing like this before," Mr. Tompkins replied.

"Why is he coming here?"

"Must want to speak with General Bragg. No other reason that I can see. It's a little late to remove Bragg for his failures in Kentucky, so maybe they have a new plan to hatch. Maybe we will go on the attack soon and re-take Nashville from those Yankee devils."

* * *

As they walked back from the general store, both Anna and Lockett were lost in silent reflection, which was just as well. There was no opportunity for Lockett to confer on anything with Anna. There was too much commotion on the sides of the street as people prepared for President Davis's arrival the next day. Even at Bragg's headquarters, Lockett could see soldiers weaving green garlands through the railing of the balcony that covered the front entrance. There were also red, white, and blue buntings dipping over the railing that had not been there when they had first come this way.

It was hard to comprehend what he would see tomorrow.

Lost in his own thoughts, he did not notice the soldier coming from the opposite direction who veered his path directly in front of theirs.

"Anna, what a pleasant surprise?" came the deep voice. The words were directed to Anna, but the man was staring aggressively at Lockett.

A tall, well-dressed young Captain with long, curling brown

hair stood in front of Lockett, studying him with a critical eye. As Lockett turned his head to meet the gaze, revealing the bandaged area, he could feel the man's blue eyes settle on the burns poking out from the edges of the bandages.

"I don't believe we have met," the words were said more grudgingly than in a friendly manner.

"William," Anna said, "I did not see you."

"Yes, you seemed lost in your own world."

"The news of the day," she replied airily.

The captain nodded. "Yes, it is not every day that President Davis visits this part of the country."

"Captain William Ellicott," he said, stretching out a hand.

Lockett took the handshake, while Anna answered. "His wound has damaged his throat."

Ellicott cocked a head sidewise and studied what he could see of the wound. "Must be worse than looks," he said skeptically. "Who are you with?"

"He's a friend from Savannah," Anna answered.

Ellicott nodded but returned his gaze to Lockett. "Which Tennessee regiment?"

There was a brief moment of awkward silence. Then Lockett raised four fingers.

"Fourth Tennessee? Provisional or regular?"

Lockett nodded.

"Regular?"

Lockett nodded again.

"Colonel Strahl is a good man," Ellicott said. "Part of Stewart's Brigade. They have seen some fighting over the last year... Of course, I don't recall them doing any lately."

"Are you on your way back to headquarters, William?" Anna asked. "William is part of General Bragg's staff," she explained to Lockett. "He is always very busy for the General."

"I am," Ellicott answered, "There is much to do before tomorrow."

"I can only imagine," Anna answered, "Will you get to meet the President?"

"That would be customary for the General's staff."

"How wonderful for you."

"Many preparations to go still. Perhaps, you would let me call on you afterwards?" Ellicott looked boldly at Lockett.

Lockett tried to hide his rising temper and clenched his teeth slightly, but Anna's response was said with a disarming evenness. "I think I shall be otherwise occupied right now, William. I have already promised much to Aunt Molly. It is a very busy time right now for everyone."

"Of course," he said stiffly with a slight bow. "Until later then."

"Until later," Anna answered, and Ellicott departed.

After he left, Anna and Lockett continued on their way.

"He's suspicious," Lockett said softly.

"He's not smart enough to be suspicious," Anna answered, drawing a surprised look from Lockett for her bluntness. "He's jealous, James, not suspicious."

* * *

It was the middle of the afternoon when John Hunt Morgan's latest prisoners arrived. Using his height and standing on his toes, Lockett looked over the top of the crowd as hundreds of on-lookers jeered the half-frozen blue coated prisoners coming through the main street of Murfreesboro.

The day had turned cold and windy. The icy gusts cut right through Lockett's clothing, but it was the sight that chilled him more than the weather. Some of the prisoners were in bad shape, limping through the streets on frost bitten feet. Most had been stripped of their boots, no doubt re-acquisitioned into service for a needy Confederate.

The crowd heckled and cursed the prisoners with surprising vehemence. He was glad that the prisoners were accompanied by a strong contingent of Morgan's raiders, if only for their own protection from the crowd. Murfreesboro was not like Savannah, he realized.

In Savannah, the presence of the Union Army had worn on the patience of many people, but the town had been a mixture of Unionists and Confederate sympathizers that perhaps over time leaned away from the imposing blue army, but Murfreesboro was different.

This was a full-throated cry for the Cause, for Secession. It was not just because of the current presence of the Confederate headquarters. These emotions were real and raw. They could not be faked.

It only made Lockett more sad. He felt the same nauseating despair that he felt after Shiloh. It was the bitter realization that the war was far from over. There was serious doubt that such emotions could ever be repaired. How could they ever live together as one nation again, whenever that someday was? He had trouble imagining how something torn apart so violently could ever be sewn back together.

Anna seemed to be feeling the same thing, because she pulled him down to whisper in his ear, "Let's go."

Lockett shook his head. It was difficult to watch the humiliation and pain of his fellow soldiers, but if he and Anna were to walk away, they would be the only ones in the crowd to do so, and he did not want to draw attention to himself.

Slowly, the pathetic trail made its way past the crowd. Most kept their heads down and trudged onwards, but one bearded corporal shook his fist and spat in return to someone in the crowd who threw something at him. For his defiance, the man received a rifle butt in the side from a Morgan's raider, and his comrades pulled him into the middle of their mass lest he be tempted to get into more trouble.

When the parade of humiliation was finally over, Anna and Lockett thankfully headed home.

December 12

Daniel stood next to Patrick McManus and a number of other men from the company. Solemnly, they watched the punishment drill in front of them. Twenty men were wearily dragging railroad ties behind them. Lap after lap of it had rutted the rocky soil. The ties bounced as they jolted over exposed rock that would not be carved away like the dirt had been.

This was eighth hour for the men, and nearly all of the men staggered beneath the load. At first, it had been little trouble for them, but now fatigue and thirst tortured their muscles and throats. The pile of canteens sat nearby, visible on the backstretch on every lap as an additional vindictive stab, but there was to be not one sip until the punishment was completed.

"I'm glad it's not us," Daniel muttered.

There was a murmur of agreement before Prosper T. Rowe added, "'Cept next time, the whole company will get the punishment. The Colonel ain't just talkin'."

With too much time on their hands and too little discipline from their oft drunk captain, things were spinning out of control. A simple argument had led to claims of thievery, which had led to counter-claims of card cheats, which had led to shoves, which had led to blows, which had led to others joining the fray until there were 30 men from two companies engaging in an outright melee.

The irate Colonel Blair had promised punishment to all involved and to the entire company next time.

"Definitely glad it is not us," Daniel repeated as one man fell to his knees and then face first into the ground in exhaustion.

Levi Thickle nodded silently, gently touching his fat lip. He was one of ten who had escaped punishment by claiming successfully, albeit untruthfully, that he had only been trying to break it up.

They all watched Sergeant Bosworth yank the fallen man from the ground, ordering him to continue until the full punishment was delivered, exhausted limbs be damned.

"Wouldn't be in this mess if the captain would keep everyone busier during the day," John Messern grumbled. "Ain't gonna say I liked it then, but Lieutenant Lockett was good about preventing idle time and the Devil's hands."

"When do you think the Lieutenant will return?" young Sam Baker asked.

There was no answer to that.

* * *

In the dark of evening, Lockett closed his eyes and listened. The bandages lay next to him, as they hoped that letting some air get to the burn would help the healing process. He sat in the parlor with Anna and Aunt Molly. The older woman worked on her omnipresent needlework while Anna read aloud from the Bible.

It reminded Lockett of the peaceful time that he and Anna had spent together in Savannah. She would read the Bible aloud on the front porch of the Tucker house.

Those had been moments when Lockett forgot there was a war on; those had been moments when Lockett realized he had feelings for her like he had never felt before; those had been moments before he realized that there was so much more to the Tuckers.

His musings were interrupted by a knock on the door. He stole a look at Anna, knowing that they were not expecting any visitors. Aunt Molly answered the door.

"My dear Mattie, come in," Aunt Molly said as bright-eyed Mattie stepped in, an exuberant smile on her face. "Oh," continued Aunt Molly. "Colonel Morgan, isn't it?"

"Ma'am," a deep voice answered. The visitor took off his short brimmed kepi, "Evening."

"I apologize for coming over unannounced, Miss Molly," Mattie said, "I just had to share my excitement with Anna."

"You are always welcome," Aunt Molly said, her own voice excited at the prospect of visitors, particularly a colonel in her house, "Please have a seat, Colonel." She motioned Colonel Morgan toward the empty seat next to James. "Can I offer you some refreshment?"

Lockett blinked in surprise at John Hunt Morgan. This was the man who had plagued his army for the last six months, standing directly in front of him!

Dumbfounded, he stared at the sturdily built man who carried himself with the confidence and dash that accompanied his reputation. Goateed with a strong jaw and thick nose, he looked to Lockett like a man ready to lead men into battle at a moment's notice.

"No, thank you, ma'am. We have just come from the Ready household, and they treated us to a feast."

"We have splendid news," Mattie told Anna. She paused. "John has been made a brigadier general."

"Congratulations, sir," Anna said, "Well deserved from all that we have heard."

Morgan chuckled, "Mattie is having some fun with you. That was not the news that she wanted to share with you."

Anna looked questioningly at Mattie.

"We are getting married in two days!"

Anna gave a cry of joy and hugged Mattie. "Oh, Mattie! Oh, congratulations, Mattie!"

Lockett, seeing Morgan look at him, stood and offered a wordless handshake. Morgan took Lockett's proffered hand with a crushing grip.

"You must be the young soldier that Mattie told me about. James, isn't it?" He eyed the nasty burn and scarring on his unbandaged neck and jaw. There was a flicker of soldierly recognition in seeing the gruesome wound, but beyond that, there was no sympathy. Both men knew such was the price in war. "No need to reply," Morgan added quickly, "Mattie told me about the difficulty of your voice."

"A Christmas time wedding," Anna interrupted intentionally, squeezing Mattie again.

"No time like the present with a war on," Morgan added.

"The Confederacy needs him off terrorizing Yankees, so the time seemed right."

"Actually, tomorrow seemed better," Morgan joked, "But there is the slight matter of President Davis's arrival. I suppose I will play second fiddle to him."

They all laughed except for Lockett who forced a quiet smile.

"I take it from Mattie's first news that the President has finally arrived," Anna said.

"Finally," Mattie answered, "Much delayed, but President Davis did arrive. He is at Oaklands tonight."

"That's the Maney's house," Aunt Molly commented, "What a privilege!"

"Train schedules are never very accurate," Morgan explained, "And with all of the adoring folk along the rail, he was much delayed, but the great man did arrive."

"But his first action upon his arrival was to duly promote my dear John," Mattie broke in proudly.

"Congratulations all around indeed," Aunt Molly added, "A General in my house? I am so honored."

"And you would honor us, ma'am, with your attendance at the wedding in two days' time."

"Imagine all those Generals, Miss Molly," Mattie said teasingly, "It will be the likes of which Murfreesboro, or any place else, has never seen."

December 13

The morning cook fires had been extinguished, but the normal routine had been disrupted by the delivery of mail. That was one benefit to being in one place so long, Daniel mused. The mail found them much easier and with greater frequency, but there was no mail for him today.

He had not noticed McManus idling up behind him. There was never any mail for him with his wife being dead and his father illiterate.

"Your brother used to look forward to mail call so much," McManus remarked.

Daniel turned his red-rimmed, sleep-deprived eyes towards the familiar voice. The voice was familiar, but the light blue Irish eyes did not look back at him with their normal vitality. Since their initial confrontation after being released from jail, things had been cool between the two old neighbors.

Feeling some remorse, Daniel replied, "Yes, I can see now why he would look forward to a letter so much. It does seem like we are a thousand miles from home."

The two old friends looked at the other's drained countenances.

Finally, McManus said, "Looks like you have not been sleeping well."

Daniel opened his mouth, but then shut it quickly. He wanted to tell McManus about the nightmares, tell somebody, but he could not. How could he? It would just add to his fouled reputation as a coward.

Seeing the initial hesitancy and that the younger Lockett was not going to respond, McManus continued in a low, almost whispering voice. "You're not the only one who gets nightmares, you know."

"How did you know about that?" Daniel said, stunned.

"I know a lot about what goes on in this company," McManus replied patiently, "Very little happens here without me knowing about it." He paused before adding. "Besides, sometimes I get up and wander a bit at night myself..."

Daniel clenched his hands together and looked at the ground. "I keep seeing her face, Patrick." He squeezed his hands tightly together as the image of the blood and the sightless eyes came back to him.

"Whose face?"

"The whore. The spy. Whatever she was. The dead one. It's horrible, Patrick." The look of surprise on McManus's face was unmistakable, and it stopped Daniel from clenching and unclenching his hands. "What? Why are you looking at me like that?"

McManus tilted his head. "I always said you two were more alike than anyone realized," he muttered to himself. "I used to describe you two as two sides of the same leaf."

Daniel looked at him quizzically. "So what are you saying?"

"No one else knows this but me," he said solemnly. Only in his old friend's confidences would James Lockett share his problem about the nightmares of little Amelia's death.

"Are you talking about my nightmares? James? He would think me a coward again for having such dreams," Daniel said sourly.

"No, he would not," McManus replied so fervently that it startled Daniel. "You see, he has the same sort of nightmares involving the death of a little girl in Missouri."

"James? He does?"

McManus nodded.

"What girl in Missouri? I don't know anything about this."

"There's a lot that you don't know about your brother."

"He killed a girl in Missouri? Is that why you two came home from the Sharpshooters? I thought it was because you were ill."

"He did kill a girl in Missouri, 'cept it wasn't his fault. But that hasn't stopped him from getting nightmares about it. He was trying to save her when it happened. Your brother is always putting his neck on the line for somebody other than himself. Remember Otto Klugge?"

"The big German who was killed at Perrysville?"

McManus nodded. "Your brother stuck out his neck for him. For the girl in Missouri. For you, obviously... God knows how many other people."

As close as they were, even Patrick McManus did not know about Lockett's most surprising example, risking it all for the Tuckers back in Savannah.

"Is he coming back, Patrick?"

McManus bit his lip. He did not want to reply, not to spare Daniel, rather he just couldn't bear to utter the words aloud. Finally, he said softly, "I don't know, Daniel. It's been weeks now. Something did not go right."

"Things never go right in the army," Daniel answered with the wisdom of a wizened soldier.

"Never," McManus agreed. "Except in times past, there were others there to help your brother. Me, Milton, the boys... This time, he's on his own, Daniel, and it's cutting me to the bone."

He stopped and wiped a tear from his reddened Irish face.

"James has got no one to help him this time."

* * *

The blue sky and nearly spring like temperatures seemed to match the mood in Murfreesboro, Lockett thought to himself. The town was alive with exuberance and excitement.

The President was in town, meeting with the Confederate generals and receiving a grand review of the army, or so it was told to Lockett by Henry, an adolescent slave in the Ready household.

Lockett sat in the garden next to the Ready's house. Henry was, in theory, to attend to anything that he might need, but given that Lockett would not speak, it was a strange silence as he sat on the bench, occasionally punctuated by Henry spouting the news of the day in short bursts to him.

Anna was inside with Mattie, preparing for tomorrow, talking, doing things that Lockett couldn't figure out.

This house, this place, was not like what he was used to. There were a few large, stately houses like this back in Kalamazoo, but those were a far cry from his own home. There was no comparing someone who lived in a little farmhouse like his, working dawn to dusk, with someone who lived in such elegance. And of course, there were no slaves in Kalamazoo.

The elegance and prosperity of any big house always made him uncomfortable, but never more so than now as he stared at the ebony slave across from him. The boy was the only one around who seemed to be doing nothing. All around the house and garden, there were other slaves in a whirl of activity. Winter and holly berries were strung in decoration. A large wreath was being hung above the door, and no doubt, the inside of the house was even busier. As for the Ready family themselves, Lockett had seen little of them.

He wondered now if his insistence on accompanying Anna here was so wise. She had explained that one of Mattie's seven siblings was on General Hardee's staff. He hoped that the brother would not return home while Lockett waited outside, a sore thumb to be observed. But he also knew that he could not just sit inside of Aunt Molly's house and let the war go by.

Finally, Anna emerged from the house with two packages under her arm. Clothes for each of them, she explained, clothes appropriate for a gala like tomorrow would be. Lockett fingered the material she handed him, knowing that he had never worn such fine clothing as that before. He could only shrug. He was such a long way from the dark soil of his little farm.

Chapter 30

December 14

Orrin Long licked his fingers and counted through the paper currency again. He didn't like the newfangled money; gold was more to his liking, but the greenbacks seemed to be holding their value for now, unlike the Rebels' worthless scrip.

He counted again and came up with the same number. Satisfied, he put it in the heavy metal strongbox that he kept. With a look of disgust, he hefted it one last time to test the weight and then locked it.

This new assignment with Colonel Wilks kept him too busy to be as directly involved in his money making schemes as he had been in Missouri, plus he needed more middlemen now to pull it off, and middlemen cost shares.

On the other hand, the Army of the Cumberland was far larger than the army had been in Missouri. There was far more opportunity here to pilfer blankets, uniforms, and other goods intended for the army and resell them to the ubiquitous sutlers. It was lucrative and ridiculously easy as long as you knew which hands to grease with a bribe here and there.

With his personal business taken care of for the moment, he returned his attention to the report that he was writing for Wilks to share with General Rosecrans. The report would say that, sadly, there was no word from Lieutenant Lockett, and given the weeks that had passed, it was assumed that he was captured or dead. Unfortunately, Wilks would have to report that there was no other way to retrieve the information. The General would have to decide what to do without it, but that mattered not at all to Orrin Long.

Rather, Orrin Long smiled to the empty room. Lockett was gone, and he had his revenge. He knew in his heart that Lockett was dead, probably at the hands of the filthy lump of a man who was his guide. He could not remember the man's name, but it was of no consequence. All that mattered was that the impudent, self-righteous farmer, who had been such a thorn in his side, was now dead.

* * *

"You look like a dignified Southern gentleman now," Anna said as she adjusted Lockett's loaned clothes, "Except for this, of course." She gently caressed his cheek and bandaged neck.

They stood in the tiny attic, and Lockett looked back at her in the fine dress that she had borrowed from Mattie. She was more beautiful than ever, and he could not take his eyes off her.

The blue gown was like nothing he had ever seen her wear before, far from the conservative and almost homely dresses that she normally wore. The dress exposed her shoulders and graceful neckline, all the more so with her dark hair curled up in combs. A long, solitary curl dangled from each temple, covering the front of each ear.

She pulled herself close to him.

"What about Aunt Molly?"

"Auntie is not here."

"Really?" Lockett said with some surprise.

"She already left for their house. I think she's quite distracted by all the goings-on tonight."

They held each other tightly in silence, and he could feel her heart beat drumming against his.

"You don't have to go tonight, James. It would be easy to claim that you do not feel up to it." She paused and then added, "But I know the answer already."

"And miss a real Southern wedding?" he joked.

"It will be your best chance," Anna admitted. "Whoever this spy is, he will be there tonight. Anyone with any real connections in Murfreesboro will be there tonight, though I still don't know how you sort that out."

"Neither do I, but it will come to me."

"Such confidence," she said with her own mock bravado before turning serious. "There is something else that has occurred to me,

James."

"What's that?"

"Maybe you never find your spy and get their information, but what if you return to your lines with your own information?"

"What do you mean?"

"I mean, what if you subtly collect your own information on General Bragg's plans tonight? He will be there, as will the rest of his command and all of their staffs."

"You want me to ask General Bragg what he is planning for us Yankees?"

"Not you," she said slowly, "You are a mute after all... I mean... me."

"You're going to ask Bragg?" he said, frowning.

"Not so directly mind you."

"Never, Anna," he snapped, "I can't ask you to do that. I've already involved you too deeply as it is... Not to mention the fact that you are not a Unionist."

"I... I suppose I don't know what I am anymore," she said, hesitating.

He blew a slow breath out through puffed cheeks. "I know the feeling," he replied, thinking back to Savannah.

They held each other for minutes. The silence coated them like a second skin, trapping their unspoken thoughts.

Finally, he said, "We best not be late." Although he had little desire to move from that spot at this moment.

"Best not," Anna agreed without moving either.

Lockett quietly contemplated what lay ahead. He was about to enter a houseful of Confederate generals and other officers. The chances of discovery seemed high. Discovery would mean death, and not just for him alone anymore. Even though Anna and Aunt Molly were women, there would be no mercy for them either. If he was discovered, then they would surely be seen as accomplices.

"James," Anna said softly, sensing the same enormity of the night.

Fearing that he might not ever have the opportunity again, Lockett bent down and kissed her passionately.

* * *

They were admitted to the house by a pair of handsomely dressed house slaves, who took Anna's heavy winter shawl and quietly retreated. The large house was alive with light, noise, and people. It seemed to him that all eyes in the place turned toward them when they entered, but he knew that none of those eyes were focused on him. Anna laid a dainty white lace gloved hand on his elbow, and he escorted her out of the large hall and into one of the large parlors.

The candles were bright against the winter darkness. Their light glinted off of an ocean of gold braided officers, ceremonial swords at their sides. Their smiling and well-dressed Southern belles stood by their sides or mingled with each other.

It was like nothing that Lockett had ever seen before or could even imagine. The elegance and richness of both the men's and women's attire amazed him. He found himself staring at one Confederate general. His gray uniform was unlike any that Lockett had seen on a battlefield. There were gold epaulettes on his shoulders and swirling golden stitching that signified his importance from his wrists past his elbows. A gold tassel belt dangled next to a long sword whose sheath glinted brilliantly in the candlelight. The boots and buttons were polished to such perfection that it would have made Fulkerham envious, Lockett thought.

As fine as his borrowed clothes looked, better than any clothes which Lockett had ever worn before, he paled miserably in comparison with the dash and elegance of the officers in the room. And it wasn't just the Generals either. There were Colonels, Majors, and Captains - all were the picture of perfection - crisp, clean and without blemish of any sort. These were not the tattered, holed, and ragged uniforms with which Lockett was familiar.

The crowded room was difficult to maneuver through, and he found himself extremely uncomfortable and self-conscious. He felt slightly dizzy, feverish, and even nauseous. What was he doing here, he cursed himself. He didn't belong here.

He pawed at the bandages at his neck and grimaced. The tender skin felt hot beneath the fresh wrapping. He would need to sit down soon. If he passed out or, worse, vomited across the splendor, he would be anonymous no more.

He forced his hand down to his side and clenched a fist tightly. He would get them killed if he did not keep it together.

Awkwardly, he let Anna steer him across the room, and he found himself standing back to back with a cluster of Confederate officers in conversation while Anna introduced him to one of Mattie's sisters, Alice. Fortunately, Alice had little attention for him and spoke in excited tones only to Anna.

Lockett stood absently and listened to the goings-on around him.

"General Bragg, sir," he heard from behind him. Unable to resist the temptation, Lockett turned and found that the group of officers behind him contained a short, well-dressed general. The general looked back at him with dark, brooding eyes. He was a short man, much shorter than Lockett, with a grizzled, bristling dark beard flecked with gray. Dark eyes beneath a heavy and bushy brow seemed to study Lockett and his bandaged neck for a moment. General Bragg scowled, as if it was some sort of affront that a wounded man in civilian clothes should be here, but then the General turned his attention away.

Lockett looked back at Mattie's sister, stifling an insane desire to laugh aloud. This was crazy, he thought to himself. How in the world did he end up here? He had no business socializing with his own generals, much less Confederate ones.

He looked into the distance and strained to hear the conversation going on behind him. What was Bragg saying? Was that gravelly voice his? It must be based on the man's authoritarian tone.

Despite the noise echoing around the crowded parlor, Lockett could catch parts of the conversation, but the topic was of no military value to General Rosecrans. It was a discussion on how such a small town as Murfreesboro could contain so many attractive women.

* * *

In awe, Lockett watched the wedding ceremony. The whole leadership of the Confederate Army of Tennessee surrounded John Hunt Morgan and Mattie Ready. Some of the faces were familiar to him already. Whispering, Anna detailed the others to him as the proceedings began.

General Cheatham stood behind the couple. Hands held behind his back, he attentively watched General Polk, who was presiding. General Polk opened the brown leather Bible and began to address the couple.

The gray haired, goateed General Hardee stood behind Polk. Blithely, Lockett remembered this was the general who wrote the book on infantry tactics that Captain Bibb kept with him at all times.

Next to him, there was the dapper, mustached former Vice President of the United States, John Breckinridge, now a general himself.

Mattie's face glowed with exhilaration and her irrepressible smile. Next to her, John Hunt Morgan, in his new general's uniform, looked serious and reserved.

General Polk raised his strong stentorian voice. It was a voice useful for commanding on a battlefield, or delivering a sermon as the bishop was known to do. It carried through the lower reaches of the house and beyond.

Lockett imagined that it could even be heard outside where hundreds of Morgan's soldiers and others had gathered to celebrate the occasion. Through the corner window, Lockett could see their bonfires burning brightly.

His mind wandered as Polk continued to speak. He realized more than ever how correct Anna was. If there ever was a place for a Union spy to be on this night, it was here. The entire brain trust of the Confederate army was here, and there was no doubt that the alcohol would flow in celebration tonight.

He wondered which generals he should try to put himself in the proximity of and how he would do that without creating suspicion. He pondered this deeply, losing track of time. The tug at his elbow from Anna snapped him from those thoughts, and he recognized that Polk had stopped speaking.

It was the conclusion of the ceremony, and Morgan kissed Mattie, a prim and proper kiss. Somehow, a signal must have been made because the crowd outside cheered loudly. Mattie Ready was now Mattie Morgan.

The dancing began after the supper, a stunning feast. There

were hams, duck, turkey, and game. There were also wine and spirits. Celebrants consumed all, and the merriment continued. Lockett had never seen such a joy filled occasion. It was particularly stunning to him in its obsequious obliviousness. Nattily attired house slaves waited on the celebrants, celebrants who for the time being thought nothing of their martial duties.

At least for tonight, there was no thought of war or of shortages.

Lockett watched the Confederate generals and their staffs revel in the food, drink, and company. They spoke of home, friends and relatives that might have in common, or the generosity of the Ready household.

Silently, Lockett watched and listened, but it was a one-sided fascination. Their eyes passed over Lockett like they passed over the black faces of the slaves. Most eyes were on the Southern belles, particularly once the regimental band began to play.

He looked across the room for Anna. He held a small drink of sugared lime juice for her in his hand. Even in the crowded room, he had no trouble spotting her. His eyes were naturally drawn to her like a magnet. But he was not the only one. From the corner of his eye, he spotted a Confederate officer staring at her and then angling towards her. They arrived at the same instant.

"It would be a great privilege to have this dance," said the well-dressed major, coming up to Anna.

"I am afraid that this dance was already spoken for," she answered, looking at Lockett.

"Of course," the major replied, masking his disappointment, "Perhaps, later in the night." He gave a polite nod and disappeared into the crowd.

"We should dance," Anna said, her eyes motioning to the crowded dancing area.

He looked at the glass in his hand and then placed it on a nearby table. Grudgingly, he led her to the corner of the dance floor. She tip-toed to speak in his ear, "You are not a dancer, are you, James?"

He did not need to respond. She already knew the answer. He was a simple farmer, who had never even thought of dancing before, much less actually done any. Clumsily, he tried to dance without attracting attention, but it felt as if dozens of eyes were upon him. It only increased his missteps.

Her gloved hand squeezed. "Just look at me, don't look at anything else." He listened to her. Slowly, he cared less and less about his awkwardness, and more and more about the dark brown eyes that looked up at him. He stopped hearing the music and only saw the brown eyes staring back at him. Trance-like, he moved stiffly around the floor with her. When the music ended, he did not notice. It was only when Anna halted and smiled up at him that he realized the pause.

She disengaged and took his elbow, and they headed back to the outer ring of merry people. "It's time for me to dance with some of Bragg's staff," she whispered in his ear. He looked at her, trying to figure out how to argue with her without using his voice, but there was a steely glint in her eyes. She had already decided for the both of them.

She was going to help gather this information, consequences be damned.

* * *

"It's a beautiful home, isn't it?" the feminine voice startled him as he watched Anna dance with a blond haired captain.

Lockett turned, revealing the bandages and burns on the far side of his face.

"Oh! You are the one that my sister's husband mentioned," she said, "You're staying with Molly Tucker. I'm Mary McNeil," she introduced. "I live with my sister and her husband, Preacher Hornsby."

Lockett nodded.

"Rather difficult to hold a conversation with someone who can't speak," Mary McNeil said absently. "Well, it is a beautiful home."

Lockett could only nod. Burgundy carpeted floors, finely papered walls with expensive looking draperies, and polished furniture, there was nothing that seemed to be missing.

"You should be careful letting Anna dance so freely with all of those eligible officers. She has caught the eye of many a man, although I must say that tonight she is not as off-standish with them as usual." She saw the sour look on Lockett's face. "Not a dancer?"

Lockett shook his head slowly, wishing that she would go away. He had specifically picked this seat because it was within earshot of the Confederates drinking and conversing with increasing volume. It was a group that included three generals, and he could hear them plainly, all the while not looking like he was trying to listen to their conversation.

"Then we shall sit in companionable silence," she said with finality.

His eyes were focused across the room, but his ears strained to hear what was behind him.

"We should attack Nashville, but Granny would never be so bold," one complained angrily. Lockett assumed from the presumed authority in the tone that it was one of the generals.

"Granny Bragg," another snorted, "He had Buell. We were rock solid between Buell and his supplies in Louisville this summer. Had them right there! Across the only route available to Buell, but then we pull back."

"Bloody well lost his nerve," an oddly British voice remarked.

"That he did, San Leger, that he did! Did again in Perryville for that matter. Lost his nerve there too!"

"But he is friends with President Davis, as we all saw yesterday."

"General Polk could have told you that. The Bishop went to Richmond after Perryville to complain of Bragg's conduct, but the President would hear no wrong about his friend."

"Damn foolish mistake of the President."

"Not as foolish as the one he is making now."

"Which one?"

"Carter Stevenson's."

"Yes, bad business. Sending him and his 8000 men away to Mississippi with the Yankees scant miles away from us? Lunacy. Good for us that the Yankees are tucked away in Nashville until spring. Hopefully, Carter and his men will be back by then."

"It's Davis's home state," a new voice explained, "Mississippi and Pemberton need those 8000 men more than we do, and President Davis will do all he can to protect his home state."

"I wouldn't say that Pemberton needs them more, but I would agree that President Davis will do all he can to protect his home state of Mississippi."

"And what will Rosecrans do when he realizes that 8000 men have left Bragg's command? I'd attack!"

"By God, Hanson, it is a good thing that you are not in charge of the Yankees then," another laughed.

"It is no matter. The Yankees don't know about Stevenson leaving. Even if the Yankees did, they won't attack. They are holed up in Nashville for the winter. We won't see them until the first blossoms." They all laughed heartily at the certainty.

"We should still attack," repeated the first voice.

"Even without Stevenson's men?"

"Our boldness would win the day."

"Sounds more foolhardy than bold to me."

"Regardless," another voice interjected, "It won't happen. That is not Granny Bragg's objective."

"He has no objective, Breckinridge."

"That is where you are wrong. He has an objective. It's politics, you see. He has a political objective, not a military one."

"Spoken like a former Vice President," grumbled another general.

"Come now, Cheatham, if there is one thing I've learned as a general, it is that the army is just as rife with politics as Washington ever was. And Bragg has an objective. This is his objective. He wants Murfreesboro."

"It is a fine town," came the British sounding voice again, "But I don't see why you say that."

"Politics. That is why I say that," Breckinridge said. "As long as he can hold middle Tennessee, he can claim victory. All those movements in Kentucky, that was a feint, a maneuver to pull the Yankees out of middle Tennessee and the rich lands around it. The Yankees left to defend Kentucky, and now Granny can claim victory to Richmond. 'Look, see, I have re-captured middle Tennessee, just as ordered.'"

"Sounds like an excuse to me, and a poor one for all that was lost in Kentucky."

Still, there was a murmur of agreement with General Breckinridge's logic.

"All in all, there are worse places to spend a winter, gentlemen. We can relax here, recoup, and hit the Yankees come spring."

So focused was Lockett on listening to what was going on behind him, that he did not notice that there was someone standing directly in front of him.

"So this is where you have been hiding, Mary."

Lockett lost track of the conversation behind him and looked up to see Preacher Hornsby and his wife.

"Why are you sitting so far away, Mary?" the preacher asked, "Oh, sitting here with the Tuckers' guest." he added, noticing Lockett.

The wispy haired preacher's face was a glowing red, flushed with drink. "Congressman Ready has been generous enough to open his cellar to celebrate with the guests." He held a glass of wine in each hand. "You must try some, Mary."

"You know that I don't drink, Samuel," Mary McNeil answered with a frown.

"Your sister was once a temperate Presbyterian too," the preacher grinned, "But look at her now." Mary's sister held her own glass of wine and smiled blandly back at them.

"I still say 'no, thank you'," Mary replied with a touch of curtness in her voice.

"Presbyterians, even worse than Methodists," Preacher Hornsby commented. "Alas, alas, now I have an extra glass." The preacher turned to Lockett with mock gravity. "Perhaps, you would like a glass? It is a vintage of its own, one that I am not accustomed to myself."

Lockett shook his head.

"Abstaining from alcohol?" he asked Lockett with some surprise, "A rare quality in this army, or any army, I am sure."

Lockett shrugged, glad that he did not need to answer any of these questions in words. He just wished that the man would go away. It was impossible to hear what was going on behind him now.

"Your loss is my gain, young man," the preacher said, downing a glass in one swallow. He belched visibly but silently.

Lockett noticed the look of indignation in Mary McNeil's eyes.

"Come, dear Mary," he said, "You can't sit here in the corner on such a splendid night. Look around you. Have you ever seen anything so grand?"

"I have been here before."

"Not the house. Look around the room, the cream of the Confederacy is here. The only shame is that President Davis had to return before he could attend but no matter. Look at the tailored uniforms, the gold trim, the silver of the swords... Why it is a dignity and class of its own!"

"You know that such things do not impress me," Mary said guardedly.

"Come now, even you must admit to the splendor of tonight! Why, look at the obvious superiority of the night!"

"You have had too much to drink."

The preacher ignored her rebuke, "Very well, I shall leave you alone as you seem to wish." He turned towards his wife, "Come, Ruth, let us dance." He took her hand and led her off to the dance floor.

While Lockett had been sitting stiffly, trying to inconspicuously overhear any bit of conversation, he was unaware that Anna had not been on the dance floor for some time. Rather, three handsome Confederate officers vied for her attention.

A lieutenant colonel, one of General Hardee's staff, stood confidently next to her. The broad shouldered officer looked completely at ease in his immaculate uniform. The gold thread on his sleeve was particularly new and bright against the gray wool.

Of his two competitors for Anna's attention, one was a major and the other a mere captain. They also bandied about her. The lieutenant colonel and major kept most of her attention, even though the captain already seemed to know the dark-eyed belle.

"... but I do fear that the Yankees might return," Anna coaxed the major with faked distress, "You said that General McCown's division is in Readyville. That seems so far away."

"The Yankees would never dare. They have no heart, you see," the major replied. "They have no stomach for a battle with us. With McCown in Readyville in the east and General Hardee's men in the west at Eagleville, we are well prepared should they try to slink around us..."

Anna nodded blankly as she expected that she should do. Naturally, she made no comment on how far apart the Confederate wings seemed to be. It must be 30 miles between, she thought. How the Yankee General Rosecrans would like to know that, she thought to herself.

"… of course, there is a screen of cavalry in front to keep prying Yankee eyes from us. But they have no heart for battle, not like us," the major continued, "Not like our Southern boys. That's why the Yankees will stay in their camps until spring."

"Damned Abolitionists!" the captain broke in. "Army of abolitionists," he slurred. Captain Ellicott glared at an unseen enemy. He had been drinking throughout the night, increasingly so as his attempts to monopolize Anna Tucker's attention had garnered less and less attention as the more senior officers had arrived on the scene.

First, he had needed to get her away from that crippled old flame of hers. He had seen them enter the house together tonight. He had smiled gleefully as he had watched the clod stumble around the dance floor like a cow on ice. Ellicott had thought it the greatest of good fortunes when the clumsy fool had made a wreck of the dancing and then made himself scarce. For a moment, he had Anna all to himself…

And then the major and the lieutenant colonel had butted in. He wished now that he had dismissed them immediately, except that Anna had welcomed them into the conversation so happily that he did not know how to expel the two interlopers. Now, he found that she placed more attention on them than in him!

The major looked at him sternly, but it did not slow Ellicott.

"Emancipation!" he said, raising his voice even more, "That villain Lincoln and his army of … of… villains!"

It was the lieutenant colonel who artfully steered the conversation away. "Were you able to see President Davis during his short stay, Miss Tucker?"

"He was a busy man," Anna said in a delicate and dainty voice.

"He spent yesterday reviewing the troops," the major added.

"Indeed," the lieutenant colonel interjected, unwilling to cede the floor this time, "Many of the troops had to march three or four miles to the review. Most didn't believe that he was really here."

"Didn't believe?" Anna asked.

"It's the rumors," the lieutenant colonel said patiently, "There's often rumors of a general so and so or President Davis being near camp. Usually this is to hustle the men to reviews and so on, and of course, it's never true."

"Tricks of the trade," the major added, trying to get back into her line of sight as he said it.

"But not this time," the lieutenant colonel continued, "There the great man was in a plain broad cloth suit. Some of the men still didn't believe it was Jeff Davis at first, but as he shook a few hands, the recognition spread in a matter of minutes. Funny how it straightened the backs of the men," he laughed.

Anna smiled, as if delighted. "It's been an eventful last couple of days here," she said.

Completely shut out of the conversation now, Captain Ellicott slunk away, head hanging.

With the evening winding down, Lockett made eye contact with Anna. She was disengaging from the gaggle of officers who had hovered around her most of the night. He had lost count of how many different officers she had danced with. Each time he saw it, the sight was so galling that he had to fight the impulse to rush right out on the dance floor. He tried to remind himself that the smiles that she gave were surely faked, necessary instruments of deception for her to find the information... information that was for him...

Despite all of the levity and joy in the room, the evening had been an interminable one for him. He was oddly tired considering what little he had been doing. The pain in his neck had been rising, and his stomach was queasy. He badly wanted to lay down.

Still, it had been a useful night. Hearing the generals complain about Bragg and each other had been interesting, but hearing about how Stevenson's 8000 men were leaving was more than interesting. He just wished that he knew when. They had probably said something about that, but he had lost that vital piece of information when Preacher Hornsby had shown up. That had been a touch of bad luck, but overall, he could not complain.

It was valuable information. He was sure that General Rosecrans would want it. Having Bragg's numbers go down by 8000 was no small number.

He watched Anna make her way through the thinning room to him. It occurred to him that she seemed to be the only one here who ever saw him. Most of the night, he had been close to invisible. Even Aunt Molly had walked past him twice before she noticed him, and at that, she had made little comment other than to wonder aloud where Anna was.

Anna summoned one of the Ready's slaves to get her heavy winter shawl. She approached Lockett with that same fixed smile that she had worn all night, but as she spoke, he saw the weariness in her eyes too, "Ready?" she asked.

He nodded.

The slave appeared out of nowhere with the shawl and handed it to Lockett, who helped place it around her. Anna did the buttons in front and adjusted it around her neck. Then they exited the Ready house.

General Morgan's troops and other revelers who were not so privileged as to enter the house were still celebrating outside and around their bonfires. Lockett could hear two fiddles sawing away. One was hopelessly out of tune but no less exuberant in its playing. Nearby, other men sang lustily; their spirit making up for their lack of talent.

There was laughter too.

It reminded Lockett of good times around his own camp. It could have been Prosper T. Rowe and John Messern on the fiddles. It could have been Levi and Milton singing bawdily out of tune. It could very well have been a Union camp, he reflected, and the thought saddened and perplexed him.

They were one country; they shared one common language; they shared a history of fighting for their own liberty; they shared a God; they shared common stories of pain and toil to get here; and yet...

And yet, they were killing each other by the thousands!

He clenched a fist and stiffened.

Anna, who was holding his arm, looked up at him. "What is it?"

He could only shake his head. It wasn't the cover story of his throat that prevented him from saying anything. He was at a loss for words for this terrible tragedy. They shared too much for this!

Chapter 31

December 15

It was a brisk morning. The men in blue stamped their feet and blew on their hands. In the early morning light, none had trouble seeing their breath. Given the temperatures, all were anxious to start loading the wagons that stood empty near the quartermaster's warehouse. Work or not, any sort of activity might keep their blood moving.

Patrick McManus stood next to Daniel Lockett, Levi Thickle, and Prosper T. Rowe. Prosper smoked his clay pipe contently. Daniel blew on his hands for the umpteenth time and stuck them in his armpits trying to get some feeling back. McManus himself waited with growing impatience for Captain Bibb to clear up whatever confusion reigned.

This was the second day in a row that they had marched over to the quartermaster's to draw the regimental rations, as well as procure heavier blankets and a few other basic items.

Somehow, when they had arrived back in camp yesterday, they had arrived with only two-thirds of what the records showed them as having drawn. Now, Captain Bibb was trying to clear up the matter with the quartermaster but to no avail apparently.

"What's taking him so long?" Thickle grumbled, "I bet it's all sorted out and the captain is just warming his arse in front of a nice fire in there while we're out here freezing."

Prosper answered with a shrug and continued to smoke his pipe. It was quite possible that Levi was right, he thought. Captain Bibb was not one for sharing their hardships, unlike the lieutenant had been. They would never see Captain Bibb strip off his jacket and work with the men digging a mass grave like the lieutenant had done.

"It's probably something else," McManus answered, although

he would not have disagreed with Prosper's unspoken thoughts. "You've been in the army long enough now, Levi. More 'n likely that they can't sort it out because someone has already gone and taken our supplies."

"Already taken?" Daniel said, mystified. "They gave them to someone else? Why not just give us theirs then?"

"That's not what I mean," Patrick began patiently. He had been taking a more patient tone with Daniel lately. The chasm between them was slowly growing closed.

Prosper took the long thin clay pipe from his mouth. "I think he's talking about sticky fingers, a pilfer here, a snooker there."

"What does he mean?" Daniel asked McManus.

McManus opened his mouth to answer Daniel, but he stopped before he could utter a word as he watched a familiar face exit the quartermaster's. At the same moment, the individual turned and looked over his shoulder, as if he knew that he was being watched. Instantly, he made eye contact with McManus.

A low, animal breath escaped subconsciously from McManus as he stared at the smooth, mustachioed face of Orrin Long.

The conflict was truly between James and Orrin Long. McManus had never had a direct conflict with the man, but he knew all about his friend's troubles. He knew enough.

Orrin Long continued to stare at his old private as he slowly walked away.

"What is it?" Daniel asked.

There goes your brother's enemy, McManus thought to himself. That's the man your brother stopped from pillaging and raping in Missouri. That's the man who set up your brother for the murder that plagued his dreams. That's the man who ran out on his men at Shiloh. And that's the man who lied and gave this regiment the stain of perceived cowardice in Savannah. The thoughts churned in his head, but his mouth stayed quiet.

Instead, it was Levi Thickle who answered. "There goes a real bastard, Daniel." Like the others in the company, he would never forgive Orrin Long for what he had done to them.

McManus continued to stare hard at the officer. The look of hatred reddened his face and etched deep furrows into his weather-beaten brow. He was not like James. He could not hide his emotions. The Irish in him was coming out.

"Easy, Pat," Prosper cautioned, seeing the look on his face, "Ain't no good to come from what you're thinkin'."

The look did not frighten Orrin Long, but he did stop and stare back. Slowly, a strange, knowing smile spread across his face. He knew full well who the men were who stared at him. They were Lockett's men. The sly sinister snake of a smile spread from ear to ear. He looked back at them for a moment more, and then he turned away and mounted his horse.

McManus continued to glare, but the knowing smile had taken him aback. What treachery was the man up to now, he thought in a flash. I've seen that smile from Orrin Long before.

"He knows," McManus said aloud without thinking.

"Knows what?" Daniel said innocently. "Who is that?"

But McManus did not answer the younger Lockett. Orrin Long knew something about James. That was what the smile on Orrin's face had to be about. And if Orrin Long knew anything, then that could not be good. An unshakable sadness gripped McManus. It had been weeks, but in the back of his mind, he was still holding out some hope that James was all right. But now...

Orrin Long's satisfied smile could only mean one thing.

James was dead, and Orrin Long probably even had a hand in it. What else could give that son of a bitch such a look of satisfaction!

* * *

Lockett struggled out of bed the next morning. Though he had been one of the few to not indulge during the prior evening's reverie, his head pounded, and he felt a fatigue as if he had done a hard march through the night.

But it was a small price to pay for what he had learned, especially the part about Carter Stevenson's men being sent to Mississippi. It was obviously information that General Rosecrans would be interested in.

Anna had learned the same information with even a more detail from her time on the dance floor, plus the location of Bragg's wings. Still, Lockett had hated every minute of watching her on the dance floor with other men. It was a silly jealousy, he knew. He had reminded himself countless times last night that there was no reason to be jealous. She was committing treason for him after all. There was no doubt how she felt about him, but he had hated the sight in any case.

She had also been told that the 1st Louisiana and 6th Kentucky were sponsoring a ball the next day in honor of John Hunt Morgan. He had no doubt that some of the men were already decorating the new courthouse for the occasion.

Anna suggested that she attend since all of the belles of Rutherford County were invited. He did not like the idea.

That evening, Lockett liked the idea even less.

Aunt Molly was surprised that Anna had wanted to attend but was supportive. So Lockett read the Bible quietly in the parlor while Aunt Molly worked on her ever-present needlework. They worked away in silence for a considerable time before Aunt Molly set aside her work and looked over at him.

"Do you ever have things that you don't understand, James?" she asked abruptly.

He blinked, shrugged, and then nodded in agreement.

"There are things that I don't understand. I have been thinking about them most of the night. The needle keeps my hands busy but not my mind. And so, I have been thinking about my niece."

She took a breath. "For months since she arrived here, I had been trying to introduce her to any number of suitable bachelors, many with pedigrees that no one in this family ever dared aspire to. But she is a smart, lively girl, and clearly more beautiful than most that this bloodline has produced. And indeed, there was no shortage of young men whose heads she turned since she arrived here."

Aunt Molly picked up the needlework and continued working, perhaps to keep herself from looking at him.

"But Anna turned a cold shoulder to all of them. I could not understand it for the life of me. And then you came..."

The flashing fingers paused, and she looked directly at him.

"Then I saw how she looked at you... And I thought that I understood. Anna was suddenly alight with something that had been missing." Aunt Molly tilted her head to the side and looked at his wound. "Yes, James, even with that hideous wound and all, it was different. I thought that I finally understood why those

307

prior months were like they were. Indeed. Indeed. I thought that I understood." Aunt Molly arched a brow. "Except then there was last night, she dances with every available man and a few who weren't, and tonight she is gone at another ball. Indeed, I don't understand it at all now."

Lockett shrugged, hoping that his surging nervousness was not showing.

"Makes no sense." Her eyes narrowed. "Did you two have some sort of falling out?"

When Lockett gave no reply, he could see the frustration building in her. "When will you be able to talk? What are your intentions with my niece?"

December 16

"She is getting suspicious," Lockett warned Anna the next day.

He was in a foul mood, and he struggled not to show it. Not only had Aunt Molly's comments bothered him, but they were further exacerbated by the fact that Captain Ellicott had escorted Anna home last night after the ball. The man's intentions were plain, as was the man's disdain for finding James waiting in the parlor at the end of the evening.

The discomfort was palpable, and Lockett could see by the man's face that Ellicott had no intention of ceding to him.

In the back of his mind, Lockett harbored some worry for Anna once he left, but he shook the thought from his head. He knew by now that Anna could take care of herself, plus he had no intention of leaving without her although he had not mentioned that to her yet.

"Auntie?" Anna replied, "Suspicious? Of you?"

"Letting you go to that ball last night was a mistake. She doesn't understand it. I guess you could say that it is out of character in her eyes."

"Why? Because I had refused such things in the past?"

"Exactly."

"But if I had not gone, then you would not know the location of Bragg's various commanders. I am sure that your generals will find it interesting that General Wheeler is in LaVergne or how many men have been granted local leave for Christmas."

Of that, Lockett had no doubt. She had been able to learn a great deal.

Anna looked at him, opening her mouth but holding back on the words.

"Go ahead," Lockett prodded, seeing that she was hesitant to continue.

"I don't know that there is that much more for you here, James. There can't be much more to learn."

He took a breath. "Time to leave?" he mused.

They were silent together. Neither wanted him to leave, yet they both knew that there was no choice ultimately. The longer he waited, the more dangerous it became... for both of them.

"I can't return without the information from Wilks' spy," he said slowly.

"Why?" she said with some indignation. "What more could this spy know? You have already gathered so much. Much more than Father and I were ever able to gather for... for *our* side." She flinched at the word, and they looked at each other, not knowing what to say or how they had ever got here.

"...You know that Bragg is not attacking Nashville," she eventually added, "You know that he does not expect the Yankees to attack either. He is expecting a quiet winter. You know where his various commands are located. You even know his troop strengths. What more is there to tell your generals, James?"

He looked thoughtfully at her. "You know what this means, Anna?"

"Of course, I do," she said with a serious look, "I am providing your General Rosecrans with all the intelligence that he needs to attack Murfreesboro."

Chapter 32

December 17

Lockett worked the plan over in his head again, step by step. It was time to go. That was clear to him, but how to get back? That was a difficult question. He doubted that he could make his way north using the deer trails like McGowan had done. As the crow flew, Nashville was not far, but he could not fly as a crow. There were two armies between him and Nashville, fanned out broadly. On top of that, there would be cavalry roaming.

It had taken some time and a number of discarded ideas, but he had finally settled upon what seemed like a workable plan.

He had arrived by train, and he would leave by train.

The Southern train schedule was unreliable, but Anna had learned for him that there should be a train running south to Tullahoma. From there, he could connect to another heading east. He would swing wide around both armies, find a horse, and with all haste get this information to General Rosecrans.

He figured the still grievous wound and scars on his neck would provide a simple enough explanation for his departure. He was merely another wounded soldier on his way home to recuperate. He would rely on Anna to be his voice, as she had been here.

He knew that the cavalry man's daughter could ride, far better than he in fact. Once they reached the end of the rail line in McMinnville, then they would ride towards Sparta and then turn north. From the information that they had learned, this would keep them well clear of Confederate cavalry and prying questions. Then, when they reached the Union lines, he would be able to talk them through by using Colonel Wilks' name.

He only needed to wait two more days for the scheduled departure to Tullahoma and keep his fingers crossed that for once the Southern train schedule would keep remotely close to schedule.

Anna, of course, could tell Aunt Molly that she was seeing him home to family. Aunt Molly would think that they were going south to connect to Chattanooga and then points west, an easy enough subterfuge to pull off, he figured.

He had been working on the plan most of the night and into the morning. He was anxious to share it with Anna, but she was out with Aunt Molly this morning. They had told him not to expect them back until the afternoon.

As he waited for Anna to return home, he glanced out the window and watched a passer-by. It was Mary McNeil, he recognized.

With a mild grimace, he remembered her interruption to his eavesdropping of Generals Hardee and Breckinridge. If only she had not intruded, he wondered what else he would have heard.

Of course, she had been a quiet companion for the most part, he admitted. It was really her brother-in-law, Preacher Hornsby, who had distracted.

He shrugged and turned away from the window, reflecting on how she seemed to walk past the window, heading the same direction, each day. He wondered where she was headed, but he put the thought aside and mulled his planned escape again.

He and Anna would get back to his lines, and he would give Colonel Wilks the information. He wondered if Colonel Wilks would believe him. The colonel was expecting some sort of written information to be retrieved. Something in code no doubt. That was something that Lockett could not deliver, but he had all that was needed in his head.

He smiled. Just knowing that Carter Stevenson's men were leaving should be enough to make Wilks happy. It had been a stroke of luck to hear that, he thought to himself. At the party, he had landed in that perfect place to overhear the information. It was the perfect place to eavesdrop, even after Mary McNeil arrived.

"The perfect place?" he said suddenly to the empty room.

In fact, it had been ideal. He had parked himself near the generals, but in such a way as to be inconspicuous, and then Mary McNeil had joined that spot nearly at the same time.

The thought struck him like a bolt of lightning, startling him with its simplicity.

What if it had not been a coincidence that Mary McNeil had joined him at that spot and at that point in time? What if it was not just good fortune that she had been a silent companion, allowing him to listen to the conversation?

What if she too had been listening? She had seemed as annoyed by the interruption from Preacher Hornsby as he had been.

It could be a coincidence, but what if it wasn't?

If it was not a coincidence...

That would mean that she wanted to overhear the generals too!

And if she wanted overhear the generals...

That could mean that *she* was Wilks's spy!

Did she walk by each day because she was checking where the signal was supposed to be made?

Lockett dashed to the kitchen and grabbed a coat. Putting it on while he ran, he hurried to catch up to Mary McNeil. The more he thought about it, the more certain he became.

Where had she gone?

Frantically, he looked down the empty street. He walked with a briskness that was far from inconspicuous as he hurried down the tree lined avenue. As he passed the intersecting road, he looked to his right and then left, and then he saw her.

More sure than ever, he followed Mary McNeil.

He kept at a discreet distance, watching where she was going.

Is this what she did every day, walk to some prescribed point to check for her signal?

For thirty minutes, she walked on. They left the ordered streets of the town and were out in the open land interspersed with farms, woods, and the various limestone ribs that seemed to poke forth from the Middle Tennessee ground.

The dirt lane curved around a copse of trees, disappearing around a bend, and over a small knoll.

As Lockett came around the bend and looked down the rest of the lane, he was surprised to see the road empty. He stopped in his tracks, puzzled at where Mary McNeil had gone. He looked left and right. Finally, he heard some movement behind him.

Whirling, he found himself facing Mary McNeil who had a small Derringer pistol aimed at him.

"You?" she said with surprise that equaled his own at walking into a trap.

He had thought that she was unaware of his presence until then. "Why are you following me?" she asked.

He swallowed and took a deep breath.

"Speak," she insisted. "Who are you? What do you want?" She waved the Derringer for emphasis.

"I'll speak alright," he said slowly. "I'm here to see you. I've come a long way to see you."

She blanched at the sound of his voice and turned pale. "What... what do you mean?"

"The Garrett farm, the family cemetery," Lockett continued, "There will be a large oak stump in the middle of it. I'm to retrieve your message there."

At the mention of the Garrett cemetery, Mary's eyes grew wide and her mouth hung open. For a second, her aim wavered with the Derringer, but then she stiffened. "I don't know what you are talking about. Who are? Who sent you?"

"My name is James Lockett, from Kalamazoo, Michigan. Colonel Wilks sent me. He's anxious for your information."

"You lie," she said sternly, lining up her aim, "There was no signal."

"It's no lie," Lockett said calmly, taking a small step towards her despite her agitation. "The signal died with my guide." He gestured towards his neck, pulling the bandages down to reveal the horrific scarring and tender pink skin. "Two men, each with one part. One with the signal, one with the drop location. Just the way that Colonel Wilks likes to do it."

"You lie," Mary repeated, but not as convincingly.

"Do I sound like a Rebel?"

"No," she admitted, half lowering the aim. "How did you know? How did you know it was me? And by the way, two men, two parts is not the way that Colonel Wilks likes to do it. It is the way that *I* instructed *him* to do it."

"Sorry," Lockett apologized, "And it was the wedding. That was how I knew." He took another step forward. "I was trying to listen to the generals, and then you came over too. It took me a while to realize that it was not a coincidence. We were both trying to do the same thing."

"But Anna? Molly? They're Unionists?"

Lockett shook his head. "Aunt Molly doesn't know who I really am, and neither of them is a Unionist."

"Neither of them? But then why? Anna knows?" Mary said, truly puzzled. The widow looked at the young soldier, studying him. Then she arched one brow in perceived comprehension.

Lockett ignored her and said, "Do you have any additional information for me to take back, Mary? I'm leaving soon."

"Back at the house," she said, "It's in cipher, but Colonel Wilks will have the key. I have much to share. My brother-in-law does a prayer meeting with the generals. They have much to pray for, and even more to voice when they think they are alone with him."

"Then let's go back. Fetch it for me and bring it to Aunt Molly's house. I'm leaving in two days."

* * *

Lockett could hardly contain his excitement as he entered the house. He wanted to shout at the top of his lungs for Anna to share the news. It took all of his self control to stay silent, even though he knew the house was empty.

As he entered the backdoor, he took off his coat, unable to suppress the broad smile on his face. He could hardly believe the good fortune. Anna would never believe that he had figured it out. The hours of self-doubt in those first days as he laid in agony in bed were fully washed away by this tremendous exhilaration. In many ways, the information itself was secondary in his mind to the sense of accomplishment that he felt.

He hung the coat on the peg and walked out into the front parlor.

His pure joy turned instantly to bile as he heard the click of a pistol cocking and a shockingly familiar voice.

"Hello, James," Ambrose Tucker greeted ominously.

Lockett turned to see him seated in the same chair in which Lockett had spent so much recuperation time.

Chapter 33

"Ambrose," Lockett said with a calm that he did not feel.

Anna's brother aimed a large LeMat pistol squarely at him. All other words caught in Lockett's throat as he stared at the unusual double barreled heavy revolver.

"You look surprised to see me," Tucker said, rising, his face becoming taut with anger. "Yes, I was able to start my leave sooner than expected. I saw Aunt Molly with some of the other women organizing medical supplies as I rode into town. Imagine my surprise when she said that a friend of ours from Savannah named James was staying at the house while he recovered from wounds."

Ambrose stepped to the side to get a better view of the bandage around Lockett's neck. With the LeMat, he motioned for him to lower the wrapping. Lockett obliged and revealed the scarring.

"Nasty," Ambrose said without feeling. "Yes, imagine my surprise, because I could not think of any family friends from Savannah named James. The only James that came to mind was *you*." He said the last word with a dark tone.

"Surprise," Lockett said with mock enthusiasm.

"I couldn't imagine it was you, but Anna was not to be found, so I came straight here, and then the house was empty. So I waited and waited. Where were you?"

"I needed some air," Lockett lied.

Ambrose seemed unconcerned with the answer. "What are you doing here, James? You are a long ways from your lines."

Lockett contemplated telling him that he was here because he could not bear to be away from his sister any longer, but he decided against that. Given Ambrose's previous comments, Ambrose might find that statement as offensive as Lockett being a Union spy.

315

When no answer was forthcoming, Tucker scowled.

Lockett silently calculated how far away he was from the hall that led back into the kitchen. Could he dash back around the corner and sprint from the house before a heavy LeMat ball hit him in the spine? Or before the second barrel, loaded with buckshot, flayed him? He had never seen the LeMat in action before. There were few of them, and only Southerners used the peculiar weapon. The only one that he had ever seen was when one of his men found one on a Rebel officer as a battlefield souvenir.

He had heard that they were notoriously inaccurate, but in these close quarters, he had no doubt how deadly their firepower could be.

No, he decided, it would not be possible to spring around the corner. Even if he made it out of the house, then what? He was surrounded by 50,000 Confederates.

"You're a spy," Ambrose said. It was a statement, not a question.

"So what are you going to do?"

"Do?"

"Yes, you can't just hand me over to the authorities."

"Why not? Because you saved my neck once? No. That does not matter to me."

"That's not what I'm getting at," Lockett answered, "I mean Anna."

"Because my misguided sister won't like to see your neck stretched? That is the least of my concerns."

"No, Ambrose," Lockett said patiently, "Because if you turn me in as a spy, then you are also turning your sister and even Aunt Molly in as spies. Truth be damned, they'll both be strung up with me."

From the clouded look on Ambrose's face, Lockett could see that Ambrose had not thought that far ahead yet. "You got a point there," Tucker said slowly.

But the mental standoff only lasted a matter of seconds. "March," he commanded, waving the pistol. "Out through the back door."

"Where are we going?" Lockett said, feeling a chill on his body that felt unnaturally physical, as if a cold draft had just swept into the house from the outside.

"Because you're right, I can't turn you in. So instead, I'm just going to kill you myself. We're going out back cuz I don't want a mess in Auntie's house. Now, turn around and start walking. If your secrets die with you, then that should work well enough."

Lockett nodded slowly and took a hesitant step towards his impending death. "Give a dying man a final wish?"

"What's that?"

"Don't take it out on Anna. Protect your sister to the end. It wasn't her fault. Promise me."

"What kind a damn trick is that, Yankee? Of course, I'm going to protect her. She's my sister."

"You swear on it?"

"Swear on it? Of course, I'd swear to it. But I don't need to. She's my sister!" he said hotly.

"Okay, then." Lockett took a stride forward, down the hall and into the kitchen. As they entered, he saw that he had left the back door open in his earlier excitement. It was slightly ajar, explaining the cold draft that he had felt on his legs.

Then with his next step, his peripheral vision picked up flashing motion, and there was the clanging sound of metal on bone. He twisted around and saw Ambrose slumped on the floor. Anna stood over him with a skillet in her hand.

"Where did you come from?" he gasped.

"From down the road. I saw the horse tied to the post in front of the house. I had a terrible feeling about it so I came in the back."

"How long were you back here?"

"Long enough," she said, dropping the skillet and retrieving the LeMat. She uncocked it and carefully handed it to Lockett. "You better keep this."

"Is he dead?" Lockett asked, bending down to feel if there was any breath coming from Ambrose's nose or mouth. "Alive," he answered his own question.

"That's the second time that you saved me like that," he remarked, remembering their encounter with Bloody Bill Coulter. Even though he was still surrounded by 50,000 Confederates, he couldn't stop himself from smiling like a wild man.

"And that's not even counting me finding you on the train,"

Anna corrected, a wry smile at the corners of her mouth. "But we'd better hurry. There is some rope in the back," she added, ducking out momentarily.

When she returned, they quickly bound Ambrose hand and foot.

"Aunt Molly will be back in about two hours," Anna said, "I'll have to untie him before then."

"Untie him? You can't," Lockett said in confusion, "What are you talking about? You have to come with me."

She looked at him in surprise. "I can't leave. It was never my intent to leave with you, James. Where would I go? Back to your army camp? I know no one in the North."

"But you can't stay!" Lockett said in shock.

Anna interrupted him. "You said this morning that you had a plan for getting back to your army. Well, follow it now. There is no time to spare."

Lockett shook his head slowly. "That plan required two days, a train, and *you*..." It was the latter that plagued his thoughts. He could not bear the thought of leaving, especially like this.

"Anna, you can't stay," he repeated. "What about Ambrose? He'll turn you in!"

"I know my brother. He's a lot of things, but two things that I know above all else are that he loves the Confederacy, and he loves his family."

"Those two things are in conflict now, Anna."

"He'll choose his family."

"And if he doesn't?"

"He will," Anna said with full determination.

"I wouldn't be able to live with myself for leaving you here."

"You will. You have to! James, time is wasting! You must leave now!" She grasped him in a fierce bear hug and buried her face in his chest. "Leave, James. Stay alive. You will find me again. I know you will."

He returned her embrace, feeling her chest heave slightly.

"Ambrose's horse is out front," Anna said in a softer voice.

He squeezed her tightly. Releasing her, he stepped back and tilted her chin upwards. There were tears in her eyes that matched the tears in his heart. He felt utterly drained, and yet, he knew what he had to do. He knew she was right. With a last memory searing stare, he looked into the dark eyes one more time and drew her close. "I will find you again," he promised.

She reached up and pulled his head down with two hands. He felt her warm tears on his face as they kissed passionately. It was a reminiscence that would have to sustain him, he knew.

And then he left.

"Find me," he heard her say, her voice just a whisper on the wind as he mounted the horse.

Chapter 34

When Ambrose Tucker started to come to, he was surprised to find himself in the parlor, bound tightly, and diligently guarded by his sister. She said nothing as her view switched from looking out the window and then back to him. She knew he was now conscious and still said nothing, which Ambrose found odd.

Finally, he asked, "Aren't you going to say anything? Untie me."

She looked back at him with lips pursed and returned to gaze out the window.

"What are you looking out the window for? For James?"

She did not switch her gaze as she answered, "I'm watching for Auntie. I figure that if I see her at the top of the street that it will give me just enough time to untie you. So that way she continues to have no idea what has gone on."

"Untie me now!" he demanded.

"You were going to kill him. I heard you."

There was a hard edge to her tone, decidedly bellicose and unfeminine.

"He's a spy, Anna!" he said angrily, "I had no choice! And you? A traitor? What would Father say? I thank God that he is in a grave and not alive to see such a thing."

"How dare you!" She turned irately. "How dare you say that about Father! In his grave? I wish every day that he was still alive with me!"

"Oh! And what would father say if he saw you helping a Yankee spy!"

"He would say that one good turn deserves another," Anna said with total certainty, "Especially in this crazy world!" Her tone turned softer, and her eyes glazed in a faraway look. "Father liked James, and that was even before James risked his life to save

320

Father."

"Anna," Ambrose said in a more reasonable tone, "Untie me. This is doing nobody any good."

Anna said nothing, so he continued in a more vindictive voice. "You think that you are helping James by doing this? Nothing is further from the truth! You've sent him to his death."

He paused, but there was no reaction from his sister. "Certain death, Anna. What is he to do? Find his way to Nashville? He's no horseman to begin with. You've told me that. He can't outride a cavalry patrol. He doesn't know the country. There are thousands of Confederate troops between here and Nashville. He won't know where they are. He'll probably ride right into their camps by accident or into some loyal farmer or town folk. They'll find that Yankee voice of his more than suspicious."

There was still no reaction from his sister. In exasperation, he added, "He has no chance, Anna! He'll be captured and strung up as a spy, probably after being beaten half to death to see what he knows. He's as good as dead."

But Anna only answered in a quiet, confident voice. "He'll find a way. You don't know James Lockett like I do."

* * *

Night was falling by the time Lockett took even the slightest break. He had ridden the horse hard. Anna's warning that Aunt Molly would be home in two hours impressed upon him the immediacy of putting as much ground between him and Murfreesboro as possible in those two hours.

But he had probably overdone it. Even as he had slowed the pace hours later, the horse was broken and, in fact, had come up lame. Grudgingly, he abandoned the animal and swallowed the instinct to put it out of its misery. He just did not want to risk the prospect of the pistol shot.

He had ridden hard with his mind in a frenetic tornado. He had forgotten about Mary McNeil until he was well outside of Murfreesboro, although he decided that even if he had remembered her, there was little he could have done. He didn't have time to ride to Preacher Hornsby's house, even if he knew where it was, not to mention the risk involved with all that. No, he decided, he had enough locked in his brain to make Colonel Wilks happy, even without Mary's coded messages.

Having put aside thoughts of Mary McNeil, he had tried to focus on a plan. How would he get back to Nashville? His plan with the train had been sound, he thought wistfully, and he struggled to put it from his mind, just as he struggled to put visions of Anna aside.

As he had walked quickly through the tangled forests, he tried to envision how he could get back to Nashville. Back in Murfreesboro, he could really only come up with one decent plan, and he needed Anna for that.

He was on his own now. There was no one to help him this time.

Or was there?

He tried to picture the map that Octavius Matson had laid out for him before he left Nashville. Could he remember enough from that brief study weeks and weeks ago?

Lockett paused in the snarled underbrush, his feet ankle deep in wet leaves. Around him, the trees were barren. Their gray skeletal branches spread behind him like a multitude of demonic limbs. In front of him, there was chest high evergreen underbrush, as tangled as could be. He would need to walk around it in order to reach the isolated cabin that beckoned from the clearing ahead. The tiny woven green leaves of the underbrush provided some cover, but he felt naked as he watched the cabin for signs of life.

By the time he finished studying the cabin and questioning his own memory in the intermittent moonlight, the clouds had fully taken over the night sky. Was this the cabin on the map, one of the handful that the Pinkertons had directed him to memorize?

It seemed that it must be. He had gone through the crossroads, turned eastward through the trees, walked a mile to the small creek, then followed it northwest, and here it was. It had to be this cottage, didn't it?

But there was no sign that this depot of the underground railroad was open. He was supposed to see a candle in the window to the left of the door, but there was no window to the left of the door. The window was to the right.

Had he remembered incorrectly? If all was safe, the candle

should be in the left window. If not safe, there would be no candle in the window. What did a candle in the right hand window mean? Was it the wrong cabin? Was there another further down the creek trail? Or was he supposed to look for a ribbon on the gate to the garden? That was another sign, but he did not see a garden next to this cottage?

He shook himself as the cold set deeper in his bones. Now that night had come, the temperature had dropped precipitously. He had been cold throughout the day, but this was something else altogether.

He weighed the decision of moving on and finding another depot versus the quality of his memory. Had the Pinkertons given him confused guidance? Had he forgotten it? He shook himself, knowing that fatigue and cold were sapping his alertness and judgment.

The hunger also started to claw at his belly now, and he stared once again at the cabin, smelling the smoke that trickled up from the chimney. Inside the cabin, a figure passed through the background on the other side of the room.

This had to be it, he convinced himself. He had switched right and left hand windows in his cold-addled memory, he decided. He crept across the barren winter meadow. There was a large tree that when in full bloom of summer must have given the little cottage much needed shade, and he headed for it, still studying the candle in the window.

He was nearly to the tree when he heard the tell-tale clop of horses. At first, they were so faint that he thought he might have imagined them, especially when the sound disappeared for a moment, but then he heard it again, louder and approaching. He turned but could not see anything. The hooves were starting to sound incredibly close.

His heart surged into a pounding within his chest.

He looked back over his shoulder. The underbrush from where he had studied the little house seemed a mile away now. He could make a dash for it, but would the riders see him? Clenching his teeth, he decided that it was too far. Instead, he quickly hurried to the large tree and crouched by its thick trunk, careful to keep it between him and the little cottage.

Out of the gloom, dark formless shapes appeared. As they

approached the dim light of the cabin, he could eventually make out four men on horseback. They dismounted in front of the cabin, their carbines protruding from saddle holsters.

"Auntie Mae," one called out, "It's Sam."

Seconds later, a small, hunched woman appeared at the door, a blanket wrapped around her shoulders. She beckoned them in.

In the crisp, still air of the night, Lockett could hear them as if they were right next to him, but of course, they were only a mere fifteen yards away from his hiding spot. He pressed against the trunk but could not resist poking his head around the side for a second to look at the riders. They were partly illuminated by the little light from the cabin.

"What are y'all doing out on a night like this, Sam? It's bitter cold out," she said.

"Colder than a Yankee's heart, that it is," answered another of the riders. His Irish lilt reminded Lockett of Patrick's father's intonations.

His comrades chuckled, and the leader, Sam, answered. "Huntin' for a deserter, Auntie."

"On a dark and cold night like this? That's plum crazy. Ain't there plenty of deserters in the army this time of year?" she answered.

"This one's special," Sam answered.

"Our lieutenant is offering a reward, thirty dollars!" one of the other horsemen blurted out.

"Thirty," the old woman whistled in surprise, "In Confederate script?"

"No, greenbacks!" Sam answered, starting to dismount. "Let's warm up for a few minutes, boys."

"Three months' worth of pay," the other rider added.

"A pretty penny, it is," the Irishman added. Following his leader's example, he slid stiffly from his saddle.

"For one deserter?" the old woman said, still astounded, "What did he do, attack a general on his way out?"

"Not sure," he answered, "The lieutenant didn't say exactly, but it seems to have something to do with his sister."

"A matter of honor, or so he said," the Irishman added. "And having seen the lass, thirty dollars is too little if this bastard dishonored her."

"A beauty she is," Sam agreed.

Lockett pressed against the tree, knowing exactly who they were talking about. They were hunting him!

"There's whole squads hunting in all directions for him," Sam continued.

"Thirty dollars is a lot of money," the woman replied as she went back into the warmth of the cabin followed by the four riders, shutting the door behind them.

Outside, Lockett shivered from the cold and the knowledge that he was much more of a hunted man than he had expected. He had hoped that his only challenge would be finding a way through the lines without getting caught, but now he knew that he was being tracked from behind as well.

It seemed doubtful that he could even get to the lines. It was ingenious of Ambrose, he thought to himself. He had hoped that Ambrose would not call out a search for him for fear of exposing his sister and Aunt as Yankee spies. He had thought that, at worst, he would have only Ambrose trailing him.

But Ambrose had been smarter than that. The idea of a reward based on somehow dishonoring his sister was plausible and plenty of incentive to launch a full-fledged hunt for him. He suspected that it was a dead-or-alive type of reward on top of everything else.

Now more than ever, Lockett knew that he had to find his way to the Underground Railroad. It was his only chance for escape. He crept away from the cottage and disappeared back into the brush. The cabin on that map must be somewhere nearby, maybe further up the creek, and he had to find it.

Chapter 35

General Rosecrans' aide ushered Colonel Wilks into the office. The red cheeked general smiled congenially at Wilks and motioned for him to sit in the chair at the front of his desk while the general finished writing out something.

There was one other man in the room, and Wilks looked curiously at the man.

"I don't believe that you know Father Michael," Rosecrans said. He was still looking at his papers, but he seemed to sense that Wilks was studying the other man.

"We have not met," Wilks said cautiously. He had heard that General Rosecrans, a devout Catholic, traveled with his own personal priest, but he did not realize that jokes of the priest attending councils of war and other meetings were truth and not fiction.

Father Michael reached across the way and shook Wilks' hand.

Rosecrans attached his signature to the bottom of the paper and carefully placed it aside for the ink to dry. He calmly folded his hands atop his desk and looked at Wilks. "So, is there news?"

"News, sir?"

"From your man, the one that you sent to Murfreesboro."

"Oh," Wilks started. He had not thought about the man in a couple of weeks now. For a second, he even forgot the man's name. Lockett, that was it. "No word from him."

"Lost, killed, or captured?"

"Hardly makes a difference at this point, sir, but I suspect he's dead."

"And no other information on Bragg's dispositions?"

Wilks shifted uncomfortably in his seat. Even the last cavalry patrol had turned back in a fright. Bragg was fully screened by Wheeler and the rest of the Confederate horse soldiers.

"You realize, Colonel, that Washington is anxious for action. They are insisting that I attack before I am felled by the same fate as General Buell."

"Yes, sir," Wilks answered. He was fully aware of Washington's constant drumbeat to attack and move forward.

"And I have little idea what I am facing. Where are General Bragg's wings? How thin has he spread his forces? Are they close enough to support each other? And how many does he have anyway? Has he been reinforced?"

Wilks nodded dumbly.

"Are these not fair questions to ask? Are these not fair questions to understand before committing men's lives?"

"Very fair questions, sir."

"And yet, here we are." He looked coldly at the intelligence officer. "I will be committing men's lives and the fate of the army on nothing more than prayer and my superiors' insistence that we *do something*... I hope your conscience can bear the weight of committing such action on nothing else. I depended on you, Wilks."

* * *

It seemed ages until the dawn finally started to break through the darkness. Lockett had stood plenty of sentry duties during the night but never one as interminable as this. He had also done plenty of difficult marches, but nothing compared to the stumbling, frozen trek through the tangled Tennessee brush. He had eventually found his way back to the creek in the darkness, but the forest of slicing, unseen branches had unceasingly flayed his face as he battered his way through the blackness. He knew that his face must be a terrible sight, surely criss-crossed with scratches.

But he had found his way. Twice during the night, he had dashed into the closest hiding spot, thinking that he had heard his pursuers nearby, particularly as he tried to follow the creek bed. He felt terribly exposed, but the creek bed was his lifeline on that memorized map. The true depot must be somewhere ahead. He must have overestimated how far he had gone, he thought.

He paused and rubbed his numbed hands across his grizzled

and battered face. He expected to feel some dampness of blood on his hands after doing so, but he could not feel anything. He blew on his hands and tried to clench them into fists.

As the black of night turned gray, he knew that he was running out of time. Once it was light, then the hunt would truly be on. In the barren woods of winter, hiding spots would be difficult to find, but he plunged resolutely onwards.

It was fully morning when his nose first sniffed it, smoke, the smell of warmth. Both trepidation and hope surged in him at the same time. It was a net numbing effect to match his physical state. He followed the scent, praying that it was coming from a depot and not his pursuers' morning cook fires.

He ascended a small knoll, conscious that the woods cleared to the left. Was that a road or path there, he wondered?

At the top of the knoll, he looked down into the open meadow where a small clapboard house with a garden sat in lonely vigil. Smoke curled from the stone and mud chimney, but it was the garden that instantly captured his attention. There was a red ribbon tied to the gate post of the little garden next to the house!

Hope warmed him like he was standing in front of the fireplace already.

He was still staring, rejoicing in his good luck and dead reckoning skills, when the door to the cabin opened. An old man in a dark overcoat exited the cabin and headed straight for the garden. He moved purposefully to the gate and removed the ribbon. Without another thought, the old man turned around and went back inside the cabin with the ribbon.

His mouth hanging open in shock, Lockett paused. No ribbon meant the depot was closed, that something too dangerous was nearby, but he made up his mind instantly and impetuously. He stormed down the hill to the cabin at a full run, stumbling crazily on his exhausted and half-frozen legs. It seemed minutes until he reached the front door of the cabin, but eventually, he was there, pounding on the door urgently with his fist.

Chapter 36

"Who the devil are you?" snapped the voice.

The door had been yanked open, and with his fist poised in midair, ready to pound on the door yet again, Lockett found himself staring at a shotgun pointed at his midsection.

He gaped at a small, wiry old man. The man had a weather worn, creased face that was dominated by bushy black eyebrows that suggested he was a younger man than the wispy gray hair of his dome suggested.

"I said, who the devil are you?" The old man jerked the shotgun for emphasis. "And what are you doing on my property?" He stared suspiciously at Lockett, who knew he must make a strange sight. His clothing was damp and muddy. His face was smeared with dirt, dried blood, and a multitude of small cuts and scratches, not to mention the horrific burn on his neck and jaw line.

"I'll not ask again, stranger."

Finally snapping out of his daze, Lockett recalled Octavius's instructions. "I'm a soul in need of refuge."

But the old man just blinked at him and gave no indication that the code words were correct. He just looked at Lockett, and the shotgun did not alter one iota. Lockett began to wonder if he had picked the wrong cabin again, but knowing that he was committed now, he continued on. He ignored the shotgun and stepped into the cabin, closing the door behind him.

"Please, there are people out hunting me. I can't stand in your doorway. It's too dangerous."

The old man did not lower the shotgun. "It is dangerous. You can't stay here."

"I need your help."

"Sorry. Not sure, who you think I am or what I can do for you, but you need to leave."

"The Underground Railroad is my only chance."

"Underground Railroad?"

"I saw you remove the ribbon from the gate post."

The old man's frown deepened slightly. "Not sure what you mean," he said slowly.

"Please, I need to get back north."

"No doubt about that," the old man said, "You sure sound like a Yankee. You're a little far south for a tongue like that."

"You can help me get back to my army."

"Lost are you?" the old man cackled suddenly. "I'll say you are lost, Yankee."

"Look, they're hunting me, and they might not be very far behind now!"

"Who is?"

"The Rebels. Who do you think?"

"What makes you think that I'm not a Rebel? I could just hand you over to them."

Lockett studied the old man. He had a tough, weather hardened face. The man's blue eyes, partially shrouded by the heavy black brow, stared back at him unflinchingly.

"You're no Rebel," Lockett said slowly. "And I know what you are. You're the guide who is going help me get to the next depot."

The old man was about to respond when he stopped in mid-thought. His eyes flickered from Lockett's to something that caught his attention in the small window behind Lockett.

"Cor-," he said, continuing to mutter some sort of oath that Lockett couldn't understand.

"What is it?"

The old man pulled Lockett away from the window while he continued to stare at a group of horsemen on the knoll, looking down at the house.

"What the devil? What the devil? There's no room. No room," he said, showing anxiety for the first time.

Lockett started to turn and wanted to look through the window to see what had changed the man's demeanor so quickly, but before he could peek through the window, the man pulled him back.

"Don't, you fool! You want them to see you?"

"Who is it?"

"You bein' hunted by Confederate cavalry?"

"Among others."

"What the devil, what the devil, what the devil!" the old man repeated, sounding more anxious with each utterance.

"Hide me," Lockett ordered. "This is a depot, isn't it?"

"Yes, yes, it is," the old man snapped.

"Then hide me."

"I'm not sure that there's room." His eyes widened as he continued to look out the window. "Mercy, they're coming."

"Hide me, now."

"Mercy, mercy. There will have to be room. Hurry, follow me."

He led Lockett to the back room. It was dimly lit. The only light was that which trickled in from the front room. He shoved aside a small unkempt bed and started pulling up two loose floor boards. This time, the hiding place was not a clever false space. It was merely a small crawl space underneath the flooring.

"You must make room. Hurry, hurry!" he pleaded.

At first, Lockett was confused by what the old man was saying, but then in the gray light, he was vaguely aware of two black faces staring up at him from the coffin like crawlspace.

"Get in," the old man said. "Hurry!" he added, unsatisfied as Lockett tried to gently lower himself into the tight space. The man gave him an unceremonious push, and Lockett fell into the shallow crawlspace. The old man used his boot to slide the rest of Lockett's long body into the space and immediately began replacing the floor boards.

"Open up!" came a yell from outside, and there was a pounding on the door.

The old man nudged the floor boards into place, and they all heard the front door open. There was no chance for the man to put the bed back on top of the floorboards.

A horse whinnied, and a gust of cold wind raced through the tiny homestead.

"You there! Where are you?" commanded a voice.

"What are you doing in my house?" the old man answered, stalking out from the back room.

Lockett could both hear and feel the footsteps. He lay awkwardly in the tiny crawlspace. His cheek rested on someone's leg, and his left arm and shoulder were trapped between two bodies. He opened his upward facing eye and could see a crack of light between the boards, just above him. He tried to shift ever so gently but could feel the floorboard on his right shoulder. He stopped shifting and tried to roll his shoulders so as to not disturb the boards.

"I said, what are you doing in my house?" the old man demanded.

He was answered with the audible click of a hammer being cocked. "You alone, old man?"

"I am and what is the meaning of this?" the old man asked indignantly.

"You'd be well served, old man, to treat the soldiers who are protecting you from hordes of Yankees with more respect."

"Then the army should treat my house as more than an open stable," the old man grumbled, but his voice was softer as he said it.

"What's your name, old man?"

"Samuel Cooper."

"Wahl, Mister Cooper. W'are lookin' for somebody."

The old man was silent, and Lockett could hear a number of footsteps in the outer room. He was conscious of his heart pounding through his chest. It seemed as if it made the small tomb reverberate. As tightly as they were pinned together, he had no doubt that his two new companions could feel his throbbing, fearful heart.

He was also aware of his breathing. He tried to take shallow, quiet breaths, but in the trapped space, it seemed that there was little air and less so by the second. A moment of panic seized him as he thought that they were running out of air, but he calmed himself and listened to the activity in the front room.

"Ain't nobody here," he could hear the old man say.

"We'll be the judge of that, Mistah Cooper. If ya alone as ya say, then ya won't mind if we takes a look around."

Lockett could hear no answer and had no way of knowing that the old man had shrugged with resignation as the leader of the troop waved a cocked weapon in his face.

"Damn poor excuse for a house," a different soldier commented, looking around the sparsely furnished cabin.

"What's back there?" the leader asked.

"My bed."

"Mowrie, go check it," the leader commanded.

The footsteps came closer and closer. Lockett could feel one of the bodies in the crawlspace stiffen. If his heart had been pounding before, it was now surging with a rapid fire staccato.

The footsteps paused near the floorboards, and Lockett had a sudden fear that the man would be able to smell him.

The stench of body odor was strong in the hovel, and Lockett knew that he smelled something fearful.

The floorboards creaked above, and the small crack of light disappeared as the soldier stood over them. A tendril of dirt and dust trickled down onto his face. He held his breath. Then the man got on his knees to look under the nearby bed. Through the crack, Lockett could see the man's mud splattered trousers.

The man paused in that position for a moment, and Lockett thought that all was lost, but then the soldier stood up and called out, "Ain't nothing back here but one poor excuse for a bed."

The footsteps trailed out of the room, and Lockett felt one his new companions physically relax in relief.

"Ya seen anyone in the last day, Cooper?" the leader asked.

"Out here?" the old man cackled, "I go for weeks without seeing nobody, and that's the way that I like it too."

"Wahl, there's a dangerous man on the loose out here. Ya catch wind of him, ya best find me, Cooper."

"Some sort of criminal?"

"Something like that, Cooper. There's a reward for him. Ya help me find him, I'll cut ya in for a piece."

"A reward?" the old man said with renewed interest. "A reward, why didn't you tell me that in the first place?"

"Oh, so ya seen him now, have ya?"

There was a slight pause, and Lockett cursed Ambrose Tucker's deviousness. The pause could mean only one thing, and Lockett wondered if he could at least get a swing at the old man as they dragged him out of this coffin hole.

Then the old man laughed. "Still ain't seen nobody, but ifs I do now, I will let you know. How much would my share be?"

"Depends on yer amount of help, Cooper, but it is a fair reward, enough to go around."

"If I sees him, and I can't finds you, then I go into town and find the sheriff?"

"Ya find me, old man."

"But if I can't find you, then the sheriff can help with the reward?"

"It ain't a matter for the sheriff. He don't know a thing about the reward. It's a matter of honor. So if ya see him, then ya find one of us. That's the only way ya get the reward. Don't go thinking that ya can go straight to sheriff and collect the whole. Ain't gonna work that way."

"Never a thought," the old man snorted. "Then I'll be sure to let you know."

"Ya do that, Cooper. All right boys, mount up, let's see if we can pick up his trail." There was a gust of cold air as the door opened and closed, and then it was silent.

It was a full fifteen minutes before the old man ventured to the back room and removed the floor boards. With his first deep breath since entering the hovel, Lockett pulled himself stiffly from the hiding spot.

"That was close."

He didn't notice until he was completely out that Cooper held a shotgun pointed at him.

"I don't like being taken for a fool," he growled at Lockett. "I don't risk my life to hide criminals. Matter of honor? What does that mean? What'd you do?"

Startled, Lockett scrabbled backwards. "Easy now, Cooper. I'm not a criminal in spite of what they said."

"You sayin' there ain't a reward for your capture."

Lockett hesitated and looked at the man behind the gun. What kind of man was he dealing with? Was this another McGowan? Was he honest? He obviously hid slaves. Did he turn those in for rewards too? He had heard of that happening before.

Did Cooper just wait until the soldiers were gone so that he could claim the full reward for himself? Or did he wait because there were innocent fugitive slaves down in the hole with him?

"No, Cooper, there is a reward... at least I think so," he

admitted, "I'm not a criminal. That's not why there is a reward."

"Not a criminal?" Cooper said skeptically, "Then why the devil would there be a reward for you? Of course, you're some sort of criminal. Them soldier boys can say that it is a matter of honor and that the sheriff don't know a thing, but I don't believe that for an instant. They just want a larger share of the reward. So what did you do? I'd say you were a horse thief, except you walked here, so what is it? Murderer?"

Lockett paused and said in a low voice. "I'm not a murderer."

"You tellin' me you ain't killed before?"

"I've killed plenty," Lockett said in a controlled voice, but his temper was starting to rise. "Soldiers kill plenty. There's a war on. But I am not a murderer, and that is not why they want me."

"So what then? Why a reward?"

"Because I'm a spy."

The words hung heavily in the room. Cooper instinctively flinched, and all was silent.

Chapter 37

"A spy?" Cooper eventually uttered.

"Yes," Lockett answered slowly, "I have information that General Rosecrans needs. I need to get back through the lines. I need your help, Cooper."

Cooper chewed on his lower lip, and the shotgun dipped but only an inch. "I dunno," he said. "A spy? I ain't a Yankee. I jus' help them slaves escape."

"I've been in Murfreesboro, Cooper. I have information that will help the Union Army, help us greatly."

"Dunno," Cooper repeated warily.

Another voice entered the conversation. "So if you git back to the army, Father Abraham's army can win a great victory?"

Lockett looked in surprise. His two new companions had climbed from the hiding spot, and to his astonishment, both were female. One was just a young girl of ten or so, and he assumed that the other one was her mother. It was the girl who had spoken. She was a spindly little thing, more limbs than anything else. She wore a thin, soiled dress. Her face was dirty and short hair matted, but she looked at him with a pair of inquisitive eyes that searched him.

"You will win a great victory?" she repeated.

Lockett nodded finally. "Yes, with this information, we can win." He turned back to Cooper. "Help me, Cooper."

Cooper sighed and looked from Lockett to the two fugitive slaves and then back again. "Devil be served or Angels be served? Ain't sure which one you is." He blew out a long breath and lowered the weapon. "Very well, very well."

* * *

They had started the journey that night. Warily, they had departed in the black of night.

"Those boys from earlier today are still around. I can feel it," Cooper commented as they left.

Lockett knew that they would have to dodge patrols, encampments, and both sets of lines in order to get back. One more set of horsemen did not overly worry him. What worried him more was the young girl. Poorly dressed for the conditions, even with Cooper's borrowed jacket and pants, he worried that she would slow them down, but Cooper had openly laughed at his concerns.

"You think that she will slow us down?" he had said with disbelief. "More 'n likely that you'll be slowin' her down. I know she's a young thing, but when the flame of freedom burns in your heart, it gives an energy like you've never seen before."

And Cooper had been right. Never once during the night had they slowed and never did the girl stumble or make a peep. Doggedly, the three of them followed Cooper throughout the night, and by early morning, he had directed them to a small cave where they would wait for the next cover of nightfall.

It had been a quiet night as they had followed Cooper. At times, it had been a meandering path through the woods, and it reminded Lockett of how he had been forced to follow McGowan so blindly. The lack of control irked him greatly, but he did not see that he had much choice. Could he trust Cooper, or would it end up like McGowan?

He knew that Cooper was part of the Underground Railroad, but he had heard stories that there were a few scoundrels who would turn in their passengers for rewards. The question lingered in the back of his mind.

Silently, the three of them had followed Cooper. He had learned before they had left that the mother was named Linzy and her daughter was Clarissa. But that was all that he knew about them, and they did not say a single word during the night. At first, there had been a palpable fear and tension, but as the night went on, the three of them were certain that there was no one in these woods except the three of them. Still, there was no talking.

Even if he had felt like it, Lockett was also not sure what to say to them. Normally, he would ask where someone was from or where they were heading, but in the case of escaped slaves, those were foolish questions.

And so it was only upon reaching the cave, and only in muted whispers, that any of them spoke. Even so, when Clarissa spoke in that first hushed whisper, it startled everyone.

"You are part of Father Abraham's soldiers?" she asked with a voice that was both slightly anxious and curious.

Lockett looked at her. In the dim light of the cave, he could see little more than a pair of eyes looking at him. "Father Abraham? Lincoln, I guess. Yes, I am in the Union army."

"You have fought battles?"

"Yes," he said, thinking back to Shiloh and Perryville, "Some terrible ones."

"You have seen men killed?"

"Hundreds. Thousands," he said in a sad whisper, "More than I ever would have thought possible."

"For me?"

"For you?" he said confused.

"You fight to free us."

"I…" he stammered. "I don't know."

"But you must fight for us?" Clarissa said with honest confusion. "If Father Abraham wins, there be no more slaves."

Lockett thought about the Emancipation Proclamation that had caused such consternation in parts of the army. Given Lincoln's official proclamation, then the girl was right. The outcome of the war would lead to no more slavery, at least in the South.

"Well, that is true," he said slowly. "There would be no more slavery."

"Then you fight for us," Clarissa said with an unequivocal confidence and satisfaction that belonged with her youthful age.

"I suppose," he answered slowly, but he was really not sure. He had not thought of it in such simple terms before. Everything was so complicated now.

Chapter 38

They had hiked steadily through the second night but only with painfully slow progress. Lockett wished that they could travel during the day. He knew that they could cover far more miles in the daylight, but it was risky and Cooper was not willing to do it. Linzy and Clarissa said nothing, but he could sense that they agreed with Cooper. Speed was not important to them, only a successful escape. If it took a week or a month, it made no difference to them. All that mattered to them was to make it. He could understand that, but General Rosecrans needed his information sooner than later.

By early morning, they had stopped under another rocky outcropping near a small hill. Lockett climbed to the top and carefully peered around. They were in the middle of nowhere, no sign of civilization in sight, and so the four of them relaxed under the outcropping. A misting cold rain began to fall, and the rocky spur provided only the slightest cover.

Still, the drizzle did not matter to Lockett who quickly curled against the rock with his hand buried inside coat, resting against the butt of Ambrose's LeMat revolver. He did not think that he would be able to fall asleep, but he figured that some nervous dozing was better than nothing for his tired feet and cloudy mind.

The others seemed of like mind, and nothing was said as the quartet recuperated uncomfortably on the rocks.

However, in spite of his pessimism, Lockett did fall asleep. Almost immediately, his dreams turned back to Missouri and little Amelia. He could see her face. He could see Orrin Long chasing her through the house. For some reason in this version of the dream, Orrin held a bayonet in his hand, and he chased her from room to room. James could see himself in the dream, giving chase, but his feet were heavy, like he was slogging through a muddy bog and not a house. He could not catch Orrin or little Amelia, but Amelia was quick and Orrin could not corner her. The chase went from room to room until they were outside the house. James followed them out of the house and then back in, but now, he knew he was too late. She was cornered and tucked into a small, fearful ball. James yelled, but his feet could not move.

In the dream, Orrin Long looked over his shoulder and sneered in triumph. The oily, greedy smile stuck daggers in James, but still, he could not move, but then he realized that it was not Amelia in the corner; it was Anna.

With a choked cry, he burst awake. Wildly, he looked around, unsure where he was for a moment. Linzy just looked at him. Clarissa and Cooper both slept peacefully, oblivious to his startled yelp.

Lockett felt himself breathing heavily, and he felt hot, even with the cold rain now blowing in on his face.

"I have dreams like that too," Linzy said simply.

They looked at each other, neither wanted to know the details of the other's nightmares.

He found himself staring at her, noting her calm presence. She returned it with a look of neither sympathy nor anything else, just a placid look. She was not an unattractive woman with a round face, and a full figure that could not be hid even by the men's trousers and rough shirt that she wore. Cooper had supplied both mother and daughter with them, telling them that it would be necessary for the arduous trek.

Gently, Lockett touched the burned side of his neck and jaw. There was always a constant smoldering sensation that made him want to grind his teeth, but for the past day, it hurt worse than usual.

"You need to clean that," Linzy commented.

Lockett nodded. Anna had taken pains to make sure that the wound was clean and re-bandaged regularly. He knew that the hardships and haste of the past few days had turned him into a wreck, and he could only imagine how bad he looked.

"It is a bad burn," she added, "How did it happen?"

Lockett snorted and gave a wry smile. "Had a disagreement with someone, a bad someone." He paused and added, "Normally, he'd be hunting someone like you..."

"Is he dead?" she asked.

"Yes," Lockett nodded.

"Good," she answered, "I was not able to do the same for my scars."

Lockett looked quizzically at her. She responded by taking off the jacket and raising her shirt. She faced away from him. Her back from top to bottom was a criss-cross of thick ugly scars. In parts, it looked like scars upon scars. Lockett had never seen anything like it. He could not imagine the whippings that it would take to create such a mass of torn flesh. Even with all that he had seen since he had left little Kalamazoo, his mouth fell open in astonishment.

She lowered the shirt and turned back to face him again. "So if you killed him, why do you sleep so fearfully?"

"My dreams? It's someone else," he said darkly, "Someone who is still out there."

"Then I hope that you have a chance to ease your dreams."

Lockett nodded, but he knew that the dreams were with him to stay. Regardless of what happened to Orrin Long, that would change nothing for little Amelia. Worse now, his dreams were starting to be filled with fear for what would happen to Anna.

* * *

At dusk, they departed again. They had eaten all the stale bread and small cheese that Cooper had packed for them, but he assured them that there would be something at the next stop.

After being so well fed by Anna and her Aunt Molly, the last few days had been a grim reminder to Lockett of how much he disliked going hungry. Yet, he knew that he could not say anything about the knot of pain in his belly. He had seen how Clarissa had devoured the stale bread and knew that she must be far hungrier than he. From her bony frame, he doubted that she had ever enjoyed full meals.

It was still three hours before the dawn when Cooper drew them to a halt at the edge of the woods. He paused and looked across the black, broad expanse of a pasture.

"What is it?" Linzy asked in a scarcely audible voice. Her eyes strained in the darkness.

"It's the ford," Cooper said. "It's down yonder, and we need to cross here. The next passable place is a good three miles."

"Then why are we waiting?" she asked.

"I thought that I saw a flicker of light."

"I don't see anything," Clarissa whispered.

"Same here," Lockett said.

"No, no, I'm sure I saw a brief light," Cooper said cautiously.

Lockett peered through the inky darkness, but he did not see anything that was amiss. With only a sliver of moon, the night was nearly as dark as could be. A steady cold breeze gusted from behind them, causing him to shiver. Was there something waiting for them on the other side?

"Can we go around?" Linzy asked.

"No," Cooper answered. "It is pasture land here, and this is the ford where need to cross. The next passable place is too far."

"Then let's go," Linzy said, displaying impatience for the first time on this journey.

"No, I'm sure that I saw something," Cooper paused. "Let me check it. If it's clear, then I'll come back for y'all."

"We'll come too," Linzy said.

"No," Cooper said stubbornly, "If I wander into something up there, then what am I supposed to do? I cain't talk my way out of it with two escaped slaves and a Yankee. I'll be back. Don't worry."

Lockett said nothing. He could not see Linzy's face in the dark of night, but he could sense her disapproval and worry as the old man set off across the pasture.

The hunched figure melted into the darkness. He moved swiftly and silently, and Lockett realized that the old man had been doing this for a while. Just before he disappeared completely into the night, he stopped as if his presence had triggered something. After a long pause, he continued on and out of sight.

Lockett rubbed his jaw, deep in thought, and then pulled out the revolver. In the dark, he nervously rubbed a finger against the nine chambered cylinder. After another five minutes, he turned to Linzy and Clarissa.

"Wait here."

"Where are you going?" Linzy asked in surprise, concern

evident in her voice.

"I'm going to check on him," Lockett said with a fraternal voice, as if it was Cooper's welfare that he was interested in. In reality, it was Cooper that he feared. He recalled how McGowan had left that message in the slave quarters on the way to Murfreesboro. Was something equally underhanded afoot? He did not dare take the chance, but he also did not want to worry Linzy and Clarissa. "I'll be back shortly," he finished.

He set out across the pasture. From the woods, it looked like a dark, flat expanse, but once he started to cross it, Lockett quickly discovered that it was not. The pasture was ribbed with long thin stretches of rock protruding up from the ground. It was row after row, like he was crossing some celestial giant's ribcage. He tripped on the first outcropping and fell heavily, banging his knee painfully.

He bit back the cry of pain and froze in the shallow trench formed between the two 'ribs'. He listened intently but heard no other noise in the night. Rubbing his knee, he got back to his feet and blindly continued across the pasture. Halfway across the pasture, he paused suddenly. Turning his head, he listened to the night, wondering if he had just heard something from the far end of the pasture. But another gust of cold slapped him from behind and whistled on through the limbs of the forest at both ends of the pasture. Reluctantly, he decided that the noise was just the wind and his imagination.

He put the revolver back in his pocket and blew on his cupped hands. The frigid gusts were sapping the feeling in his fingers. Nervously, he clenched and unclenched them, and in a crouch, he crossed over the next two outcroppings and stopped again. There was still no sign of Cooper or anyone else ahead, but he sensed that something seemed wrong. He wondered if he was letting his suspicions get the better of him. He so desperately wanted to get back to General Rosecrans. With this information, the army would have to move, and they could have that decisive victory that could propel them to the war's end. He wanted to believe that Cooper was just the man to help guide him back, but he just wasn't sure.

Of course, nothing was ever for certain in this war. He had friends in the South; he even admired some of the Rebel generals and certainly the courage of their soldiers. Of course, there were some Southerners hunting him down, ready to kill him like a dog if they could. And there was little difference with his Northern army. He had blood brothers in men like Patrick and Milton, but there were also men like Orrin Long.

It was hard to tell what was up or down in the country now. And all of those thoughts were even before thinking about Anna. As he finished crossing the pasture, he could not help but let his thoughts stray from the task at hand. He lost himself in contemplation about Anna. What was she doing now? Was she safe? How long could that last? He had to get back to her too, but how was he to do that when he was heading in the opposite direction?

He was so lost in thought that it took a second to recognize that he heard voices coming from the woods ahead.

Lockett slowed his pace and crept forward with tedious patience. Each step was carefully placed for stealth. He entered the tree line, and his footfalls were gentle and delicately placed, lest there be a stick or leaves to give away his approach. It took minutes at that pace to creep close enough to make out what the voice was saying. At that same point, he could now smell a campfire's familiar smell. Another gust blew from behind, and he realized that being upwind had made it impossible to smell the fire until he was nearly right on it.

"I don't believe you, old man," the harsh voice said.

"It's true. It's true."

Lockett recognized the second voice as Cooper's, and even the first voice sounded vaguely familiar.

"Why should I believe you?"

"Why else would I be out here? On a night like this?"

"If you had information on the man we're huntin', you could have told the sergeant when we were at your cabin."

Lockett then recognized the speaker's voice. It was one of the men from Cooper's house, one of the men hunting him, but it was not the leader's voice.

"I didn't know anything then, but I do now."

"I don't believe you. Why did I catch you sneaking through the woods then?"

"There's bushwhackers nowadays. I didn't know if it was you

or some brigand. How can I tell? You can't be too careful these days. It might even have been Yankees."

The last comment brought a laugh of derision. "A Yankee? Here? There ain't a single Yankee for miles."

He laughed again and shook his head. "They ain't leaving their cozy beds in Nashville. They won't venture down here til spring time." There was a pause and then the audible cocking of a hammer. "Now, tell me what you know. Where's the man that we're after?"

"What about my share of the reward?"

"We'll take of care of that, now what do you know?"

"I dunno. Where's your sergeant? I want his word."

"The sergeant is up yonder, and my word is as good as the sergeant's."

Lockett crept closer. He circled around a small bush and stepped over a fallen log, pulling the revolver from his pocket. He had half a mind to shoot Cooper first and then the Confederate.

Lockett could see between the trees into the camp. There was a small fire shielded by the pines and two small tents. Cooper sat on his haunches with his hands bound behind him. Facing him was a short, whip thin man who casually held a cavalryman's carbine pointed at the sky. A lit pipe dangled from his mouth, and Lockett wondered if that pipe had been the flicker of light that Cooper claimed to have seen. Had the man been away from camp and lit his pipe? Or was Cooper up to something from the beginning? And what was Cooper saying? Was he talking to save his own skin? Was there more to it?

A horse snorted nervously and shuffled. Lockett turned his head to the right and saw two horses tied up at the edge of their camp. Just two horses, he questioned in his own mind. One was for the short, whip thin man, but the other?

Before he could wonder a second longer, there was a jubilant voice.

"Davis, guessee what I got here?" Then there was a crashing through the forest that drew everyone's attention.

The man, Davis, took his pipe from his mouth with one hand while the other gripped the carbine in mid barrel.

Lockett followed Davis's eyes as the Rebel turned, and he saw a large, mountainous man dragging someone by their feet. The man was enormous and looked to be a full head taller than Lockett and at least twice as thick. With a cry of triumph, the Rebel giant continued dragging his prisoner across the ground and then tossed that someone a few feet from Cooper.

Lockett saw the look of fear and dejection on Cooper's face before he saw anything else. Then with a sinking feeling, Lockett watched Linzy struggle to one knee.

Chapter 39

"Well, I think we know now what you're doing out here in the dark of night, old man," 'Davis' said.

"Found her sneaking through the woods," the larger Rebel explained to his partner.

"When the sergeant said to keep an eye on the ford in case that deserter tried to use it, who knew?" Davis laughed. "Caught ourselves a damn abolitionist and a runner! If they built a gallows for that deserter, maybe they can use it on you too, Cooper."

"I don't much care for his type," the giant said. "Best hangin' I ever saw was one of his type back in Nashville before the war started, kicked a full two minutes he did." He gave a big belly laugh at the memory.

Like a cornered animal, Linzy crouched on the balls of her feet. Her eyes danced left and right in the firelight. Sensing that she was about to try to scamper away, her captor viciously cuffed her across the head. She sprawled backwards with a shriek.

Lockett expected her to be flattened by the blow, but she sprung back to her feet and flung herself at the enormous man, who had turned to laugh with 'Davis'.

Unaware of her resilience or aggressive approach, he never saw her as she crashed into him, clawing for his eyes. The giant stumbled back. He stepped in an indentation on the uneven ground and fell to all fours.

Linzy still clung to him and clawed at his face. 'Davis' laughed while Linzy attacked the mountainous man, causing him to bellow and cry out in alarm as her nails searched for his eyes. Clumsily, he defended himself by back-handing her across the cheek, but still she clung to him, clawing and hitting.

"She's a fighter, Mowrie," Davis laughed, "She'll be worth a pretty penny when we return her."

'Mowrie' used both hands to free himself from the smaller woman, tossing her angrily to the ground. "I'll show you what we do with your type!" he yelled as swung a heavy boot into her midsection and proceeded to stomp on her again and again.

"Easy," Davis cautioned, "She'll be worth more if she ain't broke." But he did not move an inch to stop 'Mowrie', and Davis seemed content to watch.

Mowrie continued to kick and stomp again and again, despite the fact that Linzy had stopped moving after the third kick.

Lockett eased the hammer back, hoping the sound would not give him away, but nothing could be heard over Mowrie's exertions.

Cautiously, he took aim at the giant. Fearing that the range was too great for a revolver of such dubious reputation as a LeMat, he eased himself closer. His aim was on the man kicking Linzy, but he wondered if perhaps he should first shoot the small man with the carbine.

Mowrie prodded Linzy with the toe of his boot. When she gave a soft moan, he pressed the boot against her neck.

Lockett decided it had to stop now. If he waited any longer, she might be dead, if she wasn't already. He raised the revolver and centered it on the middle of Mowrie's chest. His finger wrapped around the cold metal of the trigger.

But before he could pull the trigger, a shadow flashed into camp with a cry, snatching a flaming log from the fire. Clarissa dashed across the camp and swung the log at a startled Mowrie who stumbled backward, his girth pulling him off-balance once more.

Mowrie stepped on the same uneven piece of ground and fell onto his rear again. Clarissa clubbed him with the flaming log across the chest.

A braver charge Lockett had never seen before. Nor had he ever seen as foolhardy and futile of one.

The log thumped on Mowrie's chest with the effect of a willow switch falling on a boulder. Davis laughed loudly, "Another one!"

From the ground, Mowrie's meaty paw snagged Clarissa by the wrist.

Lockett lowered his aim. Now he had no shot at the man. Clarissa was in the way. He waited for the huge man to stand, which would give him a clearer shot.

But then Davis, still laughing, happened to turn and see Lockett standing just outside the edge of the camp with a gun in his hand. His laughing stopped immediately, and his mouth dropped open. He swung his carbine up while Lockett changed his aim to Davis.

Lockett's cocked revolver was faster than the Rebel. The shot banged in his hand well before Davis could finish aiming his weapon.

But the LeMat's round pulled to the right, missing Davis narrowly.

Still, it caused Davis to leap to the side. From the ground, Cooper stuck out a foot and tripped the small man.

Davis fell, and the carbine discharged as it slipped from his grasp.

Lockett fired again at Davis and ran into the camp. The smaller Confederate yelled in fear and tried to scramble behind a tent, leaving the weapon behind.

Lockett fired again through the tent, but before he could follow up, he was distracted by movement from the other side of camp where Mowrie had righted himself and had Clarissa by the throat, holding her between him and Lockett.

Lockett turned and leveled the weapon at Mowrie. The distance was short, and he judged the chances of shooting him without hitting Clarissa. He knew that his first shot at Davis had missed. Was that his aim, or did Ambrose Tucker's gun pull to one side or the other?

"Not a step closer!" Mowrie yelled, spittle flying from his mouth. "I'll snap her bony neck like a twig."

Lockett paused and aimed for the middle of the man's face. He could make the shot... right?

He had to hurry. Where was the other Rebel? Reloading? He steadied his aim.

But then like a spell had been cast, his hand wavered. He saw little Amelia's face, not Clarissa's. He felt his old Dimick rifle in his hands, not the LeMat. It was that old rifle that had discharged and killed Amelia, and his hand shook at the memory.

Emboldened, Mowrie edged himself back and to the right where his own carbine lay near his tent.

Not again, Lockett thought, what if the shot killed Clarissa?

He couldn't have this happen again.

Clarissa dangled from Mowrie's grasp. The tips of her toes scraped the ground. Her eyes bulged, and she struggled for air, powerless to prevent herself from being dragged towards the carbine. She tried to speak, to tell him to shoot, but no words or air could come from her throttled windpipe.

Mowrie was now only a foot away from the carbine.

Lockett knew that he must fire, but his arm was frozen. His heart pounded in his ears like a hundred cannon and reverberated through his whole body. He doubted that he could hold the weapon steady enough to make the shot. Surely, it would hit Clarissa. He knew that he couldn't hesitate, but still, he did.

Suddenly, there was sound from the other side of him, and in his peripheral vision there was movement. He tilted his head slightly and saw Davis mounting one of the horses.

Mowrie also looked over to where the horses had been tied up, "Wait!" he yelled, "Davis, wait!"

Lockett looked back at Mowrie and felt a steadiness that had not been there before. Off to the side, he could hear Davis's horse leaving the area.

"Wait!" Mowrie repeated, still distracted. His grip loosened on Clarissa ever so slightly. It was just enough space for her to move her head and jaw, and she bit down fiercely on Mowrie's arm. He yelled in pain, and she squirmed completely free.

Mowrie tried to grab the fleeing girl, but she ducked under his grasp, and he stumbled forward. Lockett fired, and the shot hit Mowrie in the shoulder. It staggered him, but he righted himself and charged Lockett like a wounded bull. Lockett fired again from a mere three feet away. The heavy slug caught the man in the throat, and Mowrie dropped to his knees, gagging and choking, blood rapidly spilling out on the ground at Lockett's feet.

Lockett paused, and for a moment, the camp site was eerily quiet with the only noise being the hooves of a horse disappearing into the night. Lockett looked at Clarissa who stared back at him with an equally stunned face. Then, she sprinted to her mother's side.

"Is she still alive?"

There was no answer, and Lockett noticed the tears in the girl's eyes now.

Clarissa held a hand to her mother's mouth. "She's still breathing."

Giving a sigh of relief, Lockett scooped up the discarded carbine and a cartridge box. He made his way to the one remaining horse. "We have to hurry. We don't know how far away the others are. They may already be on their way because of the shots."

He grabbed a canteen and sniffed the meat cooking next to the fire. Turning around, he noticed that he was the only one moving, which was understandable for Linzy and Clarissa. "C'mon Cooper. We gotta go." Then he remembered that Cooper was still tied up.

He walked over to the old man, but he only made it halfway before his steps slowed. There was a dark puddle under the old man who still lay on his side. "Cooper?"

There was no answer.

Lockett hurried over to the old man. Blood covered his stomach. Lockett pulled free his knife and cut Cooper loose, but the old man did not move. They looked at each in the firelight.

"Gut shot," Cooper managed through clenched teeth. "By devil, I'm as good as dead."

Chapter 40

"How?" Lockett asked dumbly, even as he remembered Davis's carbine discharging. "Can you move?" he asked, even though he already knew the answer. He had seen enough gut shot men now. There was nothing that could be done for Cooper, and it was going to be a slow, painful death for him.

He grabbed a filthy blanket from the tent and held it to the wound. He placed Cooper's hand there. "Keep pressure on it."

"Ain't no good, Yankee. I'm dead, and you know it."

With resignation, Lockett nodded. He looked over at the other two. Clarissa cradled Linzy's head, and there was silence. What were they going to do now?

"You need to leave," Cooper said after a minute.

"I know," Lockett said, silently contemplating the obvious question.

"Cross the ford first," Cooper said, stopping as a spasm of pain surged through him. "Head northeast, head for the swamp." He stopped and grounded his teeth, and his eyes closed. For a moment, Lockett thought that he might die right there.

"Then what?" There was no answer. "Then what, Cooper?" No answer. "Cooper? Cooper?" He said more urgently. "Cooper, where do we go from there?"

"The swamp," Cooper managed, but then halted in another spasm.

"Cooper," Lockett pleaded, "What about the swamp?"

Through clenched teeth and closed eyes, Cooper managed in a softer voice that forced Lockett to lean close to hear him. "The swamp is the edge. The Yankees are on the other side… There is a high ground in the middle… Git there. I have a hut there. Rest there. Then go north. Your lines are jus' north…" With that, his eyes closed, and he went limp.

Lockett turned. "Clarissa, grab what food and water there is."

"But momma..." she started.

"I'll take care of her," he said in a gentle voice.

Softly, Clarissa lowered her mother's cradled head. Lockett went over and knelt next to Linzy. Cooper's blood dripped off Lockett's hands, but he paid no attention as he held Linzy's hand. "Linzy?"

She stirred slightly, and one eye opened to look at him. The other eye was swollen shut, and the swelling was already ghastly. It was the size of a fist and seemed to grow by the second. It was a wonder that the skin could contain that much pressure. There was just a thin slit to show where her eyeball should have been.

Blood leaked from her nose, but it was her arm and ribs that worried him most. One arm hung limply, and he had seen the punishment that her ribs had taken. He had to believe that some of those might be broken as well.

"Linzy, we need to go."

She moaned and tried to stir herself, but just that slightest effort overcame her, and she slumped back to the ground.

"Linzy, can you ride?" But he knew the answer to that. He thought about laying her across the horse and leading the horse by the bridle, but then he thought of her ribs and the jarring that they would take with each step.

"Clarissa," he called, "Do you have that food and water?"

"Yes'r," she answered.

"Put it on the horse, and bring the horse over here."

She did as instructed and brought the saddled horse over. Lockett slid Mowrie's carbine into the saddle holster and handed Davis's weapon to Clarissa. She looked at him in pure puzzlement, as if he had just handed her a foreign musical instrument.

"Sling it over your back," he said, as he knelt back by her mother. Gingerly, he slid an arm under her. "C'mon, Linzy. Easy now. Let's get you up."

With a tenderness that astonished Clarissa, he helped Linzy to her feet. She staggered and would have fallen had his arms not been under her. "We have to get you on this horse. I'm going to help."

He held her steady. "Clarissa, put her foot in the stirrup so that

I can get her up there." Having done so, he slowly tried to lift her into the saddle. Even with his height, he could not do so alone. "C'mon, Linzy, you can do it. Get up there." With her one good arm and a cry of pain, she pulled on the pommel and they managed to get her onto the horse, although for a second, Lockett feared that she would fall off the other side.

Then, he swung himself up onto the horse and gently lifted Linzy so that she sat side saddle across his lap.

"Your turn," he said to Clarissa, who had assumed that she would be walking. He held an arm out to her. She reached out a hand and agilely scrambled up as he gave her light frame a pull.

She sat on the rump behind him.

Lockett put his arms around Linzy and picked up the reins. Behind him, Clarissa held onto his waist, and they rode off slowly for the ford.

* * *

Not even a mile from his camp, Davis dismounted. His head was still spinning, and he could not concentrate. He felt woozy, and all he that he could think about was how close to death he had just come. The man had seemingly come out of nowhere, and Davis still could not fathom how either that first shot or the second one that ripped through the tent had missed him. His short life had passed before his eyes, and in sheer terror, he had raced out of camp.

In puzzlement, Davis looked at the lame horse, the reason that he had dismounted. It took him a few moments to realize that the horse was lame in one of its front legs. In the dark, he felt the animal's leg. The horse could put no weight on it, and as Davis ran his hands down the leg, he felt warm, sticky blood.

Slowly, it dawned on him that the shot through the tent had missed him, but it must have nicked the horse. The animal stirred pitifully on three legs, but there was nothing that Davis could do. He did not even have a weapon to put it out of its misery.

His blood coated hands started shaking, and he sat down against a tree. He knew that he needed to get back to Sergeant Dunbar, but first, he needed to rest. His wobbly legs suggested that he had no choice.

* * *

Lockett, Linzy, and Clarissa rode throughout the night and into the next morning.

During the night, he had used the north star to help guide his way, but as night gave way to day, that became impossible. He tried to hold his course to the northeast as Cooper had instructed, but with the cloudy skies he had limited ways of knowing now if he was doing so.

There were no landmarks to go by as they went through one empty pasture after another, through woods and over rocky knolls. He could not tell if they were still headed for this swamp or even how far away it was.

Of greater concern was pursuit. They plodded along at an agonizingly slow pace, but it was the best that they could manage. Linzy rested her head against his chest, and he could feel Clarissa's head against his back. His arms were weary from supporting Linzy and holding the reins, and his back demanded that he shift position, but he did not for fear of unsettling all of them like a house of cards. Every now and then, he would crane his head over his shoulder, and every time, he was surprised that there was no one behind them yet.

If the pursuit did catch them, he did not know what he would do. There was no way that they could outride them, and despite the two carbines, he could not envision winning a skirmish on his own. Yet, resigning them to their pursuers' mercies was a pointless idea. So he rode on, praying that they could reach this swamp and salvation.

* * *

It was already well past midday when Sergeant Dunbar found Davis walking towards the rendezvous point. When no one had shown by late morning, he had gathered the others and set off for the ford that Davis and Mowrie were supposed to be watching. He just did not have enough men for this task, he thought bitterly. On the other hand, the more men, meant more shares and less of the reward that would be his.

"Where's Mowrie?" he called out from his saddle. "And where's your horse?"

"Dead," Davis answered to the former, and more softly, he added, "I think." He had not actually seen Mowrie die. The last that he had actually seen was when Mowrie had the slave girl by the throat. Of course, there were those other shots after he had ridden off... In a way, he hoped that Mowrie was dead. The man had a vicious temper and would be particularly enraged that Davis had abandoned him.

"Dead?" Dunbar said, nimbly sliding off the saddle. "Dead, how?"

"He came out of nowhere. He got the drop on us. I barely escaped as it was."

"Who?"

Davis shrugged, his thin face frozen into a pleading expression. "The man that the Lieutenant wants, I guess. He must have been with that old man back at the cabin, and there were two slave girls too."

Dunbar frowned at the information. "They killed Mowrie?" It was hard to imagine the enormous man dead. The man could be a vile drunkard, but he obeyed Dunbar's orders and was a fearsome sight in the saddle. They had been through too many battles together to keep track of.

Davis's head bobbed.

"Where's your horse?"

"Came up lame a ways back."

Dunbar remounted. "Let's go see for ourselves. Mount up with Howell," he finished.

By the time that they reached the camp, the fire had long since burned out. The bodies laid where Lockett had left them. Given the time of year, there were no flies buzzing about, but the blood soaked ground beneath both bodies was clear enough. Three carrion birds squawked at the arrival and angrily left their meal. They had been busily working on Cooper's belly, and one bird pulled free a bit of entrails as it moved off and waited for an opportunity to return to its feast.

Despite the markings left by the carrion, Dunbar clearly recognized the old man from the cabin. "So he was lying," he muttered, "I knew that something seemed off there."

"Had two slaves with him too," Davis said.

"Ain't his slaves," Dunbar remarked, "He was dirt poor, must have been helping them run. Got what he deserved. He ain't been dead too long. See how there's still steam coming from his belly?"

One of Dunbar's other men was rolling Mowrie over. "What do we do, sergeant?"

"Bury Mowrie. Leave the old man for the birds."

"Do we follow them?" The man looked at the hoof prints leading out of camp towards the ford.

"They've a goodly head start on us, but what else are we going to do?"

* * *

By the end of the day, Lockett was as sore as he had ever been. He expected Clarissa to plead for a break from the horse because he knew that he would have if the positions were reversed, but she said nothing and continued to doggedly hold onto him.

He contemplated abandoning the horse. A horse was easy to track. Going on foot would improve their chances of slipping through the forest undetected, but he doubted that Linzy was up to it. While she had stirred somewhat over the last hour, she was still in a bad way. One whole side of her face swelled grotesquely, stretching the skin to the limit, and he still worried about the condition of her arm. He thought it should be set but did not know how to do it. Their only option was to ride on.

The horse was getting worn out, but he did not care if it completely broke down. He still could not believe that there was no pursuit behind them, and he felt incredible anxiety about making as much ground as possible.

"Why did you do it?" Linzy asked softly, startling him from his thoughts.

"Do what?" he answered.

"You could have left us."

"Left you?"

"Back at the camp."

"I needed Cooper to show the way too," he said lamely.

"No, after that, I mean. You could go much faster by yourself. One man on a horse? You could get back to your people."

"The army? I suppose," he said.

"Our problem is not your problem," she stated.

He gave no answer, and they rode along in silence for the next minute.

"So why didn't you leave us?" She tilted her head back and looked him intently in the eye with her one good eye. "It would make more sense."

"I don't know, Linzy," he said honestly, "Abandon you? Wouldn't seem right."

"There ain't much right in the world."

"No," he shrugged, "I reckon not. I have a mission for the army, but…" He paused. "I don't think I could live with myself if I just abandoned you and Clarissa."

"You are strange," she said, tiredly lowering her head, "For a soldier. Or a spy, whichever it is."

* * *

By the end of the day, the terrain had become thicker and more difficult for them to maintain their northeasterly course. Dense glades of cedars with branches that stretched to the ground slowed their progress to a meandering crawl. Fortunately, they had the north star to guide them again and put them back on course from their many alterations.

They had mostly consumed the little food that Clarissa had gathered before leaving Davis's camp, and there was little water left in the canteens. What they would do tomorrow, Lockett had no idea. Still, they plodded on, but by the middle of the night, Lockett could go no further.

Exhausted, they slid from the saddle and horse. He contemplated starting a fire, deciding that no one could be tracking them in the dark, but in the end, decided against it, mostly because he was too tired to make one.

Wordlessly, the three of them huddled together. Almost immediately, he fell asleep. He wanted two hours before heading out again.

* * *

It was Clarissa who woke him in the morning light. "You, soldier, sir," she shook him, "It's morning."

Groggily, he rubbed his eyes. "The name is James," he said. "What's going..." He stopped, it was too bright to be the beginnings of the morn. Cursing himself, he jumped to his feet. It had been hours longer than he had intended. Angrily, he tried to shake some sense into his head. How could he have let this happen? He had given away some of their lead, he knew.

Gingerly, Clarissa moved from the ground and roused Linzy.

"We need to get moving," he said unnecessarily.

They had ridden in near silence for the next couple of hours. The only times that they spoke were in hushed whispers. All three of them felt the impending sense that their pursuers were closing on them. They skirted an open pasture and again ducked into the woods below a long sloping set of hills.

It was Clarissa who first spotted them. She tugged on his shoulder. "Behind us," she whispered.

Lockett twisted in the saddle. It took him only a second to spot the horsemen on the crest of the hill behind them. The cavalrymen had paused under the barren branches of the large oak that he had just passed under only fifteen minutes ago.

They disappeared from sight as Lockett and his two new companions merged deeper into the woods.

"Did they see us?" Linzy whispered.

"No," he answered, "But they don't need to. They are clearly having no trouble tracking our path."

"Will you fight them?" Clarissa asked.

"I'd rather not. There are too many of them." He paused with a grim look. "But we might not have a choice."

The forest sloped downhill, and in the distance, he could see blue sky. If it was open ground, then he was in a real predicament, he thought. The Rebels would have no trouble riding them down and making short work of them. Flat pasture land was exactly the type of ground that a horse soldier loved.

But as they neared the bottom of the slope, he was surprised to see that it was not pasture land ahead. Rather, it was the low expanse of stunted trees mired in a swamp. The swamp itself was buttressed by a thick band of thorn forest that stretched remarkably deep into distance, ringing the swamp.

He paused in this elevated position to study the thorn trees. Cutting across the front of the thorn forest was a dirt road. It was the first road that he had seen in days, and as he looked beyond it and the thorns, he knew that he was looking at Cooper's swamp. Roads could not go through swamps, but they always went around them.

"Which way?" Linzy asked, looking at the road.

"Neither," Lockett replied, seized with an idea. He dismounted. "Hurry. We don't have much time. Grab what you can."

Clarissa obediently slid from the horse's rump. She took the canteen, and the spare carbine still dangled from her back. Lockett pulled the other carbine from the saddle holster and slung the cartridge box.

With a muted cry of pain, Linzy dropped to the ground.

Lockett's eyes scanned the wall of thorns that ran from left to right as far as the eye could see. Finally, he saw an opening in the thick, tangled growth.

A childhood memory of playing hide and seek with Daniel in a thorn forest sprung to his mind. It was a happy childhood memory, one before his father had died. For just a second, a smile played at the corners of his mouth. What fun he and Daniel had! They were just boys then, crawling through the tiny openings like it was the entrance to a separate, magical world.

He looked at the opening in the thorns across the dirt road. It was smaller than the opening in his childhood memory, or perhaps he was just so much bigger than when he had played hide and seek, but he was still convinced of the plan.

"Into the maze," he said, pointing to the burrow like opening.

"What maze?" Linzy asked.

But Clarissa obeyed instantly, and her tiny frame was darting across the road and into the thorns like a rabbit diving into its lair.

"In there?" Linzy said dubiously.

"You can do it," he said.

He squeezed into the gap and crawled through into the thorns. It was just like the one that he remembered as child. It was like another world, a separate kingdom. Two inch long thorns sprouted like a hundred tiny daggers from every tangled branch. They wove in and out of each other, so thickly and tightly that they nearly blocked out the sunlight. Only in tiny rays did the slivers of light break the shadowed world of the thorn forest, but there were tiny meandering gaps at the floor of it, just enough for a person to crawl and squeeze through, if they were creative and determined enough.

He scraped his scalp on one of the spear like daggers but ignored the warm blood that oozed from his head. It had been easier to maneuver through such things when he had been a small child.

There were sections that forced him to crawl flat on his belly. Even in the largest of the gaps, he needed to move on all fours like an animal. Ahead, Clarissa waited for them to catch up to her. At her size, she could squat comfortably, crouch, and duck beneath the lashings of the thorn trees.

It was hardest for Linzy to keep up. She moved with the stuttering pace of a lame horse. Unable to use the one arm, she hobbled and crawled on three limbs.

"Over here!" came a hoarse, masculine cry from outside the thorns.

Lockett could hear horses and men beyond their thorn umbrella.

Linzy fell flat on her face, gasping in pain. Clarissa wiggled around a tumble of thorns as she made her way back to her mother.

"They're in there!" came the shout again. The call was followed by a blast fired blindly into the massive net of stabbing thorns.

"Over here! Over here! I knew I saw 'em duck in there!"

Biting back a cry of alarm, Clarissa helped her mother and tried futilely to support some of her weight as she crawled deeper and deeper into the shadows.

There was a flash of light back from the opening as another blast from a shotgun emptied itself. Lockett could not tell where the shots were aimed, for there were no tell-tale snapping of thorns and branches around them. Still, he paused and took a percussion cap from the cartridge box to complete the loading of the carbine.

Clarissa gave a small cry as a thorn branch snagged the carbine that she had slung across her back. Shaking herself free from the sling, she moved on deeper into the thorns, leaving the weapon behind. Lockett let Linzy and Clarissa work on ahead of him while he paused with his weapon to see if anyone dared follow them into the burrow.

After a couple of minutes, satisfied that no one was foolish enough to chase them in here, he moved on to catch up with the two escaping slaves. In a way, he wished that the Rebels would pursue them in here, because a firefight in these tight quarters, with such limited trails, would even the odds substantially.

But they moved further into the shadowed depths of the thorns, and no one followed.

They carried on for over an hour. It was a completely circuitous route, dictated solely by what openings there were in the kingdom of the thorns. A few times, they backtracked to find a different opening after crawling to a dead end, and once Lockett had to use the butt of the carbine to bash a better way into a new avenue.

The long thorns slashed at their clothing, faces, and hands as they slithered through. Their clothing and skin snagged on the wooden daggers, despite the care that they took crawling through one gap after another.

Linzy doggedly moved on, using her three good limbs until she needed to pause to recoup. She was in obvious pain but said nothing. Lockett could not help but admire her determination. Cooper had been right. The fire that burned to be free was like nothing that he had ever seen before. For all their bluster and bravery in facing down muzzle flashes and whipping balls of canister, Lockett knew few soldiers who could bear up as well as Linzy, and certainly none without complaint.

Finally, they reached the edge of the thorn kingdom. Ahead of them lay the swamp.

It was cattails, dormant tall grasses, and trees growing from the shallow, scum coated water. Bloody scrapes and all, Lockett wished that the thorns would go on further. There was something foreboding about this marshy swamp land. He hesitated.

Linzy and Clarissa looked at him expectantly.

"I believe that we found Cooper's swamp," he murmured.

"Freedom is not far away now, Momma," Clarissa said in a soft voice.

"Cooper said that there was high ground in the middle with some sort of hut," Lockett thought aloud. He hoped his voice showed more enthusiasm than he felt as he stared at the bleak marsh.

* * *

As the sun began to sink in the sky, Lockett became increasingly concerned about their situation. He had prayed more than twenty times in his head for God to show them the way to Cooper's high ground. They needed to find that and Cooper's hut. If they couldn't find it before dark, he was certain that they would die.

Even as it was, that might still be the case. They had slogged through knee high and in some parts waist high water. The mud was a leeching, treacherous mire. Many times, he had to slow and pay close attention, or else the mud would take his boots.

But it was the cold that was their worst enemy. Their feet had long since gone numb, and Clarissa's constant teeth chattering was incredibly loud. At one point, she had asked him if the noise would bring back their pursuers. He smiled, trying to give them some levity and told her 'no.' Only the most desperate of madmen would attempt to cross this frigid swamp, he joked. He forced what he hoped was a genuine sounding chuckle, but neither the mother nor her child joined him.

Their pace slowed precipitously. Exhaustion was setting in, and he knew that the chill was rapidly sapping their physical and emotional reserves. Linzy leaned heavily on him for balance. They had only covered a mile, but it felt like ten.

The orange glow in the sky was rapidly giving way to the black of night. Even if they managed to make it near Cooper's high ground, they could miss it in the darkness. But they couldn't stop. There was nowhere to stop. Stopping would mean freezing to death. The black water of the swamp would just draw their bodies under, never to be seen again.

The despair was so great that he could feel it physically

weighing on him. With each step, his feet seemed to sink deeper into the muck than the previous step. With each muscle wracking effort to pull it free, he cursed the inevitability of it all.

He had come so far! Damn it all! He had survived McGowan! He had found the General's information! How could he have come so far to perish here!

Finally, with the last spark of light before it disappeared for hours, he spotted a small rise to their left.

Blinking, he wondered if he had truly seen it. Had it been real or imagined?

"Praise the Lord," Linzy managed in a soft voice.

He gave an audible breath of relief. "You saw it too? I thought that my mind was playing a trick on me."

Linzy was too tired to say another word, but she clutched his arm even more tightly in response.

Lockett could not agree more. He had never been so fatigued.

With their last ounces of energy, they had pulled themselves onto the dry rise of ground.

It was scarcely more than a half acre in size. In the middle, surrounded by trees, was Cooper's "hut". It was only slightly larger than an outhouse with a small mud chimney. They staggered in, collapsing on the dirt floor.

Lockett weighed whether or not to start a fire. As Clarissa's teeth continued to chatter and his own dripping trousers clung to him like a frozen second skin, he decided to chance it.

Once the fire was started, he squeezed in next to the already sleeping mother and daughter. He was asleep in seconds.

December 23

The sun was already high in the morning sky when he awoke. This time, he felt no panic about it. He knew that they had desperately needed that rest. Clarissa still slept, but Linzy was awake, and she lay next to him, looking at him through her one good eye. Curiously, she was grinning at him and even gave a small chuckle.

"What's so funny?" he said, propping himself into a seated position.

"You are very dirty," she said.

He rubbed a filthy hand against his cheek. Dark muck from the swamp coated his feet and legs like ebony plaster. His left arm was equally obscured by the mud from catching himself after stumbling multiple times yesterday. He wondered what his face looked like. It felt like it was caked as well.

"And it's funny that I'm dirty?" he said, puzzled.

"No, I jus' think that you are now as black as I am."

He looked at her, and then they both laughed. It was a cathartic moment. For just a moment, they were two people laughing at a joke. They stopped and then laughed again, if only because it felt so good.

He nodded, sure that she was right. He was dirtier now than when he had arrived in Louisville last September after that difficult march with Buell. He remembered the bystanders saying the same thing about him and his men as they had filed into the city, but that level of grime paled in comparison to now.

He closed his eyes and forced his mind to contemplate the day ahead. He wanted to slide back into sleep.

He had never been so worn out in his life. He had always prided himself on his stamina, whether it was day after solitary day toiling behind the plow or whether it was a long day's march, but now he knew that he was near the end of his limit.

It was sorely tempting to declare that they would rest all day before carrying on, but he knew that the generals were waiting for his information. But would one more day matter?

He argued with himself in his head, but it was the growling pain in his stomach that determined the answer. They had no food. Another day of waiting would only make them weaker. They were close. Cooper had said that the picket line was just beyond the swamp. They just had to get there.

"Do we leave now?" Linzy asked, interrupting his thoughts.

"Soon," he answered, "Soon."

"You will reach your army today?"

"I think so."

"You are not like the others."

"What others?" he asked.

"Soldiers in blue."

"How so? Where are you from?" he asked, realizing how little he actually knew about Linzy and Clarissa.

"I lived my whole life near Athens," she said.

"Athens?" he said, remembering rumors of General Turchin sacking the Rebel town. It was what that reporter Hoskins had wanted to report on, how General Buell wanted to court-martial Turchin for his actions.

"It was terrible," she said, reading his face, "The blue soldiers... they were as bad as any overseer, worse."

"Our soldiers?" he said. "What do you mean? They burned the houses of the Rebels. They retaliated after their citizens attacked our hospitals and other cowardly attacks?"

"Yes, they burned the houses and stole from the owners, but that is not what shocked me."

"What then?"

"It was their assault on us."

"On you?"

"I escaped and hid in the woods with Clarissa. We were lucky."

"They attacked slaves?"

"The women."

Lockett looked blankly at her. He had once heard a rumor that insinuated such, but he had disregarded it. "They attacked some women?"

"Not just some. Many, many. The entire army was like a horde of devils unloosed."

Lockett looked at her blankly. At first, he wanted to deny it, to say that she was exaggerating, but he knew that she had no reason to do so. Even more compelling, he started to remember Missouri. He remembered Orrin Long and his cronies. He remembered Orrin's first failed attempt, and then he remembered Orrin's plans for little Amelia.

That had been just a small handful of men, but an entire regiment out of control? The thought was revolting and frightening.

"This war is a vile, vile thing, Linzy," he said in a sad voice.

"This information that you have, it will help end the war?"

"I suppose," he said, still thinking about the images that Linzy had planted in his head, burning houses, looting, slave women running for their very lives.

"And when you win, we will be free?"

"What?" he asked, his mind still elsewhere.

"When you win, we will be free?"

He looked at her battered face and saw her one good eye looking expectantly at him. Clarissa had asked him the same thing days ago, and Linzy's gaze was much the same. It was a look of hopefulness, yet disbelieving at the same time. The struggle was clear on her face. She wanted to believe, but it must surely be too good to be true.

Finally, he nodded. "President Lincoln decreed as much, Linzy. It didn't please a few in blue, but he gave an Emancipation Proclamation last fall. Slavery will be gone after the war... if, when, we win."

She gave no answer, apparently satisfied.

* * *

"It will be one lean Christmas," young Sam Baker remarked.

"Makes you wish you were still home," Prosper T. Rowe agreed, his head bobbing on his long neck.

"What I wouldn't do for a bite of turkey or goose."

"You'll be lucky to get a second bite of rancid salt beef," Levi Thickle joined in.

"It's one thing to live like this day after day, but Christmas? Surely, they're saving some special rations for us for that day." Baker looked expectantly at his older and more experienced comrades.

"Be sure that there are some special victuals," Thickle guffawed, "But they been saved for some colonel or general to eat, not us,"

Baker looked at Prosper T. Rowe, knowing that he could trust the gangly farmer, but Rowe only nodded in agreement. "Too true." He paused. "But at least there be no fightin' that day. With General Rosecrans, I think we can be sure of that."

"There ain't been no fightin' for weeks," Thickle interjected. "Cain't count no little skirmish for forage parties or what our cavalry does."

"Still, with the General bein' such a devout man, we won't be fightin' that day."

Thickle shrugged. "If it meant a goose for Christmas dinner, then I'd fight."

* * *

There were still about two hours of daylight left by the time that they reached the end of the swamp.

When they had made that first step onto the dry land, they had given each other broad smiles. No words were spoken, but they all shared the same thought, *they had made it.*

Clarissa looked triumphantly at her mother.

The fringe of forest surrounding the northern edge of the swamp thinned quickly. Lockett worried that it might empty into pasture land, in which case they would have to wait until nightfall to cross, but while thinner, the forest provided just enough cover for them to keep moving. That is, until they came to the road.

The dirt strip barred their way. They waited a moment to see if the stretch was empty.

Lockett feared his own side and the pickets now as much as anything. He had to be close to the line. He just had to be!

"What are we waiting for?" Linzy whispered.

Lockett gave no answer. He rested the stock of the unloaded carbine on the ground and contemplated loading it. He had not done so as they had moved through the swamp and forest for fear that he might stumble and accidentally discharge the weapon. But now, something played with his instinct.

"There's somebody out there," he said eventually. He scanned the area in front of them, seeing nothing, but something bothered him. To their left, the road curled away, and he could see the land drop off. There was a hill beyond that drop. He strained to hear anything, suspecting a creek of running water in that gap between the road and the rising hill.

He also examined the hill. It was an obvious position to place pickets. They could be on the wooded high ground with a stream to their front to slow any sudden advance from the enemy. It was then that he saw movement on the hill. It was not much, just a soldier in blue shifting his position behind a tree.

"We made it," he breathed.

It was then that Clarissa tugged on his sleeve and pointed in the other direction. He turned and saw it too. It was a squad of infantrymen, probably the Confederate pickets' relief... and a troop of horse soldiers.

One rider dismounted. From a distance, there was something familiar about him.

"It's the man from the camp," Clarissa said, her sharp eyes spotting the short, whip thin man, 'Davis.'

"Should we go back?" Linzy asked. The men were moving slowly in their direction. "We can hide until night."

Lockett was contemplating just that when he muttered a sudden, scarcely audible, curse.

"What is it?" Linzy asked, seeing the concern on his face.

"We are so close," he agonized. "I can see our men on that hillside, but..."

She looked at the hill to their left. "It is too far to run. The horses would catch us."

Lockett nodded in agreement.

"Then let's jus' hide until tonight," Linzy said.

"We can't," he said, trying to keep the despair from his voice. "Look." He pointed. "They have dogs with them now."

Linzy and Clarissa then saw what had caused his sudden curse and kept his attention, bloodhounds.

"We could edge back into the trees," he started, "But those dogs... I think they'll catch a scent of us." He looked back towards the Union pickets, gauging the distance to that hillside.

Maybe they could make it, he tried to persuade himself.

"If you get back, your information will help win Father Abraham's war?" Linzy asked abruptly.

Distracted, Lockett did not even bother looking at her as he continued to study the hill. "Win? Yes, yes, of course," he answered absently.

Even if they could sprint across the distance safely, they would have to cross the creek and then climb the hillside. The Union pickets might provide some cover fire, that is, if they didn't shoot him too. He knew that he was fairly swift. He might be able to make it. Could Linzy and Clarissa? What if he loaded the carbine and gave them some cover? How many horses did the Rebels have with that group that was hunting him?

He could hear Linzy whispering something to Clarissa, probably trying to reassure the young girl, but Lockett put it from his mind. There was too much that he still needed to weigh.

There was so much to consider. What was beyond that dip in the road just before the hillside? Was it just an empty gully? Was it something that could be climbed out of easily? What if it wasn't? Would they be like rats trapped in a barrel? He could climb, but what about Linzy? With one good arm, she probably could not climb.

Too much to think about! He scowled fiercely. The dash would be near suicide, but what choice did he have? Those bloodhounds would pick up their scent any second now, right?

"Linzy, I think we're going to have to run for it," he said, trying to determine how many Union pickets were on that hillside. He could only see that one clearly, but he knew that there would be more. "Linzy, can you make it?"

There was no answer.

"Linzy?"

When there was no answer again, he turned his head. But Linzy was gone.

Chapter 41

Lockett looked uncomprehendingly at Clarissa. He couldn't understand where her mother had disappeared to. "Clarissa, what happened? Where is she?"

Clarissa looked blankly at him and gave no answer.

"Clarissa?" he repeated anxiously, and then he noticed that the carbine was gone too.

"Clarissa, where is she?" he said, grabbing her by the shoulders. She pointed to the right, but by then, he had already guessed that much. "What is she doing? She can't fight twenty men." He left out the fact that the carbine was unloaded.

Clarissa finally spoke. "She said she loved me and to listen to you. That your escape was more important."

"More important!" he said astounded. "More important?"

"You can help free us all."

"My God!" he gasped, knowing exactly what Linzy intended. He had half a thought to chase after her and stop her, but he stopped himself. Cold, practical logic invaded his thoughts. He hated it, but he knew that it was their only chance. Linzy apparently knew that too. It was then that one of the hounds started barking.

"Come on, Clarissa," he said, pulling her to her feet. They crashed through the forest to their left as fast as possible. The dogs were howling now, there was no need to worry about stealth.

In a second, they would be clear of the forest's protective grasp, and they would have to dash across the road and into open area towards the hillside.

There was a shot from behind them as they burst across the road. His long legs quickly outdistanced the spindly legged child. He paused, waving his arm to urge her on. As she caught up, he could clearly see the chaos behind them.

In surprise, the Confederates looked on as Linzy emerged from the other end of the woods. She too was running, running straight for the Confederates with the carbine dangling from her one good arm.

Linzy cried a high-pitched, screeching war cry that pierced the air so loudly that Clarissa turned her head while she was running. "Keep running!" Lockett ordered, "Look ahead!"

They were nearing the creek bed in the dip beyond the road. They were going to make it! Behind them there were more cries and muskets cracked the air.

A couple of the Confederates finally noticed Clarissa and him, and both fired in their direction, but the others were still consumed with Linzy who was nearly upon the Rebels now. She raised the weapon. The soldiers, now realizing that she might be a real threat, quickly readied and aimed their own weapons. Eight separate shots went off in the frame of a second.

Linzy staggered and spun crazily. She landed on her knees momentarily, somehow propped up by her bad arm. She tottered and fell permanently backward with her legs corkscrewed under her.

The rest of the Confederates now seemed to realize that there were two others escaping, and Lockett could hear the horses starting to gallop behind him.

He had again outdistanced Clarissa. He turned and pulled free the revolver. "Keep running," he yelled, and he loosed three hopeless shots in the direction of the riders before turning and chasing after Clarissa again.

He could see the drop off into the creek bed now. It was indeed a creek cut into the bottom of the hill, but it was steeper and deeper than he would have guessed. They wouldn't have time to slide into it and then climb up the other side. The Confederates would be upon them in seconds. They would be trapped in the ravine!

But Clarissa had seen something else. She angled towards a fallen tree that had landed across the opening. It would have to be their bridge to salvation.

She reached it, and nimbly, she dashed full speed across it. A slab of bark kicked off to the right, but she did not lose her footing, and she was across, making her way up the hillside.

Lockett turned and fired two more shots before following her across. About half way, he nearly lost his footing and he could imagine himself tumbling to the bottom of the ravine. But somehow, he kept his footing for one more stride and dove clumsily across the last stretch, landing on his knees just on the other side. A shot winged the tree next to him, and another kicked up the dirt. Spurred on, he clambered to his feet and made his way up the hill.

They were halfway up the hill when the other Confederates arrived at the ravine, but most of their weapons were unloaded due to emptying them into Linzy. Hurriedly, they reloaded.

"That's close enough, Johnny!" came a call from the top of the hill.

But it did not deter one of the dismounted horsemen from trying to cross Clarissa's bridge. A smattering of shots from the top of the hill changed his mind.

Another Rebel reloaded faster than the others, and his shot snapped an arm-thick branch just above Lockett's head. That drew a quick response. A half dozen shots from the Union pickets cracked.

There was a cry from behind Lockett, but he paid no attention. He hustled up the hill after Clarissa. She had scurried past the first staggered line of pickets, and he caught her at the top of the hill, out of sight from the bottom of the hill. A burly sergeant now had her by the scruff of her neck, and a heavily bearded lieutenant stood next to him.

As Lockett reached her side, the Union lieutenant aimed a revolver at the muddied, disheveled, and thoroughly spent looking human being in front of him.

"What the hell is going on here?" the hirsute officer demanded. He motioned with his pistol for Lockett to surrender his weapon.

Lockett dropped the LeMat and tried to answer, but he was breathing so hard that nothing intelligible could come out.

"Johnny, you better tell me why your friends are chasing you! You a deserter?"

"I'm not... a Rebel," Lockett finally managed between gasps.

A number of other blue coated men gathered around now in curiosity.

"You look like a Rebel."

"Don't even look fit to be a Johnny," muttered someone in the cluster. A couple of them snickered at the comment.

"Do I sound like I'm from the South?" Lockett said angrily, his breath returning.

The bearded lieutenant's gaze narrowed. With one eye nearly closed, he studied Lockett. "You could be an actor."

Lockett looked at Clarissa. She looked back at him. There was no fear or uncertainty on her young face. She just looked expectantly at him with a peculiar confidence that he would resolve this.

"An actor? Escaping with a fugitive slave?" Before the lieutenant could express any more skepticism, Lockett quickly added in a more imperious tone, "Look, I'm Lieutenant James Lockett from Blair's Independent Regiment. Take me to your commanding officer. *Now*! I have an urgent message for Colonel Wilks and General Rosecrans. There is no time to waste."

"A lieutenant you say?" the officer said skeptically, not the least cowed by Lockett's authoritative tone. "I should hardly think so, but I'll take you to the Colonel." Happy to hand the decision to someone else, he shrugged. "I'll take you to Colonel Easton, but I doubt it'll make a difference."

Section V

The Slaughter Pen

Chapter 42

Colonel Brewster H. Easton wrinkled his nose as Lockett and Clarissa were brought before him. "Good God," he breathed, "I never thought a man could smell so bad!"

He edged back, and his eyes narrowed. "Or look like such. Even the worst hog would be cleaner!" He pulled a monogrammed handkerchief from his pocket and held it to his nose. "A corpse in the field would smell better!"

Lockett ignored the comments, knowing that the past days on the run, and particularly the last two days and the freezing swamp, had turned him into a filthy beast. But he felt no shame, only pride in it. He had survived.

"Colonel, I am Lieutenant James Lockett from Blair's Independent Regiment. I have been on a special mission for Colonel Wilks and General Rosecrans. I have urgent information that must be presented with all haste to Colonel Wilks. I need a horse and a guide to the Colonel's headquarters."

Colonel Easton looked aghast at him. He eyed Lockett from head to toe. Then, he started laughing. "What do you take me for?"

"Sir..."

But Easton cut him off sharply. "You take me for a fool!" He glared at Lockett. There was no more laughter from him. "A horse? A guide to headquarters? To do what, assassinate him? To make me look a fool? You are some sort of Rebel and will be treated as such."

"I'm an officer in Colonel Blair's regiment," Lockett protested.

"Never heard of him," Easton cut him off sharply. He stuffed the monogrammed handkerchief back into a pocket.

Lockett could feel his temper rising dangerously. He had not gone through so much, skirted so close to death so many times, to have this happen.

"I have urgent information for General Rosecrans," Lockett snarled, his eyes blazing.

"And just what is that?" Easton answered, unimpressed.

Their voices were rising with each sentence, and Lockett was vaguely aware of other soldiers surreptitiously trying to get a view through the window.

"I am not at liberty to share with you," Lockett said with a tight jaw, "It is for Colonel Wilks and General Rosecrans only."

Easton laughed haughtily. "Scofflaw! You are a scofflaw, and a Rebel one at that!"

"I'm no scofflaw!" Lockett shouted back, pounding a fist on the desk. Easton jumped back, startled by the aggressive motion.

"Sergeant, take this man into custody!" Colonel Easton ordered, motioning towards the sergeant in the corner of the room.

"Sir, you can verify my story easy enough. Have a message passed to Colonel Wilks," Lockett persisted, "He will vouch for me! He's anxious for this news!"

"And send a valuable man off on that! Nonsense!"

The sergeant now stood next to Lockett but had not yet put a hand on him.

"Sergeant, take this man. Get him cleaned up and burn those putrid clothes. I won't have my camp smelling like a sewer. Then shackle him. Put him in that stable and post a guard."

"Yes, sir," the sergeant saluted. "And what about his, er, servant, sir?"

"Servant?" Easton looked flummoxed, as if he had not noticed Clarissa's mere existence. He looked at the equally soiled wretch. "Take care of that too."

"Sir, you don't understand," Lockett protested as the sergeant pulled him away. "Sir! Sir!"

"C'mon, you," the sergeant said gruffly, giving Lockett a firm shove to get him moving.

"Sir!"

The sergeant used his rifle as a staff and gave Lockett a two-fisted thrust in the back that nearly knocked Lockett from his feet.

"He ain't gonna listen," the sergeant said in a low voice, taking Lockett firmly by the elbow. "C'mon, sir, ifs you are a sir, that is."

"I am who I say I am, sergeant."

"Then walk with me now, sir. You ain't gonna help yourself trying to argue with the Colonel. He ain't the type, ifs you know what I mean."

Obediently, Lockett let the sergeant lead the way, and Clarissa followed them.

"There's no time for this," Lockett muttered.

"Ifs you don't mind me askin', what were you doin' over with the Johnnies, sir?"

"I was on a special mission, sergeant," Lockett said with resignation.

"Mission? One man?"

"I was a spy, sergeant. Does that help explain it?"

"A spy? A spy in General Bragg's camp or something?"

"Exactly, sergeant. Yes."

"Reckon that would explain why the Johnnies were after you."

"It was a near thing, too many times to count," Lockett commented, "I need to get to Colonel Wilks."

"The Johnnies do that to your neck, sir?"

Lockett touched his neck. Despite the filth, it was still a grievous looking thing. "Yes, in a way, yes."

"Ain't look too good, sir. Someone ought to look at it."

"It's not nearly as important as getting a message to Colonel Wilks," Lockett breathed tiredly.

The sergeant ignored the last plea. "And who is this exactly?" He thumbed back at Clarissa.

"Clarissa? Well..." he paused. "She's escaping the south too. Without her and her mother, I would not have made it. Her mother sacrificed herself to get us to these lines, sergeant."

The sergeant seemed unmoved. "Where you from, sir?"

"Michigan. You?"

"Indiana, sir."

"I need to get a message back, Sergeant. Colonel Wilks can clear up this whole mess."

The sergeant pondered for a moment. "Tell you what, sir. I'll try to help. There's some cavalry boys from Kentucky passing through here. They leave camp in an hour. I'll talk to one of them to see if he can pass a message for you. I'll let the colonel know later when he's in a better mood. If the Kentuckians pass the message, then the colonel won't need to worry about having one of the men up in Nashville."

Lockett saw Clarissa look up at him quizzically. She was probably wondering why the big issue with having one man leave, but Lockett thought he knew the reason. This regiment was probably having some issue with desertions, especially over the Holidays. Southern Indiana wasn't too far away.

* * *

Lockett sat in the dirt of the empty stable. There was not even a single blade of straw, such was the thoroughness of the foraging, he thought. His legs were shackled in leg irons, which were connected to the post in the middle of the stable by a long chain. They did not bother to do the same to Clarissa.

Both of them were cleaned up and wearing spare army blue pants, shirts, and private's jackets.

He half-expected Clarissa to question if this was what freedom was like and wonder why his own side treated him so, but she said nothing. She merely sat patiently and looked at him with an oddly expectant stare, as if she was waiting for him to share what they would do next.

But Lockett had no idea where to go from here. Shackled, with an armed guard outside, there was no chance to escape. His best hope was that the sergeant and his friend in the Kentucky cavalry would come through and deliver the message that he had written out for Colonel Wilks.

If there was anything to be thankful for, it was the army blanket and the chance to rest and sleep. So he slept until the regimental surgeon woke him to check on the burn on his neck. Pronouncing it a hideous and permanent 'disfigurement', the surgeon nonetheless cleaned it and declared there was nothing else he could do about it.

Once he left, Lockett immediately fell back asleep. For once, he slept without dreaming.

* * *

Another day had come and gone, and it had left Patrick McManus in a melancholy mood. The warm temperatures and the fact that Captain Bibb had been sober all day did nothing to lift McManus's spirits. He decided that Bibb was only readying himself for a real bender on Christmas Eve and Christmas Day, and the warm weather made him think back to the autumn, when James had still been around.

He had James's journal in his hand and the Stuart family sword that James had "borrowed" laid across his legs. The others in the company had declared James dead already. They wondered how long Patrick would keep a dead man's things. It would have been best to give them to his kin now that he was dead, most thought.

The only person who did not agree was Daniel Lockett himself. It wasn't that he held out any hope that James was coming back. He had no such illusions. Rather, he knew how Patrick clutched those items as his last bits of hope. It would be cruel to take them away from him, and besides, Daniel did not really want them.

Patrick had recently spent time talking to Daniel and explaining how frequently his brother had written in the journal. He related how they had found it after the battle of Shiloh in the tent, just where they had left it at the first blows of the bloodbath. Daniel had asked Patrick if he had ever looked at what James had written. The response was a scowl like one he had never seen before, as if the suggestion was some horrid desecration.

And as for the sword, what need would a private have for that? It would just be more weight to carry on a long march. Daniel had learned that much during the march north to Perryville and back. Newcomers were fond of their battlefield souvenirs, but only until the weight in their packs started to break their backs.

Patrick wordlessly ran his thumb along the soft edges of the paper in James's journal. He wondered where his old friend was at the moment. Was he in a shallow grave somewhere, and if so, where? Was he in a prison camp somewhere? Where was he?

* * *

It was early afternoon when the Kentucky cavalry returned from the outer picket line to Nashville. While most of the men took care of their mounts and eased their jostled joints, Private

Edward Beedon asked for the location of Colonel Wilks and made his way to the small house.

He was tired and hungry. He knew that many other men would have simply crumbled up the message and forgotten about it, or at least delayed delivery of it until it was more convenient. But that was not how Private Beedon had been brought up. If he said that he would do something, then that is what he would do.

He didn't know why he had agreed so readily when that Hoosier had asked him to deliver a message for him to some unknown colonel. Beedon hoped that if he ever fell on the battlefield that someone would go the extra mile to deliver a message for him to his loved ones back near Louisville.

He did not know what was in the message or why it might be important, maybe that Hoosier sergeant was friends or kin of this Colonel Wilks. No matter. He said he would deliver it, and so he would.

No matter that the first two soldiers he tried had no idea who Colonel Wilks was or that the third one had sent him incorrectly into the camp of General Thomas.

Night would fall quickly in these winter months, and Beedon knew that he needed to get back to camp immediately when he finally located the headquarters of Colonel Wilks.

When Beedon entered the door, he found a smooth cheeked captain behind a desk. The captain looked up when he entered but then paid no other attention for a full minute while he finished his writing.

"Yes?" the captain said, without pausing in his scribble, "Are you purely a dolt, or will you tell me why you stand there, Private?"

"Ah, yes, sir. I mean, no, sir."

"Which is it, Private Dolt?" the captain sneered.

"I have a message to deliver, sir. A message for a Colonel Wilks..."

"The colonel, you say?"

Beedon had the captain's attention now. The captain smoothed his moustache with a thumb and forefinger as he paused in his work. "Well, what is it?"

"It's written, sir." Beedon handed him the folded piece of paper that he had kept in his saddlebag all day.

Frowning, the captain took the paper and unfolded it. There was a quick intake of breath, and a startled look passed over his face. "Have you read this message, Private?" the captain demanded angrily.

"No, sir, no!" Beedon answered truthfully with an equally honest fear on his face. He had no idea what was on the piece of paper that prompted such a reaction.

"You swear to me?" The captain rose and took an aggressive step towards him.

"I do, I do. On the Bible, sir. I haven't read it."

"Who is it from?" the captain said skeptically.

"A sergeant gave it to me, out with the 37th Indiana. Asked me to deliver it. But I don't know what's on the paper, sir! I swear!"

The captain eyed him skeptically. Then, apparently satisfied with the answer, he nodded. "Why did you have it?"

"The sergeant gave it to me because he knew that we were heading back to Nashville. He said it was urgent and asked me to deliver it to Colonel Wilks."

"Yes, yes," the captain said, starting to pace with a thoughtful look on his face. He tapped a finger on his cheek as he pondered what to do with the message. Then he seemed to remember that the Private was still standing before him. "You are dismissed, Private. I will see that the Colonel gets it."

With that, Private Beedon gratefully departed, promising himself that he would not be so quick to volunteer to help a stranger again.

Captain Orrin Long held the message in his hand a moment longer. When he heard the cavalry private depart on his horse, Long wadded up the message and tossed it into the fire.

Lockett had been gone so long that both he and Colonel Wilks had assumed that he was dead. It had been weeks and weeks without word from either Lockett or McGowan.

Orrin Long scowled. He had been sure that Lockett had been killed, but yet again the damn farmer had slipped death's grasp and eluded one of his surefire plans! And not only was Lockett alive, he apparently had the Colonel's information if the message on the paper was to be believed! And Orrin Long believed it.

What to do? What to do? The colonel was gone now, and he

would be none the wiser if the message never made it to his hands, Long surmised.

Yes, he decided, smacking a fist into his other palm. The message was destroyed. He would act as if it had never been received. Without a response, Colonel Easton would have to assume that Lockett was either a spy or a Union deserter. And Orrin Long knew Colonel Easton's reputation. He was a Pennsylvania man who commanded a regiment of Hoosiers, Hoosiers who had deserted in droves during the merciless heat and thirst in Kentucky last September. Galled by how many had slipped away once they reached Louisville, Colonel Easton now had a reputation for quick and severe justice for all those who had been caught.

Yes, spy or deserter, it made no difference to Orrin Long. Either way, with any luck Lockett would be hung in the next week. If the Rebels couldn't accomplish that for him, then at least this Pennsylvanian would.

Chapter 43

December 25

Milton Bosworth warmed his hands over the fire. It seemed hard to believe that on this day of all days, they were moving out, or at least moving out in search of forage. At least they were motivated, he thought. Their best chance of a decent Christmas meal was to take it off the table of some Rebel as part of this foraging expedition.

Captain Bibb staggered to the front of the column. He was ashen and holding his head with both hands. He had clearly dipped deeply into his personal cache of whiskey last night, unaware that today would be such an active day.

Colonel Blair looked in disgust at the officer and instead focused his attention on the sergeant. "Well, sergeant, the men will be ready to move out in fifteen minutes?"

"Yes, sir. I might have to kick a few in the arse and give some other *encouragements*," he frowned, "But we'll be ready."

Colonel Blair mounted his horse. "Where would this army be without its dependable sergeants?"

"Probably much further north, maybe in Ohio, sir," Bosworth answered cheekily.

Colonel Blair looked harshly at Bosworth, and the sergeant reddened. Lieutenant Lockett might appreciate his humor, but he forgot that he was talking to the colonel.

"Sorry, sir," Bosworth added regretfully.

Colonel Blair grunted but gave no other response.

The colonel sneezed mightily three times before riding off to check his other companies.

Bosworth hoped that the Colonel was not getting sick. He was a decent man, for an officer, and there were certainly plenty of men getting sick now. Many regiments were down a third of their strength as the mumps, measles, and various poxes had run amok.

He spied Daniel Lockett and Sam Baker settling into the column.

"Let's go!" Bosworth bellowed to hustle them up, "We got some foraging to do. I'm sure there's a Secesh out there with a turkey on his table, and I want this company to get it, not some other company!"

* * *

Two days had passed, and Lockett was surprised that there had been no news. The friendly Hoosier sergeant was sure that the Kentucky cavalryman had been the honest sort, but Lockett was starting to wonder. Had the Kentucky cavalry man absconded with the message? Did he fail to deliver it? Had he been unable to find Wilks? Had the company of horsemen been directed somewhere besides Nashville before he could deliver the message?

Lockett couldn't believe that there had not been a rider, if not Colonel Wilks himself, dashing hurriedly into camp, anxious to get the information.

In fact, most everyone seemed to have forgotten about Clarissa and him. The sergeant brought food and water each day, but that was all. Colonel Easton seemed to have no recollection that there was a prisoner in his stable.

Lockett had asked the sergeant what the colonel intended to do. The Hoosier had shrugged and said that the colonel had not mentioned him at all, and that maybe it was better if he forgot, given his commander's view of deserters and traitors.

"You need to walk," Clarissa said, interrupting his thoughts.

At least, he was not alone, he reflected. She was not particularly talkative, but when she did talk, she shared a few stories of where she came from. She had not shed a tear for her mother in front of him, which he thought strange, but when she didn't think that he was looking, he would catch a glimpse of silent tears on her face, which she would quickly wipe away.

"What?" he said.

"You've been shackled for two days now. You'll waste away. When you walk, it will be like newborn colt."

"I think you are exaggerating, but it sounds like something that you've seen before."

"I ain't never going to see it again," she declared. "Not after you get us out of here." She was confident that the injustice would be rectified soon, more confident than he was.

He frowned at her. "Like I said before, you're not shackled, and they have no cause to keep you, Clarissa. You can walk out of here right now."

"And like I tol' you before, no." She looked at him stubbornly. "I ain't got nowhere to go anyhow."

It was the third time that she had made such a statement since their confinement in the stable. Each time, it left Lockett with a perplexed feeling of where to go from here. She was right. She did have nowhere to go, but what would happen when he got back to the army?

He had previously figured that he could find some other escapees for her to join up with, but he was starting to wonder if Clarissa would agree to such a plan.

"Well," he said slowly, "We won't be able to stay here much longer. Message or no, I'm going to find a way to get back to Colonel Wilks myself."

"We'll need a horse."

"We?" he started, causing the young girl to frown at him. "Yes, 'we', I suppose," he relented. "Yes, we'll need a horse. Of course, I'll have to get out of these leg irons first."

"That's easy," she said.

"It is?"

Her head bobbed excitedly. "When I help the sergeant get our food and water, I'z seen where the keys are."

Lockett looked at her, and a smile slowly broke across his face as a plan started to take form.

December 26

Daniel and the rest of Blair's Independent Regiment awoke before dawn. A cold mist coated their ragtag collection of tarpot hats, kepis, and ordinary broad-rimmed farmer slouch hats. Their woolen jackets gave some protection from the damp and glistened with the fine spray of droplets in the firelight.

Clouds obscured the moon, and the men could smell some heavy rain in the air. They were in for a drenching in a matter of an hour most of them guessed. After the mild and dry December that they had seen so far, it gave them a strong sense of foreboding.

Today, of all days, it was going to rain? The one day that the generals had stirred them and ordered a march?

Even without those clinging thoughts, they could hardly believe that they were marching south all of a sudden. Two months of inactivity had ended abruptly and right at the Christmas? All of the men knew of General Rosecrans's devout tendencies. The timing of the march was a shock.

A cold wind from the north propelled them down the Nolensville Pike with the rest of Sheridan's column. Three corps of Rosecrans's army marched parallel courses. Theirs was the middle column, and all three columns had one destination, Murfreesboro.

* * *

When Colonel Brewster H. Easton awoke, he found that the Kentucky cavalry regiment had returned to his camp. They carried new orders with them. The horse soldiers were to scout ahead, secure the crossroads, flush out Rebel vedettes and positions, and generally shield General Thomas's column from prying eyes as it made its way south.

Colonel Easton's orders were to follow along behind the cavalry and provide infantry support if the horsemen ran into any stiff resistance.

But the written orders were not all that were on the colonel's mind when he met with the Kentuckians. Immediately, he summoned his sergeant to seek out the particular horse soldier to whom he had given the message. Despite opinions to the contrary, he had not forgotten about the prisoner in the stable.

Twenty minutes later, his sergeant returned with a young private. The Kentuckian saluted and stood at rigid attention in his tall cavalry boots.

"This is him?" Colonel Easton asked airily before sneezing and then blowing his nose vigorously into his monogrammed handkerchief.

"Yes, sir," the sergeant answered.

"Private Beedon, sir," the private answered, looking at a point above and to the right of the colonel.

"And so, Private, did you deliver the message to this Colonel Wilks?" Colonel Easton blew his nose one last time and then stuffed the handkerchief back into a pocket.

"Took some finding, sir, but yes, I delivered it."

"And so?" the colonel said impatiently.

The private hesitated and blanched, not understanding. "And so? I don't understand, sir."

"What was the colonel's reaction? Do we have a deserter? A spy? A liar? A thief? What is he?"

"I don't rightly know, sir," Beedon said with a confused look. "I just delivered a piece of paper."

"Well, what did the colonel say?"

"I don't rightly know, sir. I delivered it to his aide, a captain. He said that he would take care of informing the colonel."

Colonel Easton pursed his lips. "Very well. You are dismissed, Private." After Beedon left, Easton turned his attention to his sergeant.

"I knew it! Bring the prisoner here, sergeant. If the message was delivered and there was no response from this Colonel Wilks, then the prisoner is clearly lying! A deserter, most likely! I'll give the man one last chance to clear his conscience, not that it matters much. Looks like a hanging before we depart, sergeant!"

He dismissed the sergeant and said to the empty room. "A good way to begin this jaunt today... A little demonstration to all to show the consequences for a lack of loyalty! This ought to stiffen the backs of the louts."

It was only a matter of minutes before the sergeant returned with a shaken and timorous lieutenant. Wide-eyed, the lieutenant cleared his throat and struggled to make sound come out. His gaze dropped.

"Well, what is it damn it all?" Colonel Easton growled.

It was the sergeant who answered. Unlike the young officer, his stone face gave no clue to which emotion he may have felt.

"The prisoner has escaped, sir."

Slack-jawed, Colonel Easton's mouth hung open momentarily. With a quick intake of breath, he then straightened and glared at the lieutenant, ignoring the sergeant. "How is this possible? What is he talking about?"

The lieutenant stammered and made an incoherent reply. The sergeant filled in for him. "They're gone, sir."

Easton looked blankly at him, not sure who 'they' were. He had forgotten completely about the contraband who accompanied the deserter.

"The guard was knocked unconscious, sir," he added.

A low, gurgling sound came from Colonel Easton. His face visibly began to turn purple, which was interrupted by a knock on the open door and a discrete cough.

"What?" Easton fairly yelled at the corporal.

"Beggin' yer pardon, sir," the corporal said, "'fraid I have some bad news, sir."

Easton's shoulders hunched forward, and he clenched his fists. "What is it now?"

"Yer horse, sir. He's been stolen overnight."

* * *

"You're getting good at this," Lockett grinned at Clarissa as they rode through the narrow path in the woods. He tapped the multiple canteens of water and the saddle bags full of food. Two beds rolls were also tied onto the back of the saddle, not to mention the heavy great coats that they now wore to protect them from the gusting wind. A quartermaster could not have outfitted them better.

"More practice," she said simply, but she too shared the giddy feeling as they made their escape.

Everything had been organized by the young girl, right down to stealing the horse. Lockett tried to not think of whom she stole the horse from, but he had a pretty good idea. Ever since Buell's orders last summer, only senior officers had kept their mounts. He imagined the scowling gray haired colonel's reaction and smiled broadly.

It had been surprisingly easy. After knocking out the lone guard, they had quietly ridden northwards. The pickets were well deployed, but most were all positioned at the other end of the camp, to keep an eye on the enemy to the south, not to prevent anyone from going north. Apparently, Colonel Easton decided that his threats to scofflaws were enough of a deterrent.

The only dilemma that gave Lockett pause was the weather. When they had left, they had been able to see the north star, and guided by that, they had headed north. However, shortly after their departure, the clouds had obscured the moon and stars. He had tried to keep a northerly course, but he wasn't entirely sure that their direction was true now, although he did not share those thoughts with Clarissa.

Still, she seemed to read his mind, just as Patrick had a tendency to do. "Do you know where you're going?" she asked.

"We've marched through these parts a couple of times on the way to Nashville. I want to avoid the main roads to be safe, but I'll recognize some landmarks as we go through, I'm sure. If we hit the Cumberland River, then we know that we'll need to turn east." He looked at her face. "Don't worry."

"I'm not," she said brightly. "Besides, this time you have the right uniform on."

At that point, the downpour began, and they clawed their way through the strengthening breeze. He actually shared her optimism now that he was behind his own lines, but he also knew that it would be a tough ride to Nashville.

* * *

Daniel and the rest of General Sheridan's column pushed further down the Nolensville Pike despite the weather.

It was a dreary landscape, Daniel thought, and it wasn't the weather. It seemed that nearly every structure south of Nashville was a charred shell. Only chimneys seemed to be standing. Most were not recent victims of the war. The houses looked like they had been burned weeks or months ago.

In any case, the aftermath of the no-man's land between the two armies startled Daniel. He wondered where those families had disappeared to. Were they dead? Were they killed on the precipice to their own homes? Had they abandoned the structures long ago, resigned to the fact that one side or the other would destroy it?

The sobering thoughts were interrupted throughout the day by moments of scattered gunfire, some of it sounding as if large forces were engaged, but then it would die down.

Riders would come back to order some infantry to the front, but then the fire receded and the Confederate horsemen melted away into distance, only to reform miles down the road. At that point, the entire cycle would restart.

Another of these delaying actions was beginning again. This time, it was Blair's Independent Regiment who double timed to the front in support of the thin screen of Union cavalry that rode in front of the column.

"To the left, to the left!" An officer directed them off the macadamized pike and into a drenched, muddy field. "Form on Major Peters' left."

They crested a small rise and saw a small line of blue in the tree line at the bottom of the slope. Prosper T. Rowe slipped in the mud and went down face first, sliding for five feet before coming to a stop. He had the forethought to keep his right hand, which clenched his rifle, elevated and out of the mud. He came up with a uniform and mask of brownish red mud, but his weapon was clean. That was more than Sam Baker could say. He had fallen on the up slope and instinctively plunged his hands downward to break his fall. He had tried to wipe the clump of mud from his weapon, but everyone doubted that it would fire now.

"Form up, form up!" Captain Fulkerham was bellowing at them as they came down the hill. "Form on me! And hurry up, you clods! We flank them, thrash them, and then put an end to this nonsense!"

Daniel shuffled into position next to Patrick and Prosper. The rain had paused and there were a few isolated cracks from the skirmishers' rifles in front.

It seemed to take a long time to form the line, and Daniel looked down the length of it to see the delay. He could not tell the reason, but he did see Vaught who nodded back at him. They had hardly spoken since the incident in Nashville, although Daniel bore him no ill will. It had more to do with the fact that he seemed to have been accepted into his brother's old inner circle than a conscious decision to spend less time with the gambler.

Finally, the order came for the line to advance, and they tromped forward, ready to engage some dismounted cavalry, but as they approached, the Confederates withdrew, satisfied that they had slowed the Yankees sufficiently.

In the rear, one horse soldier would hold the reins on four or five horses each. The others would race back to that spot, mount up, and ride back further south.

And slowly, General Rosecrans's Army of the Cumberland advanced down the pike.

December 27

Lockett and Clarissa awoke to a dense fog. They had sheltered the cold night in a half-burnt farmhouse. Most of the roof was gone, but the chimney still stood, and they kept a smoky fire going all night. Even with the heavy great coats and the blankets that they had taken, it was a tough night.

As he had shivered throughout, Lockett was thankful that the Army was still in its winter quarters. It would have been a terrible night to be on the march and without any shelter at all. He wondered how Daniel was doing and equally wondered how each of them would handle that first reunion.

"Do we go?" Clarissa asked. "I can hardly see my hand in front of my face."

"The fog will hide us well. Only the truly desperate would be out in this, though I suspect it will burn off soon enough."

"Can you tell which direction to go?"

"That's a different question," he said slowly. "I think so. Though the last thing we need is to get twisted around and headed in the wrong direction."

There was a temptation to wait a little longer, but that was counter-balanced by the urgency of getting the information to General Rosecrans. In the end, he decided to give it another hour before they continued on.

* * *

The progress of Sherman's and McCook's column was equally delayed by the thick fog. Worse yet, the continuing rain had turned the fields into a sloshing mire. Cannon and their limbers sank to their hubs. Horses strained, and men heaved on extra lines or pulled on the spokes of the wheels or pushed from behind. And agonizingly, the march crept forward in such a fashion. Extra pounds of mud clung to men and equipment alike. The cold steady rain also sapped the men's strength.

Progress was exceedingly slow throughout Saturday.

* * *

The early winter's dusk was rapidly coming on when Lockett and Clarissa reined in their horse. A smile creased Lockett's face, and he clapped his hands once at the sight before them.

"What?" Clarissa asked in confusion, looking at the railroad tracks in front of them.

"I know where we are," Lockett answered, "That's the Nashville and Northwestern." He guided the horse to the right. "We'll just follow this right into town."

They did not stop that night, riding steadily next to the tracks. As they crossed a tributary that fed into the Cumberland River, Lockett knew exactly where they were. Eventually, they left the tracks and headed straight for Colonel Wilks's headquarters. With any luck, they would be there by early morning, Lockett thought to himself.

December 28

The cold drizzle and the gusting northern wind had ceased when Lockett and Clarissa dismounted in the growing light of dawn. Stiff and saddle sore, his steps were like that of a creaking old man.

A steady gray smoke came up from the chimney at the house where this journey had all started. A mixture of bitterness, relief, and a melancholy longing for Anna came over him as he stared at the house.

"We go?" Clarissa interrupted his thoughts.

"I go," he answered, thankfully tearing his eyes away from the structure. "Stay with the horse and try to stay out of sight. If someone asks, I'm with Colonel Wilks."

"I will," she answered slowly, a glint of anxiety in her eyes.

She had been fearless and redoubtable during the journey. This momentary crack in her demeanor struck him as odd, but then he remembered what her mother had told him about the blue coated soldiers in Athens.

He had told her to stay out of sight because he knew that no one would take kindly to a contraband wearing army issued clothes. They were sure to think that it had been stolen. But now that he recalled the conduct in Athens, there was even more to worry about.

"I won't be long," he promised. He patted her young head and walked briskly towards Wilks' headquarters.

There was no one in the outer office, though he could hear voices from the inner office. He knocked on the door to the inner office and was already swinging it open when he heard Wilks' voice say, "Enter."

About to rebuke the intruder for opening the door before being verbally admitted, Colonel Wilks gaped in surprise at him.

The reaction was even more pronounced with Orrin Long. His mouth hung open, and his eyes were wide at the apparition in front of him.

Together, they stared at the man in the door frame. Soaked and muddied, the dirty and grizzled face glared back at them. Lockett's eyes bore into them as their own eyes were drawn to the shocking burn marks on his jaw and neck. Even the grime and the tall collar of his greatcoat could not hide them.

As Lockett looked at Orrin Long, he felt the scarcely dormant hate rising in him. Normally, a shield would drop over his gray eyes, giving no clue to the emotions that bubbled underneath, but not today. Today, those emotions were perilously close to the surface. The angry glare on his face was unmistakable.

"Lockett?" Colonel Wilks finally spoke. There was a heavy pause and then the colonel moved closer to Lockett to get a better view of the scars. "What happened to you?"

"Your McGowan is what happened to me," Lockett answered bitterly. He pulled the collar away from his neck to show more of the pink, thickening, webs of the scar.

"Where is he?" Wilks asked.

"Dead," Lockett said through clenched teeth. "He won't be betraying anyone else again."

Wilks looked away and nodded.

"You knew," Lockett accused. "You knew he was a traitor, and you still sent me out there!"

"We didn't *know*," Wilks said quickly. "We suspected. There's a difference."

"He knew," Lockett said, pointing at Orrin Long.

"Captain Long?"

"He knew," Lockett repeated and took a menacing step forward. Though he was still a good ten feet away, Orrin Long instinctively took a step back.

"Now see here," Wilks said, "We did not know. We only suspected, and I told you as much when you left."

"No," Lockett declared in a low voice, "You both knew. That is why you sent me. You needed to persuade the generals that you were doing something, so you sent someone who was expendable."

"Now it's not like that..."

"Did you tell the general that you sent me with a guide who you *suspected* was a traitor?" He said the critical word with a harsh disdain. He took another step towards Orrin Long.

"Now see here," Wilks said, his voice gaining strength suddenly, "I will not be threatened in my own office."

Lockett turned to see that Colonel Wilks had pulled a revolver from his desk and had it trained on him. Lockett was immediately conscious that he had no weapons, not even a knife. Still, there was a bold confidence in his voice as he spoke. "I'm not threatening you, Colonel. I'm threatening him."

He paused. "Besides, I didn't go through all this to *not* deliver the information to you."

"You have it?" Wilks said, astounded.

"I have everything that a general would need."

"Well," Wilks said cautiously, "I suppose you can still give it to me." There was a profound lack of excitement in the Colonel's voice despite hearing the news. He holstered the weapon.

For the first time, Lockett felt a hiccup of indecision and surprise. He had expected a fully different response from the colonel.

"Hand me the paper. I'll de-cipher it."

"I don't have the paper, Colonel. She didn't have time to get it to me before I had to escape."

"She?" Orrin Long scoffed, regaining some of his confidence.

But Wilks's reaction was different. "You met her?" he said puzzled. "It was to be an unseen drop?"

"When you gave half of the clue to McGowan it died with him. I had to find another way. But I have everything that you need."

Wilks looked skeptically at him. "You found her on your own?"

"Troop strengths. Christmas furloughs. Carter Stevenson and his men have been withdrawn to Vicksburg. I can tell you where Hardee's men are at, Breckinridge, and Polk too. Their exact locations…"

"That might have been interesting at one point, but you are too late. Though the General would be interested to hear about Stevenson…"

"Too late?"

"Yes, too late, Lieutenant. The army has already started to march towards Murfreesboro."

"What!"

"Yes, Lieutenant. Things have changed."

"It is *Captain* Lockett now, remember our deal?"

"No, it is Lieutenant still," Wilks said forcefully. "You were to deliver this information so that General Rosecrans could make the decision of when to attack and where, but you did not deliver the information by then. He decided without you. You didn't hold up your end of the deal, so you are still a Lieutenant. Be happy that I don't put your brother back in jail!"

Lockett clenched his fists so tightly that his long nails drew blood from his palms. "Too late!" he said hotly. "Too late? Then you should have come for me when the message was delivered. Colonel Easton has had me locked up for days. You had the message, why didn't you come?"

"I don't know what you are talking about, Lieutenant. There was no message."

"There was a message…"

Lockett started, and he noticed a twitch on Orrin Long's face. The realization immediately dawned on him. "You bastard!" He started for Orrin Long again, prompting Colonel Wilks to scramble to pull the gun from the holster again. Lockett made three strides closer before the gunshot shook the small room and dust fell from the ceiling.

"Enough," Wilks demanded, "The next shot won't be a warning shot."

Lockett glared at Orrin Long. He noticed that Orrin was not wearing a holster and was unarmed at the moment, which was a good thing, he realized. Given the easy opportunity, he could easily see Orrin Long taking the opportunity to shoot him on the spot. Slowly, the two men wordlessly eyed each other.

"Your day will come, Orrin. I promise you that," Lockett vowed. The two men glared at each with pure hatred. "I should have killed you when you hid with the shirkers at Shiloh."

"You lie!"

"Enough!" Colonel Wilks interjected.

Lockett turned to face the colonel. "If there is nothing else, then I'd like to return to my regiment."

"You have nothing else to share?"

"Since you don't care to hear my information, then there is nothing."

"Then, permission granted, *Lieutenant*," Wilks said snidely. "You may return to your regiment."

Lockett exited the building and succumbed to petty influence, slamming the door behind him. He was startled to find Clarissa standing next to the front door, still trying to catch her breath.

"What are you doing here? I thought that I told you to stay out of sight?"

"I heard," she started between gasps of breath, "The shot... I knew you didn't have no gun no more so I came runnin'."

Lockett shook his head slowly. At least her loyalty took some of the sting off of the betrayal that he felt.

"You're not shot, is you?"

"Not with a bullet," he answered.

She looked uncomprehendingly at him.

"Never mind," he continued.

"Where are we goin' now?"

"We?" he said, scratching his head. "We... Well, that's a good question." He lapsed into silence as they walked towards the horse. Finally, as they reached the worn out mount, he added, "I don't know, Clarissa. The army has headed south, back towards Murfreesboro. This means that I need to go back." He sadly shook his head at the irony. "But this horse is worn out. I guess we are not going anywhere for now."

* * *

Milton Bosworth sat on the frozen ground and vigorously rubbed his bruised knee. A spew of curses came from the mouth and fogged the air around him.

The ground was treacherous in this state for both man and beast. Finally, he cautiously rose to his feet and slid off the icy patch. He made his way back to the others over by the fire.

The sun was well up now, but all of the fires still burned strongly. There was no organized chaos of packing up camp and moving on. It was Sunday, and as General Rosecrans was prone to do, there was no activity for this Sabbath day. Nearby, a few dozen men were singing a hymn to conclude their prayer meeting. There were a number of such meetings across the army, just as there would be similar such meetings south of them in the Confederate camps.

"Do we move out later today, Sarge?" Sam Baker asked him.

Bosworth shook his head. "Rosie don't like to fight on Sundays, so we stay here today. Just as well too. These last two days took too much of the army just getting this far. Damn weather. Had perfect weather for weeks, then as soon as we decide to head for Bragg, the heavens open up and the temperatures drop. Always seems to work that way."

* * *

It was late afternoon by the time that Lockett arrived upon a plan. With Clarissa in tow, he headed into town. She had followed him wordlessly until now... as they looked at the sign that read 'Hotel'.

"What are we doing here?" she asked.

"I need a little help, and I figure this is the place to start," he answered.

"What kind of help?"

He didn't answer at first. Pausing, he looked at the empty front step. He hoped that the two Pinkerton men were still here. Maybe they could tell him which direction Blair's Independent Regiment had headed. There were multiple routes to Murfreesboro from Nashville.

He knew that Colonel Wilks would have been able to answer that question, but he would be damned before he would stick his head back inside that door again.

"C'mon," he answered, and he headed up the steps and entered the empty bar room beneath the makeshift hotel rooms. The same old man stood behind the scarred wooden bar as the last time that he was here, but the bartender gave no indication that he recognized him. In fact, the stooped old man looked at him with a harsh glare as they entered.

Lockett opened his mouth, but before words could come out, the bartender snarled, "Their kind ain't welcome inside these doors."

Lockett stopped in mid-stride, but Clarissa spoke quickly and quietly before he could respond. "I'll wait outside." She slipped out, and Lockett stood still for a moment. He did fear for her safety on that front step. After all, she was still wearing the oversized Union blue greatcoat with the lighter blue army trousers poking out underneath.

But the streets were mostly empty today. All of the army was gone, save the provosts and a few troops to keep the capital quiet. The image of a provost coming around the corner and spotting her in "stolen" army clothing was not a pleasant thought though, so he decided that he better get on with it.

"The two Pinkerton men, are they still here?"

The bartender looked back at him blankly.

"MacDonald and Matson, are they still here?"

With a shake of his bald head, the old man said, "Ain't here, left here when the army left."

With a muttered curse, Lockett looked at the floor. He had been counting on them to help him with the location of Colonel Blair. He had also secretly been hoping that they could help him with what to do with Clarissa. "Do you know where they went?"

he asked.

The bartender looked strangely at him. "Ain't my job to keep track of 'em. Course I don't know where they got to."

Lockett bit his lip and turned on his heel. Clarissa was waiting in the shadow of their horse by the splintered railing in front of the hotel.

"That was fast," she remarked with surprise.

"They weren't there."

"Who?"

"That's not important now," he grumbled. "But I do need to figure out where my regiment went, and what to do with you." He mounted the horse, and she quickly scrambled up behind him.

"Me?" she said with a hurt voice.

"The army has gone south, Clarissa. That's not the direction that you need to head. You need to go north. I'm not sure which road south they've gone, but I do know that they have gone south."

"Momma said to stay with you," Clarissa said resolutely.

"I'm in the army, Clarissa. You can't follow me around."

"Momma's last words were to trust no one but you and stay with you." Her young voice was full of defiance and determination.

"Clarissa..." he started, trying to figure out exactly how to reason with her. He couldn't think of the right words, so he shook his head, and they rode along silently and slowly.

December 29

The rising sun of the morning revealed that the clouds had departed overnight. Lockett and Clarissa started off at first light, but their pace for this return trip to Murfreesboro lacked the urgency that they had felt in leaving the place. Both were only grudgingly willing to point their stolen horse back south.

The bright sun should have cheered his spirits as it warmed him, but Lockett felt little excitement for chasing his army back south. He knew that he should have felt something, anything. After all, he was heading back, closer to Daniel, closer to Patrick, closer to his men, closer to Anna even. Any of those should have been more than enough motivation, he told himself, but his body was weary and his spirit more so.

And Clarissa? Her eyes were a mixture of dread and determination. This was clearly the wrong direction for her to head, but she was no less insistent than before. Glumly, she clung to him from the back of the horse.

Lockett tried to think of what else he could do to help her, but invariably his mind kept wandering. It kept returning to Colonel Wilks's little office and the satisfied look of triumph on Orrin Long's face at the end of it all. Thoughts of Anna, Clarissa, Daniel, Patrick, and all others were fleeting. The wound was still too fresh to his psyche, and it was the face of Orrin Long that kept reappearing, mile after clip-clop mile astride their worn out horse.

What he really wanted to do was corner Orrin Long, corner him out of sight from all eyes. Lockett had never considered himself a killer before; he still considered himself a farmer, even after all of these battles. But now, there was some forced introspection due to his lingering, odious thoughts.

Were it not for Orrin, he would have succeeded in plenty of time to help General Rosecrans and the army. Rosecrans could have used that information.

Yet, as Lockett rode along in silence, he was forced to admit that the knot of anger in his chest had less to do with consequences to Rosecrans's army and more to do with the knowledge that Orrin Long had successfully outmaneuvered him again.

Given his moroseness, it was no surprise to Lockett that he and Clarissa said virtually nothing throughout the day. The sky had soon turned gray again, and the past few hours had alternated between mist and steady rain. Wordlessly, Clarissa had clung to his back, and when she finally spoke late in the afternoon, it startled him.

"Is that the battle?" she said.

Lockett knew exactly what she was referring to. Ahead of them, further down the pike, a long trail of black smoke hung low in the sky. The low clouds forced it from drifting high into the air, and the drizzle broke it up such that it was scarcely visible above the tree line.

"No," he said, "That's not from a battle."

The smoke ahead was dark and black, not the gray smoke

caused by the relentless firing of weapons. Something ahead was burning.

"I've been watching it for the past twenty minutes," he added.

"I had my eyes closed," Clarissa replied. "If it's not a battle, what is it?"

That had puzzled Lockett for the past twenty minutes as well. There was no sound of a battle, and it was clearly not gun smoke, but something was burning. Out of an abundance of caution, he slowed their pace to even more of a languid crawl than it already was.

"I'm not sure," he answered.

The pike rose over a small knoll and from its low summit, he could see a bit further into the distance. Whatever it was, it was about three miles away from the looks of it.

To his left, he saw a muddied field with ruts in the reddish brown earth. The army had camped here, he realized. The earth was churned, and he could see that the ruts were quite deep, up to a wagon wheel's hub possibly. He could picture the heavy cannon and their limbers mired, men and beast hauling with all their strength to pull them free.

A little further, he could see the telltale signs of a small skirmish. A makeshift barricade of stones and fallen logs had been created between two thick trees. From its vantage point, it would have had a commanding presence over the pike. The two trees had been scarred and scoured by shot.

One tree in particular had numerous nicks in the one side, head-high, Clarissa noticed.

"Was that a battle?" she asked.

"Skirmish," he replied. "The Rebels must have been trying to block the road from there."

"So they lost?"

"No, not really. They would want to slow our army down. It's just a delaying tactic."

"You sure that's not smoke from a battle ahead?"

"Very."

It would be dark soon with the early winter sunset, and the smoke had nearly stopped rising into the darkening sky. Only a few vaporous tendrils existed by the time they neared the spot.

Lockett was still unsure what the smoke was all about until they were nearly on top of it. It was only when he saw a few dead horses near the road that the idea popped into his head. With a sudden jerk of the reins, he halted.

"What is it?" Clarissa asked.

He shushed her and looked around. He saw and heard nothing, but he also knew that they were so close now that if he was right, there was little chance to escape, especially on this tired horse.

"Raiders," he answered.

Confederate horsemen had a long history now of swinging around Union armies with impunity and attacking supply and communication lines. Had the raiders already departed the area?

Another hill hid the rest of the pike from view. Cautiously, he nudged the horse forward. When he reached the top, he saw that his suspicion was correct. Even so, the scale of the destruction startled him. The carnage ran the length of the slope and then up to the top of the next rise.

Wagon upon scorched wagon littered the pike, some still neatly in line, but others were pointed chaotically in all directions in the adjacent fields.

There were wagons on their sides; wagons pitched forward on their broken axles; some burnt to the ground and others still smoldering; dead horses by the hundred lay in their harnesses

The bodies of the teamsters could be seen in the fields or even in their wagons with the reins forever locked in their fists.

Nothing moved other than the trickles of smoke from the long line of burned wagons.

"How many wagons is that?" Clarissa murmured in awe from behind him. "Gawd, it smells terrible," she added.

The cold, damp, clammy air smelled thickly of burning horseflesh.

Slowly, Lockett and Clarissa continued to pick their way through the carnage on their horse, twisting here and there in a ponderous path through the wreckage. Lockett said nothing, but he quietly counted the number of burned wagons as they went by. In some cases, the wagons were completely burned to the ground with little more than their wheels remaining. In other cases, the wagons were just charred. Charred, but empty, he noticed.

He stopped counting, and the only sound was the slow steady

clop of their horse's hooves, but what was fully overpowering was the incredible stillness in the area. It was a stillness that Lockett was all too familiar with by now. Nothing stirred here.

They were maneuvering their way around two charred wagons that must have collided with each other in the chaos when Lockett sensed some movement ahead. In front of them, a man in brown civilian clothes, a teamster from the look of it, was propped up in a peculiar sitting position against a large dead horse. The man's head lolled to one side, but his eyes followed the riders.

"He's alive," Clarissa said, seeing it too.

They dismounted.

The man made no movement or sound, even though his eyes tracked their every action as they approached. He had an oddly, incongruously peaceful look on his face, despite being situated in a large puddle of blood. It was too much blood for one person. Much of the blood pool must have come from the horse that he leaned against.

"They alread' took my money," the man said in a weak voice, mistaking the lone soldier and escaped slave for battlefield looters, ready to rifle through the pockets of the dead and kill the wounded if they resisted.

"We're not here for that," Lockett said, taking no offense.

"You a deserter?"

Lockett shook his head. "I'd be going the other direction, wouldn't I?"

"Reckon so," the teamster said softly. "In that case, can you give a dying man some water?"

"Of course." Lockett returned to the horse and unstrapped the canteen. He brought it to the man and offered it, yet the man made no motion to take the proffered item.

"Cain you pour it in my mouth? Cain't feel my limbs no more."

Lockett looked at the grotesque wound in the man's belly and realized that what had looked so odd about the way the man was seated was the flaccid way that his arms lay next to him.

"There's anoth' in the back. Must've hit my spine."

"What happened here?"

"Wheeler's cavalry. Came out of nowhere and made short work of it. Some more water?"

Lockett obliged, and then the man continued. "Picked us clean too. Took what they could, burned the rest."

At the pause, Lockett turned to Clarissa. "Scout around and see what you can find. We need a weapon most of all."

"Ain't goin' find nothin'," the man interrupted. "Done real thorough, they did. 'Nough guns and reloads for a whole brigade. That's what the Johnnies took, plus about five hundred prisoners. I'd be one, 'cept, I cain't move." The man laughed sadly. "Said they goin' clear 'round the whole army and ain't anyone to stop 'em. Bastards." He added softly.

"Well, I'll go look too," Lockett answered. "Must be something useful here." There were a hundred wagons. "Anything I can do for you?"

The man scowled, as if the offer was some sort of insult. "Jus' give me some water when you come back." He closed his eyes.

The man had been right. Despite his best efforts, Lockett had not been able to find anything particularly useful. What had not been taken away had been burned. Of what was left, he had no use for things like iron pots.

Lockett returned to the man, canteen in hand, but the teamster was already dead. The rain was starting to fall harder again, and night was falling quickly. Through the dusk, he could see Clarissa dragging something through the mud.

"You found something," he commented, meeting her. She was dragging a charred box of hard tack and a few other items.

"One wagon didn't burn through, just smoked. Rain must've have put it out. Found these inside."

There were no weapons, but she did find food, two pup tents, and a couple of gum blankets that would be useful on a rainy night like tonight.

December 30

The artillery barrage that Lockett and Clarissa had heard a few hours ago had ceased, leaving an ominous stillness to the air.

It was late afternoon, and they had known for a few hours now that they had reached the backside of Rosecrans's army. At the crossroads ahead of them, they saw wagons parked near a small farmhouse. A few large white tents were positioned nearby.

As they slowly rode along, a man was urinating in a clump of trees. Finished, he turned around. He did not give Lockett or Clarissa a second look and headed back towards the farmhouse, but the sight of him made Clarissa gasp. His white shirt sleeves were completely reddened with blood past his elbow and the short apron that covered his front was equally crimson.

Lockett felt Clarissa stir behind him as she scanned the pasture around the farmhouse. "What is this place?" she asked. "A butcher? Where are the cows?"

"No, it's not a butcher," Lockett answered and then paused. "Not exactly anyhow."

He knew what this place was, and he did not need to see the black lettering on the crates in the wagon that read "U.S. Sanitary Commission" to know what it was.

"But I guess many soldiers would consider this place a butcher shop," he added softly.

His eyes focused on the farmhouse. There was no pile of amputated limbs outside the windows... yet.

But with a major battle looming there would eventually be a pile of arms and legs that would grow and grow until it was taller than a man.

"It's a hospital, Clarissa," he answered with a faraway sounding voice.

As he said that, the quiet was broken by an excited voice shouting, "Lieutenant! Lieutenant! Over here, Lieutenant!"

Lockett looked at the house and tents.

"Lieutenant!" came the cry again.

He looked into the pasture where there were already a handful of wounded, and it was then that he saw an arm waving from the winter grass. He drew the horse to a stop and dismounted with Clarissa in tow. His actions were slow at first, and then he recognized the face of the man who propped himself up on his elbows. Spurred on, Lockett jogged quickly towards the man.

"Prosper!" he yelled excitedly. As he reached him, Lockett looked with concern at the crimson soaked bandage around Prosper's thigh. Bending down to his knee, he and Prosper clasped forearms tightly, and he placed a brotherly left hand on the wounded man's shoulder.

"Prosper, what happened?" He looked anxiously at the leg.

"Don't worry, sir. The surgeon said it missed the bone. He won't need to take the leg."

Looking at the gangly man, Lockett wondered how it was even possible for a bullet to hit Prosper's leg without hitting bone, but he was heartened to hear the news.

The moroseness and dejection that he had felt for the past two days was lifted by the sight of his old comrade. Suddenly, he was anxious to see the faces of Daniel, Patrick, Milton, and the others.

"Gawd, the boys will be so glad to see you, sir! We thought you was dead! Dead by gum! Ain't you a sight!" Prosper looked at him with such a wide-eyed expression of pleasure that it seemed impossible that he was wounded and in pain. Lockett had never seen such a happy, wounded soldier. "I feel like I want to get up right now to tell 'em!" Prosper exclaimed.

"I think you better just rest easy there, Prosper," Lockett chuckled. "Now, what happened?"

"Nuthin' much to tell, sir. We were up in the picket line today, trading a few shots here and there with the Johnnie's pickets. Just a lucky shot. Never saw 'em. Then a couple of boys dragged me back and eventually brought me here. Battle ain't started yet, sir."

Lockett was about to ask where the regiment was exactly, but he couldn't get a word in.

"Who's the boy?" Prosper asked.

Lockett turned and looked behind him. It took him a moment to realize that Prosper was talking about Clarissa. With her short cropped hair and bony frame cloaked in Union blue, he could understand the mistake. He opened his mouth to correct Prosper, but before the words could come out, Clarissa spoke quickly.

"My name's Charlie," she said.

Lockett looked quizzically at her, but the quick movement of her eyes told him not to correct her now.

"Where'd you come from, sir?" Prosper asked, turning his attention back to him. "Where were you? What happened? God Almighty, I can't believe you're here!'"

Lockett asked his own question before Prosper rattled off another. "Where are the boys, Prosper?"

"Part of Sheridan's and Sill's men now," Prosper answered.

"Sheridan?" Lockett frowned. He still remembered the

General's inactivity at Perryville. He remembered how Sheridan had sat while Starkweather's men bore the brunt of the Confederate attacks alone.

"Yes, sir. God Almighty, the boys won't believe it when they see you! We was so sure that you were dead. You was gone so long. What happened, sir?"

Lockett ignored the question. "How are they? Patrick is ok? Daniel?"

Prosper gave a large gap-toothed smile. "They're all good, sir. You'll be impressed by your brother too."

"Daniel?" Lockett said skeptically.

"I know you two ain't seen eye to eye on somethings, but he's growing up, if you don't mind me saying, sir. We kinda took him under our wing after you left, sir. We ain't never talked about it, but I think all of us thought it was something that we should do considering that you was gone. He joined up with our mess, kept to the straight and narrow, been a real soldier, sir. Been volunteering for extra time up in the picket lines with us and everything…"

The last sentence gave Lockett pause and mixed feelings. On one hand, he was proud to hear that Daniel had changed course and was developing a reputation for something other than running out on them at Perryville. On the other hand, the old fear of something happening to his younger brother cropped up again.

"Patrick, Milton, the rest of 'em are good too, sir, though they'll be a mite better once they catch sight of you."

The spitting rain started to come down heavier, and Lockett turned to Clarissa. "Go fetch the gum blankets and tents from the horse."

"We staying here?" she asked, turning around and heading back to the horse.

"You are," he replied.

The answer caused her to stop in her tracks and spin on a heel. "What about you? I'm going wherever you are."

Lockett walked over to her, and Prosper remarked in the background, "Strong-minded little fellow."

Lockett walked by Clarissa's side as they went back to the horse. "You can't follow me where I'm going, Clarissa. See this field?"

His arm swept across the open pasture that surrounded the farmhouse and the three large white tents. "This field will soon be filled with more wounded like Prosper, and there will be twice as many dead where I'm going. It won't be like anything you've ever seen before, and I don't want you to see it. You shouldn't have to see it."

His voice dropped a notch, and he looked away, adding softly as if he was talking to himself. "There will be blood, fire, smoke, and chaos. It will be a hell on earth." He said the words slowly and deliberately. Blinking, he cleared the vision from his eyes and looked back at her. "And I'm not taking you there."

The quiet passion and caring quieted Clarissa. She hung her head and followed him to the horse. When they reached the animal, she tilted her head upwards, staring at him, and he saw her eyes welled with tears that streamed down her face, mixing with the drops of rain.

He stopped unstrapping the gum blankets from the saddle and paternally put his hands on her shoulders. She looked squarely at him, her dark eyes wide with fear and sadness. "Look, it will be all right, Clarissa. Trust me. You'll be safer here, and I'll come back for you. Understand?" She gave a dazed nod. "Take care of Prosper for me. I'll be back. He's a good man too. You can trust him."

She gave another mournful nod and then began to remove the tent from their makeshift contraption where it was lashed to the saddle.

After they had removed everything and started to walk back, he asked, "And what's this about Charlie? A boy?"

"It will be easier if they think I'm not a girl, right?" she answered.

Lockett shrugged. "I suppose." He paused. "But why 'Charlie'?"

"It was the first boy's name that came to mind," she said. Unprompted, she added, "It's my brother's name."

"Your brother?" he said with surprise. He had never considered that she might have other siblings.

"Yes, my brother. Charlie and my father were sold further south after we was caught after our first attempt."

"South?" he said dumbly.

"Yes, that is what they do when you'z caught." She looked surprised that he did not understand such things.

They put the gum blanket over Prosper to keep him from getting any wetter than he already was, and they proceeded to put the first tent up. As they did so, Lockett asked Prosper where the regiment was located.

"I can tell you how to get there, sir, but when they were pulling me out of there, I heard that General Sheridan was taking us off the line and putting us in reserve for a rest. I think that both spots are a ways from here. It seemed that we went on forever before the boys found a surgeon."

"Well, tell me where you think the reserves will be then. I'll head there." It was quickly getting dark, and he had half a mind to wait until morning out of fear of blundering about in the dark and sentries with quick trigger fingers, but the thought of reuniting with Daniel and Patrick was overwhelming.

"We were more towards the south, sir, but I think the reserves are more towards the middle. I can point you off in the right direction, sir. I think you go further down this lane here that you came in on, when the road curves around a woods, leave the lane and go right and due south. You should run into the reserves eventually."

Lockett nodded. He turned to Clarissa. "Charlie," he said deliberately, "You tend to Prosper, I'll be back later, battle or not."

She nodded with a pensive look.

After Lockett left, she did not look any better. The tension and fear were clear on the young face.

"Don't worry, Charlie," Prosper said, mistaking the look for one of a singular fear of self-preservation. "We're a long ways from the lines back here. The battle will never get this far..."

Chapter 44

But Blair's Independent Regiment had not been pulled back into a reserve position. They had hardly started when they learned that it had been a miscommunication. Used to such things in the army, there was the usual grumbling as they headed back towards the lines.

Daniel and the rest of Blair's Independent Regiment shivered as darkness fell. The fires did little to warm them as a bitter wind from the north blew through their camp. None of the men had blankets or tents. Something had happened to the supply train, and no one knew where their supplies were.

There were rumors that the quartermaster and teamsters had taken a wrong turn and were headed back to Nashville. There were also rumors that the baggage train had been caught and burned by more Confederate raiders.

There were always rumors of the latter, but all that mattered to Daniel and the others who shivered was that it was going to be a frigid night and impossible to sleep.

Daniel blew on his hands and tried to warm them against the fire. He looked across the fire at Patrick who stared intently into the flames. "Will tomorrow be the day, Patrick? Do we attack tomorrow?"

"Up to the generals to decide that," he answered, "Us or them? Can't stay this way with Rebs within hailing distance. Someone will attack."

Daniel nodded and, as if on cue, General Woodruff's regimental band started to play "Hail, Columbia".

No sooner had the song ended when from the woods across the way, where the Rebel pickets had wounded Prosper, a Rebel band began playing "Dixie". After "Dixie" concluded, General Woodruff's band played "Yankee Doodle" with a noticeable increase in gusto and volume.

Many of the men chuckled at the musical contest, a welcome interruption from their brooding thoughts of tomorrow.

After patiently waiting for the Yankees to finish, the Confederate band began "Bonnie Blue Flag." When the Southerners had finished, one of Woodruff's men good-naturedly jeered his own band, "I think they're louder, MacKenzie!"

The Union band began to play "Home, Sweet Home". Immediately, the Confederates joined in, and both bands played with a remarkable echo of each other. When the final bars were done and drifted across the camps in the frigid air, the Union camp was left still and silent in reflection. No words were said, and each man was left to look into the flames or into the distance and contemplate their futures.

Daniel had never felt anything like it. It was as if a spell had been placed on the camp, an unbreakable spell. He was both alone in his thoughts, and yet, part of a massive communal one.

Finally, three minutes later, the sound of a single singing voice came from across the picket line. The voice was somewhat faint, and probably only heard because of the immense silence and stillness.

It was not a croaking or out of tune voice like he had often heard in the camps singing on any given night. No, this was a baritone singing voice like Daniel and most of the men had never heard before, full of richness and seamless tonality. Whoever this Southerner was, he sang "And Can It Be That I Should Gain" with an impassioned perfection.

"I've never heard that Charles Wesley hymn sung so well," Levi Thickle said in a soft whisper next to Daniel.

Daniel looked in surprise at the irascible soldier, who gave a slightly embarrassed look and shrugged, knowing what Daniel's unspoken question was.

"My father is a Methodist minister," Thickle admitted quietly and then resumed listening to the song.

At its conclusion, there was again silence, this time in appreciation for the man's talent. Finally, there was a hooting call from another part of the Yankee camp. "You sing like an angel, Johnnie! I hope we don't make you one tomorrow!"

* * *

Lockett rode along slowly in the pitch black. The lane was a straight arrow shot, but in the inky night, he wondered if he would be able to spot the sprout of trees at which he was supposed to turn south.

And while the sight of Prosper's familiar face had spurred Lockett with a renewed sense of purpose to get back to Daniel and the others, it had also left him with a lurking fear for the next day. The night was as quiet as could be, and he could not shake the foreboding. He tried to tell himself that it was all exaggerated due to the fact that he was riding alone in the darkness of an unfamiliar place. Yet, with each clip-clop of the hooves, it only grew.

Worst of all though was the fatigue. Very quickly, his head began to bob, and he struggled to stay upright in the saddle. He had always taken such pride in his stamina. As a soldier, he had never faltered on those long hot marches. Years of endless toil on the farm, doing a man's full day's work from the time that he could remember, particularly after his father had died, had built up a well of reserves that he had always been able to draw upon.

But now? Now, he had little left.

The events of the past days and months had taken its toll. With regret, he decided that he should have stayed behind with Clarissa and Prosper. At least, with a night's sleep he would have recovered. Instead, his head drooped, and he closed his eyes to save what little strength he had left while the horse with equal weariness slowly tramped along the dirt lane.

Finally, the flicker of campfires caught his eye. It was to the left of the lane, not the right, but deciding that he might get some better directions, he pulled the weary horse towards it.

As he neared the camp, he saw a series of tents and realized that it was not the encampment of a regiment, but rather a headquarters. Outside the camp, he was stopped by the picket and asked who he was. Answering, that he was Lieutenant Lockett with Blair's Independent Regiment, the guard asked if he had a message for one of the generals.

"I'm looking for General Sheridan or Sill," Lockett answered.

The guard did not know if either was here. This wasn't their headquarters. It was General Rosecrans's, but it was possible that

413

they were here. He directed him towards the tent of General Rosecrans's aide.

With some trepidation, Lockett approached, knowing that General Rosecrans's adjutant had better things to do than directing one lost officer, but deciding that he was committed now, Lockett tied up the horse and approached. The candlelight made the tent glow despite the late hour. Inside, he could see the shadowed shapes of three men.

He paused near the tent opening, second-guessing himself. He had just decided not to interrupt whatever may be going on in there when he saw a familiar face, or rather bald head, through the tent opening. "Octavius?" he exclaimed in a tired voice.

The Pinkerton man turned in surprise and was joined by Bobby MacDonald in the opening.

"Good Heavens, lad!" MacDonald said in a stunned voice, "Where did you come from? We heard you were dead."

* * *

The early northern wind that had half frozen Daniel Lockett at the start of the night seemed to have passed, or at least, it could not reach him here in the dense cedar thickets of sentry duty.

"Do you see it?" McManus said from nearby. Daniel could hear the whisper but knew that the question was not directed at him.

There was no answer from Colonel Blair, or from General Sill, who both stood next to McManus. Blair and Sill were not sure if they saw what McManus had been seeing for the past thirty minutes. In the flickering of the camp light through the dense trees, on again, off again. The intermittent light meant to McManus that there were men marching past the light. It was hard to tell if that was it, or not, but the sounds clearly caught the attention of the two senior officers.

It wasn't much: the rustle of movement, the occasion jangle of canteen on cartridge box, the stamp of feet, and even the occasional creak of a wheel axle. But they too were convinced that the Rebels were on the move.

"How close are their pickets, Private?" General Sill asked.

"Fairly close, sir. We've traded shots a couple of times

tonight."

"Can we get a little closer?"

"Sir?" McManus said in surprise. "I'm sure that I can get a mite closer, but I don't reckon that you ought to come, sir. As a general, I mean."

"Nonsense," the youthful general responded good-naturedly. "I can be just as stealthy as you."

McManus shrugged. He liked the sandy-haired boy general. "Well, sir, that isn't exactly what I meant, but if you want to get a closer look, I'm happy to go with you." He walked over to Daniel's position. "Wait here," he said, "And when we come back to this position, call out, don't just shoot."

With that, McManus and General Sill crept further ahead and to the right. They did not need to go far before Sill tapped McManus on the shoulder. It was far enough. From this position it was clear to see what they had heard and what McManus had surmised in the flickering light. In fascination, they watched large bodies of Confederate soldiers marching west, clearly illuminated by the camp fire and clearly heading around the Union right flank.

* * *

"I owe you my life, Octavius." Lockett concluded after relating the tale of what had happened and his escape from Murfreesboro. "Without the Underground Railroad, I never would have been able to escape."

"Remarkable," was all that General Rosecrans' adjutant could utter. The tale seemed too fantastic to believe, but the scarring on the young officer's neck and his total conviction in relating the tale left him with no doubt about the veracity.

"And Wilks," MacDonald asked, "I assume that you tried to find him. He's still in Nashville. Did you find him? What did he say?"

Lockett looked away from the Pinkerton and then cryptically at Rosecrans's adjutant. He was not sure if he could trust the senior officer like he could the Pinkerton men. He had not related his suspicions about Orrin Long's role in the affair, including his withholding of the information that caused Lockett to be detained.

He decided to opt for discretion. "The Colonel said that I was too late and that my information was not important any more. The army was already on the move. So here I am, looking for the whereabouts of my regiment."

"Well, I am sure that we can help with that," the adjutant said, "And you are just in time to bear witness to a crushing defeat that General Rosecrans is about to hand to the Rebels."

Lockett looked quizzically at him.

"We launch our attack at day break, Lieutenant Lockett. We have massed our divisions and reserves on our left flank. We will crash through the Rebels' right flank and sweep into Murfreesboro. Bragg has no idea of what is about to hit him."

"My regiment is apparently with Sheridan and Sill. Where are they at?"

"Sheridan?" the adjutant answered. "They are on our right flank. Sadly, for you and them, they will not be part of the attack. They only have to make a small demonstration and keep the Rebs from knowing where the true bulk of our army is…"

* * *

On the far left of the Rebel flank, Ambrose Tucker watched yet another brigade of infantry march by in the dark of night. Rains, Ector, McNair, Liddell, Johnson… the cream of McCown's and Cleburne's divisions had already gone by. The assault on the Yankee right flank would be shortly before dawn.

Absently, Ambrose wondered where James Lockett had disappeared to. Despite his best efforts and the offering of a healthy reward, the Yankee seemed to have escaped.

He shook his head to clear his thoughts. In a few hours, they would deal the Yankees a death blow, like the one that General Lee had delivered in Virginia. They would crush the Yankees here and now. They would make middle Tennessee safe for all freedom loving people again.

* * *

The drops of cold water fell intermittently on Clarissa's head. The rain had stopped, but at Prosper's direction earlier, she had pitched the two small, one-man pup tents beneath a tree. Prosper laid in one of the tents. The drops of water falling from the tree sounded like tiny drumbeats on the canvas.

Clarissa clutched the gum blanket around her and shivered. There was a second pup tent, but after setting it up, she had stumbled in the dark across a prone figure lying miserably in the mud. The soldier was missing his arm below the elbow and was in such a weakened state that he had hardly managed a protesting sound when she had tripped on him.

As the rain had fallen in that early part of the night, she had taken down the second pup tent and erected it over the man, although Prosper had warned her that he figured the man would be dead by morning, tent or not.

Still, she had no regrets about it as she shivered in the gum blanket next to Prosper's tent. It was well past midnight when she finally managed to drift off into a fitful sleep.

* * *

"What do you think?" Daniel Lockett asked after they had been relieved from picket duty.

McManus gave no answer aloud. Silently, he reflected on how much blood would surely be spilled in the coming hours.

"The Rebs are preparing to attack the flank," Bosworth answered for him. "That should be clear to even the densest general."

"I heard that General Sill sent a warning message to General Sheridan three times tonight, even went to see him personally the last time," Sam Baker added.

"Now, how would you know that?" Bosworth said skeptically.

"I was taking a piss, and I overheard two of the general's aides talking," Baker said with mock indignation.

The chatter blended into the background as McManus let his own thoughts consume him. This night was sounding all too familiar to him. It was just like Shiloh again. The signs had been there, but most of the generals could not believe them. Tonight, it was even more obvious that something was afoot. He prayed that this time it would be different.

* * *

It was shortly before four in the morning when General Sheridan strolled through their camp. They had been ordered to breakfast quietly and now formed in line of battle. The cannoneers were at their pieces, and the little general personally inspected each of his twelve regiments. Satisfied with their positioning and alertness, he quietly congratulated some as he walked by, energized and confident. The Rebels would come and they were ready, or at least General Sheridan's men were.

An hour passed when Colonel Blair summoned McManus. The colonel was sharing a tin cup of coffee with a tall, young captain. For a second in the flickering campfire light, McManus thought that the silhouette looked like James, but then sadly, he reminded himself that James was not here anymore. He had let him down and allowed his friend to go off on that fool's errand alone, and now, he was dead, McManus thought morosely.

"Captain," Colonel Blair started, "This is Private McManus. He can find his way in the dark better than anyone I know, plus he knows where General Willich's headquarters is." He turned to his soldier. "Private, you need to guide General Sill's aide here, Captain Garr. With the Rebels moving further around the right flank, the General wants to make sure that the old German is aware and ready for them."

When McManus and Captain Garr reached the camps at the far edge of their right flank, they were surprised to find men asleep in their tents and others going about the normal business of making breakfast.

Speechless for a moment, Captain Garr finally spoke aloud at the sight, "What is this? I know that General Sheridan's warning was delivered earlier this night." The lack of preparedness and urgency seemed to have stunned him into a motionless state.

"Shouldn't we inform General Willich, or at least General Johnson, of the threat?" McManus prompted, worried about the Captain's lassitude.

"Of course. Of course," Garr repeated. "We need to find Willich right away."

* * *

Octavius Matson and Bobby MacDonald looked quietly at the snoring James Lockett. His head was tilted, and with his chin resting on his chest, the pink scarring and criss-cross of scrapes and scabs of the tender, scarred skin was easy for them to study now. It crept over his jaw line and then fanned out across his neck before disappearing below his shirt line in an inverted V-shape that suggested that there was much more scarring below and out of sight.

"Remarkable that he came back alive," MacDonald said softly.

"We all knew that McGowan could not be trusted," Matson replied. After a long pause, he added, "But it was worse than I thought."

"I feel like a general," MacDonald said. The comment caused his partner to look at him quizzically. "We sent him off to die. Generals send men off to die every day," MacDonald explained, "It's a feeling that I could not get used to, Octavius."

"Except that this one did not die."

"Somehow... somehow. The shame of it is that if he had been able to return a week earlier, the march here may have been different. Imagine what could have been with his information?"

"You don't have faith in General Rosecrans's flank attack for the morning?"

"It could work," MacDonald answered his partner, "I'm no general." He looked back at the snoring lieutenant. "Should we wake him?"

"He looks like he needs the sleep more than anything else. He's done enough for now. Let him rest. Besides, his regiment is on the right flank. There is little for him to do down there."

* * *

The young Captain Garr turned and gave McManus a bewildered look. It was then that McManus noticed how young the captain was, younger than himself and younger than James, but he was a captain. Obviously, he came from somewhere besides a poor farm in Kalamazoo, Michigan.

McManus ignored him and looked at General Willich. The German general, whose long brown beard hung low like a hairy tapestry covering his neck, looked severely at the captain and then the private, but McManus was not cowed. He needed to speak his peace.

"It's true, sir. I saw the Rebels myself with General Sill. They have been moving around the flank all night and in large numbers."

"T'ank you, *Private*," General Willich replied with clear annoyance at being addressed by the private. "But vee sent out a patrol hours ago and sie found nichts... er, nothing." He pointed to the woods beyond them. "It's quiet as you can see. The Rebels are gone."

Willich turned his glare to Captain Garr. "You can tell your young General Sill that he is over-reacting. Dere is nothing to vorry about."

"But, sir," Garr tried again, "General Sheridan and General Sill..."

"You are dismissed," General Willich said curtly. He turned on his heel and stalked away.

Garr and McManus stood there dumbfounded for many minutes.

The men around them were slowly stirring. Some were up, starting breakfasts or pots of coffee, calmly chatting. Finally, Garr uttered, "I can't believe that. They look like they think they are in reserve. I can't believe it."

"I can," McManus answered. "It was more or less the same at Shiloh."

"You were at Shiloh?" Garr said with a note of surprise and awe.

"It started much like this."

"Let's hope not," Garr replied.

"We should start to head back, sir. It will be light soon."

"Yes, General Sheridan will want to know what is happening on his flank."

Suddenly, in the gloomy first light of the coming morning, there was a smattering of shots from the picket line.

The soldiers at their cook fires turned their heads curiously, but when there were no responding shots, they turned back to their goings-on.

"Just nervous pickets?" Garr suggested.

"No," McManus said cautiously. He craned his head toward where the noise had come from, his face a mask of concentration. Like a rabbit alert to a possible danger, he tried to make sense of the quiet. "That was too many at one time. Nervous sentries would have been more like one after the other. This was all at once."

"But it's quiet. If this was the Rebel attack, wouldn't there be an answering volley or a Rebel yell."

"Not sure about the yell," McManus said, knowing that the Rebel yell was always a part of a Confederate attack, "But they could be holding that volley until they get closer."

They waited again in the silence until McManus's instinct took more control of him. "Sir, I think we should edge back now, sir."

"Edge back?"

"Something's not right, sir. I can feel it." He started to back away from the camp, and obediently Captain Garr followed suit.

Then from the woods beyond them, a single blue coated soldier came dashing through camp at full speed. "Run!" the man yelled. "It's the Rebs!"

Curious, some soldiers looked up from their fires. A couple poked their heads out from their tents at the noise. None took him seriously. Many jeered him derisively, but the soldier never broke stride as he ran through camp.

As the men laughed, there were a few more scattered shots, though this time they sounded closer.

Captain Garr stopped backing away and started forward out of inquisitiveness.

"Sir," McManus warned, "Sir…"

Then a number of other pickets broke from the line of trees. Their yells of warning were accompanied by a strange background noise.

For many of the men, it took a moment to recognize it, but McManus knew what it was immediately. It was the sound of thousands of men marching through the brush and thick cedar forests.

Almost paralyzed, McManus stood rooted as two long, majestic gray lines emerged from the mist. They were massive lines of men that moved steadily and wordlessly straight for the encampment a mere 200 yards away. They marched with a profound oneness, their flags stirring the still air behind them. Through the thin fog, their individuality was blurred, but with each step, they became more clear and distinct.

The Confederates' quiet mechanical progress was contrasted by the startled yells and flurry of activity in the Federal encampment. Men ran for their weapons which were still stacked. The lucky few who were close enough to grab their rifle struggled to load the weapon frantically.

One Union cannon managed to fire a load of canister into the advancing gray wall. It seemed to make no dent in it, and instead it prompted the gray line to move quicker.

In the encampment, men tried to hustle together to form a line or present any sort of impediment. They were still trying to sort out their ranks and ready themselves when the first approaching rank opened with an immense volley.

The thunderous, rippling volley shattered the morning. It seemed to go on and on and then reverberate after that.

The lead balls crashed through the encampment. The men who had vainly tried to organize a line of resistance were instantly knocked from their upright positions. Screams of agony joined the newly brewed cacophony. They crumpled into bone shattered, bloody pools.

Other shots whipped though the encampment, tearing holes in canvas tents, ricocheting madly off of campfire cookware, battering men and rifles alike near the stacked weapons.

Captain Garr staggered backward. His hand clutched his neck from which red blood squirted madly six feet from his body. He sank to his knees, and after a few seconds pitched forward.

Meanwhile, a pitifully few brave soldiers fired in response. Their puny answer either missed or was absorbed into the encroaching gray wall, seemingly without slowing a single target.

Further to the right, McManus noticed the long Confederate lines overlapping or seeping through gaps in the Union front. Many of Willich's men were faced in the wrong direction and struggled to reform when the Confederates hit their flank, killing dozens where they stood and sending hundreds on the run to the rear. In their confusion, some of the running men in blue ran straight into another advancing gray line. More shots fired and echoed in a continuous pattern now. The dazed men in blue died quickly.

The Confederates were now in the camp and had already captured eight artillery pieces, most of which had never fired a shot. One courageous knot of blue soldiers clustered near a small tree and fired repeatedly into the lines. Other soldiers, seeing some resistance, joined them at that location and tried to rally others to join them.

A group of Confederates near the captured cannon kicked aside the dead blue coated bodies that blanketed the ground around the weapon. They manhandled two of the guns and pointed them towards the small knot of resistance. Without even needing to load the pieces, they fired into the small, but growing cluster of blue.

The twin blasts of canister shredded the Federals. They disintegrated in a mist of red. Two lone survivors stumbled backwards and helped each other slowly limp away, though at the speed they were moving, they were sure to be overtaken by the other advancing gray wall.

McManus slowly walked backward, as if entranced by the carnage. He saw another Union battery fire a load of canister into the gray wall. Again, it seemed as if the Rebels were invulnerable to shot and shell. If any hole had temporarily been made in the human wall, it was immediately filled.

The Union battery brought forward their horses and made ready to pull the cannon and limbers back, but the gray line fired another crushing volley that swept across the battery. Instantly, dozens of horses were killed or sent thrashing to the ground. The animals flailed grotesquely in the pain. Even the rare horse that managed to stand back up on all fours was entangled in a harness and attached to other dead and twisting beasts. Crazed, the animal bucked wildly against the constraints.

Gunners, who seconds earlier had been anxiously working to evacuate their weapons, were cut down also. The surviving few, seeing that they had no chance to remove their heavy guns from the field without their horses, took off on foot. One man cut a harnessed horse free and mounted it bare back, riding off wildly away from the growing disaster.

The mist of the morning was now further clouded by the gray gun smoke from the volleys. Appearing like specters from the clouds, additional Confederate brigades emerged. Some headed after the fleeing Yankees; others headed off at confused angles towards other areas of the flank, like where Generals Post's and Sheridan's men would eventually be. A few Confederate regiments even headed for each other in the misty morning.

Even though he had been shuffling backwards throughout most of it, McManus suddenly realized that was about to be taken. Turning, he took off in full flight along with many of the others.

As he ran, he saw that other parts of the Confederate armies had already reached these rear areas. He swerved wide around that pasture so as to avoid their interest.

Many of those Rebels had already paused in the onslaught to rummage through the Yankee encampment. He saw men in butternut stopping to drink from the coffee that was still on the burning campfires, poke into tents, and then re-emerge with trophies.

Much like that first blow in Shiloh, McManus realized that the only things slowing down the Rebel army were empty Union encampments and the promises of food and booty. He stopped to catch his breath and watched the pillaging.

Then from beyond the encampment, he saw a single horseman dashing straight into the encampment. In surprise, he recognized the rider by his long, thick beard. It was General Willich. He could even hear the iron-lunged General as he rode into the middle of the camp.

"Hurry, ve must get into line! You dere, stop vhat you are doing! Dis is no time for kaffee!"

The bemused soldiers looked curiously at him but gave no other action.

Enraged by their disobedience, Willich shouted and waved his arms even more wildly, "It's an order, damn you! Vhat don't you understand!"

A single shot was fired, killing his horse. As the beast fell, the German slipped his foot from the stirrup and landed gracelessly, though unhurt, with a thud.

Still, it was only when the soldiers around him raised their weapons and pointed them at him that General Willich realized his mistake.

"The Yankees use color blind generals, boys!" The Rebel

captain looked at his men and laughed loudly. Looking back at the Yankee general, he added. "Case you didn't know it, we ain't wearing blue, General!"

With their pillaging spell broken, McManus decided that this was a good time to retreat deeper into the thick woods.

* * *

The steady staccato of rifle and musket fire, punctuated by intermittent crescendos of artillery fire could be clearly heard back at the field hospital.

Anxiously, Clarissa peered into the gray morning mist that coated the field and obscured the first five feet the trees beyond. She could see their leafless tops, but nothing at ground level.

For a breath there was a lull, and then it began anew. She tried not to jump at the sound but twitched nonetheless.

"Don't worry none, Charlie," Prosper reassured from nearby. "It ain't that close."

Clarissa turned to look at him. His voice sounded confident, but she wasn't so sure.

"How do you know?"

"'Cuz I've been in a battle or two. It's a ways off."

"Did you fight with him?"

"Him? The Lieutenant? Of course. I warn't there with him at the very beginning of Shiloh, bad business that war', but ever since."

"Can you tell where it is coming from?"

"The fighting? Sounds south of here to me."

"Isn't that where you sent him?"

"That's where our regiment is, yes." Prosper said nothing else. The status of his friends was on his mind too. He did not need a runaway slave to remind him. His face darkened slightly from the positive countenance that he had tried to display earlier for Charlie's benefit. The only thing worse than being wounded, he decided, was being wounded and unable to be there for his friends.

"Will James be there already?"

"The Lieutenant? Mebbe. Hard to say really, Charlie. It almost sounds to me like it is further to our right. The Lieutenant and our men should be to the left. We're probably not even engaged."

There was another steady rattle of shots, and they both lapsed into silence.

Clarissa bit her lower lip as the bangs and cracks continued.

"So tell me, Charlie," Prosper began. Watching the child's apprehensiveness was starting to make him nervous too, he decided. The more he listened, the more it *did* seem that the sounds were getting louder and closer.

"Tell you what?" she asked, anxious herself to talk about something else.

"The Lieutenant didn't have time to tell me, but I saw those burns on his neck. Do you know what happened?"

"I do," she answered.

After she did not elaborate, Prosper added, "So? How did he get them? War' you there?"

"No, I wasn't there. But I heard him tell momma about them. A bad man did them to him."

"A man?" Prosper said in surprise. "I figured that he got caught in some sort of fire."

"No, he fought with a bad man. The man did that to him. Then, he killed the man."

The last sentence was said with a sense of satisfaction that sounded almost personal.

* * *

The firing off to his right sounded louder and far more ominous than what Daniel had heard during Perryville. The volume and scope of it easily convinced him that this was a different scale than Perryville.

He looked anxiously at the others. The temptation was still in his mind. He wanted to run. He wanted to get as far away from that sound as possible. Tightly, he clenched the stock of his rifle and tried to swallow the fear. He tried to think of something else, but the idea kept worming its way back into his mind.

Again, he looked at the others in the regiment and the rest of Sill's Brigade. General Sill had moved them slightly forward about twenty minutes earlier. The current acreage that they occupied was an odd speck of land, he thought to himself, trying to focus on something other than his fear.

It was wooded, though not heavily so, but what made it odd were the multiple limestone ribbings that came up from the rocky soil. Some of the ribbings were only a foot high, but others were three or even four feet. There were narrow channels between the ribs, some barely wide enough for a man to stand in. They ran mostly parallel to each other, with the occasional channel between them, as if men had somehow dug narrow walkways out of solid stone.

Milton Bosworth knelt in the channel behind one of the three foot high sections. Beyond him, the rock ran flat like a table for five yards before dropping into another indention, and then the same pattern beyond that.

The men of the brigade were scattered throughout these natural trenches, facing the edge of forest and then the open field beyond their position. Each man looked out across the expanse, lost in their own private thoughts of what would be coming across the field.

Daniel looked at the burly sergeant next to him, and the older man returned his gaze.

"You get enough to eat this morning?" he asked before looking away.

"Enough to eat?" Daniel said in an astounded voice. It seemed like a particularly strange question to ask at this moment.

"Yes," Bosworth answered. "It's going to be a long day. We can hold this ground for a long time when the Rebs come this way, but there ain't goin' be much time to fill your belly in between."

Daniel looked at him blankly, unsure what to say.

When Daniel made no sound, Bosworth looked back at him. "Snap out of it, boy. You look like you alread' seen the elephant, but you ain't." He gave Daniel a hardy whack on the shoulder. It was so fierce that for a second Daniel couldn't feel his fingers, and he winced.

"That's better, boy. Soon enough now. Soon enough."

Daniel rubbed his shoulder, and though it hurt, he felt a touch better. "What about Patrick?" he asked.

"McManus? What about him?"

"He went off with that Captain in that direction and he's not back yet." He pointed toward where all the firing sounded from.

"McManus, bah! He's too bull-headed to get killed. Don't worry none. Durn fool was probably already on his way back here when all the excitement started. Damn sure that he got himself lost trying to get back here. Them Irish ain't so good with the sense of direction, you know."

Though he spoke with full confidence for the benefit of the young Kalamazooan, the sergeant was worried about his closest friend.

* * *

The distant and sporadic thunder sounded again, although Octavius Matson and Bobby MacDonald knew that it was not thunder. This was the beginning of Rosecrans's battle.

MacDonald held a tin pan and swirled a few pieces of bacon awash in a sea of grease, with an unusually fresh looking biscuit island in the middle.

"At least Sheridan's demonstrations down south seem to have gone off on time," he commented as he chomped on a rubbery piece of meat. "Biscuits are fresh, Octavius. You ought to try one. I brought that second pan back for you."

"Not hungry right now," his cohort answered, "I'll let the lieutenant have it when he awakes."

"I figured that the sound of battle, no matter how distant, would wake our warrior friend, but he still sleeps," MacDonald said as he slid the biscuit around in the grease.

"He still sleeps," Matson echoed, "If you can call it sleep. He twitches every ten minutes or so. Whatever dream world he is in is one that I don't want." As if on cue, Lockett's whole body trembled in his sleep, and for a second, it seemed that he would awake, but then the snoring continued.

"Well, he ain't going to miss a whole lot of battle at this point," MacDonald remarked. "McCook may be keeping up his end of the bargain by having some sort of demonstration down on the right flank, but there is some sort of hold up on the left flank. We haven't even launched enough of an attack to bump into their pickets yet. The army is always one of such slow going."

There was another brief echo of thunder from beyond, and though it too was scarcely loud enough to hear, this particular one snapped James Lockett awake. He bolted upright. His hands clenched an unseen rifle. Wide-eyed, he looked rapidly around the tent, confused by his surroundings momentarily. With a sharp breath, he resumed breathing, and his gaze slowly focused in on MacDonald and Matson.

Still, the confused look on his face prompted MacDonald, "Tis all right, Lieutenant. You just fell asleep last night. You're still here with us at General Rosecrans's headquarters."

"What's going on?" he asked in a dumbfounded voice. He wiped a few drops of sweat from his forehead that had appeared despite the cold temperature.

"The battle has started, Lieutenant," Matson said.

"Slowly," MacDonald added.

Lockett paused and listened, but there were no sounds that could be heard.

"I need to find my regiment," Lockett mumbled to the constant drumbeat in his head.

He stood stiffly, bent at the back like an old man. Slowly, he tried to straighten himself. He felt like an old man, he mused sadly.

"Morning, General, sir," MacDonald piped enthusiastically.

Lockett looked up and saw General Rosecrans and his aide at the tent opening. Sore back or not, he stiffened into his best salute.

"As you were, Lieutenant," Rosecrans acknowledged. "My aide told me that you had returned and with a harrowing tale. You'll have to tell me about it when this battle is done."

"Yes, sir."

As Lockett said that, a courier trotted up to the tent and dismounted. Behind him, Lockett could see another rider about a quarter mile out speeding in this direction also.

The first rider bounced from the saddle and saluted. "General McCook's compliments, sir, and I have a message. His forces are engaged, and he requests reinforcements, sir."

"Excellent, excellent," Rosecrans turned to his aide. "I could hear it underway, but it is hard to say how well engaged they are. I told McCook that I wanted a spirited demonstration, and it sounds like that is underway. That should draw Bragg's focus from our real target, a nasty left hook is coming for his jaw.

Excellent, *excellent*." He drew out each syllable of the last word with flourish to demonstrate his satisfaction.

"And reinforcements, sir?"

"For McCook? No, no. He is just over-reacting a little, probably wants some more men so that he can turn his demonstration into a full-fledged attack. Beat the left hook to Murfreesboro. No, he needs those not, just a General with the usual demand of more, more, more."

As he finished saying that, the second rider rode up and dismounted. He too saluted quickly.

"Lieutenant White, sir. Captain Otis from the 4th Cavalry sends me, sir. I'm sorry to report, sir, but the right flank is smashed, sir. They're broken, sir. The enemy is driving them back."

Rosecrans sighed and shook his head slowly.

The milquetoast reaction was not the one that Lieutenant White was expecting. He wondered if the General heard him correctly. He was about to repeat the message, so certain was he that the General did not hear him.

"Nonsense," Rosecrans said. "Tell Captain Otis to hold his position like the others. It is just a demonstration that we launched to draw the Rebel's attention."

"Sir?"

"Lieutenant White," Rosecrans said with unusual patience for a general, "This is General McCook's courier. He arrived shortly before you did. The demonstration is underway. McCook would have told me if something so dire as 'smashed' or 'broken' had occurred."

General Rosecrans looked at McCook's courier. "Tell General McCook to contest every inch of ground. As he holds them, we will swing into Murfreesboro with our left and cut them off." He looked over at his aide. "It's working," he reassured.

* * *

McManus knew that he needed to head east to rejoin his regiment, but that was easier said than done. He could tell that he was actually caught up in the flow that went northward, pushed and pursued by various Confederate brigades.

It was a chaotic mess. Thousands of blue coated men streamed north, many fleeing at top speed, without their arms or any regard for anything other than pure survival. Other small groups, company sized not even regiment sized, stopped in their fleeing to take up positions behind fences or farmhouses, but the stands were brief affairs where the outcome was fully predictable. These little bands would halt momentarily, fire off a few rounds, but then the crushing mass of Confederate brigades would near, and then the Federals would sprint off without any order to flee the next crushing volley.

The confusion was further exacerbated by the fact that the attacking brigades were not always appearing from the expected direction. Some elements seemed to have gotten behind even the rapidly fleeing Union right flank. A few Confederate horse soldiers also swept in, and in the confusion and desperation, many Yankees fled directly into the on-coming Confederates infantry brigades.

Despite the nearly irresistible flow northward, McManus decided to break away and head in a more easterly direction. His mind told him that it would be wiser to go north. He was one man and on his own, and there was no telling when a group of Rebels, infantry or cavalry, would sweep up unseen and capture him, especially if he went east instead of north.

But he was compelled to do the unwise. He had to get back to Daniel. He owed it to his dead friend, James. James had done all he could to protect that younger brother. Now who would watch out for him since James was dead? He had to get back there.

So like a man trying to wade against a strong river current, he broke from the flow and started to head more to the right.

Ten minutes later, as he tried to dash back into the next cluster of trees, praying that there were no Confederates already waiting there, he saw an entire brigade of Confederates across the pasture just south of him. Oddly, they were stopped, waiting and unengaged. There were no tents there to pillage, so all that McManus could figure was that they had expended all their ammunition already and were waiting for the ammunition train to be brought up.

Not willing to linger, he hurried even more quickly through the woods.

Fifteen minutes later, he angled slightly northwards when he saw a line of about 200 men crouched below a line of brush in an otherwise open pasture. It took a moment for it to register that they were wearing blue and facing southeasterly, anticipating something from that direction.

From beyond them, McManus saw ammunition wagons spurring frantically forward from the south west. Dumbfounded, he watched the ammunition wagons quickly getting closer to the waiting blue line. Both sides were oblivious to the presence of the other. Finally, the Yankees realized that something was coming.

Astoundingly though, the blue line of men bolted from their position and ran from the scene at full speed as the misguided Confederate ammunition wagons chased them from their positions.

With demoralization that severe, McManus decided that he had better hurry onto Daniel all the more.

* * *

Ambrose Tucker rode along slowly behind General Cleburne's men. He was ready to carry any messages back to the generals that were required, but he really hoped for a chance to ride wildly forward with the advancing infantry.

He had already seen General McCown and his men sweep away the Yankee flank like mere dust. Their shots and shouts were now far into the distance. Besides the fact that he was not riding along, enjoying the rout with them, the only thing wrong was that they had advanced so quickly that General Cleburne's men, who expected to be in a second line behind McCown, actually found themselves in a new front line, headed in a slightly different direction as it turned out.

When they had butted against Yankees, that shock had stunned and slowed them, but only momentarily. Regrouping, they outnumbered and outflanked the Yankees whose right hand brigades had already fled the field.

Ambrose Tucker's reverie was broken by the sudden thunder erupting from the dark woods that had concealed the next batch of Yankees. The woods were so thick and the volley fire so compact, that there was an instant shroud of gray smoke. Even though the Yankees were only yards away, he could not see any individuals, just flashes in the darkened cedars.

It took a number of bloody moments, but Cleburne's right hand units were not deterred despite their losses. They gathered themselves while the left hand regiments moved to flank the Yankee position.

The Yankees were equally stubborn, Tucker mused, but the outcome was as inevitable as all of the previous ones.

It took near twenty minutes, but the Yankee flank fell back, exposing the next Yankee brigade in the line to the same inevitable fate.

* * *

Daniel looked off towards the flank. The sounds were coming closer and closer, but he still saw no Rebels coming.

"Don't worry, Daniel," Bosworth said. "Woodruff and his men are still there. I know those Illinois boys. They won't run so easy from a fight."

Daniel nodded absently at him. He wanted to believe him.

"Now, what we need to do is watch our front and don't let any Rebels split between our brigades."

Minutes later, Daniel blinked as the first butternut line appeared across the way. The Rebels were here.

An Alabama state flag waved dramatically three hundred yards away, across the empty cornfield. After redressing their lines, the Alabamians stepped off and headed towards the Yankees that they could see, Woodruff's brigade.

The Illinoisans waited behind a fence line on a low ridge, backed by another thick growth of cedars.

A Rebel yell rose triumphantly from the butternut line as it slogged across the wet field, awkwardly making a right wheel to bring them in better alignment to the waiting Yankees. The yell rose up again, but it did not stir the waiting Yankees.

"Hold your fire until we give the word," Colonel Blair said from behind him. He moved cautiously over the ankle and knee twisting limestone ridges, going the length of the line, repeating himself.

To Daniel, it was an unnecessary order. The Rebels were not in range yet and were heading for Woodruff anyway.

"He's right, Daniel. Make sure you wait til I tell you."

When Daniel looked questioningly at him, Bosworth continued, "They don't see us in here, Daniel. They think it is just Woodruff. Damn fools or damn arrogant, not sure which. That's just one brigade there. We can give them a good thrashing." He smacked a fist into his hand, but the sound was drowned out by the eruption of fire in the cornfield.

The ridgeline rained smoke and fire, and the butternut line shuddered to a stop. Men fell dead or writhing as the lead balls crashed into their previously unbloodied lines.

Stalled, the Confederate line returned fire at the Yankees behind the fence on the ridge.

Daniel found himself staring in shock at the parallel lines of fire. Back and forth, back and forth.

The air crackled and thundered. He felt himself trembling and clenched his leg to steady himself.

In the angle between Woodruff's and Sill's men, a battery of Union artillery added to the din. To Daniel, it seemed that the air itself was alive and buffeting him.

His heart pounded in his ears, mixing with the sharper cracks of weaponry. He tried to lick his dry lips, but his tongue had no moisture.

The volleys continued to pour forth from the two sides, and he again tried to lick his dry lips. He thought that he should look over at Bosworth, hoping that the sight of the steady veteran would give him some stability too. He was breathing hard and felt incredibly dizzy.

As he turned his head, he realized that Milton Bosworth was already looking at him, studying him. Embarrassed, Daniel looked away quickly, back to the battle that continued. Wide-eyed, he continued to stare into the cornfield where more and more butternut forms lay crumbled on the ground.

Finally, a gruff hand shook him by the shoulder. It was only then that he realized that something was going on amidst the limestone ribs. Sergeants rousted men from their scattered positions and tried to form their companies into lines.

General Sill, his aide, and Colonel Blair walked right past him.

"Make sure that they hear the recall," General Sill was saying to Colonel Blair as they passed by.

Daniel did not know what that meant exactly.

"We will be vigorous but not foolhardy," Sill continued as they walked away.

Daniel watched them go. The general was about as handsome of a man as there was. So young, and a general! He was the true depiction of what a hero should look like. Even more amazing, Daniel realized, most of Sill's men would agree with that. From what little Daniel had seen so far, officers like General Sill were few and far between. He was admired and respected by both the men and the other officers.

"Stick by me," Bosworth interrupted in his ear, rather loudly.

"Stick by you?"

Bosworth nodded.

"I'm not goin' run off, Sergeant."

That wasn't what Bosworth had intended to mean, and the snappish response gave him a pause. "Just stay close and don't do anything stupid. I owe your brother that much at least."

Before Daniel could make any response, he heard cries of "forward" and "double quick" echo around him. He felt himself propelled forward. Out of the trees, Sill's Brigade came surging across the cornfield.

The sight of the counter-attacking blue uniforms caused the Union artillery to stop, but oddly, the Alabamians seemed oblivious to the approaching danger from their flank. It was only after they were well within the range of the Yankee rifles that the right hand parts of the Confederate line noticed the threat.

"Now!" the officer near Daniel yelled. A terrific ripping and tearing sound shook the air around him as the brigade loosed its volley. Caught off guard, Daniel now raised his own weapon and fired. He did not look for a target, but he aimed into the cloud of smoke and fired his first shot. The rifle kicked back into his shoulder painfully, and he stared into a cloud of smoke.

A cheer went up from the ridgeline. Through a gap in the smoke, he realized what the cheer was for. The Rebels line staggered backward over its own dead and wounded. Many Alabamians turned and ran with no shame back across the cornfield for the safety of the trees beyond.

Additional shots chased them back as Sill's men reloaded and fire again. A few bold ones started to run forward, eager to chase some of the retreating Rebels, only to be held back by their officers and sergeants.

Daniel stared for a moment longer, and then reached into his cartridge box, knowing that he should be reloading. He looked over his shoulder and saw the approving look on Bosworth's face as the sergeant's practiced hands did the same exercise, just more quickly and deftly. Bosworth nodded at him and then shouldered his weapon, firing off another round into the Rebels.

A few more rounds convinced the rest of the Alabamians of the futility of staying in the cornfield. Daniel watched them hustle off the field. He raised his voice in a cheer with a few more men, though he noticed that Bosworth did not share in the reverie.

He looked questioningly at the older man as the recall was passed down the line. They were to head back to the security of the limestone outcroppings.

Bosworth saw the look on the younger Lockett's face. "Their friends are here now."

"Friends?"

"Tennessee and Texas." He pointed to the distinctive state flags that were on the other end of the cornfield that was now covered with dozens of butternut casualties. "They'll be back once they reorganize."

"But we can still lick them, right?"

Bosworth grinned at the innocence of the question. "If they keep coming piecemeal like that, then for certain. If they press Woodruff and us at the same time, it will be a hot fight."

In the distance, there was the sound of other fighting, but it droned on unrecognized by Daniel. As he settled back into his old spot in the limestone ribbing, his only thought was on the Texans and Tennesseans across the way. When would they come? And in what strength?

It was a shockingly brief matter of minutes before the questions were answered. The red backed flag of Tennessee waved and another brigade launched itself out across the same ground as the Alabamians. With a greater sense of urgency than the first doomed attack, the Rebels quickly marched in line of battle towards Woodruff's ridge. The battery between Woodruff and Sill did not wait this time for the Rebels to near. Immediately, it began sending a hail of solid and percussion shells. The first salvos used timed fuses within the shell, but the gunners had cut the fuses too long. The shots sailed over the line of men and exploded behind them, sending gouts of earth and smoke into the sky, but causing little damage.

That battery was soon joined by another artillery battery further behind Woodruff's right, and its shells screamed in. Their percussion shells exploded upon impact. The muddy ground absorbed some of the explosion, but they too sent all sorts of matter skyward, including one particularly well aimed shot right at the feet of the advancing men. A detached limb arced visibly through the morning mist, but as the earth came raining back to the ground, there was no sign of the men anymore.

Gaps began to appear in the Confederate line. Men recoiled in pain and horror as their limbs were snapped like so many twigs. Others just seemed to disappear, leaving gaps in their well-packed lines of battle.

Daniel himself recoiled at one sight. His eyes had been following the color guard surrounding one of the Tennessee flags. One moment, his eyes saw the color sergeant turn to beckon the men forward. The next moment, he was beheaded by a screaming solid shot that also killed another man ten yards behind him.

And yet somehow, the other Rebels trudged on through the horror. They stepped over the collapsed forms of the Alabamians who still laid in the field. As they did so, Woodruff's line erupted with a rifle volley again. More Tennesseans thrashed and fell to the ground, some dying literally on top of the Alabamians.

It was horrific, but Daniel could not tear his eyes away. It was butchery, sheer butchery. Surely the Rebels must fall back. They must run! Daniel knew that he could not withstand that. How could they?

But they did not run. Heavy losses or not, they actually charged forward, angling for a part of the ridgeline where two cannon were positioned.

Then, they were only twenty yards away from those cannon, and the nearness of the prize spurred a collective banshee yell from the suffering Tennesseans.

The Union gunners turned and fled at full speed. One of the

gunners still carried the large ramrod in his hand.

That handful of Tennesseans had reached their prize, but it was not to be theirs. They were too few in number now. More shots winged into the area, a number of them ricocheting off the barrels of the cannons.

The Rebels tried to trade shots, but it was a one-sided mathematical affair. There were not enough of them anymore. Three companies of Union troops counterattacked, and in less than a minute the cannon were back in Union hands. Only a few Rebel soldiers were able to hop the fence and sprint away... back to the maelstrom of the cornfield.

The attack was broken.

The survivors staggered back across the cornfield to the tree line where yet more regimental flags were appearing. Even once they had made it back to the relative safety of the trees, the Union artillery sent more shells cracking like giant hammer blows into the woods.

Woodruff's men had won again, but Daniel had seen enough today to know that it would not be long until this was repeated. For every Rebel regiment that they destroyed in the cornfield, another two seemed to appear in the trees behind it.

Chapter 45

Prosper T. Rowe continued to listen to the sounds of battle, and he did not like it.

For the past half hour, what started as a trickle of men flowing from the south was now a steady stream. Some were wounded, or bringing wounded comrades to the now fully hectic field hospital, but some had no physical injuries.

Doctors ignored those men and worked with cold efficiency as the wounded were brought into the small two story farmhouse. Patients were carried into the building and then back out, placed in the field around the house, usually still alive but not always.

The pile of limbs beneath the second floor window was growing at a steady pace.

Frazzled orderlies struggled to bring some order into what seemed a haphazard process.

Forty minutes ago, the army had also drafted Clarissa into their service to fetch continuous pails of water from the nearby well. When one of the orderlies, a particularly harsh-looking and grizzled one, had come and told Clarissa/Charlie to start fetching water, it was clear that he expected instant obedience. It was not a request. When Charlie had looked at Prosper, who was still quietly sitting by, that had only enraged the orderly. With his face in a hateful scowl, he swore viciously and made it clear that he held Charlie and his people responsible for the death and carnage that surrounded him. For a moment, it seemed certain that he would strike Charlie, but a soft word from Prosper averted that.

"It's all right, Charlie," Prosper said, "Fetch them some water. I'll be right here. You can check on me a little later."

But now, Prosper wished that Charlie would reappear from the latest water run.

The stream of refugees was larger than anything he had ever

seen before.

Far too many were wide-eyed and consumed with fear, like panicked horses. There were always some like that at every battle, but this was different.

As they bolted past the wounded, many of them told of a horrible rout that was underway and warned those in the hospital to flee now, that the Rebels would be there in a matter of minutes.

Something was not right, Prosper knew. Where was Charlie?

Finally, the youth appeared. Despite the cold temperatures, Charlie was perspiring heavily. Prosper watched him draw near, his bony shoulders sagging under the weight of the twin pails of water.

"Charlie," Prosper beckoned, sitting up a little higher. He waved frantically, worried that Charlie would not see him.

Clarissa obediently veered her course so that she would pass by him. As she reached him, she gratefully set down the splashing water and breathed a sigh of relief.

"Charlie, I need you to do something," he said as another crackle of musketry sounded again. It was too close, he thought to himself. It was definitely closer than earlier this morning.

She nodded, and he continued. "When you drop those pails off, you see that crutch by the side of the house?"

She looked over at the chaotic farmhouse. Bleeding men were sprawled all over the front step so that the orderlies had to carefully avoid tripping over them as they brought men into and out of it. With all the activity, it took her a moment to spy the solitary crude wooden crutch propped absently against the house.

"Yes, I see it."

"Fetch it, and don't let anyone stop you. Bring it straight here."

She looked blankly at him. "Why?" And then she decided that perhaps he needed to go into the woods to relieve himself, the privacy of which seemed an unnecessary chore given the other sights and smells that were going on around here.

"Just fetch it and bring it straight here. Now hurry."

Obediently, she went on her way.

As Charlie went away, slowly since he struggled with the pails of water, Prosper wished that he had told the boy to leave the pails behind and hurry, but he did not want to panic the boy. As Charlie continued towards the house, Prosper scooted over to where his rifle and cartridge box were. Even the slight jarring sent bolts of pain through his leg and up his back, but he ignored it and proceeded to load the rifle, just in case.

Though he did not want to panic the boy, Prosper felt some himself. Something was wrong. The sounds of battle were coming ever closer... and quickly. They were leaving now while they still could. For once, he believed the shirkers.

* * *

James Lockett prepared to depart from General Rosecrans's headquarters. As best as he could figure from Octavius and the one member of Rosecrans's staff who was willing to talk to him, Colonel Blair and the others were in the center of the line. They were probably already engaged in this demonstration that was critical to the General's plan of bringing an unseen left hook into the town of Murfreesboro.

He was glad that he had listened to MacDonald and eaten the meal that the Pinkerton had brought for him. He had not eaten well since leaving Anna behind in Murfreesboro. Aunt Molly had fed him well. He prayed that Anna and Aunt Molly would be safe as Rosecrans's plan for the battle moved in that direction, but he could already see in his mind's eye the shells tearing into the prosperous, manicured town. And then there were the soldiers themselves.

Lockett had seen the strength of the townsfolk's convictions when John Hunt Morgan had brought the prisoners from Hartsville through town. He could imagine their defiant reaction to an invading blue army. He hoped that Anna and Aunt Molly steered well clear of that, but it would be a chaotic and dangerous time in that town. He knew how soldiers could be once they were locked into the bloodlust of fighting. Plus, they would not be sure of friend or foe. Tragedy was sure to occur.

These dark thoughts continued to fasten their roots ever deeper into his brain. One moment, his only desire was to rejoin Colonel Blair. He needed to find Daniel, Patrick, and the others. The next moment, he started to wonder if he should find his way into this 'left hook', if only to give him a chance to protect Anna from his own invading army.

He was so lost in conflicted misery that he did not notice General Rosecrans heading towards him.

But Rosecrans was not coming to see Lockett, rather he was meeting the rider in the distance, who was galloping hurriedly to them. As the General passed him, Lockett turned and watched.

The older man's ruddy face tried to look impassive and calm, but Lockett saw the flicker of impatience, impatience for news of what was going on.

At that point, General Rosecrans must have realized that he looked anxious, so he drew himself to a stop and waited for the rider to make his way into camp. Eventually, the rider was pointed in his direction, and he dashed on foot over to the waiting commander.

"General, sir!" the courier saluted, "I have a report from General Johnson."

When he added nothing else, General Rosecrans frowned, "Well, get on with it, man."

"Yes, sir. Sorry to report, sir, that General Willich has been captured." The messenger paused, expecting some reaction, but little was forthcoming.

"I see, never mind that. We must win this fight. And the battle?"

"General Johnson reports that he is heavily engaged with a full division, maybe two. He requests reinforcements."

"I think your general exaggerates the scale. Surely, there is not a full division on the flank, much less two. Tell him to maintain his position and contest every inch. If he is facing such strength, all the better for our attack on the left. Dismissed, soldier."

Rosecrans turned and walked back in the other direction. Looking up, he saw Lockett standing nearby. "Lieutenant Lockett, still here I see."

"Yes, sir. I was about to leave."

"Walk with me a moment, if you will."

Obediently, Lockett followed at the general's shoulder. For a minute, the general said nothing, and they walked along in an awkward silence. The older man was clearly deep in thought.

Being a general was a lonely business, Lockett decided as they tramped along. The waiting for information from various quarters, the complete reliance on others to follow through with plans or react as needed… It would require a patience that Lockett knew he did not have.

Abruptly, the General stopped and looked Lockett in the eye. "My apologies, young man."

"Sir?"

"I misaddressed you. I said 'Lieutenant', but I do believe that the arrangement was that you would return a Captain. It's Captain Lockett now."

Lockett looked at him, visibly flummoxed. He nearly blurted out that Colonel Wilks denied the captaincy due to his tardiness, but instead, he said nothing. When the General continued to look at him, Lockett replied, "No apology necessary, sir. None at all."

"Very good, Captain." The General then turned away, scanning the vacant distance. He spoke up as if he was only talking to himself. "That river beyond," he started and paused. "It should not be taking us so long to cross that infernal Stones River. Our left hook should be further advanced by now… but I suppose we are finally across those fords in the numbers required. It won't be long now. Not long at all."

Uncomfortable in this next pause, Lockett made no reply. He wasn't sure if he should mutter some sort of agreement or just remain quiet. He finally decided that he should voice some sort of confirmation with the general, though he did not know what value his opinion would really have. Then the general startled him by turning to face him again.

"You have a horse, correct, Captain Lockett?"

"Yes, sir."

"Good. Stay in camp a while longer before you rejoin your comrades. They've survived this long without you. They can surely manage a little while longer, and I may need another messenger later." He looked Lockett up and down, and he added. "In the meantime, find my steward. Tell him that I want him to find you a proper uniform. This army can't have its captains walking around in a plain private's uniform."

* * *

Milton Bosworth toed the thin strip of dirt between the

limestone ribbings. "If I had a spade, we could make this deeper."

Where he and Daniel waited, the limestone was about waist high. "It's good ground to kill Rebs for sure and certain, but it could be even better." When Daniel said nothing, he added, "We could use our hands, but the soil here is so rocky, it would be a waste of strength."

He looked over at Daniel who leaned his side against the stone. The channel between the two ribbings was so narrow that it was not possible lean his back against it. "Just make sure that you're on a knee when you reload," the sergeant advised.

Daniel shifted stiffly. He wished that he could spread his legs out in front of him and lean back against something, not one or the other. It seemed perverse to him that it was scarcely eight o'clock in the morning. It felt like it should already be well past noon.

He looked around him. The men from the company were scattered into their positions in the limestone. Levi Thickle and John Messern squatted in a similar trench to his front right. Sam Baker lounged on the flat limestone table. He laughed at something that Messern said, or maybe he was laughing at Thickle. Either way, he seemed ridiculously relaxed to Daniel's mind.

Further to the right, he saw Lieutenant Renaud walking behind his French Detroiters, chatting with them to relieve the tension. The lieutenant saw Daniel looking at him and nodded.

Behind him, Daniel saw mostly men from another regiment, but there were some of theirs mixed in as well. Vaught was one of those men. He sat atop a section of limestone, his rifle across his lap.

Absently, Daniel wondered what Vaught would be like in this battle. Was he as nervous as Daniel felt at this moment? He was near the back of their position. It would be easier to run from there, he speculated.

Daniel let the thought slip from his brain. It was not his problem. He had enough to worry about with keeping his own cowardice in check. Instead, he concentrated on their position.

As good as the position was in the limestone trenches, they were not in the straight lines like an army engineer would design. These were designed by Mother Nature, and they criss-crossed and staggered such that once the shooting started, some of the men in the back would be shooting over or around their own comrades. Milton was right, he thought, he would really need to keep his head down, and not just for the Johnnies' lead!

There was a murmuring of commotion that brought Daniel's attention back to the front.

From his right, at the edge of the woods, two men from the 88th Illinois, who were posted there to watch for signs of movement, came scurrying back.

"They're readying their lines across the cornfield again," one of them said, dashing up to his Colonel.

"Not long now," Bosworth said to Daniel.

"They're going to try to cross that cornfield again?" Daniel asked.

"We can only hope we're so lucky."

Seconds later, the sound of firing started again, but this time, it was not from Woodruff and the cornfield to the right of Sill's Brigade. This time, it was a frontal assault on Sill's position in the wooded limestone trenches.

From the tree line in front of them, the smattering of the skirmisher fire started. A crack here, a bang there... Then the Yankee skirmishers were hurrying back to the safety of the main line.

Bosworth knew what that meant. With only that little skirmishing before rushing back to the relative safety of the main line, it meant that the enemy was coming in force.

"Not long now, Daniel," he repeated.

Oddly, Daniel could sense the veteran soldier's tension, and the fact that someone like the sergeant could be nervous actually calmed his own nerves.

"Just make sure that you wait until you hear the command. And aim low. Make every shot count." Bosworth then snorted. "You know who I sound like? I sound like your brother, God rest his soul. A quiet man, but a devil in a fight that he was..."

But Daniel's attention was on the front edge of the woods. They had let the Confederates cross the thin strip of open land in front of the woods unmolested, and the first butternut forms started to appear amongst the trees.

"Wait for the command!" Daniel heard someone hiss.

More Confederates appeared directly behind the first, but

unlike the attack on the cornfield, these men were not in line of battle. They were in a column. To Daniel this meant nothing, but many of the officers recognized the opportunity.

They let the Rebels advance deeper. Daniel was ready to fire, anxious to let that rifle kick back into his shoulder, anxious to slow that advance. They were well within range now.

"We will fire by echelon!"

Daniel heard the first order ring out, but it was subsequently repeated down the line.

More seconds went by, and more Rebels pushed deeper into the woods. They were nearing the limestone ribbings now.

"Fire!"

Daniel heard the distant call from his left. Soldiers from the 24th Wisconsin fired in unison.

In the Rebel column, the first row of soldiers was obliterated.

A second after the Wisconsinites loosed hell upon the unsuspecting Rebels, the 36th Illinois did the same. The next rows of Rebels tumbled and thrashed. The dead hit the ground with unheard thuds amidst the raging noise. The Confederate rows immediately behind looked on in horror as they were doused with their comrades' blood and brain matter.

But the momentum of the column pushed them from behind. Some Rebels were already tripping over the bodies at their feet when Blair's regiment wiped away yet another row.

Daniel felt the sting of the rifle kick, but he was already squatting to reload, mindful of Milton's advice.

There were only a few shots in return from the Confederate column. It was then that even the inexperienced like Daniel realized the precarious position that the Rebel general had placed his own men in.

By approaching in column, only the few rifles in the front of the column could fire, the back rows would have to wait for fear of hitting their own men.

But the Union positions were in a line of battle. Every man could fire into the column. It was simple arithmetic. However deep the Confederate position might be in men, they were hopelessly outgunned by the line of Union soldiers.

The 88th Illinois added to the slaughter, and seconds later, the quickest reloaders of the Wisconsin men were already hitting the column again.

Men hurried to reload, worried that they had let the column advance too close before opening up. In their haste, many sent the next round of shots high, over the heads of the Confederates, showering them with branches and dead leaves but little more.

Regardless, the sledgehammer blows of the echelon fire had brought the column to a shuddering halt. The men in the front of the column tried to dig in their feet, but the mass of humanity behind them pushed them forward slowly. A few tried to return fire, but the Yankee line that they faced seemed to be firing from everywhere. More men went down. A few tried to scatter to the sides, which only opened up a new rank of butternut soldiers to receive the hail of minié balls.

For a short time, this grotesque dance continued with the dead piling upon each other. Finally, the ranks further back in the Confederate column realized the horror that must be going on in front. The column wavered for a moment, and then many started to flee.

"On them, boys!"

It was General Sill himself. He leapt upon a limestone table, waving his sword for the men to counter-attack.

"Drive them!"

A guttural, excited roar erupted from the brigade. It was not like the shrieking banshee Rebel yell, somehow it was deeper. But it was just as ominous and effective at that moment.

Enthusiastically, men jumped up. The limestone ridges were knee and ankle twisting traps that slowed them at first, but they were quickly after the stunned Rebels who were now fleeing in a panic without any cohesion.

Daniel jumped from one limestone table and ridge to the next, nimbly sliding across a slick one. Soon, he found himself in the front of General Sill's charge. He yelled wildly, his voice mixing in with the mass of others.

Quickly, he was at the slaughter point were so many rows of Southerners had died over the top of each over. He skirted the pile of death. Most of the Rebels in his vision were running back now, tripping over each other in self-preservation, but one Rebel had paused behind a tree to shoot at the charging blue coats. Daniel raised his rifle to fire, but before he could, the man's head exploded into a red mist. So instead, he redirected his aim to the fleeing mass. When he squeezed the trigger, there was no stinging kick in his shoulder. Realizing that he had not reloaded after the previous shots, he paused for a second. Other blue coats dashed by him, yelling like fiends.

Unconcerned about his empty rifle, Daniel ran after them, motivated by some unknown reason to be in the front of the charge.

More Rebels scattered in front of them. Surrounded, the demoralized Southerners dropped their guns and raised their hands. Without a wasted breath, the blue coats were upon them. One Federal fired his weapon at a surrendering man who crumpled to his knees and clutched his abdomen. The other blue coats swung rifle butts and jammed the stocks of their weapons into the defenseless faces of the butternut gaggle.

The men in butternut went down in a heap, and the beating continued. Without thinking about it, Daniel joined in, slamming his rifle butt against the ear of a man cowering on the ground.

But more bluecoats were passing him, and he ran after them, leaving the bloodied and battered Rebels to be collected by someone else.

They were out of the trees now, and the counter attack continued across the stretch of open ground. Just feet ahead and to his right, Daniel saw General Sill himself slashing at the air to encourage the men forward.

The Rebels were in full flight now. Many had already made it to the trees beyond, but it did not seem that they had stopped there. There were only a handful of shots from the cedars at the rampaging Yankees.

Another guttural yell rose up from the bluecoats. They were going to push their counter attack all the way through. Daniel saw the color guard of some Rebel regiment near the tree line, and a chorus of shots brought the men down. Their colorful flag dipped in the dying man's hands and then fell grudgingly to the ground.

He had sudden visions of taking the Rebel colors! They would be within his reach in seconds at this rate.

He could see that General Sill, who was still just ahead of him, had seen this also. The General started to point his sword in the direction of the colors, when his head snapped back violently.

The sword fell from his lifeless hand, and General Sill dropped straight on his back, dead before he hit the ground.

A regiment of bugles or a battery of canister loaded artillery could not have had a greater effect on the Federal counter-attack.

Many men, not just Daniel, must have been looking at their beloved young General at that moment. Instantly, the attack stopped in its tracks. For a moment, there was an eerie, echoing silence ringing in Daniel's ears, even though he felt the zip zip of minié balls near his own head. He stood dumbfounded at what he had seen, his eyes disbelieving.

"Back! Back!"

No one ever knew who shouted the first words, but they were all thinking it, and immediately, the attack ended. Men were dashing back for the safety of the limestone.

When they reached their own tree line, the commanding voices of the regimental commanders were waiting for them, ordering them to take up their old positions.

Chapter 46

Patrick tried to make his way back east, but try as he might, he kept finding his course being more northerly. Some of it was to avoid the Rebel skirmishers or cavalry that blocked his way, but more often than not, it was just a feeling that compelled him to head north.

He wanted to get back to Daniel so badly. He owed it to James to do that, but the fear was overwhelming him.

He had been through Shiloh, through Perryville, through countless skirmishes, but he had never felt fear like this. Before there had been others to rely on; there had been others around who needed him to put on a fearless face.

But now... Now, he was alone. He had never felt so utterly alone. Any moment, he could stumble across even a small handful of skirmishers and be unable to defend himself. He didn't know what was worse: the idea of being taken and dragged off to a Southern prison or the idea of dying here alone in some field in Tennessee.

The fear weakened his legs and loosened his bowels. The rifle that he carried felt heavier and heavier. He was sorely tempted to drop it altogether, but then he thought of James. He might not be here with him, but he would be looking on from above, and he would not approve of that degree of cowardice. Solemnly, he clutched the weapon against his chest and continued on, redoubling his effort to at least head northeast.

* * *

Daniel rubbed a hand against his face. Was his face as blackened by powder as Milton's? The man looked like he had crawled out of a chimney.

It was only a lull, but the last Rebel attack had left his ears ringing. Lieutenant Renaud was only feet away from him, but his French-tinged voice sounded distant.

"Corp'l Bouillard, you z'ere, take z'ose men, be'cos we need to gather ze cartridges from ze dead." With his revolver, he pointed at the death pile of Rebels.

"That's a good idea," Bosworth muttered, wishing that Lieutenant Lockett was here. Bosworth bemoaned the fact that he was just a sergeant. These types of things often did not occur to him, not fast enough anyway.

Captain Bibb had been killed seconds into the latest attack. One moment, Bibb had been walking behind them, mostly drunk, but still encouraging the men. Then the next set of Rebels had appeared through the thin woods, and Bibb had leapt up onto a limestone table and whirled his revolver in the air, yelling something incomprehensible. The next moment, two shots hit him simultaneously, one in the foot and the other in the heart.

He had been a sorry excuse for a captain, Bosworth lamented, but he was still an officer, and the sergeant sorely felt the burden now. There were no more officers in their shrinking company, and technically, he was in charge. He looked at Renaud and echoed the Detroiter's orders. "All of you, check your cartridges."

Then in a louder voice, he yelled, "Baker, Thickle, Perkins! You men there, make your way up yonder to those dead ones, and bring their ammunition back."

Daniel could scarcely believe how quickly the Rebels had followed up that first attack with a second.

It had only been a matter of minutes from General Sill's fatal charge to the next Rebel attack. The follow up attack had not been in column, rather they had come in the line of battle that time. The firing had been continuous, and he felt deafened by the unceasing cracks and bangs as the two sides had hammered each other in the lightly wooded forest. Shot and smoke had obscured their vision, but the two sides still fired blindly into the fog. The limestone ribbings were proving to be a very defensible position though.

Between the fire of Sheridan's infantry and the percussive shells of the artillery lobbed into the flanks of the long Confederate line of battle, the Southerners had been forced to retreat once more.

So again, their corner of the battle was at a brief respite. However, the cost of the stubbornness was all around Daniel now. The dead Rebels were sprawled throughout his front, and it was plain to see that their own losses were heavy as well. There were blue coated, crumpled forms sunk down in the limestone ribbings; others lay collapsed face down or flat on their back atop the limestone tables. Their lifeless eyes saw no more. He recognized many of the faces who were now victims of the merciless war. Gordon, Payton, Riggs, Beall, and many others who had made that march from Detroit with him, plus a score of other Blair men...

Next to him, Milton Bosworth watched the party collect cartridge boxes from the dead. They would need every round. The rate of fire had been faster than Daniel had imagined doing it. His brother had drilled the company to fire and reload in fifteen second increments. He had told them that their ability to keep up a fast rate of fire would be the difference between living and dying someday. Today was proving him correct, Daniel thought grimly.

The downside of that, however, was that they would need more ammunition eventually.

Daniel rubbed his face unconsciously. The latest wave of fear had washed over him for now. It was strange. He had felt little fear when they counter-attacked and charged the fleeing Rebels, but standing toe-to-toe with them, he had felt the fear rising in him at times. It was only the practiced regimen of reloading and firing, reloading and firing that kept the fear from overcoming him, he thought. He wondered if that was what it had been like for James at Shiloh. Looking from on high, he hoped that his brother was proud of him. He was not running; he was fighting; he was preserving the family honor.

He wished that James could have lived to see this moment.

* * *

Ambrose Tucker watched the two Confederate generals argue and complain about their lot. All across the battlefield, the Yankees were in full flight. It was only this stubborn knot of blue bellies that was slowing them down.

Multiple attacks had failed on the position to this point, and the two generals complained that it was the Yankee artillery that had doomed every attack. There were two Yankee batteries situated about 600 feet apart and supported by infantry. One battery was positioned behind the line on an open ridge near a brick kiln. The other was in the trees farther east. They were arranged so devilishly that an attack on one position exposed the attacker's flank to the other battery and vice versa.

It was patently obvious to Ambrose Tucker what should happen, but it took the debating generals much longer to come to his conclusion. Each battery should be attacked simultaneously. They had the men to do so.

However, the execution of such proved to be another matter. The timing had been off as well as the communication. For some reason, the attacking Tennesseans thought that the cannon in the trees were theirs, not Yankees. Rather than returning fire or charging the guns, their colonel ordered them to lie down in the field while he hopelessly tried to signal the artillery that they were shooting at their own men.

He tried to send individual officers forward to tell the cannon to cease, but they were killed. Even then, the Tennessean leader maintained a belief that they were Confederate guns, not Yankees. It was not until a solitary sergeant took it upon himself to demonstrate to his commanders that they were horrifically wrong. Seizing the Rebel flag from the color guard, he ran forward boldly waving the banner back and forth.

Shells followed him, exploding and sending spouts of earth into the sky and shards of shrapnel screaming in all directions, yet the sergeant somehow survived and moved on. More shells followed. By then, it was clear even to the Tennessean commander that he had been mistaken. They were Yankee guns after all!

Rising from the ground, the regiments opened fire on the battery. The zip of minié balls was a swarm of angry wasps down upon the gunners. Many were slaughtered at their posts, but the remainder stayed on, grimly reloading their pieces. They knew that their survival depended upon it. The Confederates anxiously reloaded and then charged forward.

Ambrose Tucker watched with satisfaction as the attack hit home with a vengeance. The ground was covered with dead Yankee gunners and at least 80 horses.

The fighting continued in seemingly every direction. With their flank finally freed, the Rebels were able to start flanking the brigade of Yankee infantry on the small ridge behind the cornfield. Rebel infantry also pressed again at the lightly wooded area where Ambrose had heard that the Yankees were positioned behind rows of low limestone rocks.

It had taken time, but they were finally getting the upper hand on this one resistant part of the battlefield. If they could drive off this one last sector in a panicked flight, then the day would be theirs.

The Yankee army in middle Tennessee would be forever crippled.

* * *

"So 'Captain,' is it now?" Bobby MacDonald said cheerfully to Lockett, who paced nearby in his new captain's uniform, complete with a new holster and revolver.

Lockett frowned at him. The man's cheerfulness irked him at this moment. The distant thunder of the guns seemed closer and more ominous to him now. It could well be his imagination, he knew, but it had rekindled his impatience to find Daniel and the others.

"I need to find my regiment," he said sourly.

"Could you really find them so easily?" MacDonald said, suddenly serious. "It sounds like chaos to me, and that is discounting the messengers coming into camp here. Do you think it is not so bad?"

Lockett paused before answering. "I've never been in headquarters before during a battle. Perhaps from afar, it always sounds like this, but I feel something is wrong, MacDonald. I just feel it."

As he said that, he noticed another rider bolting into camp.

MacDonald noticed him as well. "Let's see what the latest is."

By the time they reached General Rosecrans and the messenger, the messenger was nearly finished. He took a breath and added, "Also, General, I'm sad to report that General Sill has been killed."

A grim mask appeared on Rosecrans's face. Like the others, he had held the young general in high esteem.

Lockett felt his stomach drop. He did not know this General Sill, but he knew from Prosper that Blair's Independent Regiment was in Sill's brigade. If the fighting was so intense that their brigade commander had been killed...

"We cannot help it. Brave men must be killed," Rosecrans said sadly. The general looked at the ground briefly. He re-gathered his confident outlook quickly, but in that flash, those around him could see his uncertainty for the first time that day.

"General, sir," Lockett said, interrupting the mood. "My men are part of Sill's Brigade. I'd like permission to rejoin them. I can take a message if you wish."

Rosecrans looked at him. He seemed about to deny the request, but then he nodded his assent.

"Thank you, sir," Lockett said, already turning to find his horse.

"Captain," Rosecrans then said abruptly, "On second thought, you will accompany me to Sheridan's headquarters. You can find your brigade that way, and I need to see for myself what is happening there."

* * *

Daniel's eyes stung from the smoke that hung in a stale state across the lines. It obscured what he was shooting at, but he kept up his fire nonetheless. The sounds of battle were all around them. The Rebels were pressing his front and his right, where Woodruff's men held the ridge.

There had also been sounds of battle to his left as the Rebels pressured Sheridan's left flank as well.

It was a maelstrom around them. There were unceasing cracks and bangs from rifles. Overhead, there was the peculiar zip zip sound of minié balls slicing through the air. The better aimed shots made their own unique sound as they ricocheted off the limestone. Beneath all that were the low moans and cries of dying men.

He grabbed another paper cartridge from his quickly emptying cartridge box. Using his teeth, he tore open the paper cartridge.

By now the taste of black powder was all that there was in his mouth and nostrils. The powder had long since parched his pallet into an arid condition that he never would have thought possible. He poured the black powder down the muzzle of his rifle, stuffing the lead minié ball in after it. With practiced conditioning, he rammed it down the barrel with the ramrod, not even flinching as another Rebel shot whipped off the rock nearby. He set the ramrod down next to him, rather than re-slotting it beneath the rifle. Lastly, he took the tiny percussion cap from the cartridge box and secured it on the nub beneath the trigger hammer.

Then he peered out into the smoke.

There were other flashes and blooms of gun smoke from the trees where the second Rebel Line had once ventured. Through the clouds, he could not make out distinct forms, but he aimed for the flashes. Squeezing the trigger, the rifle kicked back into his now heavily bruised shoulder.

He did not bother to see the effect. Instead, he dropped to a knee and started the process all over again.

As he dropped to his knee, he felt a wet sensation as he knelt. He looked down to see that he was kneeling in a growing puddle of blood. For a second, he thought that he had been hit, but then he looked further up the limestone trench. The numbers of dead and wounded were growing quickly. Their blood emptied from their bodies and pooled beneath them until it flowed down the slight descent in the trough to where it gathered beneath Daniel.

One corpse stared unseeingly back at Daniel. His front was drenched with more blood than Daniel imagined possible. Another of Renaud's men clenched a hand against his upper chest as more crimson liquid rushed through his fingers. He saw Daniel looking at him and seemed to say something, but the sound was easily lost beneath the rage of the weaponry.

Daniel jerked his eyes away and finished reloading his weapon. The growing residue of black powder caked to the inside of the barrel was making it increasingly difficult for him to ram the projectile all the way down. He rose slightly again and aimed out across at the white-gray haze and fired blindly into it again.

The replies came increasingly quick. A shot thudded solidly into the small tree a few feet behind him. Another clanged off the rock behind him, drawing a shriek of pain.

He dropped back down lower than before and fumbled around in the box for another cartridge, thinking for a second that he had no more, but then his palsied fingers grasped another, and he choked the cry down. He tried to swallow, but there was no moisture in his mouth.

At that moment, an unknown officer came dashing up from behind and splashed down between Daniel and Bosworth.

He looked around for a half-second at the carnage. "It's a Goddamn slaughter pen in here! It's like a Chicago slaughterhouse!"

Bosworth ignored the comment and fired again.

"Sergeant, we are falling back to a new position. Woodruff's been flanked and is falling back. The 36th is out of ammunition and doing the same. Roberts Brigade is setting up a new line of defense just south of Wilkinson Pike."

Bosworth fired another shot into the smoke, and then turned to acknowledge the captain.

"We'll be there," he said.

"In good order, Sergeant! Keep them in good order!"

"Yes, sir." Bosworth looked over at Daniel. "Load now, we go back loaded."

"Blair! Blair!" Bosworth shouted to get their attention.

As he did so, the Chicago captain stood and started to climb over the next limestone barrier to repeat the message. Daniel lowered his head to finish reloading, when amidst the crackling roar of battle, he heard a sharp crack like a dried out branch snapping in two and then a horrific yell, seemingly in his ear.

Startled, he twisted to see the cause of the noise and fell on his buttocks into the blood pool, but he did not feel anything. His eyes gaped wide at the Chicago captain who was still screaming in pain. He was holding his arm at the elbow, but above the elbow, the forearm dangled grotesquely. The bones were snapped in half, and only the sinews held it from dropping to the ground.

He gave loud gasping moans, interspersed with "Oh, God!" He slumped to a sitting position atop the limestone, oblivious to the on-going fusillade around them.

"Take him back," Bosworth ordered Daniel. "I'll let Renaud and the others know that we are falling back."

Numbly, Daniel nodded. The captain swooned, but Daniel

caught him under shoulder. "C'mon on, sir, I'll get you back." He tried to hoist the captain to feet, but the man's legs wobbled, and they both sagged under the weight. Still, Daniel manhandled him back five feet, into the next limestone ribbing.

But the effort was great, and he wondered how he would get the captain over the subsequent rows of rocks. It would be a tricky enough proposition to do alone and in haste, and that was without trying to help the captain. Still, Daniel tried to pull the gasping, sobbing captain up over the next batch of rocks. The hail of fire continued behind them.

He slipped on a bloody patch caused by another Blair company corpse and nearly fell. He landed hard on his knee, and captain pitched forward. Daniel clung tightly to him to prevent the man from falling face first into the rocks. He righted himself and then the captain. They staggered forward, but then the captain was mule-kicked out of Daniel's grasp. He pitched forward and hit the rocks heavily but made no sound and no motion.

Dazed, it took Daniel a second to realize that the captain had been shot again, this time square in the middle of his back. More shots whipped around him. One ricocheted off the rock, just inches from Daniel's foot. Brought back to his senses, he stumbled over to the captain.

"Captain! Captain, sir, can you hear me?"

But the officer gave no reply. When Daniel squatted over him, he saw the all too familiar lifeless stare.

Not sure what to do now, he looked around. The chaos still swirled amidst the smoke. He searched for Bosworth but did not see him. Then he remembered that the sergeant was going to find Renaud, so he looked to where the French Detroiters had been. Sure enough, he saw Bosworth in a crouch next to Renaud.

Without thinking another thought, Daniel bolted in their direction, which was closer to the increasing Rebel fire. He tripped over an unseen piece of limestone and went sprawling across a limestone ridge, rolling and falling into the trough next to Renaud and Bosworth.

Bosworth looked at him blankly. "I thought I told you to take that Captain back."

"I tried. They shot him again. He's dead."

"We are all going back now," Renaud remarked. "We just

need to tell Captain Fulkerham." He pointed to the far left. Fulkerham's men had become more distant from the rest of the company, mostly through attrition and his company's more advanced position in the limestone. "The rest of the regiment has heard the order." He pointed around them, and the men were falling back, all with the exception of Fulkerham's men.

"I'll tell 'em," Daniel blurted out, as much to his own surprise as to theirs. Before there would be any debate, he ran down the trough to a lower area and then vaulted over the limestone.

"Daniel, wait!" Bosworth yelled, but it was too late to stop him.

Daniel ran quickly and nimbly over the limestone furrows like a squirrel crossing from tree to tree. He was only partially aware that the sound of resistance behind him was dying off and that the bulk of the remaining fire was coming from Captain Fulkerham's company, directly ahead of him.

He did not know what had possessed him to volunteer to do this. The words had jumped from his mouth before he could stop it, and once they were out in the open, he knew that he would have to follow through, but his fear was such that he knew the quicker he did it, the better.

He skirted his way past a trio of dead Blair men and hurdled another.

Breathing heavily, he sprinted across the final stretch and slid to a stop next to Captain Fulkerham. Instinctively, Daniel crouched as the minié balls whipped overhead, but Fulkerham seemed to think that he was impervious to them for he stood erect and directed his men as he thought any officer should do.

"Sir!" Daniel said between breaths.

Fulkerham frowned at being addressed by a man on his knee. He contemplated ordering the private to stand when addressing him.

"Sir," Daniel continued, unaware of the frown on the officer's face. "The regiment is falling back to a new position. You are nearly surrounded."

Fulkerham scowled, but then looked around and noticed that the others were falling back.

There was a yelp next to them as another soldier was shot. The man fell back and expired without a second glance from anyone.

Fulkerham looked back at the younger Lockett. He wondered if the younger Lockett knew that there had been no love loss between the boy's brother and himself. But he did not give it a second thought, "Sergeant Holdman!" he yelled.

"Dead, sir," someone yelled back.

"Corporal Walker!"

"Dead!" the same voice replied.

"Company, fall back!" he yelled.

Another crashing fusillade from the Rebels knocked more men back. Fulkerham decided this was not the time for an orderly retreat.

"Everyone! Back, back!"

And Daniel fled the limestone ribbings that had become a true slaughter pen.

Chapter 47

Lockett and the two Pinkertons rode along behind Rosecrans, his staff, and a protective troop of cavalry.

"You sure that you want to ride along?" Lockett wondered aloud, turning to MacDonald.

The short Chicagoan looked even more uncomfortable on a horse than Lockett. He shrugged and tilted awkwardly in the saddle as he did so, taking a hand to press his bowler hat even more firmly onto his head. "No point in waiting by headquarters."

The sounds of the battle were far clearer here and sounding far closer...

They had already seen a number of dazed men in blue going in the opposite direction. A regiment of Indiana infantry tried clumsily to stop the retreating, beaten men.

"Don't worry none, Lieutenant, er, Captain," MacDonald added. "I won't stray too close to the firing."

"Let's just hope that the firing doesn't stray too close to you then," Lockett quipped, trying to hide the unsettled feeling that gurgled within him.

General Rosecrans had stopped and was issuing orders to two of his aides. The aides turned around and galloped off in the opposite direction.

Lockett and the two Pinkertons trotted up to the cadre of staff.

"Where are they off to?" Octavius Matson said to one of the remaining aides.

"New orders for General Thomas and Van Cleve too."

"Really?" Matson said, knowing that both divisions were part of Rosecrans's flanking attack.

"Recalled," the staff officer added, a serious look on his face. "Van Cleve took his good time crossing that ford this morning; he better not do so now when he re-crosses it. They'll be needed here for certain."

There was another barrage of thunder in the distance, and Rosecrans spurred his horse forward through a path in the woods.

From the headquarters camp, the sound of battle had stirred all morning, but only in fits and stops. There had been the distant thunder of guns and even moments of sharp sounding fighting, but there had also been acoustical lulls where nothing was heard. As they rode closer to the right flank, they all realized that the dips in sound had been an auditory mirage. The fighting was continuous.

Lockett feared what he would see as they got closer. Remembrances of the thousands of shirkers hiding below the bluffs after the first day of Shiloh filled his brain.

General Rosecrans urged his steed on with more alacrity. More men fled in the other direction, but the tumult increased exponentially as they burst from the forested trail and into the broad opening.

A horrible sinking feeling consumed Lockett as he stared at the catastrophe.

Union infantry, artillery, and cavalry were flying backwards in inextricable confusion and haste. There was no attempt at order. Officers and the lowliest privates alike were bewitched with a consuming desire to escape.

Some soldiers still carried their rifles as they fled, but many ran away weaponless. Other men were trying to escape by riding bareback on artillery horses that had been cut free from their harnesses. The lead elements of those groups raced past them and into the woods.

"Colonel Knefler!" General Rosecrans shouted at a unit of bewildered, unblooded infantry. "Colonel Knefler!" he shouted again and rode closer to the regiment that watched the fiasco with wide eyed wonder. "Form line and halt those men!"

"Yes, sir," Colonel Knefler said, but his voice betrayed his uncertainty to the task.

"Halt them here. Use your bayonets if you have to!"

Lockett was frozen to inaction by the chaotic vision. He could only stare as more and more men emerged from the woods beyond the broad pasture. There were hundreds and hundreds of men in total flight.

Not all were in a total panic, he realized as he watched the exodus continued. As the stream continued, there was an increasing reminder that some of these men, though panicked and defeated, had not forgotten all of their duties.

Artillery teams raced at dangerous speeds away from the scene. Many teams still had their cannon. One group of gunners rode atop the steeds with two remaining men perilously mounting the bucking cannon like jockeys. As the cannon jolted across the field, Lockett expected at least one of them to be tossed from the cannon with his skull crushed into the mud by the heavy wheels behind him, but none did.

More infantry fled as the stream became a wave. Intermixed among those terrorized waves, there were still brave souls. With their horses killed, a group of gunners was slowly tugging and pushing their own cannon and limber away. Lockett had to admire men like that who could still struggle with those heavy guns when all around them there was the sheer pandemonium to flee the scene.

Rosecrans had ridden off to issue another flurry of orders, but Lockett, the Pinkertons, and a remaining aide all sat stiffly in the saddle watching the debacle.

Men yelling; men weeping; men running away; men limping away... Some carried wounded comrades.

"Just before the General issued that last round of orders, another messenger told him that the Rebels had reached so far that they had even overrun the field hospital," the aide remarked, still stunned at the sight.

A stab of guilt thrust deeply into Lockett's chest. He thought of Prosper and Clarissa. He had told Clarissa that she would be safe there and to stay with Prosper. Good God! He should have had her come with him. He had not even had the opportunity yet to talk to Octavius or Bobby MacDonald about her. He had planned on asking them to help get her to Chicago or someplace north.

Two more horses burst from the trees with another fifty men. One horse was riderless and rode in abject fear, incapable of avoiding some of the men in its path. The other horse dragged its dead, headless rider behind it, his boot trapped in the stirrup.

"By God, is this battle?" MacDonald asked in a dazed voice.

"No, this is defeat!" Lockett answered angrily. The sight was stirring a passion and rage within him.

More and more men emerged from the woods beyond. Some even rode mules cut free from the wagon trains, with two and even three soldiers astride the beasts.

From behind Lockett, another regiment arrived, sent to block the escapees. Seeing Lockett and the others astride their horses, their regimental commander mistook Lockett for a high ranking officer. He did not even look at Lockett. His eyes were locked on the incredible exodus.

"Ninth Michigan, sir. What shall we do? Is all lost?"

There was another resounding crackle of musketry, replied to with an equal barrage and then cannon.

"You hear that? No, someone is still fighting like the devil up there!" Lockett snapped back, "But we need to stop this, this panic. Get your men in line now!"

"But it's a cyclone, sir."

"Then fix bayonets!" Lockett barked.

"Yes, sir," the colonel replied, still not noticing that he was being addressed by a mere captain.

"Bayonets! Bayonets!" The call echoed down the line and the Ninth Michigan hurried into line.

"That stampede stops here!" the colonel yelled.

* * *

Daniel breathed a sigh of relief as he reached the cedars beyond the Wilkinson Pike. This was their third position of the day now. They had held that second position briefly and bloodied another Confederate regiment, but when more of Sheridan's men ran out of ammunition, they were forced back.

But this was no disorderly flight, it was a fighting retreat all the way. Even now, as Bush's battery limbered up and dashed further back, the Confederates filled the opening, only to learn that they had made themselves a target for Houghtalling's battery. The spherical case shot exploded over and among the Rebels. Geysers of earth, smoke, and Rebel blood filled the area. Like a punch drunk fighter, the Rebels lingered in the area and absorbed more punishment for no apparent reason before falling back as their own artillery arrived on the scene. The artillery batteries exchanged fire.

Amongst the thunder, Milton Bosworth leaned close to Daniel. "While they let us catch our breath, how many cartridges do you have?"

"Nine," Daniel replied. "I grabbed every cartridge box off the dead as we retreated. He pointed to the seven boxes at his feet. "But they were all virtually empty too."

Minutes later, two more great gray and butternut lines advanced. The first was pounded by artillery to such a degree that it wavered and then fell back. The second line halted its progress and dropped back as well. The ground smoldered from burning shells, and the fortuneless writhed in agony in the field.

"Whaddaya think?" Levi Thickle said next to them. There was a bloody knot of cloth around his arm, and his hand was jammed inside an open button on his jacket to act as a sling. It had been suggested that he fall back since it took an inordinately long time for him to load his weapon with one hand, but he had responded to the suggestion with language that would have startled his Methodist preacher father.

"Well?" he added belligerently when no one answered. What was left of the company was hopelessly intermixed with Renaud's and Fulkerham's companies now.

It was Renaud who answered. "You as' that becos' I don't hear much to ze right?"

"That means that it's only a matter of time until we're flanked again," Captain Fulkerham completed the thought.

They did not need to wait long, but instead of sound to their right, it was an assault to their left, an assault large enough to capture the attention of the artillery so that when a second set of Confederate regiments appeared across the cornfield, these Rebels were able to march unmolested straight towards Daniel and the others.

The old furrows in the soil and the short, dead stalks of the cornfield slowed their progress, but the Rebels headed straight for them.

Colonel Blair came up behind them. He had lost his hat somewhere during the course of the morning, and his brownish red hair was matted to the side of his head by a cut that had trickled a constant supply of blood. "We have to make every shot count now, boys. We wait until I give the command, and I'm going to let them get *real* close this time."

If the Rebels had been supported, it would have been a treacherous strategy, but these two regiments appeared on their own.

Finally, at only 30 yards, Colonel Blair gave the order. The volley flattened large portions of the Rebel line. Those who weren't dead tried to crawl into the furrows, but they were too shallow for real protection. They could do little but die there as the bluecoats in the cedars fired remorseless into those who still stood or those who wiggled in the earth. Finally, the Southerners who were able fled back across the field as fast as their feet could take them.

To Daniel's amazement the entire episode replayed again, as two more regiments tried individually to root them out of the cedars with the same result. If they had supported each other and attacked together, Daniel knew that he and the others would not have been able to hold. They would have expended their ammunition further out and to lesser effects. They would have been forced to fall back.

Even so, they were in that same position now. Sheridan's men did not have the cartridges to repel another attack.

* * *

The irony was not lost on Lockett as he allowed himself a second's pause to look at the men that he had spent the past hour cajoling and organizing. He and Rosecrans's staff officers had taken on the job of trying to halt the tumultuous exodus and reorganize some of the men into reserve battalions. The men and remnants of their units were hopelessly intermixed now. Lockett had a shrunken battalion of about 200 men from Illinois, Ohio, and Indiana, all from numerous regiments and brigades.

There was a dream-like, repetitive quality to these actions that was impossible for him to miss. At Shiloh, he had been promoted to an officer for his actions. His first task as an officer had been to take the broken, milling men from the bluff, men whose units had been trampled and shattered during the day, and form them into emergency reserves in case they were needed. The motley mix of beaten men, like Milton Bosworth, Prosper T. Rowe, and Levi Thickle, had become his company, a core of men whom he had come to depend upon so heavily.

Here, outside of Murfreesboro and along the Stones River, his first act as a captain was to do the same thing. He looked at their drawn faces with their wide, nervous eyes. Some men's faces were blackened by gunpowder, some wore uniforms stained with the blood of their comrades, but the others were just dirty and exhausted.

A few stood about aimlessly, but most just sat on the damp ground, leaning back against trees or rocks. A handful had closed their eyes, but most looked around warily. To Lockett, they looked like at any moment they would take off like startled rabbits. The rumble of cannon and the rattle of musketry still raged and seemed to be coming ever closer. Morosely, he wondered how close it would get before many of them tried to flee again.

The large, bare cotton field on the other side of the Pike was no longer a riotous flood of humanity, but there was still a steady stream of men falling back across the open ground. As those men would near his position, the sergeants and the men posted along the pike would block them like a cordon and bully them into joining his battalion's growing ranks. Lockett was about to order one of his sergeants to collar the next cluster of men when General Rosecrans rode up from behind.

This was not the first time that Lockett had seen the General in the past hour. He seemed to be everywhere, giving orders and encouraging the men. Despite what was obviously happening, he was full of confidence and determination. As broken and beaten as these men were, Lockett could not help but notice a change in them when General Rosecrans came around.

"Ah, Lockett!" Rosecrans said, hopping out of his saddle and briskly shaking Lockett's hand. "I see that you are equally employed now getting these fine men together."

"Yes, sir," Lockett replied.

He had been so busy trying to stop the flood of men that he had momentarily forgotten his instinct to seek out Daniel and the others, but seeing the General reminded him of that primal motivation.

"Get them together, Lockett. Indeed, get them ready. This battle must be won." He sounded so energized and confident that it struck more than a few of the men listening as odd. This was, after all, the whipping of a lifetime, and the entire army seemed to be teetering. If the Rebels kept coming and cut off the Nashville Pike, there would be no good avenue of retreat for the army. Still, if the General was so positive, then...

"I'll get them ready, sir."

"That's what I like to hear," the General said. "I asked a similar question to a colonel a few minutes ago at a ford that we need to hold. He said that he would 'try'. I had to correct the man. This is not the time for trying; this is the time for doing. Perhaps, I should make you a colonel, Lockett." Rosecrans laughed, even as a thunderous barrage of artillery started up from nearby. "That would be those boys from the Chicago Board of Trade battery. We have massed a nice lot of cannon on the high ground not far from here. The Rebels will need to cross 800 yards of open ground with the shell bursting. The cannon will bleed them, then you men will finish them."

"Yes, sir."

"Come along, Garesche," Rosecrans said to his ever-present chief of staff. "Time to check in with General Rousseau."

"Please, not so close to the front this time, General. We need you."

"Nonsense, Garesche. Make the sign of the cross and go forth. We will be fine, I assure you." He turned as he rode off and called out loudly his refrain, "This battle must be won!"

With that, the General and his aide were off again. When Lockett turned around, he noticed that the eyes of his new 'battalion' were upon him, particularly his small leadership cadre, which consisted just of two lieutenants and three sergeants.

"What do we do now, sir?" one of the lieutenants asked him. He was young, so very young looking, like Daniel, Lockett thought to himself. Even the mud, powder stains, and flecks of dried blood could not hide the fact that his angelic face had yet to see a razor. He looked expectantly at him. All of them did. They did not know who the tall, gray eyed captain was, but he was friendly with the General himself. They assumed that must be for good reason.

"Do you know where the reserve ammunition train is located?" Lockett asked.

The boy shook his head.

"Find it. We will want to know once the shooting starts in earnest." He looked at the other lieutenant.

"Lieutenant Weathers, sir," he offered when he realized that Lockett had paused and tried to remember his name.

"Try to find some food for the men, Weathers. If they aren't hungry yet, they will be, and they'll fight better if fed. See if you can find something, but be quick about it."

Lockett turned to the eldest looking of the sergeants. "Help Sergeant Pierce with the line of men at the pike. There are still some men falling back. I want to gather up any man that we can get." He turned to the last sergeant. "And you, make sure that no one leaves the area, not for any reason."

The men hurried off, and Lockett looked at the ground, wondering what he needed to do next. His patchwork battalion, and the similar one next to it, both reported to one of Rosecrans's lieutenant colonels. Lockett supposed that he should give him a readiness report of some sort. He wanted to tell the man that they were ready and able, but he had a nagging doubt about some of these men. Based on the dazed look in their eyes and limited organization, he privately wondered if they would fight.

He was still looking at the ground when a pair of muddy boots halted in front of him, but what he noticed more was the worn stock of a rifle planted next to the boots. It was the familiar shape of a Dimick Deer Rifle, and he knew only one person who still had one…

Slowly, he lifted his disbelieving eyes from the mud and into the face of Patrick McManus. Neither man said anything for a moment. The tears streaming from McManus's face said enough.

"Thank God," Lockett said softly, as he gave a brotherly embrace that lifted McManus off the ground.

"You're alive," McManus croaked after a moment. He stepped back, and each man held onto the other's shoulder as if letting go would cause the dream to end. "Is that really you, James?"

Lockett only nodded. Words would not come.

"We all thought you were dead. You were gone so long. How

did you get here? What happened to you?" As he said the latter, he frowned with concern and looked at Lockett's neck, peeling the collar back slightly to reveal more of the scars. "Good God."

"There's a lot to tell you," Lockett said, finally finding his voice.

"When I saw you standing there as I came across the field, I was certain that I was losing my mind."

"It's me, Patrick, but where are the others? Daniel?"

"Don't know. I've been trying to get back to them all morning but never could get back. Colonel Blair had me deliver a message to General Willich this morning, and then the fighting started. I could never get back." He saw the look of concern on Lockett's face. "He's with Milton. He's fine, I'm sure, James. Look, you won't believe the model soldier he's becoming. He's not like when you left."

The statement gave Lockett a distinct sense of unease. If Daniel had run away like at Perryville, then he would have been far safer.

* * *

The perpetual zing of minié bullets thrashing through the trees, mixed with the winging sound of shots bouncing off the limestone ribs, was a constant numbing tune punctuated by the galling thuds of shots finding human flesh. One such horrible thud sounded just a foot away from Daniel as another Blair man went over backwards.

Somehow, they were finding enough ammunition to continue the fight, but only the bare minimum. Daniel had lost track of how many times they had pulled back to another position to resume the fight, and every time the Rebels followed, blasting away at yet another position, whatever the cost.

The firing would slow and then intensify, slow and then intensify, but it never seemed to really stop anymore.

Daniel fired again, and then his hands repeated the exercise of loading the rifle. The barrel was hot to the touch, such that it burned his hands. The inside of the barrel was so fouled with spent powder that it took all his strength to ram the next minié ball down the barrel, and even then, he could not quite completely ram it all the way. He imagined that this lessened the velocity and accuracy of his shots, but he had no choice. There was no hot water, or time, to clean the caked residue from his weapon. He had seen one man urinate into his barrel to loosen the deposits. It seemed like a good idea to Daniel, but when a stray shot had killed the man while he was doing it, and he fell back exposed with his pants dropping to his knees, Daniel decided that there was no time for that right now.

As he looked up to aim his next shot, something glinted and gave Daniel a moment's pause. Squinting through the acrid, saltpeter haze, he spied something that gave him alarm. It was a Rebel cannon coming up along their flank. Once positioned, it would surely be loaded with canister, and like a giant shotgun, those little balls would tear the flesh and bone right off the men. When amplified by bouncing around the narrow limestone channels, its damage would be catastrophic.

"Sergeant!" Daniel yelled to Bosworth, "Look! Cannon!"

"Go find Colonel Schaeffer's adjutant. I just saw the major back there," Bosworth pointed behind him while scarcely pausing in loading his weapon.

Carrying his rifle, Daniel slid out of the first limestone trench and ran towards where Bosworth had pointed. He hurdled another limestone rib only to land on a bloody blue corpse. His ankle twisted, and he slammed heavily against the next piece of limestone. Pain surged through the knee that he banged, but he did not pause.

He pulled himself free and limped on. After a few more strides, the pain lessened, and he was hurried on his way by a Rebel minié ball chipping stone from the rock next to him. He saw a few men standing together in the general area that Milton had pointed out.

He headed that way and arrived, puffing heavily. The two men standing there gave him no attention though, instead their eyes were riveted to the ground.

Daniel looked down at what had locked their attention. It was the bloody body in a major's uniform with half of his face shot away.

Daniel flinched even though he had seen hundreds of dead men today. He looked away, momentarily confused, and it was then that he noticed an officer on horseback another 50 yards away. With no hesitation, he ran towards him, but when he was half way there, another series of shots toppled the colonel from his horse. As the man fell, dead before he hit the ground, Daniel recognized that it was Colonel Schaeffer, the man in charge of Sheridan's second brigade.

The Rebels had reached the flank again.

Unaware that Colonel Schaeffer's dying act was to order another charge to free up the rest of the brigade to fall back, Daniel turned around and raced back to Milton Bosworth and the others. He had already decided for himself that it was time for them all to go and find another position.

* * *

Ambrose Tucker winced and flexed his arm again. The sling was wet with blood, but he could still move his fingers, and he was sure that the piece of artillery shell had missed the bone.

For a moment, he reflected back on his good luck. After they had driven the Yankees from their holes in the woods just beyond the Wilkinson Pike, he had ridden to the Harding house to get a better view.

It had been then that the Yankee artillery had filled the area with shell after shell, such that it actually seemed like the ground had become alive with bursting geysers. Many of the shells had plowed into the house itself.

It had already been a nightmare of blood inside the house since the Yankees had turned it into a hospital and nearly every bit of space held a wounded Union soldier. Countless Yankees had their misery shortened by their own side as shell after shell had struck the wooden structure.

The shelling had continued on, and Ambrose had flattened himself as best he could into the ground.

When it finally ended, Ambrose entered the structure to see if there was a living doctor to attend to his arm. He saw no living souls. Instead, he saw a room that was splattered with blood and flesh across all four walls, ceiling, and floor.

Chapter 48

It was the afternoon of what had become the endless day.

Lockett and his rag tag reserves laid flat in the open area between the Nashville Pike and the railroad.

Some men could not bear to look. They buried their faces in the ground as the spent balls whipped overhead. Other men peered ahead into the thicket and cotton field beyond where Rousseau's men were being steadily driven back toward them by the Rebels. The Rebels were paying a heavy price, but they were still pushing the Yankees back. Their goal was nearly in their grasp. The Nashville Pike was nearly in Bragg's hands.

More Union reserves came from across the railroad bed. Lockett could hear their officers yelling, "Battalion, lie down! Battalion, lie down!" as they made it to the area next to his men, although one unfortunate man was struck by one these stray shots before he could flatten himself to the ground. He howled in agony, and his cries seemed to go on for minutes.

"Someone needs to shut him up," McManus muttered as he laid next to Lockett. "These men are already shaken enough as it is. More of that, and a few more stray balls, then who knows what will happen." As if to underscore his point, a Rebel ball smacked solidly into the immature tree to his front and other shots buried themselves in the dirt, just feet from them.

Lockett made no answer. Instead his tried to peer through the tangled web of brush and small trees. The sounds were coming closer, but he couldn't see much.

The hail of overshot minié balls continued to whine, and Lockett heard another man cry out.

"I see them," someone yelled from nearby. Lockett scrambled over to him and peered through the gap in the thicket. Rousseau's men were slowly falling back, loading and firing as they went.

Grudgingly, but surely, they were coming back.

Rousseau's men reached the edge of the thicket when suddenly there was the sound of a shot from Lockett's men, and then another. Lockett looked right and saw the puffs of telltale smoke. He was on his feet instantly, running towards those men, yelling at the top of his lungs. "Hold your fire! Those are our men, damn you! Hold your fire!"

He ran across towards them, jumping over the forms of his own men as he did so. He felt a shot race near his face and then another, but he continued to run. Another panicked man was raising his rifle to fire into the thicket just as Lockett arrived. Lockett stomped down on the barrel with one foot and kicked the man in the face.

"Hold your fire!"

The dazed man looked up at him blankly.

More shots whizzed by, but Lockett knew that now was no time to find cover. He needed all of his men to see him now, and they all did.

"Hold your fire until my command!"

He pulled his revolver free from the holster for emphasis. He had not meant it to be such, but many of the men took that to mean that he would shoot them first if necessary.

The stray shots coming into this area increased in volume and velocity, but Lockett knew that he could not lie flat with the others, not now. They needed to see his confidence, feigned or not.

Slowly and deliberately, he forced himself to walk in front of them, oblivious to the whining minié balls and the fact that the first of Rousseau's exhausted men were coming back through the area.

They said nothing, but their worn and dirty faces said all that could be said. The fighting had been hot and heavy. They had little physical reserves left and even less ammunition. None spoke as they walked over and around Lockett's men, lying flat just behind them.

"Battalion, rise up!" Lockett bellowed. Each of his three sergeants repeated the order, and Lockett felt a surge of adrenalin as his battalion and all of the others along the line rose to their feet.

Then Captain Morton from the Pioneer Brigade, the brigade commander in this sector, rode across the front. "Men, you haven't got much ammunition, but give'em what you have and then wade in on 'em with the bayonet!"

He was barely out of their line of fire when the Confederates appeared through the thicket.

"Commence firing!" they heard, and immediately the area was engulfed in smoke. The Confederates returned the fire.

The sounds were enormous, overwhelming the yells from both sides. Lockett walked behind his line, making sure that no men were slinking away.

The thuds of shots that found their marks were all around him. One man slumped into Lockett's knees, nearly knocking him down, while another fell dead atop that man. Another soul just feet away howled in agony and clasped a hand to his eye that gushed red blood between the fingers. He staggered backwards, and Lockett was amazed that the man was still alive and capable of making such noise.

He was not the only one to notice, and the young soldier between them started to turn and run, but Lockett grabbed him by the collar and shoved him back into the line.

"Load and fire!" he snarled at the youth.

The youth hesitated, but then obediently he started to reload. Each side blasted away at the other without let up. The youth staggered backwards again, and Lockett was about growl at the cowardice again when he noticed the bright red spot in the boy's chest. The youth dropped his rifle and fell dead at Lockett's feet. His unblinking eyes stared accusingly up at Lockett.

Lockett tore his gaze away. The Confederate line was less than a hundred yards away. The Rebel flag waved back and forth, as if mocking him, and he angrily emptied his revolver in that general direction. His eyes were burning from the smoke, and his nostrils filled with the smell of powder and blood.

He slammed the smoking revolver back into his holster. There was no time to reload now.

In general, they seemed to be holding their ground, although it was thinning out. There were now gaps in what used to be men firing shoulder to shoulder.

He started to pace down the length of the line. "Pour it in!

They won't stand much longer! Pour it in!" he yelled. He sounded convincing, but he doubted his own words.

The area was shrouded in smoke. He could not see the Rebel line clearly anymore. There were still shots, cacophony, and the yells and curses of men, but he could not tell if the Rebels were wavering like he knew his line was.

His mind drifted, and then a sudden panic seized him. He didn't see Patrick. Frantically, he scanned the line again and saw Patrick reloading. Reassured, he yelled more encouragement to the men.

"You are winning!" he yelled. "You are winning!" And after a few more minutes, it did seem to all of them that the pace of reply from the enemy was slackening.

Captain Morton had come to the same conclusion and was bellowing to the men to advance.

Grimly, the men advanced. There was no triumphant battle yell. They were all too spent for that, but forward they went, and the sight of the advance was enough. The remaining Confederates fled from the thicket and back across the cotton field where the artillery reopened on them, hurrying them on their way.

Lockett and the rest of the reserves paused at the edge of the cotton field. There was no thought to pursue the Rebels across the open cotton field.

The momentary respite was victory enough.

* * *

The early darkness of winter had fallen quickly across the battle lines. The nocturnal shroud covered miles and miles of carnage from sight.

Grimly, James Lockett and Patrick McManus sat back to back and huddled for warmth.

They were exhausted, as were all of the men on both sides, but there would be no sleep tonight. A freezing rain fell intermittently, and the wind stiffened. At times, the gale howled loud enough to cover the groans and cries of the wounded who still laid in the fields and beyond, but then the wind would soften, and the terrible cries reached the ears of both armies again.

There were cries of incomprehensible agony. There were

prayers to God, some for deliverance, but others for death and an end to their suffering. There were cries for help, for someone to give them water, if not remove them from the field, but in the dark no-man's land, neither side could provide help. So the men suffered in the freezing rain as the temperatures continued to drop.

Even those fortunate enough to still be alive and unwounded could only shiver in the dark. There were no fires, since the light would draw the fire of cannon or at least pickets.

McManus blew on his hands and then tucked them back under his armpits as he shivered and tried to fight off the numbness.

"Will we retreat tonight or in the morning?" he asked.

McManus really did not care one way or the other at this point, but he felt the need to make some conversation. He knew that James was brooding heavily on the whereabouts of his brother. They had already decided that in the morning, Patrick would leave and try to find Colonel Blair and the regiment. Lockett knew that he himself could not leave given his command of the rag tag reserve battalion.

The gusting wind parted the gray clouds and revealed a bright moon, but only momentarily. By the time that Lockett answered McManus, the clouds had obscured the moon again, and another round of freezing spittle stung their faces.

"I would think so," Lockett finally answered. "We secured the Nashville Pike, so the road back is an option. I imagine that we will get the order shortly before dawn to start back for Nashville with our tail between our legs… again."

McManus grunted in response, and then Lockett continued, "But that doesn't change anything for you tomorrow, Patrick. I need you to find Blair's regiment."

"I'll find them," McManus promised, "Don't worry about that. I'll find the boys."

In the distance, there was another picket firing and a solitary response.

Behind their thicket, they could also hear the squeak of the ambulance wagons, going about their grim business, all night long without stop.

* * *

Ambrose Tucker cursed the fact that General Bragg had dragged him back into the messenger business. He wanted to join up with a cavalry unit on the flank for the coming day. As the Yankees pulled back, there would be easy pickings for the cavalry as long as they stayed on the edges and did not wander too close to the main body of the Yankee rear guard.

But, alas, one of Bragg's aides had spotted him and decided that with his arm in sling, and a healthy mount, it made him a perfect candidate to resume carrying the General's orders to his now intermixed commands.

The aide was putting Bragg's latest orders into envelopes for Ambrose Tucker to deliver.

Nearby, General Bragg was dictating a telegram message for Richmond to another aide. "God has granted us a Happy New Year. The enemy has been driven from every position except his extreme left…"

The aide tugged gently on Ambrose Tucker's sling to get his attention. "You have the orders for General McCown and General Cleburne."

"Yes, sir," he acknowledged and patted his pouch. In his possession, he would carry the orders to pursue the retreating Yankees in the morning, but not too closely unless General Breckinridge and his heretofore fresh units made a juncture with them.

General Bragg lacked the cavalry units to cut off the Pike entirely since they had gone off before the battle in their encircling ride around the Yankees. Even without their availability, perhaps a little additional pressure would convince the Yankees to abandon their wagons, supplies, and maybe even a few cannon in their haste.

It never crossed Braxton Bragg's mind, nor Ambrose Tucker's, that the Yankees would not be retreating come the morning light.

* * *

Private Sam Pascoe from Alabama held the two wads of cotton in his freezing hands. He contemplated stuffing the wads into his ears to block out the sounds of misery that had followed him on his solitary march out as sentry for the night. As he made his way through the bullet scarred cedars and limestone outcroppings, the noises stayed with him.

It wasn't the groans that bothered him as much as the hysterical cries for God, mothers, water, or death. Of course, dulling his sense of hearing made little sense for someone assigned to picket duty on a dark and cloudy night. Plus, this particular stretch was eerily quiet. So instead, he stuffed the cotton back into his haversack and pulled out a pipe.

Wearily, he sat on a limestone rib. The rock had absorbed the freezing temperatures, and he felt that keenly through his thin trousers. At thirty-five years of age, he was old for a private experiencing his first battle. He had been conscripted only a month before and counted himself lucky to have avoided the fighting up until now, but after today, he wasn't sure how lucky he really was.

To reassure himself, he patted his pocket which held the daguerreotype of his new bride. They had only been married three months now. She was young and spry, already a war widow once, which was how someone like that had been made available to someone like him. He did not like to think that she could be twice widowed before the age of twenty.

There was a single crack of a picket's rifle nearby. The Yankee picket responded with a shot of his own. It was just enough for each side to know that the other was still there. It reminded Sam Pascoe that he was out here for a reason.

He placed the unlit pipe back in his haversack and stood up. Creeping forward to find a suitable position for the night, he felt his foot crack through a thin layer of ice. The puddle immediately soaked his foot through the multiple holes in his boot.

"Damnation," he muttered, "As if it warn't cold enough already, now my feet'll be soaked all night."

To calm himself, he pulled his pipe back out and struck the match. In the brief spark of light, he looked down and realized that that it was not a puddle of water that he was standing in. He stood above the blue form of yet another Yankee. Blood from the dead Northerner had filled the crevice and created the frozen puddle that had immersed his foot.

Pascoe shook his head and puffed on his pipe. He was in the process of picking up his rifle and going on his way when a voice not three feet away startled him.

"Help me," the choked voice croaked.

A primal reaction caused him to yank his rifle around at the sound.

"Please," the voice said softly again.

Sam Pascoe peered over the other side of the limestone. Beneath him was another crumpled form. The voice sounded Yankee to him. "What do you want, Billy Yank?"

"Please," the weak voice said.

"I ain't got time for you, Billy," Sam Pascoe said, straightening.

"No, don't leave!" the voice said with clear desperation.

"You shot, Billy?"

"Twice."

"Well, ain't nuthin' I can do for you, Billy."

"I'm freezing to death. Please build me a fire."

Sam Pascoe snorted derisively. "A fire? I cain't make one for myself, much less a Billy Yank."

"Please," the voice pleaded. "I'll freeze."

"Billy, even if I didn't have my orders, it wouldn't serve you no good. The light will attract your own pickets. They'll start shooting."

"I'm plenty safe from rifles down here," the Yankee answered with surprising coherence.

"No," Sam Pascoe said firmly. "Now, I got to go."

"No, please! I'm begging you!"

"None of that, lad," Pascoe grumbled. "There's enough moans out here as it is." He took a few steps to leave.

"Please, please, I beg you."

The voice was as pitiful as any that Pascoe had heard in his life. "Now, boy, don't be like that. I'm sure you fought bravely today. Don't ruin that by dying with such whimpers." The words were said with a sharpness that the wearied Pascoe had not intended, and he had not expected the words to work at all, but there was no more sound from the Yankee. Pascoe listened to the complete silence, but he could not even hear breathing. "You still alive, Billy?"

"Yes," the answer came back, but it sounded to Pascoe as if the word had been mumbled through a clenched jaw.

"Good. Now, you save your strength. Morning will be here soon enough. You'll be all right." Pascoe paused at his own words. He knew it was a lie on both accounts. Morning was still a long way off, and a good many men would die tonight, probably frozen in their own blood like the soldier whose blood now coated his toes.

Still, he headed off and tried to put the pitiful voice behind him. Yet after two minutes, his conscience nagged at him horribly, and he found himself retracing his steps back to the Yankee.

"Billy?" he whispered when he returned. No answer. "Billy, you still there?" There was no answer, and he thought that perhaps the Northerner had expired. He was about to turn around, when he heard a pained, "Yes, still here."

"All right. I think that ravine you're in is deep enough for mebbe a small fire."

"Thank God for you," the Yankee breathed.

Sam Pascoe ignored the comment and began to make a small fire near the man's feet. Once the fire was going, he allowed himself to warm his own hands by it and looked in the dancing light at the Billy Yank. He was young, much younger than himself, and in a bad way. He had been shot twice that he could see, once in the hip and once in the shoulder. The bleeding seemed to have stopped, so maybe the man might live, he thought to himself. But the boy's face was screwed in pain. Even when he spoke, he could only do it in short bursts. He had put some additional kindling near the lad so that he could keep the fire going during the night, but he wasn't sure if the lad could toss the sticks into the fire that was only a foot from his feet.

"Do you need any water?" the Yankee asked Pascoe. He paused and ground his teeth, biting back another wave of excruciating pain.

Sam Pascoe could not even imagine the pain that the boy was in.

"I have a canteen." There was a heavy pause again for the Yankee to catch his breath. "You can take it."

"I think you better keep your water, Billy Yank. You might need it."

"I can't offer anything else."

481

"I wouldn't think you would. 'Sides, if you had somethin' I wanted, I'd just take it." Sam Pascoe stood up and warmed each foot by the fire. His toes peeked out of the worthless shoes. One shoe was held together only by a worn strap of leather.

"You can take my boots."

"Billy," Pascoe said with some exasperation, "A moment ago, you were begging me to stop you from freezing to death. I think you need your shoes."

"Take them when I die then."

Pascoe flinched at the words, as if he had been physically struck by them. "You ain't gonna die, you damn Yankee. Now, I gotta go, but I'll be back in the morning, and I'll take you back to the surgeons." He mounted the limestone and made ready to leave.

"Johnny Reb?"

"What do you want now, Billy?"

"Thank you."

Chapter 49

January 1, 1863

Lockett and McManus stirred at the first morning light. Both men silently reflected on the brutal misery of the cold night. It was something that they would never forget. They could not imagine how many wounded and weakened men on both sides had perished overnight.

Warily, soldiers on both sides started to make small fires and move about. The Army of the Cumberland stirred guardedly, expecting another Rebel attack at any moment. But none came. Their surprise at the lack of aggression was only exceeded by the surprise of the Confederate Army of Tennessee's that the Yankees had not retreated overnight.

"Happy New Year, James," McManus said as they made a small fire.

Lockett looked at him in confusion. It took him a moment to realize that this was the first morning of 1863. Eventually, he puffed out his cheeks and snorted. "I had forgotten," he admitted.

"Adie would be happy. Somewhere up there, I'm sure that he is happy that this day is finally here."

Again, Lockett looked blankly at his friend. His brain must have frozen overnight, because he could not fathom what prompted McManus's comment.

"The Emancipation Proclamation is official now," McManus explained. "The slaves are free."

"You're right," Lockett said dumbfounded. His thoughts immediately went to Clarissa. She was free now, assuming that she hadn't been dragged back behind the Confederate lines.

"That young Charlie you told me about is free now," McManus continued.

To pass the night, Lockett had explained his entire tale to

McManus. He included every detail that he could think of. It had gone a long way to pass the otherwise eternal night. He had not altered any of the details, even the part about Clarissa telling Prosper that her name was Charlie, so he found it odd that Patrick had referred to her as Charlie.

He pondered it for a moment, and both men lapsed into silence.

Lockett found his thoughts going back to what would happen to Clarissa as a runaway slave on her own. The guilt that he felt was palpable. He shouldn't have let her tag along after Nashville…

"What I wouldn't do for a slab of bacon over this fire," McManus said, eventually breaking the spell. "Even a weevil encrusted piece of hardtack would be like a Christmas gift right now."

Lockett nodded grimly. What little food that Lieutenant Weathers had found had already been consumed. The men would be hungry today.

"I'll be off to find Colonel Blair and the others now," McManus stated, rubbing his hands together one last time over the small fire. It was what they had discussed last night. Lockett couldn't leave his little battalion, but McManus would seek out their old regiment and bring him word of Daniel and the others.

Lockett nodded once more. Oddly, the Rebels did not seem intent on attacking now, so this was as good of a time as any for the errand.

* * *

Sam Pascoe shivered as he headed back to camp from his sentry post. It had been the longest night of his life. The cold had been brutal. He had been fortunate enough to come across the corpse of a Yankee officer during the night. Pascoe had stripped the coat off the body, which provided scant comfort from the chill, but it was better than nothing.

He had left the coat behind now in the morning light, lest he be mistaken and shot by his own side. Someone else must have come across that officer's body earlier, he reckoned, or else the man had dropped everything and run, because there was little of value on that officer. The only thing that he had was a small embroidered monogrammed handkerchief in the jacket pocket.

But it wasn't just the cold that had made the night drag on for what seemed an eternity. More than once, Pascoe had thought about going back to check on the young Yankee in the ravine. He had been sorely tempted to leave his post, warm up by the fire, and chat with the boy, but each time, his desire to do his duty won out.

However, now that he had been relieved, Pascoe headed straight back for the Yankee. The boy had been so badly wounded that he wondered how he would get him back to the surgeons, but he reckoned that he could figure a way out. Yet, as he neared the spot, a sense of foreboding overtook him. He could smell no smoke from the fire.

"Billy?" he whispered. "Billy?" he said more loudly.

There was no answer.

"Billy?" Pascoe tried again as he reached the ravine. He looked down into the narrow crevice, and his fears were realized.

The fire had long since burned itself out, and the boy was dead. His soft features and light blue eyes looked unblinkingly up at him. His mouth hung open, as if he had been in mid-sentence.

"Damn," Pascoe said softly. "I'm sorry, Billy. Truly, I am. You seemed like a good 'un."

Pascoe slid into the shallow area between the limestone and rested on one knee. "Damn this war, Billy. Rest in peace." Pascoe closed his eyes and said a quiet prayer.

When he opened his eyes, he looked down at the boots on the Yankee's feet. "I'll find some other boots, Billy. You keep those."

It seemed wrong to him to leave the body here, unburied, but it was just one of thousands now. He rose to leave, but the boy's eyes still seemed to be looking at him. Impulsively, Pascoe bent down and gently closed the lids. Then he placed the monogrammed handkerchief that he had found overnight across the Billy Yank's face.

It was a nice handkerchief, but his initials weren't B.H.E. anyway, Pascoe reasoned as he headed back to camp.

* * *

It was well into morning when Ambrose Tucker returned to

Murfreesboro from delivering General Bragg's orders.

In the daylight, the town hardly resembled the place he had seen before Christmas. Gone were the bunting and laurels put out for the Holiday and for President Davis's arrival. It had been replaced with a tidal wave of wretchedness and broken men.

Every church and public building had been turned into a hospital, but even that was far from sufficient. A few lucky wounded were beneath tents that flapped cruelly in the cold wind, but many others were placed out in the open on the front steps and lawns of the churches and houses.

As Tucker rode along slowly towards the center of town, a gust of wind brought the smell of blood into his nostrils.

He plodded along, past a cluster of wounded Yankees on the ground being paroled. Each man had to swear not to bear arms against the Confederacy for the rest of the war. There seemed little chance of that, Tucker thought, as he looked at them. Legless, armless, or just generally maimed, he doubted many of them would still be alive a few days from now.

Still, one man refused to make the promise. He had a bloody bandage around where his foot should have been, and he was white as a sheet. Yet somehow, he was still full of vinegar. With a pained effort, he lifted his head from the ground and spat at the Confederate officer's feet. "That's what I think of your offer, Secesh!"

The officer made no reaction, but his accompanying private booted the man in the ribs and then stepped heavily on the wrapped stump.

The Yankee's piercing howls were loud enough to cut through the rest of the carnage and moans around him.

"Very well," the officer said evenly, as if he was calmly discussing the weather, "We'll make sure that you leave with the next batch of Yankee prisoners going. Course, your comrades probably won't much like the fact that they'll have to carry you all the way to Andersonville."

Ambrose Tucker left the men to their business and continued onto General Bragg's headquarters. To everyone's surprise, the Yankees had not retreated overnight, and to Ambrose Tucker's dismay, nothing much seemed to be happening on the Confederate side about forcing the matter.

* * *

It was late morning by the time that Patrick McManus was able to locate the whereabouts of Sheridan's battered brigades and Blair's Independent Regiment. They were positioned at the far right of Rosecrans's defensive line which ran parallel to the Nashville Pike.

Another random shell shrieked overhead and landed on the macadamized pike. It bounced crazily off the hardened surface for another 150 yards, barely missing a fortunate soldier who had picked that moment to cross the road.

All morning long, the men expected a wave of Confederates to emerge and challenge for the Pike again, but the only activity was the occasional shell that the Rebel artillery put up.

McManus crossed from the Pike back into the area between the road and railroad tracks. Other soldiers idled about in those trees. Some still looked dazed by the actions of the previous day, but others tried to satisfy their growling bellies.

He walked past one cook fire where a slab of fresh horse meat sizzled over the flames. It was a peculiar smell, but it tempted McManus.

Beyond that group of men, he found the partially butchered equine carcass, apparently, a victim of being in the wrong place at the wrong time for one of the shells bouncing off the macadam.

More importantly, he saw familiar faces. There was a group of men hacking at the remaining hind quarter with their bayonets.

"That would be a lot easier if you had a big ol' bowie knife like me," he interjected with a huge smile.

Milton Bosworth and the others snapped their heads around.

"Patrick!"

"McManus!"

"Paddy!"

"Pat!"

They all yelled at the same time.

They gathered around him and pounded his back so heavily that it was sure to leave bruises.

"I didn't think we'd ever see you again!" Sam Baker exclaimed.

"Nonsense," Bosworth snorted, "Nonsense. I'm just surprised it took the dumb lummox this long to find us." He smiled widely and slapped McManus on the back again.

"What happened to you?" Baker asked.

"The Rebs tore through Willich's men like a scythe through wheat. Fools were still half asleep. Tried to make my way back to our position, but every time I thought I'd get there, there were more Rebels in the way."

"Well, the good news is that you got back," Levi Thickle grinned. The normally acerbic private was unrecognizable in his good humor.

"If you like that news, I got better news," McManus said. "I just came back from James's new battalion."

"The Lieutenant!" Thickle exclaimed.

"He's alive?" Baker asked.

"Sure is," McManus replied. "I couldn't believe my eyes yesterday when I saw him standing there."

"God Almighty!" Thickle added. "He was gone so long that I didn't think there was a chance of seeing the Lieutenant again. Colonel Blair will be mighty glad to hear that. We're damn low on officers, even lower on good ones."

"Well, he'll be back soon, I'm sure. He's got a small battalion of reserves put together from those running off the field yesterday, but I'm sure he'll be back once that is sorted out."

It was then that McManus noticed that Milton Bosworth had gone very still and said nothing at the astounding news.

He looked over at him. "What is it?"

Bosworth said nothing. He only stared back at him blankly.

"Milton, what is it?" McManus then turned and looked around. After a complete circle, he stared at the Ohioan. The others had gone silent too.

"Milton… Where's Daniel?"

Chapter 50

It was late in the day with only an hour of daylight remaining, when McManus returned to Lockett's camp. Lockett saw him immediately, as well as the familiar shapes of Milton Bosworth and Colonel Blair. Excitedly, he raised his hand. "Patrick!"

McManus nodded in return but gave no other reaction.

Not only did the reaction strike Lockett as odd, but at the same moment, he realized that it was just the three of them.

The spark of pleasure at the reunion was immediately replaced with a choking swelling in his throat and jellied legs. He stood rooted as he waited for them to approach. He did not trust his legs to help cross the distance.

It was only the three of them…

"Daniel?"

Lockett could think of only one reason for his absence. McManus knew how desperate he was to see his younger brother. All three of the men approaching knew that so many of his actions had been to keep Daniel safe, even if it seemed misguided to them.

Daniel?

Lockett felt the dread ooze up his spine and over him, like a cold, black shawl of despair. He felt a physical nausea of the worst kind and fought down the retching that was in his throat.

It could not be…

As they neared, he could see their solemn faces. There was no mistaking it. Most of all, Lockett's eyes were drawn to Milton Bosworth. The husky sergeant seemed stooped, but it was Milton's face that Lockett knew he would never forget.

He was utterly dirty and blackened with powder stains and powder burns. If he had spent the past day face down in a coal bin, he could not have looked much different. But as the sergeant stared back at Lockett, the burly man's eyes welled with tears. A single solitary drop created a tendril of pale skin as it ran down his cheek. The sergeant quickened his pace and was the first to reach Lockett.

The pain on his face was so vivid that Lockett felt compelled to stiffen and steady himself for the news.

Bosworth opened his mouth, but no words came.

They just looked at each other, words caught in the back recesses, as the other two arrived behind him.

Bosworth took an audible breath and opened his mouth again but with the same result.

"You should know that his valor and steadfastness was equal to any man in the regiment yesterday," Colonel Blair said, arriving.

"I didn't know..." Bosworth finally managed. "I didn't know until it was too late."

Colonel Blair ignored the interruption. "I've never seen fighting like that before. Even your Shiloh veterans told me that they had never seen fighting like that, Lockett. It was like Hell had opened its gates with all its fire and smoke. Both sides at each other's necks all day... By God, I never want to see anything like that again. And yet, throughout... your brother stood his ground. In fact, more than once he volunteered for the most hazardous... He bore your family name proudly yesterday."

"I should have..." Bosworth began.

"Shut up, Milton," McManus snapped. "Levi told me everything. There was nothing to be done..."

"No," Bosworth said angrily. "I need to tell him. He was my responsibility yesterday. With the Lieutenant gone and you gone, I knew that I needed to keep an eye on him. And I tried, but God help me, once he got his dander up, he was more like you than I ever thought, Lieutenant."

He took a breath. "Right from the git, there was something different about him yesterday. He was the first one off when we charged the Rebs in the morning. Couldn't hardly keep up with him, fast like a rabbit. Same when he volunteered to pass the word to Fulkerham and his boys that they were about to be cut off. All day long, we'd load and fire, load and fire, same as you taught us back in Savannah. Taught us so good to get four shots off a minute that we held again and again, went through our ammunition too. And then your brother was off in the middle of it all, collecting cartridge boxes from the dead on both sides so we could keep firing."

Bosworth clenched his jaw. "We held them back, Lieutenant, every time! Just we kept getting out flanked, and we'd have to fall back again. It was near the end of the fighting amongst those limestones in the forest. We were out of ammunition and falling back again, towards Rousseau's new line. I thought he was right next to me as we ran back. I didn't know."

"Levi saw him..." McManus started.

"I need to tell him," Bosworth growled. "I need to be the one to tell him," he added, chastened. "When we got back to Rousseau that was when I noticed that he wasn't next to me anymore. I didn't see him anywhere, but Levi had. When we were leaving the stones, he saw Daniel slip or trip and land between two of the rocks. Then the smoke blocked his sight and then the Rebels were there. We would have gone back, but the Rebels were already there..."

At the anguished look on the sergeant's face, Lockett wordlessly clutched the man's shoulder.

"He might still be alive, James," Colonel Blair said. "We just don't know. He might be hiding from them, maybe wounded, maybe captured. We just don't know. Don't give up hope yet."

"Can we get back to that site now?" Lockett said, uttering his first words.

"It's right in the middle of the Rebel lines," Colonel Blair answered. He looked up at the falling night sky. "Tomorrow, maybe, we will beat off the Rebels once and for all. When we win, I'll detach some men to go back and find him and anyone else from our regiment. I promise."

When we win... The words rang in Lockett's ears.

He looked away, southeast of them. "Thank you, Colonel. When we win, I'll take you up on the offer. But if I may, I'll need another favor from you *when we win*."

Colonel Blair looked patiently at him, but Lockett continued to stare into the distance, towards Murfreesboro. He couldn't see the town from here, but in his mind's eye, he saw it as clearly as if he was right there. And he saw the town as it might be after another day of horrific carnage. He saw it as it might be when the battered and brutalized men in blue came into the town that had supported their tormenters so vocally. He saw the rampage and chaos that could ensue as those first unchecked, and by then blood thirsty, blue coats arrived in town.

"I'll need you to detach some men to go into Murfreesboro and protect someone, sir."

"Protect someone? In Murfreesboro? Who?"

"The person who kept me alive, Anna Tucker."

* * *

January 2, 1863

The slate gray afternoon sky matched Lockett's mood. He had said little throughout the day. McManus too had been quiet and unable to shake the mood. There was nothing that he could say in good conscience. Colonel Blair had suggested that Daniel might somehow be all right, perhaps in hiding, but neither McManus nor Lockett believed that. McManus frowned at the grim reality.

At that moment, Lockett was thinking similar thoughts. He was remembering his time in Murfreesboro with Anna, remembering the treatment of the captured Union soldiers being paraded through town… and that was before this gruesome battle that had slaughtered so many thousands on both sides.

He could hardly imagine life going forward. It would get worse and worse for the prisoners. He didn't like to think about Daniel somehow trying to survive that mistreatment, so Lockett forced his mind onto other things.

"I suppose that my journal and Ainsley's sword were left back in camp?" Lockett remarked.

The voice startled McManus, making him twitch. Before he could answer Lockett continued, "It's a shame to think that some Rebel is probably using my journal pages for his privy and that Ainsley's family sword has been sold two or three times already."

"Oh, I wouldn't say that," McManus answered, grateful for the break to his own musings, "I am Irish after all, and we have always been good at hiding the valuables if nothing else."

"I didn't think that the Irish had much in the way of valuables to hide," Lockett grinned.

"Your privy paper fits right into that group," McManus smirked back. Both men were appreciative for the moment of respite from their own thoughts. "But be that as it may, once we win this battle, I'll wager you that the sword and journal are still where I hid them."

"Win the battle, eh?" Much like New Year's Day, this day was also quiet. Neither side seemed willing to advance on the other; neither side was willing to retreat either.

"Oh, we'll win now. Now for certain," McManus declared.

"How do you figure?"

"There's no more element of surprise. There's no more of our general's being caught with our pants down. We know that the Rebs are out there, and we're ready if they attack again." He motioned to the area next to them.

It was a formidable view. During the morning, they had been ordered with the rest of Morton's Pioneer Brigade to provide infantry support to the consolidated artillery that Rosecrans had gathered at the top of the hill overlooking the McFadden Ford in the Stones River. On the hilltop there were forty some cannon lined wheel hub to wheel hub. Anyone trying to cross the ford to flank Rosecrans's army would be in for a horrific pounding.

Lockett nodded and added aloud, "If the Rebs try coming through there, then I would agree." He stared out across the way. Beyond the river, there was a smaller, well cleared open hilltop that would need to be mounted in order to descend down into the ford. The Union artillery was already focused on that area. "But what makes you think that the Rebels would be foolish enough to come from that direction."

"Simple," McManus replied confidently, "That is the only direction that they have not attacked from yet. They won't try for the Pike again. We already bloodied those brigades. The only fresh ones that they have remaining must be somewhere off to our left so when they attack, it will be from out there."

"If they ever attack," Lockett said. "It's already pretty late in the afternoon, not many hours of daylight left. Maybe tomorrow they'll attack then?"

"Then we beat them tomorrow, and then I'll go show you the sword and the journal."

"That's secondary," Lockett reminded, "First, I need you to go find Anna while Milton helps me look for Daniel…"

It was nearly a half hour later when Lockett and McManus heard the sound of skirmishing from across the ford and beyond the hillock. Quickly, the sounds grew into a full-fledged battle. They knew that General Rosecrans had posted a few brigades on that side of the river. Whatever Confederates they faced, these Union troops were being driven back based on the sounds of the battle. Closer and closer the sounds came.

With the rest of the Pioneer Brigade, Lockett began to ready his rag tag group of reserves should they be needed. Some elements had already moved down to makeshift rifle pits near the river to contest the ford, but Lockett's group remained up top with the cannon as additional reserves.

Another hour slowly dragged by as the sound of battle reverberated, but there was nothing for them to do but wait. Somewhere in the trees beyond the open topped hillock, there was a battle. It was impossible to say with any certainty what was happening, but it seemed to his men that the battle was not going well. Lockett could hear the murmurings between them and could see the worried looks on their faces.

Was it happening again? Were the Rebels about to break the outer lines and drive Rosecrans's army back to the very edge of desperation?

In the meantime, yet another battery of Union cannon joined him on the crowded hill. He hadn't thought that there was room for additional iron behemoths, but somehow, they crowded into the space. Expectantly, the gunners looked across the way at the distant hillock.

The gunners bore a different countenance. The infantry seemed unsettled at what they thought was transpiring, but the gunners did not. It seemed to Lockett that the artillery men were almost anxious for the Rebels to appear so that they could send them a greeting that they would never forget.

"Ah, Lockett!" a voice said from behind him.

Lockett turned and saw a small, bespectacled man. It took him a moment to place the face. The man had already continued talking, unaware of Lockett's confusion.

It was one of the battery captains from Perryville, Lockett could remember that much, but he couldn't remember the man's name, only that he was a fellow Michigander and from Coldwater.

"… and then there is the fact that you are a Michigan man also," the artillerist concluded.

Loomis! That was the man's name, Lockett remembered, now not sure what the man had been saying to him.

"Aha! Look there now!" Loomis said, pointing to the hillock. "Not long now."

A number of blue coated soldiers were streaming back over the rise, not slowing in the least as they headed for the ford and the safety of additional Union numbers.

"Not long now!" Loomis cheered excitedly. "I'd best go attend to my ladies."

The look on Lockett's face at the peculiar comment was not lost on Loomis. He chuckled. "Napoleon used to call his cannon his daughters. I have come to see why." He gave Lockett a parting wink and scurried off for his cannon.

"Gunners are a queer type," McManus noted from nearby.

Lockett gave no reply. Peculiar or not, Loomis was right. It would not be long now. With an odd sense of detachment, he watched more Northerners flow back over the hillock until it slowed to a trickle. Anxiously, the gunners waited by their pieces. Some gun captains checked their aim and elevations one last time, but most crews just stood obediently near their pieces with their lanyards or rammers in hand.

There were four men at each cannon, and three more men yards further behind, back by their ammunition limbers. Of the three at the limber, one was a runner, and he already had a large leather bag in hand with the next round of powder and shot. Near him were two others. They would cut the fuses so that the shot would explode at the best timing to cause the maximum damage, or ready to replace any of the four men at the cannon itself in case one of them fell.

Lockett watched them with curious detachment. It probably looked to others as if he was trying to avert his eyes from the seeming defeat on the hillock beyond them.

Finally, what little remained of the Union line appeared on the hill. They fired one last volley and then marched down the forward slope to the river. The Confederate line was upon their heels. They had crushed yet another Yankee brigade. They probably thought that they were on the cusp of a great victory,

Lockett reflected, but he was coming to share McManus's assessment of the ground. The Confederate infantry was about to wander into a terrible trap.

"Wait!" an authoritative voice yelled from the cannon. "Steady! Wait for my command!"

Finally, the last of the Union line of battle disappeared. The top and front slope of the hillock was now flooded with Confederate infantry. Anxiously, Lockett waited to hear the word to fire. He waited and waited. What were they waiting for! The hill teemed with Confederates!

And still they waited...

He looked for Loomis but could not find him in the seemingly endless line of cannon. What were they waiting for? The hill was black with moving forms.

And then finally...

"Fire!"

Immediately, the voice was drowned out by a deafening roar that Lockett had never heard the likes of before. Nearly fifty cannon bellowed angrily at once. Their carriages slammed back and gouged ruts into the earth. The air buffeted around him with such force that Lockett felt momentarily unsteady on his feet.

All around him was a massive smoke blanket. It was as if they had knocked down a cloud from the sky, and it had landed atop them.

Only through one small crevice in the saltpeter fog could he see across the way to the hillock.

He knew that so many cannon firing at once would be destructive, but even so, what he saw through the crevice stunned him. The shots slammed into the hillock with a suddenness and violence that he had not thought possible. It looked like the entire hill had exploded, as if the ground beneath the Confederates had erupted from underneath.

Earth and body parts continued to rain back on the hillock from high above. Seconds ago, it had abounded with men like quills on the back of a porcupine, but now there was utter chaos there. It was hard to make out that there were any men left. Then, as the earth stopped raining from the sky, Lockett could see torn earth and regiments aplenty.

Gray and butternut forms littered the ground. Amazingly, he

then noticed that there were still a few butternut on their feet, but they seemed to be staggering around the hill in no particular direction.

Lockett could still hear nothing but reverberating echoes, and it was only his peripheral vision that brought him back to the activity on his own hill.

Already, the gunners were hurriedly going about their business, covering vent holes with their leather coated thumbs, other men swabbing out the barrels and reloading with bags of powder and then the shot. Some had already progressed to prick those bags of powder with their long, slender metallic pricks. Lanyards were readied, and the thunder rumbled again.

This time, instead of one massive boom, it was a series of continuous thunder cracks as each crew fired as fast as they could.

The carriages gouged the earth again and again, and the hillock across the way was blanketed in continuous shot and shell.

Lockett watched the hillock explode. He saw one group of color guard completely disappear in one of the many eruptions. Another group of men had flattened themselves to the ground, but it was of little use on the open hillock. Another percussion shell landed right among them, leaving no evidence of the men, only a small crater.

A few of the crazed survivors fled down the front slope of the hillock toward the ford, but Union sharpshooters posted along the water's edge made quick work of them.

Again and then again, the same horrific story played out.

Dazed at the complete obliteration, Lockett lost track of time. Looking back, he would not be able to tell how long it went on, but it seemed to take an eternity as he watched the continual destruction. Even when the last Rebel left the hillock, the cannon continued to fire blindly in the woods beyond it.

Finally, the pounding of the guns ceased, and darkness fell across the area. Even though he had scarcely moved throughout it, Lockett's legs felt weak and wobbly. His brain was still having trouble registering what he had just seen. There were no words for it.

Chapter 51

By evening, it had become clear that the battle for Stones River and Murfreesboro was over. If the visual evidence of the carnage on the hillock was not enough, then the reports trickling in from the Union cavalry of Rebels making their preparations for pulling back south were the clincher.

For Lockett, that meant a night of anxiously waiting for the morning. Morning would mean that he could go look for Daniel with Levi and Milton. It also meant that McManus could go look for Anna with Colonel Blair's blessing.

The night passed with interminable slowness for Lockett as he poked aimlessly at the fire. Most of the men were already asleep when he heard some stirring behind him. He turned and saw two figures captured in the firelight of the other camp fires. It was a lanky figure with a crutch under one arm and a slender boy propping up the other side.

"Prosper?" Lockett said aloud, bounding to his feet. "Clar…" he started before catching himself.

"Reporting back for duty, Lieutenant," Prosper said happily, awkwardly raising one hand in a brief salute.

Lockett ignored the salute, embraced Prosper, and then embraced Clarissa, surprising the both of them.

"Thank God! I thought the Rebels had got you."

"Would have for certain," Prosper answered, "But thanks to Charlie here, I was able to get out just in time. Had them nipping at our heels, didn't we?" he added, looking at Clarissa.

She nodded dully, but then allowed herself a small grin. "You tol' me to trust him, so I did."

* * *

Shortly after dawn, Lockett and the others set off in a muted hope that there still might be a chance. Neither Milton Bosworth nor Levi Thickle said a word as they led Lockett and a handful of other comrades back to where Levi had seen Daniel fall.

Men from Blair's Independent Regiment were not the only ones heading back to the slaughter pens. Other Union troops went to reclaim the land and the bodies of friends. They were accompanied by additional fatigue parties to collect and bury dead Rebels.

The living Rebels had already pulled out overnight. The battle for Murfreesboro and Stones River was done. This meant a chance to rejoice that they had survived, but that was deeply scarred by the dolorous feelings for those they had lost.

For Lockett, it meant that he had to leave the urgent task of locating and retrieving Anna to Patrick, Lieutenant Renaud, and the French Detroiters, whom Colonel Blair had assigned to carry out the task.

Lockett knew that he would owe the Colonel for that.

Renaud's small group was already on their way to the prosperous town, leaving Lockett to look for Daniel.

He knew that the others still held out hope that Daniel was still alive, although perhaps a prisoner now. In his heart, Lockett harbored a deeply pessimistic feeling. Daniel was gone. He could feel it.

But the quiet optimism of the others caused him to wonder. He was torn as to whether he wanted to find the body or not. No body meant that perhaps Daniel was still alive, albeit likely suffering on his way to a Confederate prisoner of war camp. He had trouble reconciling these thoughts, reflecting that Daniel had never been the type to bear burdens and hardship well. On the other hand, the description of his brother during his absence suggested that Daniel was not the same youth whom Lockett had always known.

He struggled with the melancholy thoughts as he followed Milton and Levi across the cotton field pockmarked and charred by exploded artillery shells and patches of blood.

Had Daniel really changed? After all of these years, Daniel had changed, and he had not been there to see it? It only added to the injustice of it all.

They entered the gnarled woods and headed for the limestone

protrusions that Bosworth had mentioned. There were signs that the Confederates had taken their fallen comrades with them in many cases, as well as wounded Yankees. It seemed that all they had come upon so far were dead Federals.

"It was somewhere up there," Levi Thickle said matter-of-factly, "I saw it from about here."

They paused briefly and looked at the low, undulating sections of limestone ahead. Then without a word, they fanned out in search of Daniel and others. Behind them there was the squeak of a fatigue party's wagons. Its wretched squeal of ungreased axles only reinforced what Lockett felt in his heart.

"As we find the dead, bring them to this open area," Lockett said, "It will make it easier for the fatigue parties."

"What about the live ones?" Sam Baker asked.

Neither Lockett nor anyone else bothered to answer him.

Lockett headed straight in the direction that Thickle had pointed out. The others hung back and spread out in slightly different directions. No one wanted to be too close to him now.

Lockett picked his way around some brush and over the first set of limestone. For the first few minutes, he saw nothing, and he worked his way deeper into the setting. On the third set of rocky ledges, he climbed atop one the stones and saw the recent remnants of a small fire at the opening between two waist high slabs.

With his eyes latched onto it, he jumped down to take a closer look. Just beyond the opening there was a blue clad body near the charred wood. He clenched a fist and then slowly stepped closer.

The body was about the right size, he thought. Curiously, someone had taken the time to place a clean white, monogrammed handkerchief over the corpse's face. Lockett stared at the oddity and then noticed the nasty wounds in the hip and shoulder.

He slid down into the crevice. It had been months since he had seen Daniel, but he did not need to remove the handkerchief. He knew that frame too well.

As he stared down, a sob caught in his throat.

All that he had tried to do ended in failure!

He had tried to keep him from the army, but when that failed, he turned his back on his younger brother. He had let Daniel fall in with the wrong crowd. He had tried to save his brother's neck from a noose, but for what? To die in agony, alone, and cold?

The wounds in his shoulder and hip? How much pain had Daniel been in until he had succumbed?

Every nightmare that he had tried to prevent!

He sobbed silently.

Only to see it played out, an unavoidable destiny!

He cursed aloud, a blaspheming yell so piercing and out of character that it startled his men scattered throughout the woods behind him.

Angrily, he snatched the handkerchief from his brother's face.

He thought of his mother. Daniel had been her favorite. How would she take the news?

He glared at the face, Daniel's face.

He would tell Mother that Daniel had died quickly.

It would not be true. He could tell by all of the dried blood around his brother that he had tried hard to hang on, not to mention the remnants of the fire by his feet. Maybe he lasted a day like this?

He wished that he could at least truthfully tell Mother that there had been a peaceful look on his free-spirited brother's face, but even that would be false. Daniel's face was frozen in a grotesque mask of agony. The mouth was locked open, and the lips curled back, as if he still felt pain even though he was dead.

James Lockett clenched his fists until the nails drew blood from his palms, and he trembled with rage and conflict of what to do next.

Bosworth was the first of his men to reach his side, but he just looked at Lockett, unsure what he could say or do.

Lockett shook with misery.

Daniel was dead.

* * *

The sight of the Murfreesboro courthouse cupola in the distance spurred the little squad to march faster.

There were twelve of them, all Renaud's French Detroiters with the exception of Patrick McManus.

Ostensibly, Lieutenant Renaud was in charge, but McManus held Lockett's hand-written instructions on how to locate the house, and Renaud wisely deferred to the determined red-head.

They were already marching at a speed incompatible with their wearied bones and sore feet, but as they entered the town, they marched ever more purposefully.

The provost guard had already secured the town with one of General Hazen regiments, which was permitted the honor to enter town first. However, other than that, the only other Union troops in town were the wounded ones in too bad of shape to be taken back as prisoners by the retreating Confederates.

Every wounded soldier, from both sides, who could march had left town with General Bragg's army. Those left were in such shape that they could not be moved, but even so, the entire town was swamped with blood and misery.

Every church and public building had been turned into a hospital, as well as a number of private houses. Even then, that was not enough. More wounded lined the walks in front of the houses and the lawns around the churches.

If McManus and the others could have looked past the misery, they would have seen a fine looking and prosperous town, but all they saw was an overflowing sea of broken humanity. The wounded were everywhere.

Rebel surgeons and townsfolk attended to the massive calamity, but there were more wounded than those who could help. McManus and his comrades noticed the glazed looks on many of the unattended wounded, some were dead, but others still seemed alive, although for how long? Another day?

The small squad also saw a few nervous eyes peeking out from behind curtained windows as more Union blue soldiers came into their town.

Following Lockett's directions, they marched straight to the towering courthouse, which was impossible to miss. As they reached it, they saw even more wounded. Every room must have been filled because there were wounded lying on the front step and dozens of men in the bloody grass out front.

Outside one of the windows of the courthouse, there was a pile of arms and legs that was nearly up to the window sill. At the bottom of the pile, McManus's eyes noticed movement, and he saw a large rat gnawing at the half-frozen thigh on the edge of the pile.

He had seen horrors for a year now, but the sight made him wince and shiver. He yanked his eyes away.

"Din't she always worked in the hospital tent in Savannah?" one of the French Detroiters said, anxious to fill the eerie void with the sound of his own voice, "Should 'ee look in there for her?"

Renaud nodded and looked at McManus for confirmation.

"She's probably caring for the wounded one way or the other, but which one and where? No, we go to the house like James said. He said that Anna is living with her spinster aunt. If Anna isn't there, the aunt will at least know which building she's in."

"If she'll tell us, a squad of Billy Yanks?" Renaud pointed out.

McManus nodded slowly and shrugged. Anna knew him; Anna knew that she could trust Patrick, but the Aunt had never met any of them, and McManus knew that they couldn't let the Aunt know who James really was as a way of convincing her.

They proceeded past the courthouse and were passed by a troop of Union cavalry. A door slammed from across the street, and another pair of suspicious eyes looked at them from the corner of a window.

"Do they think that we will burn the town down?" one of Renaud's men said disgustedly.

"Can you blame zem, Francois? It would be ze same reaction if all roles were reversed," Renaud answered evenly.

As per the directions, they turned left on the next side street. Their eyes counted the houses quicker than their feet could walk it. "Is that it?" Pierre said, eyeing the house down the way.

"Looks like ze wounded came to her instead of ze other way round," Renaud remarked.

Upon reaching it, he looked through the front window into the small parlor. He could already see three wounded Confederates in there.

The squad waited outside while McManus and Renaud opened the front door and called out a "hello".

There was no answer at all, although multiple pairs of eyes looked at the interlopers as they entered. Ragged, dirty, but most of all, grievously wounded, the Confederates looked wordlessly at the two Yankees.

"We're looking for the lady of the house," McManus said.

There was no answer.

"I'll check the upstairs," Renaud said, "You check the back."

A minute later, they joined back up in the parlor.

"Just more wounded Johnnies," McManus said as Renaud came down the steps.

The officer nodded in agreement.

"Where are they?" McManus said, looking squarely at the one Confederate who bothered to make eye contact.

"Ain't no one here," he answered sourly.

"We can see that. Where are they?"

"Ain't never no one here."

"We mean zem no harm," Renaud put in.

"Like you meant me no harm?" the soldier snorted, pointing to the bloody bandage around his abdomen. He turned his head and closed his eyes.

No amount of verbal prodding could get the man to look back or say another word. McManus had half a mind to try something more physical, but Renaud saw him heading for the Rebel and pulled McManus back.

"Let's talk outside."

Outside, McManus glared and pointed inside. "We aren't leaving here without her. I'll get them to tell me where Anna is." He gestured angrily towards the house with his arm. "By God, Lieutenant Renaud, I'll get those damn Rebels to open their mouths and tell me where they are."

He spoke so angrily and with such intensity that he had not noticed that they were not alone outside. Lingering near the edge of the blue coated squad, there was a young slave listening intently. The others had not thought much of it since the contraband had a natural tendency to follow the blue coated army, but they were all surprised when the boy spoke up.

"Y'all lookin' fer Miss Anna and her Aunt?"

McManus snapped around at the question and looked at the inquisitive face that smiled with the boyish joy of knowing something that someone else did not. If Lockett had been with McManus, he would have recognized the boy as one of the Ready's house slaves, Henry.

"What do you know about that?" McManus demanded.

"Dey ain't here," the boy answered confidently, not the least put off by the soldier's glare.

"We know z'at," Renaud said patiently, putting a gentle hand on McManus's shoulder. "Do you know where zey are, or when zey return?"

"Ain't sure 'bout that. No one is. Dey both left town 'fore the battle started." He shrugged. "Even my mistress don't know, and she was dere closest friend."

"Gone?"

The boy bobbed his head. "For days now."

"Where?"

The boy looked strangely at them, "I jus' says no one knows."

"Anna Tucker?"

The boy bobbed his head again.

McManus looked at Renaud. He didn't want to be the one to tell James that Anna had disappeared.

Epilogue

Patrick McManus studied James Lockett.

Silent and lost in thought, McManus's lifelong friend stared at the bustling mass of sutlers' wagons. Two weeks had passed since the battle, and now the omnipresent tail of traveling merchants had caught back up to Rosecrans's army.

The sutlers sold everything under the sun to the soldiers, from useful daily items like paper and stamps for letters home to the most useless of trinkets.

Lockett was staring at one of the new sutlers, the embalmer. McManus's sun-battered brow carved into a frown. He knew what James was thinking as he looked at the embalmer.

It had been a morose and taut two weeks since they had found Daniel's body. McManus was sure that James's dolorous thoughts were back to that fateful event. He knew James and how he was prone to letting such thoughts attach themselves like a leech to his brain.

In the days after finding Daniel, James had wrestled with the decision of what to do with Daniel's body. He had wanted to spend the month's wages on the embalmer and another month's to pay for the body to be shipped home. His mother would want to see her son one last time, James had said.

But in the end, he had decided against that. Even though the embalmer said that he could make Daniel's face more peaceful looking, Lockett could not get the visage of the grotesque mask out of his mind, and he could not bear the thought of his mother seeing such agony on the face of her carefree son.

So Daniel was buried with his comrades here in Tennessee. His body would never again return to the rich, dark earth of Kalamazoo.

McManus continued to watch James stare in the direction of

the embalmer, powerless to do anything about the thoughts that plagued James.

Except that for once, McManus was wrong. He was not reading his old friend's thoughts accurately.

Lockett was lost in thought, but it was not Daniel that he ruminated on as he stared into the distance. No, his eyes did not even see the sutlers hawking their wares. Instead, he saw visions of what lay further south of here, and his mind continued to churn, wondering where Anna could be.

Two weeks had passed since Patrick had returned with the news that she had disappeared.

Where was she? Was she hiding from Ambrose? Had she been arrested? Where could she have gone? Had she taken Aunt Molly with her? Why?

When they had parted ways in Savannah, not so many months ago, he had found himself despondent and crushed. He had flayed himself with thoughts of how she had betrayed him, of how foolish he had been to miss the clues that she and her father were Rebel spies. But most of all, he had punished himself for the thoughts of what could have been.

Those thoughts had cast him adrift back then and made the future meaningless in his eyes.

But it was very different now. Now, he realized how true those initial feelings had been.

He loved her! He had to admit it, but more to the point, she loved him too. Anna had betrayed everything to save him.

He was not rudderless now.

Rather, he had never felt such meaning. Even his attempts to keep Daniel out of the army were insignificant compared to the burgeoning sense of purpose that he felt. He had to find her!

Her final words echoed in his brain, as if she had just uttered them, "*Find me...*"

Quietly, Clarissa sidled up next to him. She said nothing for minutes, patiently waiting for his thoughts to turn back to the present.

Finally, he looked over at her. Everyone knew her as 'Charlie', but it still took conscious thought for him to address her as that. She stood next to him in her blue drummer boy uniform. The men had long since adopted 'Charlie' for a reason that Lockett couldn't quite explain. Even more perplexing, she had somehow convinced Colonel Blair to keep her on as drummer boy.

A black drummer boy! How that would have pleased Adie! And how that would have distressed General Buell, he had thought to himself.

Lockett had only once attempted to dissuade her, arguing that she would be safer going to the North. He had said that Octavius Matson and Bobby MacDonald could help her find her way north to a family.

It was with that final word that he had lost his argument with her. It was then that she had stated that she already had a family, and they were further south: her brother and her father. And that she would find them, one way or the other.

Debated the day after he had found Daniel, Lockett could not carry on with the argument. He saw the determination in her eyes, and he recognized it all too well. He had once bore the same look when it came to keeping Daniel safe. And now, he had the same type of fortitude to find Anna.

So grudgingly, he ceased. Clarissa, now Charlie, would stay with the army and head south with them.

"Did you find anything today?" he asked her.

Almost every day for the last two weeks, she had ventured into Murfreesboro. It was far too dangerous for Lockett to show his scarred face in the town, dangerous to Anna, wherever she was, too dangerous even for other blue-coated soldiers to ask many questions about her.

But for Clarissa, she could venture into town and the fields beyond to ask her brethren if they knew anything. She had already confirmed the story that McManus and Renaud had brought back. Anna and her aunt had seemingly disappeared in the dark of night without a word or sight to anyone.

Before she could answer, Lockett added, "By the way, I can see the butt of my revolver in your belt. You need to hide that better. You know how most of our soldiers feel about ex-slaves carrying a weapon, not to mention any local Secesh seeing that on you."

He could see that she was about to argue, so he quickly added, "I know it's not safe; that's why I gave you the gun in the first place, just keep it out of sight... and remember to run first. Bring out the gun only if you have to."

She nodded and then adjusted the blue jacket to fully hide the gun. Finally, she looked up at the tall soldier with a pleased, but cautious, look. "Maybe found somethin' today. Outside of town on the Manchester Pike, there was one old field hand who remembered a wagon with two women leaving a few days before the battle. It was before the dawn, and he thought it odd."

"Manchester Pike?"

"Towards Chattanooga?" Clarissa guessed.

"Then let's pray this army continues to move in that direction," Lockett said, looking off towards the distant town. "Chattanooga…"

Historical Background

One of the joys of writing historical fiction is the research into that particular time and place. Even more so than usual, I enjoyed diving deeper into the history of Buell's Army of the Ohio, their astounding trek to Perryville, the Underground Railroad, the role of Middle Tennessee in the Civil War, and finally, the staggering courage, slaughter, and reversal of fortune at Stones River.

I took pains to be as accurate as possible with the locations and chronologies of the regiments, quotes from generals' speeches, and even the weather.

It would be easier to merely point out the fictional parts of *Lockett's Crucible*, but then I would miss out on the opportunity to highlight some of the extraordinary factual parts. In the following pages, I have attempted to give the reader a few of the notable facts and to hopefully assuage some curiosity about particular scenes.

Section I – Buell's Crawl East

James Lockett's journey from Savannah, Tennessee begins with General Don Carlos Buell's problematic march east towards Chattanooga.

Most casual Civil War readers probably remember General Buell for his arrival at the midpoint of the battle of Shiloh and possibly wonder whatever happened to that General.

A stickler with Southern sympathies, or so interpreted by many of his men, Buell was in some ways the Northern version of General Braxton Bragg, his counterpart at Perryville. He was a General distrusted and disliked by many of his own officers and men.

His conciliatory attitude and belief that the country could be made whole again, while still keeping slavery, certainly did not endear him to the Adie Graham types within his ranks.

His wife, Maggie, was a Georgian, and through her, he did indeed inherit eight slaves. Between that and his own policies, it is easy to see how those rumors could have started regarding his devotion.

The march east along the Memphis-Chattanooga rail line was doomed from the start, and to be fair, it was not Buell's idea. Despite his best attempts to persuade General Halleck to the contrary, his Army of the Ohio laboriously trekked eastwards, patching the railroad as they went, knowing that it would be torn up again by the more mobile Rebel horsemen and creating a tenuous supply situation for themselves.

They often needed to repair infrastructure that had been damaged by their own side in the preceding months, thanks to Generals Mitchel and Turchin, who were polar opposites to Buell in terms of disposition towards Southerners.

Even the traveling array of journalists seemed to be aligned against Buell, publishing a plethora of unfavorable articles, which only emboldened many of the Midwestern governors who tried to assert their authority over his army at times.

Indeed, recounting the episode with the reporter Hoskins gave me the opportunity to set the scene for Lockett's eventual discovery from Linzy and Clarissa about General Turchin's troops in Athens, who was tried for the crimes committed by his troops there.

Section II – The Race to Bluegrass

There were many captivating events for my fictional characters to witness in Kentucky. Lockett and company merely needed to follow the route of the actual armies. From the dry conditions to the Confederate army's expectation that their ranks would swell with volunteers, these were easy and obvious parts that needed to be included in any story.

I could not resist quoting General Bragg himself on his Proclamation to Kentucky, *"We come not as conquerors, but to restore you to the liberties of which you have been deprived by a cruel and relentless foe. If you prefer Federal rule, show it by your frowns and we should return where we came."*

In hindsight, it looks incredibly bombastic and, ultimately, off target, but that is easy to say with one hundred and fifty years of hindsight.

And no recounting of Kentucky could be complete without mention of the inauguration fiasco. Thank goodness for the character of Ambrose Tucker, so that the reader could visualize the attempt to swear in new Confederate Governor Hawes. How quickly that day turned on its ear!

But it wasn't just the Confederate side that had moments of dysfunction. The incident involving 21st Wisconsin and General Rousseau was a near fratricide. Substituting Blair's Independent Regiment as part of Starkweather's Brigade to nearly receive the orders to fire on their own side was an obvious thing to do, all the more so since Starkweather's troops were so heavily involved in the battle of Perryville. Lockett and company needed to be part of that brigade in order to cover Perryville.

Section III – The Hangman's Noose and Section IV - Murfreesboro

There was no Colonel Wilks, nor was there a spy like Anna Tucker in Murfreesboro that I am aware of. However, having James Lockett in Murfreesboro during this time frame did allow me to cover President Jefferson Davis's arrival, as well as the remarkable wedding of Mattie Ready to John Hunt Morgan.

From a historical context perspective, it was also an opportunity to convey the disdain for General Bragg held by his own leadership cadre. At times, their vitriol for their commander rivaled their feelings for the Yankees slumbering in Nashville.

For those curious about the Underground Railroad, there were numerous routes that ran through middle Tennessee up to the Ohio River and beyond. Only God knows how many slaves escaped via those routes, or how many white Southerners and Northerners were jailed or killed for their defiance of the Fugitive Slave Act. Interestingly, the Underground Railroad also spirited away a small number of white Southerners too, as the Pinkerton men pointed out to Lockett.

Section V – The Slaughter Pen

Coincidentally, both Bragg and Rosecrans planned to attack the other's right flank and on the same day. Delays from Rosecrans's commanders allowed Bragg's strike to land first. Chaos and confusion reigned on that misty morning, leading to sequences such as Union General August Willich charging into the midst of Confederates, thinking that they were his men.

Back at his headquarters, reports of a growing rout were initially dismissed by Rosecrans. A contemplative, devout Catholic, 'Old Rosey' was put to an extreme test that day.

By the time that he realized that his army was teetering on catastrophe, it was almost too late. With the Confederates smashing through his right flank, it seemed obvious that they would cut off the Nashville Pike and leave Rosecrans with no good route of retreat.

Fortunately for Rosecrans, he had Phil Sheridan.

'Little Phil' and his men fought obstinately amongst the limestone ribs and forests. The cost was heavy, for both sides, but the hours that Sheridan secured allowed Rosecrans to energetically put together a new line defense, and using the Union's normal advantage in artillery, he was able halt the advance.

Still, Bragg's gains that day were stunning. It is little wonder that he sent the telegram to Richmond declaring it a victory and expecting the Union to retreat. They had battered a numerically superior foe, but like Shiloh, the Confederates had not fully defeated it.

By the time that Bragg realized more needed to be done, it was too late. His fateful attack on the Union left was doomed to fail, and his generals knew it, or at least General Breckinridge seemed to know it. Launched late in the day, his initial success was only a tease to the disaster that awaited. As they crested the hill above the ford, there were 45 Union cannon with a commanding position across the river, targeting the hilltop.

Nearly one-third of Breckinridge's Kentuckians fell that day, reducing him to tears and laments about his "poor Orphans."

After nearly 25,000 combined casualties, the battle for

Murfreesboro or Stones River was complete. But remorselessly, the war went on.

And for James, Patrick, and the rest, they must go on as well.

ABOUT THE AUTHOR

A Michigan native, T.J. Johnston is the author of the James Lockett Civil War historical fiction series, including *The Boys From Kalamazoo*. A history lover and long time author, he has degrees from Hope College and Michigan State University. He currently resides in Texas where he is working on subsequent novels.

Made in the USA
Middletown, DE
29 June 2021

43377204R00305